Right in the middle of the inner ward was the cylindrical structure that had started as Hadrian's mausoleum and was now the fortified citadel of the papacy. So there was going to be an explosion *there*, and unless Tom missed his guess there was going to be an explosion next to the door right by them. As far as he could see, there was shelter from one, but not both.

The guardsmen came back from the barricade behind the river-wall gate, one of them trailing a stream of powder from the keg under his arm.

"Ruy, we are *screwed!*" he yelled, over a sudden and thunderous cheering that seemed to come from every direction at once.

"Not yet, Tom. Not until I finally get to have my wedding night, at any rate."

"Jesus, Ruy," Tom said, suddenly wincing at the thought of blaspheming in front of the pope, who didn't actually seem to mind. "Where do we take cover?"

"There," the pope said, pointing along the wall. There was, maybe twenty yards away, a cluster of blocky stone buildings just under the bastion they'd come in over. "Grain houses. Very strong."

"See?" Ruy was grinning as he stood up in the firelight. "Did I, Ruy Sanchez de Casador y Ortiz, not say that the Almighty would provide? His personal vicar on earth shows us the way."

"Right," Tom said, grinning in spite of himself, "that's what I call *service*."

1635:
The Cannon Law

ERIC FLINT
&
ANDREW DENNIS

1635: THE CANNON LAW

This is a work of fiction. All the characters and events portrayed in this book are fictional, and any resemblance to real people or incidents is purely coincidental.

A Baen Book

Baen Publishing Enterprises
P.O. Box 1403
Riverdale, NY 10471
www.baen.com

ISBN 10: 1-4165-5536-6
ISBN 13: 978-1-4165-5536-0

Cover art by Tom Kidd

First Baen paperback printing, April 2008

Library of Congress Control Number: 2006015948

Distributed by Simon & Schuster
1230 Avenue of the Americas
New York, NY 10020

Pages by Joy Freeman (www.pagesbyjoy.com)
Printed in the United States of America

To the memory of
Jim Baen, 1943–2006

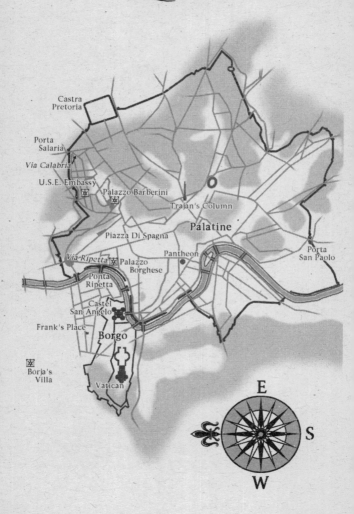

Map of
Rome

Castra Pretoria

Porta Salaria

Via Calabria

U.S.E. Embassy

Palazzo Barberini

Trajan's Column

Palatine

Piazza Di Spagna

Pantheon

Porta San Paolo

Via Ripetta

Palazzo Borghese

Ponta Ripetta

Castel San Angelo

Frank's Place

Borgo

Borja's Villa

Vatican

E
S
W

Part One

January 1635

Chapter 1

Naples

Don Vincente Jose-Maria Castro y Papas, Captain in His Most Catholic Majesty's Army in the Two Sicilies, tried sneering at the stack of paperwork and the books and ledgers of the company he commanded. It was of no use. The wretched things remained there, sneering back at him.

Somehow, the filthy business of bureaucracy was everywhere nowadays, and the profession of arms was no refuge. Especially not in a newly augmented tercio dragged from its depot and filled out by a small horde of militiamen and new recruits. And especially not when the arms he was supposed to profess were light muskets.

Certainly, they were an excellent weapon, compared with arquebuses, and far more wieldy than the heavy muskets they were replacing—had replaced, in some armies. A damnably expensive one, compared with just about anything, which was the reason Don Vincente's company had gotten so few, thus far. But the exploits of Turenne had been noted in Madrid, and the weapons had been identified as central to the small morsels of pride he had salvaged from France's shame. The exploits of the Swede with the lighter weapons had also been noted.

In times past, Spanish soldiers were expected to buy their own arquebuses. But the rapid changes brought by the Americans who had arrived in the Ring of Fire had altered military practices as well—indeed, perhaps military practices more than anything.

And so, throughout the Spanish army, which remained the best equipped and organized fighting force west of the Turk, companies and tercios that would otherwise have been unable to afford such equipment were receiving unexpected bounties.

For which they were expected to account. In triplicate. On top of all the utter, utter crap that was catching up with them after three moves in as many months around Spain before they had, with hardly any warning, been shipped out from Spain, filled out at the last minute with a collection of recruits whose appetite for war had been whetted by tales of the plunder Don Fernando's forces had received for their part in the sack of the Low Countries. Even after hearing about Don Fernando's orders to limit the looting, Don Vincente had tortured himself with visions of luckier officers filling their boots with Dutch gold. Which was a true irony, indeed. For in every other way the news out of Madrid was of deep displeasure with His Majesty's little brother for what he had done. For the recruiting parties, the word was all of how well Spanish Arms had fared. For those unlucky enough not to have gone with Don

Fernando, however, it was just another opportunity to get rich on something other than a captain's pay that had been sorely, sorely missed. He had joined hoping for plunder somewhere, anywhere he could find it. Instead, he had found himself just about staying ahead of his expenses by taking money to exchange to less and less fashionable tercios, invariably managing to exchange out of a company before it was posted somewhere with an opportunity for loot.

Which had its advantages, admittedly. He had been quietly bemoaning his ill luck in leaving his last posting just before they were sent to Flanders when the news of the massacre at Wartburg came in, in which his replacement had died in the Americans' Greek Fire.

"Don Vincente?"

It was Sergeant Ezquerra, at the door of Don Vincente's billet, an upper room in a taverna on the road out of Naples that had been commandeered. Not, it had to be said, a good inn, but the patron kept a decent if simple table and a reasonable cellar. The more exalted officers had made themselves comfortable with the local grandees, whom in theory they were there to protect from riotous mobs, but Don Vincente was being careful with his money. He could have been still more careful with it if the barracks quarter around the viceroy's palace in town had not been full to bursting before they had arrived. But Don Vincente was accustomed to execrable luck.

"Come," Don Vincente said, scooting his chair back from the folding table he had his paperwork stacked on. "I grow eager for interruptions. Even from you."

"This is good, Don Vincente," Ezquerra said, "it does

a man good to get away from the work from time to time. Especially the paperwork, which is unmanly."

"Away from the work, eh? A medicine you imbibe in large doses, I note, Sergeant." Don Vincente had never learned the man's first name, despite in theory having it among the paperwork for the company. There was a blank where the man's baptismal name was supposed to be recorded. It would hardly surprise Don Vincente to learn that the man had never been baptized. Ezquerra was the kind of fellow who, if he had remained as a peasant rather than joining the army, would have been a sore trial to his local gentry as a poacher and all-round nuisance who was just marginally too useful at whatever trade he pursued to have quietly flogged to death.

How long ago Ezquerra had left wherever he was from was a mystery. His date of birth was listed as unknown, and where exactly he was from was also unclear, except that Don Vincente had gathered one way or another that it was near Badajoz. He had the typical wiry-little-mountain-man look of so many from those parts, and the few of his claimed relatives that Don Vincente had seen—there were several in the army—had a similar look about them. Of course, a long-service soldier would have relatives in many parts of Spain, the lax approach to marriage and casual bastardy among the common soldiers being what it was.

"Not today, Don Vincente. Today I have neglected my health on your behalf." The sergeant left the statement hanging there, and waited, leaning on the doorpost, for a response.

Don Vincente glared at him. Truth be told, the

sergeant was very good at his job. It was simply that for some reason being caught actually working by any of his officers seemed to be a source of terror to the man. Don Vincente hoped one day to actually see Ezquerra doing something to ensure that the company was as well turned-out and ready for action as they usually were. Of course, they were also always ready for the whorehouse and as much cheap drink as they could get inside themselves, but that was soldiers for you. The chaplains and the inquisitors didn't like it, but after getting away from his family's estates ten years before, Don Vincente had come to take a broader view of matters of the faith. And morals. And, especially, priests.

After some moments, Don Vincente realized that he was going to have to ask. "And, pray, what has caused this unwonted self-mortification?"

"Father Gonzalez again." Ezquerra was now grinning, although humor was not the usual feeling the good father provoked.

Don Vincente raised an eyebrow. "He's found another secret Jew?" The Inquisition seemed to be paying particular attention to the army recently, and instead of only occasionally appearing anywhere they could smell soldiers—or outside their comfortable offices at all—there seemed to have been a small rain of the pestilential creatures recently. Before they had sailed from Spain they had been visited with a plague of them. A biblical plague in truth. Possibly of frogs. They croaked enough.

Father Gonzalez was the representative of the Inquisition in this small billet town just outside Naples that Don Vincente and several of his brother officers had been visited with. He was *exactly* the kind of priest that one would expect a senior inquisitor to put forward for a long posting away from the home tribunal, with no definite date of return.

"No, Don Vincente. He seems to think that the men are given to dissipation and licentious pleasures." Ezquerra's grin grew even broader. They had been putting up with Gonzalez for nearly two months already, and it seemed to have escaped his notice until *now*? It was certainly not a subject that seemed greatly to exercise the company's regular chaplain, although his being sober enough to notice was not a common event.

There was a long pause. Don Vincente stared at Sergeant Ezquerra. Sergeant Ezquerra stared at Don Vincente. At length, Don Vincente said, "And have you said anything to the men about this?"

"Naturally," Ezquerra said, grinning from ear to ear, "I told them to stop it."

"Did you make it an order?" Don Vincente asked, suddenly overtaken by morbid curiosity.

Ezquerra snorted. "Of course. I ordered them not to let the good father catch them fornicating or insensible with drink."

Don Vincente parsed that one with no small care. It seemed to pass muster in every useful way, and was, indeed, technically an order to the men to stop doing those things. "Surely this small exertion came as no great threat to your health?"

Ezquerra sighed deeply. "No, Don Vincente. What has brought me to the very brink of ruin, Don Vincente, was going about every billet to pass on the order, and then getting around all the whorehouses in

Naples before Father Gonzalez got to them so I could be sure none of the men were in them at the time."

"And why did you not tell me first?" Don Vincente realized as he said it that he had laid himself wide open.

"I checked the whorehouses before coming here, Don Vincente," Ezquerra said, not a muscle in his face moving as he pounced on the opportunity. And, of course, did so without once saying anything that could be—quite—construed as disrespect for an officer.

"Most diligent of you." Don Vincente kept his face just as straight as the sergeant did. In the nearly three years he had known the man, he had never caught Ezquerra in outright disrespect once, but heard him say things that would earn a demotion and flogging from an officer with less of a sense of humor hundreds of times.

The man had been tentative at first, certainly. Had covered up his slack ways with obvious displays of punctilio when he thought Don Vincente had been watching. Over time, Don Vincente discovered that Ezquerra and his fellow sergeants and the cabos who assisted them had turned the company into something that ran itself. The previous captain, from whom Don Vincente had bought the commission as an investment in his ongoing project to improve the modest family fortunes, had been an absentee like many officers. In his absence, Ezquerra had quietly taken over the company as a body of fighting men.

Lieutenants had come and gone, not taking much time or trouble over the company as they sought advancement. No officer had remained long enough to bring any subalterns to the company, for which Don

Vincente was grateful. He had himself learned much as a young man just left home from the sergeant he had had when he first bought an ensign's commission. What would happen to an ensign left in the clutches of Ezquerra did not bear thinking about. Except, possibly, by a theologian contemplating possible routes to utter perdition.

"Thank you, Captain Don Vincente," Ezquerra said, grinning.

"Is there more? Doubtless I shall now be able to say with perfect truth that our soldiers have been ordered to stop being soldiers. But I feel certain you would not have strained yourself by coming up the stairs behind you if there had not been more to report. Usually, you hang around until I come down."

Ezquerra nodded. "There is more, Don Vincente, yes." The man's face grew serious. "While visiting an establishment with which the Captain will doubtless be unfamiliar, it being a house of prostitution of high repute and even higher prices, I chanced to meet my third cousin, who is orderly to Colonel—"

Don Vincente interrupted him with an upraised hand. If the sergeant had a fault, it was that if he was speaking of someone he was in some way related to, he could be quite tiresomely long-winded. "What did your cousin tell you?" he asked.

"*Third* cousin, Don Vincente." Ezquerra had a hurt tone in his voice. "And he told me that there is a reception in town tonight for the cardinal, who is visiting. Which may explain why Father Gonzalez, indeed all the inquisitors, are acting like their crabs are biting particularly hard."

"Which cardinal?"

"Borja," Ezquerra said, "the one that was viceroy in Naples before."

"And so Gonzalez's crabs are—hold on, Gonzalez has *crabs*? How?" Don Vincente felt rather pleased to have spotted this one.

"The good father uses the same whorehouse as my third cousin's colonel."

"That was what I was wondering about. Surely even whores have standards?"

Ezquerra shrugged. "True, the ordinary sort. But these are the kind who service gentlemen, so their standards are lower."

Don Vincente grinned ruefully. It was too much to expect that he would out-shoot his sergeant. He much suspected the sergeant was a very clever man who, had he not been born in a one-room shack somewhere in the mountains, would have made a great deal of the opportunities he would have had. And yet God in his wisdom had chosen to place a man of such talent in the station he occupied. "Still, knowing *why* Father Gonzalez has even more of a hair up his ass than usual does nothing to help deal with the situation. Will the men be sensible about this, until Gonzalez calms down at least?"

"The old-timers, yes. All of these new fish we got in Barcelona? I can only hope. We need a fight to get them steadied down."

Don Vincente stroked his beard for a moment. "And there seem to be no prospects of that at the moment, I think. We missed Don Fernando's expedition, and it looks like we're going to miss whatever they've got planned for France. Maybe we'll get to crack some Italian heads?" He left the question hanging for Ezquerra to speculate on. Not, strictly, proper to invite a common soldier into one's confidence, but he had come to find Ezquerra's experience useful.

"Who knows?" Ezquerra shrugged. "From what I hear, everyone hereabouts was ready for revolt last year, but it seems a little quieter this year, so far. Although it's not really the rioting season right now. Prices are low."

That would be about right, Don Vincente mused. The harvests were only a few months past, and food remained plentiful. So prices were low, the winters hereabouts were not particularly harsh, and as far as Italians were ever content, the Neapolitans seemed to be content.

"That said," Ezquerra went on, "they won't like having so many of us billeted here. We've only been here a week, but there have been soldiers arriving for a month. And I hear that some of the grumbling has already started."

"What about?" There were some predictable answers to that, but it paid to ask.

"Requisitions and foraging, mostly," Ezquerra said. "The usual. There will be more. We have a lot of kids who've just joined. Many of them away from home for the first time. There will be trouble. We seem to have gotten away with it so far, though I hear someone killed an Italian in a tavern brawl a couple of nights ago. There wasn't much of an outcry over it, but it's the kind of thing we can expect."

"I know, I know," Don Vincente said. "Well, I suppose we can hope and pray that Borja's arrival does not portend more trouble. I understand he was not popular when he was viceroy."

Ezquerra shrugged. "The Captain will know more of such things than I."

Don Vincente thought back over what he had, in fact, heard. "Now I think about it," he said, "it does seem strange. The holy father ordered Borja out of Rome last year, as I recall, and ordered him to live in his diocese. I wonder why he's back in Italy? It might be thought disobedient to the holy father."

Ezquerra made the little hiss-spit noise he had for the occasions when he was annoyed by something. Don Vincente had only heard it before when something the men had done when practicing their drill displeased him. "I don't think the rules apply to such as him," he said, after a quiet moment. "You or I, Don Vincente, we face the Inquisition if we disobey a priest. The cardinal? He can disobey the pope and no one can tell him different."

"True," Don Vincente said, and it was. Not least because Borja was one of the Inquisition's senior cardinals. "Still, I want the men mustered for musket drill tomorrow, and every day until Gonzalez calms down. I don't know what the other companies will do, but I think training the men might well stop them finding idler pursuits until we have real trouble to deal with."

"The men won't like it, Don Vincente." Ezquerra's tone betrayed how little he cared about that. The man was a veteran, and had himself walked the Spanish Road to the wars in Flanders. Don Vincente could tell how much he approved of training the men by the simple fact that there was none of the usual obfuscation and delay whenever the suggestion arose.

"They aren't meant to like it, Sergeant. They're

meant to have a reason to be up early in the mornings so they start to think twice about spending their wages all night on whores and drink."

"I shall give them the terrible news, Don Vincente," Ezquerra said, relish in his eyes and voice. "Will there be training with powder and ball?"

"Not every day." Don Vincente was now thankful that he'd been going over exactly that paperwork when the sergeant arrived. "I only have so much money to spend on powder. Two or three volleys, I think, tomorrow morning, so the idiots who get themselves hangovers really suffer. After that we'll run them until they puke if they turn up looking hungover."

"As the Don wishes," Ezquerra said, grinning.

Don Vincente decided, as the sergeant left, to let the paperwork go hang for the afternoon, and bellowed for a bottle of wine to sit in the afternoon sun with. He would beg off messing with the other captains tonight, to ensure he had a clear head for the firing in the morning, but for now a short break to recruit his strength before an arduous couple of weeks was just the thing. He wondered, for a moment, if the sergeant's attitudes were contagious?

Chapter 2

Venice

Frank Stone slammed the door behind him. Giovanna looked up at him from the table where she was going over some of the Committee's paperwork—the interminable minutes of one of Massimo's interminable theory workshops, from the looks—and her face suddenly grew pensive.

Uh, oh, Frank thought. *Shouldn't bring it home with me.* He forced himself to take a deep breath and stand up straight, relax. "Sorry," he said. "Been talking with your dad again."

"I hope it wasn't too bad, this time?"

Frank chuckled, feeling his bad mood evaporate. "I guess we're sort of feeding off each other a bit. Massimo's no help, either. He gets all prickly and defensive about everything, these days."

"What was it about?"

Frank waved it away and went over to pour himself a glass of wine. "Wasn't anything, really."

"Then why could I hear you from three floors above?" The tone of her voice was . . . ambivalent.

Not that Frank could blame her. She'd been Daddy's Little Girl when they'd met, on the very day that Frank first arrived in Venice, and then she and Frank had fallen head-over-heels in love. After that there'd been all that stuff that had happened when they went to try to rescue Galileo, although describing it as just "stuff" was on a par with describing the Civil War as a bit of a disagreement—which had somehow managed to culminate in their wedding.

Now they were settling down to as near a normal married life as you could get in a family that was still doing most of the work of the Committees of Correspondence in Italy, work that was organized on traditional Marcoli family principles. Everyone pulling in three directions at once, followed by a huge argument.

And when it came to arguing, the Marcolis were Italian to the bone. Frank had tried sweet reason a few times—and the mess that that had gotten him into was still causing minor political shockwaves—and had slowly found himself going native in fine style, complete with full volume and waving arms.

Usually at Messer Marcoli, Senior, Antonio of that ilk, a man who'd very nearly made himself seventeenth-century Italy's own John Brown, hanging after Harper's Ferry included. Injury had kept him off that particular mission, which would then have failed if they hadn't happened to have had a mad Frenchman along to supply, with hindsight, most of the planning and, just to put the cherry on the top of it, an assassination attempt on the pope.

Frank wondered what his own dad would have made of it. He certainly wouldn't have approved of making Giovanna suffer the spectacle of the two guys she cared most about, her father and her husband, getting into blazing rows about . . .

What had it been this time? Frank was already having trouble remembering how it started, but he seemed to recall something about organizing the soccer league.

How it had ended was with Antonio Marcoli telling Frank he was a poor excuse for a son-in-law, disobedient and wayward. In return, Frank had reminded Antonio of some choicer passages from the Venetian Committee's statements as to the rights of free people, and all but called the old guy a fascist.

Not that that would have made much of an impression, but the yelling and swearing probably did. And would be the cue for a good couple of days' sulking. On both sides, Frank realized, thinking back.

He sighed. "Giovanna, it's going to be a lot easier when we get some help down from Germany. Your dad's going to have someone else to rail at instead of me."

The Committee in Germany had promised some help, training if nothing else, but for the moment they were all busier than they could handle up there, what with the wars and the other mayhem. The promise of aid—reading between the lines, on Mike Stearns' all-but-orders—had become increasingly abject apologies that the assembly of a team of activists was being delayed by one urgent necessity after another.

It wasn't that Frank didn't believe them. Given what he'd heard about what was happening north of the Alps, at least some of that "urgent necessity" was pretty damned urgent. That still didn't make him any happier about the fact that he'd have to maintain the daily walk on eggshells he needed to make in order to deal with his in-laws for some time to come.

"Frank," Giovanna said, and then stopped.

"Yeah?" he said, encouraging her to go on.

"Maybe we shouldn't wait for the German Committee."

Frank frowned. "What do you mean?"

"I think maybe we should start working on Massimo's plan to spread the Committee elsewhere in Italy, no?"

Frank noticed she was chewing the inside of her lip, the way she did when she was thinking hard and deep about something. That made him feel good about the way the conversation was going for two reasons:

First, because Giovanna was probably the smartest of the Marcolis, if only because she had the same brains her dad did without the hairy-eyed temperament that went with it. And, second, because it was cute as all hell.

Frank cleared his throat. "Okay, lay it out for me—how are we going to do that with your dad dragging his heels all the way?"

"We should go back to Rome," she said. "I think."

It was all Frank could do not to sigh. There were also some disadvantages to having a smart wife.

There was no point lying to her, either. Giovanna had an ability to detect Frank telling lies that bordered on the supernatural.

"Well, yes," he admitted. "Venice is just too . . . different, I guess, from the rest of Italy. It's ultimately a sideshow, here. Politically speaking."

She seemed to be only half-listening to him. "Naples, maybe? Instead of Rome, I mean."

Frank was paralyzed, for just an instant. It had suddenly dawned on him that, from the standpoint of the danger involved to Giovanna, Rome was almost infinitely better than Naples.

Slowly, he sat down at the kitchen table, while he thought about it.

True enough, they'd have to be careful in Rome, what with the Papal Inquisition right there on their figurative doorstep. But with some experience, Frank had come to realize that the "Inquisition"—the papal variety of it, anyway, if not the Spanish—wasn't actually the pack of slavering torturers he'd vaguely remembered from his up-time history reading. They could be awfully scary, at times, to be sure. Still, they tended to respect certain limits—and, whatever else, they weren't usually given to precipitous action.

Naples, on the other hand . . .

Naples was a political powderkeg. To make things worse—much worse—Naples had the Spanish army sitting on top of it. And the Spanish authorities, at times, *were* given to precipitous actions.

It wasn't simply an issue of their personal safety, either. As much as he tried to protect Giovanna, Frank understood perfectly well that engaging in revolutionary activity was inherently a risky proposition—and there was no way to keep Giovanna out of it, even if he was so inclined.

But Naples was a political mess, as well as a powderkeg. A city with a long-standing revolutionary tradition of its own, with a multitude of political tendencies and unofficial parties. From the standpoint of a fledgling Committee of Correspondence, just getting off the ground in Italy, it would be an inhospitable environment. They'd probably wind up spending more time quarreling with other revolutionists than they would getting anything productive accomplished.

"No," he said firmly. "Let's go to Rome."

Giovanna nodded. "I will speak to my father about it."

Maybe he'll decide to stay behind in Venice. But Frank knew it was a hopeless wish.

Rome

There was nothing unusual about an atmosphere of tension in the halls of the *curia*. If anything, Cardinal Antonio Barberini the Younger reflected, it would be a sign something was badly amiss if at least a few of the cardinals, monsignors and what-not present were *not* pointedly ignoring each other, barbing their comments or outright yelling insults. For a body that in theory was moved and guided by the Holy Spirit, it was usually infernally bad tempered.

And, of course, the last few years had been . . . more strained than usual. And the cardinal presently rising to speak had been the source of much of it. Or, at least, more of it than any of the other purple-clad mischief-makers Rome was home to.

Cardinal Gaspar Borja y Velasco. Like every other Spanish prelate, part of the government of His Most Catholic Majesty Phillip of Spain. This one in particular was a leading member of Spain's privy council, holder of enough offices to make him almost a quorum of government in his own right. He was also firmly in that part of the Church in Spain that regarded the church as an arm of the Spanish Government, and in a very real sense could not see where government left off and the church began, or vice versa.

Only two years before he had made it plain—loudly, publicly and with the crashing lack of tact that was practically the man's signature—that that view did not apply only to the Church in Spain. Two hundred years of being the only power in Spain whose writ ran untrammeled in every one of the kingdoms of Spain—even His Most Catholic Majesty had limits to his powers outside Aragon and Castile—two hundred years of inquisitorial power unmatched anywhere outside of the papal states, and the Church in Spain clearly believed it was time for the Roman dog to stop wagging the Spanish tail.

Unlike England a century before, they had the guns and ships and tercios to give their opinion weight, not least by reason of owning enough of northern and southern Italy that they had the Papal States in a strategic vise that they could screw closed at any time. What stopped them was a need, for the time being and only grudgingly recognized in Madrid, to maintain at least a passing semblance of obedience to Rome.

Not that that had stopped Borja from loudly condemning the See of Rome's inaction against Gustavus Adolphus, failure to burn Galileo like the heretic he plainly was, and willingness to appoint a near-Protestant like the American Mazzare to the purple.

The criticism of the failure to act against the Swede had been the only one Urban VIII had chosen to answer. He had, with some accuracy, pleaded poverty. A military undertaking that had strained the resources of the entire arrayed might of the house of Habsburg, with all their imperial dominions and an annual treasure fleet from the Americas was beyond the pope's means to put in any more than the proverbial widow's mite. Two million widow's mites, to be exact, but still a pittance next to the cost sunk in failing to stop Gustavus Adolphus from reversing every success of Catholic arms of the last fifteen years.

Still, it had been grounds for Borja to accuse the pope of being, in so many words, insufficiently Catholic. He had nearly been ordered out of Rome for that, and then his performance after the Galileo affair—which had, in truth, been a whitewash but it was tactless to say so—had got him slung out.

And now he was back. He had at least had the good grace to confine himself, before today, to sulking quietly in his villa on the outskirts of Rome, but he had not wasted his time back in Spain. If Vitelleschi's reports were right—and seldom were the Jesuit father general's formidable spymasters not in possession of accurate information—then Borja was here in the van of a small horde of prelates and cardinals, each of whom was coming to Rome to demonstrate how much more Catholic than Pope Urban VIII, né Cardinal Maffeo Barberini, he actually was. And he had stopped off in Naples on the way here and apparently met with the duke of Osuna. What deal those two had done was anyone's guess. None of the channels of spycraft Barberini could access had been able to divine what had happened behind *that* closed door. But it was sure to be a devil's bargain for someone.

The Spanish prelates, meanwhile, had been arriving in Rome every few days for weeks now, all direct from Spain, and as soon as they had washed off the dust of

travel had paid an immediate visit to that villa outside
Rome, followed by long hours in closed sessions with
their compatriots all over Rome. Barberini had engaged
his own staff in imagining what they might be up to,
in more detail than the obvious "no good," as had his
brother Francesco Barberini. The results varied from
the uncomfortable to the downright alarming. At the
very least, among them they held enough offices and
concomitant rights to intervene and interfere that they
could tie up procedural business in Rome for months,
slowing down the already ponderous curial bureaucracy
to a pace that would make a snail look lightning fast.

And now Borja had presented himself for a session
of the *curia*.

"It begins," the whisper came from behind Barberini.
That was Ciampoli, Barberini's secretary, who had led
the strategy sessions and had good reason to suspect
the worst of Borja. Until the Galileo affair he had been
a private secretary to the pope, a prestigious position,
but the limited amount of damage Borja had been able
to do had included impeaching the man away from
direct papal service. Naturally, Barberini had grabbed
him as quickly as he decently could. Talented, bright,
learned in the sciences, he was visibly a coming man
and had the skills Barberini recognized as necessary
for what the new political winds in Europe would
blow through Rome.

Borja began to speak. "If Your Holiness will permit?" he said, his pinched, ruddy and choleric face
making a halfhearted effort at an unctuous smile as
he awaited permission to speak.

Barberini looked over at his uncle the pope. His
Holiness was his usual serene self, calm eyed and

affable. Of course, with fifty years' experience of Roman politicking he would be giving nothing away, although he doubtless had more than just the dark imaginings of his nephew's own staff to inform his worries. Barberini recalled a remark made by the young American, Frank Stone, at whose wedding Barberini had officiated. "Just because you're paranoid, it doesn't mean they're not out to get you."

He'd had to get Father—now Cardinal—Mazarre to explain what paranoia was, and had observed that it sounded like a perfectly healthy reaction to living and working in the top ranks of the Church. Indeed, it was those who were *not* paranoid who were unhealthy, or at least very soon would be.

Mazzare had chuckled, and told Barberini the old, to him at least, joke about the king who had brooded "I'm paranoid, but am I paranoid *enough*?" Another text for these times.

But His Holiness had nodded permission for Borja to speak.

"I thank Your Holiness," the Spanish inquisitor said, "and I would beg clarification of certain matters which I and, I fear, his most Catholic Majesty, view with no little alarm."

Barberini winced. As subtle as a joke about farting. As blatant as a street-corner whore. There was this to be said about Rome's infighting: it weeded out the dullards. Spain, on the other hand, had to find jobs for its teeming and indefatigably inbred nobility, and some of them rose to damnably high levels.

Borja cleared his throat. "Your Holiness," he went on, "has in particular elevated enemies of the church to the rank of cardinal."

That brought an intake of breath from half of the cardinals present. There had been three new cardinals in the last year—Mazzare, Cardinal Protector of the new United States of Europe, Mazarini in France, at Richelieu's behest and almost certainly another of Richelieu's attempts to preempt history with an early appointment, and LeClerc, the former "Father Joseph" and another of Richelieu's creatures.

Barberini wondered if it was worth parsing that. Enemies, plural? All of them or just the two who formed a definite group? Or just the one, and Borja was being as ham-fisted as he usually was with his rhetoric?

"In particular," Borja was saying, "there are those who have actively supported the chiefest of the Church's enemies in the north. All, in fact, of Your Holiness's recent appointments to the purple—"

The pope had raised a hand for silence. "If Your Eminence will pause for a moment?"

Borja nodded assent, and, a palpably false smile on his face, resumed his seat.

Urban VIII cleared his throat. "We are advised that there is obstinate doubt of Our policy." Another intake of breath, this time from nearly everyone present.

Barberini included. That was the form of words used in the technical definition of heresy, a most serious charge to lay against anyone, let alone a prince of the church and an inquisitor. Small wonder that there was shock. For a pope, the absolute head of the Church, Urban was known to be a genial man, little given to outright confrontation where it could be avoided. What was causing him to deliver such an obvious slap in the face to his most blatant critic?

"Let it be known," Urban went on over the sudden

and urgent whispering, "that We are saddened by the disputes among the secular princes of Christendom. As Common Father of all Catholics, We are particularly saddened by the practice of princes, a practice which has become common, of one accusing the other of being an enemy of the Church. What is enmity to the Church is for Us to decide, and no other."

That provoked another hiss, this time—Barberini was watching carefully—from the Spaniards. The decision as to who, within the dominions of His Most Catholic Majesty, was an enemy of the Church, was arrogated exclusively to the Spanish Inquisition. So it had long been, and doubtless they wished it to remain so forever. Although the reference *could* be taken to mean Maximilian of Bavaria, whose pronouncements concerning the rulers of surrounding territories and, indeed, the papacy were sounding more and more lunatic as time went by.

This time Urban waited for the disturbances to die down before speaking again. "We are also minded to consider that the practice of winning souls for the Church is a matter for the Church, and not for secular princes to attempt by wager of battle. We are, however, not yet minded to make any pronouncement *ex cathedra*."

The silence that followed was profound. The subtlety of curial proceedings had been abandoned by both Borja and his nominal master. The House of Habsburg had been a prime proponent of the principle of *cuius regio, eius religio*, and to address such a remark as that in response to the ranking cardinal of the Habsburg party present was as direct a rebuke as could have been delivered without naming names.

It was, Barberini realized, only to be expected when dealing with Borja, who had all but had to be beaten over the head with the encyclical ordering him to leave Rome before he would go.

Borja had risen to his feet, his usually ruddy complexion gone an even darker shade of red. "Your Holiness then does not support the winning of souls for the Church?"

Urban raised his hand in an admonitory gesture. "We support the missionary work of Our clergy, and no other means of winning converts. If this must be in territories where the government is opposed to Us, We observe that the Church has never wanted for brave souls called to the martyr's crown."

Borja's flush paled a little. Even *he* could pick the nuances out of that, Barberini realized. Not just territories opposed to the Church, but territories opposed to the papacy.

And then Barberini followed it all the way to the end. Was Urban expecting the worst, truly the worst, from Borja? A church of Spain, to join the church of England? Even an antipope in Madrid?

Barberini felt a shudder run down his spine. With Spain outside the church there would be no need for even nominal obedience to Rome, and the Papal States would be crushed. Even after her reverses, Spain was a power, arguably *the* power whatever the scientific wizardries of the USE could achieve. The resistance the Papal States could offer would be a token at best against an army that had lost but one battle in the last century. Was the martyr Urban referred to *himself*? Barberini looked around the room and saw a lot of faces growing very thoughtful indeed.

Not least Borja's. Doubtless he had expected a less forthright response, not a flat declaration of the pope's willingness to resist from the first. If the papacy entered into outright defiance, Spain's isolation would be complete, with their cousins in Austria already adapting to the new way of doing things and their king's brother asserting his independence. "Your Holiness . . ." he said, and paused.

"We thank you for this opportunity to make known Our thoughts on this matter," Urban said. "And We would further be grateful if Your Eminence would recall the words of our encyclical on the subject of cardinals remaining in their Sees. It is there that the missionary work of the Church goes on, and there that We depend on Our cardinals to oversee that work."

Borja remained silent. Barberini stared hard, and fancied he could see Borja's lips moving silently, although a casual glance would see the grinding jaw of a very angry man. Whatever prepared script he had had, he had clearly been diverted from it.

From behind Barberini, a whisper from Ciampoli; "We should plan for worse things from Borja, I believe."

Barberini waved him to silence, irritably. This would have to be thought over very carefully. It was far from necessary for his uncle to take his most junior cardinal into his most secret counsels, but surely some warning of so radical a response to Borja's machinations would have been sensible?

On the floor, Borja was still silent, and had been for nearly a minute. Everyone present was watching him carefully. The next words from the Spanish cardinal would, potentially, decide great matters in the life of the Church. Even, in a very real sense, how much life the Church might have left in it, for Urban had presented Borja—and by extension Borja's masters in Madrid, assuming they knew and approved of what he was doing, by no means a foregone conclusion—with a vision of the Church in ruins if Spain acted against the papacy.

Perhaps that was the plan? Barberini had to admire the audacity of it if it was. To threaten to play Samson in the temple if Borja truly challenged Rome's authority, to make the consequences of disobedience so severe that no one in his right mind would dare—it was all Barberini could do to suppress a smile. Assuming Borja was in his right mind was at best risky. Or that he had a mind to be right in, were one to be brutally candid.

Borja finally spoke, visibly trembling. "I thank Your Holiness for the clarification of these matters," he said, "and by your leave will withdraw from your presence to consider Your Holiness' words in detail."

Urban nodded. "It were better, I think, if We were to declare the day's business at an end and adjourn," with which he rose and left, not pausing to say the customary benediction.

Barberini lost all temptation to smile with that. Was his uncle *deliberately* provoking the Spaniard? It was the only possible explanation. Had Borja been allowed to flounce out in the rage he was obviously feeling, he might have saved a *little* face, a matter vitally important to the notoriously touchy Spaniard.

As it was, he was left standing before his chair on the floor of the chamber in which the *curia* had met, publicly snubbed by the pope after a rebuke that had had all the charm and subtlety of a shovelful of horse-shit to the face. He turned on his heel and stormed out, trailed after a moment's hesitation by his attendants and then, in their turn, the rest of the Spanish cardinals.

Barberini, at least, awaited his proper place in the order of protocol before leaving.

Chapter 3

Rome

Cardinal Gaspar Borja y Velasco, at no time a man other than passionate, was in a mood even he considered unreasonable. Thus far, since arriving at the small villa outside Rome that he was perforce required to use in order not to attract even more papal displeasure, he had snapped at every single member of his clerical staff, insulted two of his aides and taken a swipe at a servant with his stick. His ill temper was not helped in the slightest by the sure knowledge that the day's aggravation would be sure to lead to a sleepless night with dyspepsia.

He took a deep breath. He had serious business to conduct in the remains of the day and it would hardly do to be less than polite to such as the Borghese. Like all Italians they were notoriously touchy. A fine thing in its place, of course, but there were limits. Which, alas, Borja had to respect.

And, of course, their support was now vital. He had done no more than skirt around the possibilities with the count-duke Olivares back in Madrid, discuss in generalities what might be done to bring a clearly difficult papacy to heel and remove a potential problem in the way of the strategy that Madrid was evolving to place Spain back in her rightful place as chiefest power in Christendom. Here in Rome, after one meeting with the pontiff, he was firmly settled on the proper way to proceed. There really was no alternative, none worth pursuing, and even failure would see Urban VIII sufficiently chastised that there would be no more trouble from Rome for the ten years that the one-time Maffeo Barberini had left on this earth, if the Grantville histories were to be believed.

Cardinal Borja was a firm believer that among the secondary causes through which God worked his divine will in the world the power of His Most Catholic Majesty to order the affairs of men was among the most powerful. To allow that power to be in any way limited and constrained was in a very real way to thwart the will of God, a course of action so fundamentally sinful that any lesser sin might be contemplated in order to avoid committing it.

In the meantime, of course—

"Is Quevedo y Villega here yet?" he snapped, and realized as he said it that his tone was not yet under control. Not even the sight of gardens in springtime had calmed him. He turned from the window and forced a smile at Ferrigno, who had closed his face to all expression while his master had been simmering. Borja recognized the signs. More than once he had caused the unassuming but efficient little Neapolitan to flinch when he had let loose his passions. Borja could see that his secretary was bracing himself for the storm.

He took a deep breath. "I have no reproof for you, Ferrigno," he said. "You may take it that I am displeased, but not with you." There, that should reassure the man.

Ferrigno nodded. "Your Eminence has heard much to displease him," he said, and the relief in his tone was palpable. "I understand that Señor Quevedo is on his way."

"Good. And Sinceri?"

"He attends Your Eminence's convenience, Your Eminence."

"Send him in, then, and leave us."

Sinceri bore almost no resemblance to what one imagined when the phrase "canon lawyer" was mentioned, still less the phrase "Inquisition Interrogator." Were it not for the clerical dress it would be easy to imagine him as someone's favorite uncle, although his pedantic manner and dryness of phrase also went a long way to dispelling the illusion as soon as he opened his mouth to speak. Someone's crashing bore of an uncle, perhaps.

Sinceri's bow and kiss to Borja's ring were fussy and precise. "Your Eminence," he said. "How may I serve you?"

Borja took a deep breath. Let it out, in a long sigh. "Father Sinceri," he said, "we are, are we not, faced with a problem?"

"Your Eminence?" Sinceri looked genuinely puzzled. "I understand Your Eminence to be concerned at the import of the dispensations concerning consanguineous marriage that the Holy Father recently granted, and I have taken the liberty of preparing a legal opinion—"

He reached into the leather folder he had been carrying for a document.

Borja waved it aside. "I thank you most sincerely for your efforts, and indeed for your consideration in attempting to anticipate my concerns, but it is in regard to another matter I wished to speak with you."

Sinceri's frown of puzzlement grew deeper. "I should be most grateful to be enlightened by Your Eminence."

Borja began to pace. The afternoon's business before the *curia* still had him simmering. Walking back and forward helped to calm him. "Father Sinceri, I feel it will be helpful if I rehearse a little of the mutual history we have with the current Holy Father."

"The Galileo affair?" Sinceri cocked his head to one side. His professional attention engaged, Borja fancied he looked more than a little like a portly, yet sleek old carrion crow. One with a smattering of gray feathers amid the black, but all the more distinguished looking for them.

Borja nodded. "You are most perceptive, Father Sinceri. The Galileo affair is indeed that part of our mutual history to which I refer. You will recall, if you please, that the matter was decided wholly without regard to proper inquisitorial procedure, and indeed wholly without regard to the proper rule of canon law."

Sinceri gave a small sniff. "Most—"

His had been a career spent enforcing obedience to the church, and in particular obedience to its hierarchy, and Borja could see that the idea was giving him more than a little trouble. "Most irregular," Sinceri finished after a short, but nevertheless embarrassed pause.

"Irregular?" Borja let a little incredulity come into his tone. In truth, the sarcasm and bilious humor was not in the least feigned. The conclusion to *that* sorry business still rankled. The near-picaresque farce of the denouement at Galileo's final hearing had been a mockery of the dignity of the cardinals and of the church that not even the most ribald of the romantic writers of the day would have stooped to.

If nothing else, they would have been jeered in the streets for the shameless slapstick implausibility of the whole business. And *he,* Cardinal Gaspar Borja y Velasco, had been forced, in what with hindsight could only have been a deliberate and calculated insult, to take part in the whole degrading machination. Borja felt himself flush a little redder in his just and proper indignation at the mere memory.

"It was more than irregular," he went on. "It was a deliberate abuse of the dignity of Holy Mother Church by one whose charge it is, a charge laid on him by the Holy Spirit no less, to preserve the Church in all her glory. It was a deliberate abuse by one whose holy duty it is to preserve the Church against her enemies, within and without, whose solemn oath of office it is—" Borja stopped himself.

"Your Eminence is clearly exercised by this matter."

"Exercised, yes," Borja said, trying to collect himself. That Barberini was plainly unfit to hold that most holy of offices was plain for all to see, yet how many dared to speak of it? Borja could see that behind the professional mask, Sinceri was profoundly embarrassed by how this conversation was going. Still, let him be embarrassed.

"It is my belief that His Holiness has overstepped the bounds of what is acceptable in the behavior of a pontiff." There. Approach the matter carefully.

Sinceri thought that one over. He cocked his head upward, regarding the ceiling with its plaster cherubs and giltwork carefully as he turned the idea over. At length he said: "With the greatest of respect to Your Eminence, and to the matters of policy on which Your Eminence has sought to persuade His Holiness, I am not at all certain that that is a matter on which I entirely follow Your Eminence, in particular having regard to precedent—"

"Horseflies, Father Sinceri, horseflies!" Borja had been dealing with lawyers of one sort or another since he had been old enough to have charge of affairs, and knew the signs. It was best to stop them before they started on the hedging and obfuscation that their training made as natural to them as breathing. And canon lawyers, those who specialized in the laws of the church's governance, were the worst. All the obfuscation of lawyers with the pomposity of theologians on top.

"Your Eminence?" Sinceri raised an eyebrow.

Borja permitted himself a small smile. "You will recall that nearly every single appointment His Holiness has made since assuming the mantle of Saint Peter has been of one of his placemen, and more often than not a member of his family?"

It was Sinceri's turn to smile. "Ah. Your Eminence reminds me of the vulgar jest about the bees on the Barberini arms? That they were once horseflies? It is true that His Holiness has carried nepotism to unusual lengths, but it is not without precedent, and indeed—"

Borja cut him off again. "The man's concern for his family is, in truth, not without precedent. What I say to you, Father Sinceri, is that it is entirely revealing

as evidence of the man's character. *Entirely revealing.*"
Borja snarled those last two words. He could feel the
anger boiling up within him as he contemplated the
man whose every action of the last few years had been
to set the authority of the Church against the power
of Spain, a course of action as personally frustrating
to Borja as it was wholly unnatural and obviously
contrary to God's scheme for the secular world.

Borja took a calming breath and carried on before
Sinceri could interrupt. "It is becoming clear to all who
have eyes to see, Sinceri. The man's selfish interests
are guiding his actions, now, and quite likely always
have been. I truly fear to think what his motives
might be for impeding the progress of Catholic arms
in the Germanies—for permitting the outrage in the
Low Countries—but no matter. The question which
brought you to mind in relation to the matter I have
in prospect was the Galileo affair, as I have said.
I think we are agreed that there was much in His
Holiness's disposition of that case which gives cause
for concern, no?"

Borja watched Sinceri's face. There were other
lawyers who might be of service in what Borja had in
mind. There were certainly plenty of inquisitors who
were at the very least slighted by the pope's treatment of the Holy Office the year before. Of the men
who were in both groups, Sinceri was the one best
known personally to Borja; they had worked together
before on Inquisition business. And, when all was
said and done, Sinceri was one of the most senior
and respected lawyers in the Inquisition's prosecuting
arm. His opinion, publicly expressed, would carry a
lot of weight.

Certainly, Borja could manage without Sinceri in the scheme he was now firmly settled on. But there were definite advantages to having his support.

Sinceri's nod of agreement was almost instant, and Borja felt the first moment of genuine pleasure he had felt all day. "Indeed, Your Eminence," he said. "His Holiness' actions were quite—unprecedented."

A characterization, Borja reflected, that was quite spectacularly damning coming from a lawyer. He schooled his face to solemnity. From here, there was only the direct route to the destination. "The matter I have in mind," he said, "is nothing less than the impeachment of His Holiness."

Sinceri's response was immediate. "Impossible."

"Unprecedented, certainly," Borja replied.

"Not entirely," Sinceri said. "The antipopes, in particular, are the precedent to which I refer Your Eminence—"

Borja let the details wash over him without much attention. He had, of course, studied canon law himself and was familiar with the whole business. There had, more than once, been two claimants to the mantle of Saint Peter. Dozens of times, in fact. The polite fiction was that one was the true pope and the other an impostor, determined by which one had been legally elected. But the Church's firm statement on the subject was not necessarily the whole truth. Many of the thirty or so antipopes recorded in history had contrived to discharge real functions of the office and had only become antipopes after the event, so to speak.

In practice, the record was frequently patchy even as to some of the clearer-cut cases. It was sound theology that the Holy Spirit worked in the world through the wager of battle, and by extension through the outcome of political maneuvering, after all. Borja privately speculated that the record had almost certainly been altered or effaced after the event to insure that the eventual loser appeared as the antipope to the eyes of history.

Borja could see the way clear at every step. It was *simple*. The sheer celerity with which the plan had come to him was an indicator of its true source.

"—and so, Your Eminence," Sinceri was saying, as Borja returned from his private reverie, "while there has been at least one abdication of a pope from his office, not one has been dismissed whether by the college of cardinals or otherwise without his successor coming down to us in the historical record as an antipope. The precedent is clear: the pope cannot be impeached."

"There is no way?" Borja asked, knowing the answer from other canon lawyers, consulted before this day.

Sinceri gave a small, dry chuckle like the rustling of old parchment. "Your Eminence will recall the jest that there is precedent for nothing until it is done for the first time, perhaps?"

Borja laughed politely. "Indeed," he said. "We must simply hope that His Holiness sees the error of his ways and abdicates, no?"

Suddenly, and to Borja's mixed delight and alarm, Sinceri was every inch the inquisitor, the dryness antarctic rather than scholarly. "I am sure the Holy Spirit will guide him to the right conclusion, Your Eminence."

A statement, Borja realized, which could be parsed in many interesting ways. Sinceri would never conspire, never scheme. But if a scheme looked like succeeding,

Sinceri and men like him would be there with the right formalities, the right words and above all the right documents to turn a coup into an orderly change of government.

Borja clasped his hands and raised his eyes piously to heaven. "It shall be a conclusion to this matter that will never be far from my prayers," he said. "In the meantime, Father Sinceri, may I ask you to do me the estimable service of having ready a briefing on every precedent for papal abdication, and on the current legislations on the conclave of election? I should be most interested to study at length the scholarly conclusions you have kindly sketched for me today."

"It is the least I can do for Your Eminence," said Sinceri with a small bow of his head. With that, and a few small pleasantries, he left.

Borja passed a few moments staring out at the garden, musing on the fact that he had now taken an irrevocable step that would end in either glory or disgrace. But the possibility of disgrace was so small as not to be worth thinking about. There was a calmness in him now that he took for a sign of divine favor. Once the Holy Spirit moved, hesitation or squeamishness surely took on the character of sin.

Audacity and ruthlessness would see the matter through. The only secret that truly needed to be kept would be Borja's own willingness to shape his means to fit his end, and do so without betraying his holy purpose with so much as a hint of scruple.

Ferrigno entered silently. "Signor Quevedo y Villega has arrived, Your Eminence."

"Send him in." Borja turned away from the window. "Have wine brought. The man is an incorrigible sot, and seems unable to speak without a cup in his hand." In any event, Borja felt that a small drink of wine would not be out of order, in toast to the enterprise he was beginning.

"As Your Eminence wishes." Ferrigno bowed himself out to attend to it.

There, Borja thought, was the secret to effective statecraft. A staff who got on with the matter at hand without undue frolics of their own. Francisco de Quevedo had been pressed on him by Osuna as a useful tool in the present business. He was not a tool that would have come naturally to Borja's hand. If nothing else, the dash the man had cut at court in Madrid these past few years had offended Borja's austere sensibilities. A satirist and a humorist and a man the Spanish Inquisition had had to censure for writings once already.

Quevedo's history of wild scheming—scheming that as often as not ended in disaster—suggested that he was a tool with a mind of his own. Such were dangerous. Had he not been in Italy raising Cain because he'd had to leave Spain for a while after killing a man in a duel? And, of course, the man's most prominent failure had been the Venetian plot, which was an additional risk in using him. There was another of the Venetian plotters in Rome, a man who knew Quevedo and might recognize him.

Against that risk there was the excellent record the man had of creating complete and imaginative chaos wherever he went. It was only to be expected that that was where the man's talents would lie, since his other claims to fame were as a soldier and a poet. At once a brute and an artist, a thought that forced another bark of laughter from Borja. *Exactly* what Rome needed right now.

If Quevedo's plotting erupted into a spectacular debacle, that was all to the good. A descent into anarchy was what Borja wanted for Rome. If the anarchy ran out of control, so much the better. There would be a very present remedy for that ailment on hand at just the right time, provided Osuna kept his part of the bargain. There would be troops and to spare in Naples for anything Borja saw fit to use them for.

There came a knock. "Enter," Borja said. A servant opened the door to usher the spy in while another brought the wine Borja had ordered.

Quevedo was all that his reputation said he would be. An older man in his fifties, he nevertheless carried himself with the arrogance of a man much younger. Tall, imposing, doubtless of the kind who in his younger days would have been a favorite with the less reputable sort of lady, he carried the marks of both dueling and drink on his face. His clothes were outlandish to Borja's eye, but then he had spent too little time in Rome to have paid notice to the fashions prevailing. Still, for a man who had made part of his career as a secret agent, he cut a remarkably striking figure.

"Your Eminence," Quevedo said, bowing low and sweeping off his hat, a plain black wide-brimmed affair which lacked the feathers usually seen on such but which did sport a colorful hatband.

He straightened up and addressed Borja with a small half-smile causing his dark but graying mustachios to quiver slightly, "I, Francisco de Quevedo y Villega, am at Your Eminence's most humble and dedicated service."

"Señor Quevedo. You have been briefed on this afternoon's proceedings at *curia*?"

Quevedo tossed his hat aside, on to a couch. "I have, Your Eminence. An agent within the Vatican staff proved most informative. Am I to assume that your business in Rome is to be transacted to its most full extent?"

Borja nodded. "My plans in that regard are not fully resolved. I have great hopes that His Holiness will heed the urgings of the Holy Spirit and come to a reasonable accommodation. In the meantime, what progress can you report with the business on which you were sent to Rome?"

"Satisfactory, Your Eminence. Rome is a city with, I must regretfully say, far too much time on its hands. There is a new fashion among the lower gentry to ape the manners of the Americans. Some of these *lefferti*, as they are known, are remarkably easy to lead into bad ways. One might express a pious regret at the ease with which the devil's work is done." Again, that little self-satisfied smile.

Although Quevedo had been a fixture at court in Madrid for a few years, he and Borja had little to do with each other. Indeed, this was the first time they had spoken directly—and Borja was finding the man disagreeable already.

"The devil's work, Quevedo?" he said, arching an eyebrow.

Quevedo threw back his head and laughed aloud. "Your Eminence seeks that the devil shall make merry that God's work be done under cover of the confusion. There are plenty of idle hands with which his infernal majesty might play, be sure of it."

"I shall thank you to keep a civil tongue in your head here, Quevedo, even if your japeries are tolerated at Madrid," Borja snapped.

Quevedo bowed again. "Your Eminence justly reproves and chastises his most humble servant. I, Francisco de Quevedo y Villega, make most prostrate apology if my jesting words gave offense, which I assure Your Eminence was entirely without intent on my part."

Borja nodded acknowledgment. Clearly the man had all the polish of court, even if tarnished by incorrigible levity. "Handsomely done, Señor Quevedo. For my own part, I beg you forgive my testiness of manner. A man of my standing within the Church can abide not even jesting references to deviltry. However, do go on. The *lefferti*, you say?"

"Yes, Your Eminence. The American Harry Lefferts passed some months in Rome during 1633, and many of those with whom he kept company have taken to aping his manner of dress and disreputable ways. Uniformly low sorts of a kind with which Your Eminence will doubtless be unfamiliar. It takes little to bring them to brawling and license, as easy as leading pigs to the trough."

Quevedo gave a small sneer at the very prospect, although Borja knew full well that Quevedo's reputation—indeed, his all-but bragging in some of his bawdier poems—included a great many dalliances and the patronage of houses of ill-repute.

"It sounds like a most promising beginning. Señor Quevedo, your specific orders are now to raise all the foment you find yourself able to in Rome. You are unleashed to this task, and may draw on funds through my man Ferrigno. Anything and everything which may be done to the discredit of the House of Barberini and their governance of the city and the Church will be of assistance in our designs. Spare neither pains nor funds in your agitations."

Borja took up a cup of wine, noticing that Quevedo had not, in fact, done so already. "A toast, Señor Quevedo, to success in your enterprise!" he said, and drank.

Quevedo picked up a goblet for himself. "To the successful execution of Your Eminence's orders," he said, and drank in turn.

Borja set down his cup: the wine had been passable, at least, but he noticed the turns of phrase Quevedo had been using. "Let us indeed hope you are successful, Señor Quevedo," he said. "I should be unhappy to have to condemn a luminary of the Spanish Court before the Inquisition for foul deeds committed in Rome. It would embarrass His Most Catholic Majesty unduly, in a time when any embarrassment must be avoided by all of his loyal subjects."

"Your Eminence makes himself most excellently clear," Quevedo said, again with that little smile. "I, Francisco de Quevedo y Villega, assure Your Eminence of my most diligent efforts."

"See that it is so," Borja said, and dismissed the man.

It was, Borja reflected, good to know that someone who was, in the event of failure, utterly expendable was also so utterly disagreeable. Hidalgo himself to the core, Borja nevertheless recognized that the touchy honor and ferocious independence of those gentlemen of Spain who had not devoted themselves to the Church and its hierarchy was more than frequently an obstacle to the efficient ordering of affairs. Although, in this case, a certain inelegance and readiness to resort to violence would do no harm and might actually help.

There remained only one final piece to play in this first move. Cardinal Pietro Maria Borghese was a Genoese nobleman; therefore, at least nominally a Spanish client. Nevertheless, he and his cousins in the *curia* would have to be brought in to the fold for the upcoming enterprise as cardinals in their own right by persuasion. Since they were not directly subjects of the king of Spain, they could not simply be ordered as the Spanish cardinals were.

The interview with Borghese nevertheless promised to be a simple and uncomplicated one. At Urban VIII's election the other cardinal who had been regarded as *papabile* had been a Borghese, and the somewhat odd chain of circumstances that had left a Barberini on a papal throne that the Borghese had regarded as theirs was still a source of mild resentment. They regarded themselves as eminently *papabile* in the event of another vacancy in the Vatican, so they would be inclined to assist in any scheme that might create one. And, of course, they could read one of those so-called future histories as well as anyone else, and see the surname of the pope who would have been.

For the moment, though, Borja would be meeting with the youngest of the Borghese cardinals. Pietro Maria was a man in his early thirties placed in the church more out of dynastic convenience than any real commitment to religion on his part. There was a distance to be maintained in the early stages of a plot such as this. Not that the man's youth would be any indicator of his easiness to deal with. Like all scions of the great houses of Italy, he had imbibed politics and chicanery with his mother's milk.

Borja took up another cup of wine and composed himself to await Borghese's arrival.

Part Two

March 1635

Chapter 4

Rome

"You know, Ruy, this guidebook is next to useless," Sharon Nichols remarked. She'd had the thing sent all the way from Grantville, one of a very small number of guides to foreign cities the Appalachian town had had before the Ring of Fire. It was, if anything, worse than useless. Apart, that is, from the slightly amusing coincidence that the USE's new embassy in the eternal city was just up the street from where the up-time embassy of the United States had been. Or would be. Or something.

"My lady speaks the truth, as ever. What need have I of maps and rutters and"—he sneered, as magnificently as only Ruy could—"*guidebooks,* when I have but to know I am in your presence and can therefore never be lost?" He composed his face in a smile of such seraphic contentment that it was all Sharon could do not to crack up there and then.

As it was she chuckled, and hugged his arm where it was through hers. "There are times, Ruy, when you verge on the impossible." She looked up into his face again, and saw the beatific countenance had returned to the usual impish grin. A grin that made it difficult, sometimes, to remember that he was almost as old as her father. And was still recovering from a severe abdominal injury to boot. Technically, at least—the most she'd ever seen was him wincing a little getting up in the morning.

That was Ruy Sanchez de Casador y Ortiz. Somewhere in his fifties, he still thought getting into a sword fight against six-to-one odds was a perfectly reasonable proposition. Of course, he'd spent most of those fifty-some years fighting in Spain's wars and skirmishes on three continents and had survived everything that had been thrown at him. Come right to it, he'd put four of his six opponents down before they got him, leaving the other two for Sharon and Billy Trumble to deal with.

She'd found his courtship hard at first, perfect seventeenth-century gentleman though he was in that as in all things. She still found the memory of Hans painful, even now nearly a year and a half after his death, and with all the things that had happened since. Life did, indeed, go on, but at its own pace, and she hadn't been ready. And there, if you wanted to see a bright side, was the real beauty of Ruy. Old enough and scarred enough himself, he'd understood perfectly and been patient. Then, just as she was being relieved of her duties at the Venetian embassy by the new resident down from Magdeburg, the Day had come. A Day that merited a capital letter when she thought about it. The Day that fell a year and a day after Hans had died protecting Wismar from the Danish invasion fleet. The day she'd promised Ruy an answer to his marriage proposal.

By the Day there had been no doubt. By then she'd found a new life of her own, as a trader, diplomat and—as she thought of herself—medical missionary to the surgeons and physicians of down-time Italy. She'd also had months of Ruy's charming company to make her answer a foregone conclusion.

That just left the wedding to plan. Which reminded her, they'd come for this walk out of the new embassy—recently upgraded from a consulate by Sharon's arrival as ambassador—for a reason. The fact that Rome had been remodeled in the time between now and the future date at which this dog-eared guidebook had been written had somehow let her get sidetracked. In fact—

"Ruy? Are you trying to distract me?"

Innocence personified, cherubic this time. If, that is, you could imagine a cherub with conquistador mustachios. And wasn't that a laugh—almost the first thing Ruy had done in his military career was a term of service as an actual by-God conquistador.

"Don't give me that look, Ruy! You've been trying to duck out of planning our nuptials ever since I said I would marry you."

He had the good grace to look abashed. "Sharon, I confess, it is true. I am a simple man. For me it is only you that matters. Alas for my unpretentious nature."

Sharon snickered, and Ruy responded with a look that was old-fashioned even for the seventeenth century.

"Alas, as I was saying, for my unpretentious nature, it is only proper and right that all proper ceremonies should attend such a beautiful bride. Alas, for my grasp of these matters is not all it should be. I am but a poor, untutored Catalan country gentleman—"

"Ruy!"

"It is true!" His face was a study in wounded innocence. "What do I know of protocol and precedence and, what is the word you use, *showers*? Sharon, my love, truly I would also like to see the day of our marriage executed with all proper ceremony. But I have every confidence that, even as far as we are from both our homes, we can secure the services of very good people—"

Sharon raised her eyebrows. This was a new one on her. She'd thought he'd been being his usual testosterone-driven self and trying to duck out of Gurl Stuff.

He paused and grinned. "Sharon, the sacrament of marriage is simply the outward sign of the grace of God. Like all outward signs there are people who make an art of it. Neither of us is without means, let us simply have—" he gave a languid wave, the perfect courtier for a moment—"everything."

"Not quite everything, Ruy," Sharon chided him. "That would be *tasteless*."

Another joke that had quickly grown old and comfortable. She was so much more restrained than he was, more moderate. Putting Ruy and "moderate" in the same sentence just wouldn't do at all. She suspected that if he truly did let rip on their wedding plans, well—she had visions of cardinals, probably even the pope, dragged in at gunpoint to officiate. A lightning raid on the Vatican, to secure St. Peter's for the ceremony. And Ruy, grinning at the altar rail with a ring he'd stolen for her from—

She quashed the thought. They had come to the Piazza di Spagna, which to Sharon's disappointment had yet to have the Spanish Steps installed. Then she realized that thought had led to another. "Ruy? I've been talking about who I can get here to our wedding. How about you? Who will you want to invite?"

He stopped, remained silent, and turned around on the spot taking in the view of the piazza. He sighed gently. "This is a thing of some sadness for me, Sharon. I have passed many years in this world and made many enemies and many friends. And many of those friends, too many as I now recall, cannot come to our wedding."

Sharon realized, not knowing quite how for nothing showed on the old soldier's face, that Ruy was close to tears. She stepped closer and hugged him. His embrace in return was fierce and strong, like everything about Ruy. And yet there was that core of grief and burden, at being what he was not and the pretense that made his life possible. On top of which, the friends he must have buried, and the wives. Somehow she felt it would not be right to cry for him, though. Don Quixote-on-steroids that he was, a weeping Dulcinea did him no justice at all.

"And I suspect most of the enemies couldn't come even if they wanted to, hey?" she said, quietly. Ruy could see through flattery, and took it in the spirit in which it was intended.

He stepped back, holding her at arm's length by the shoulders, grinning fiercely. "Those few that live would not dare!" he sneered, surfing over a moment's melancholy on a wave of braggadocio. "But there are some few friends remaining who might yet come to see me marry again. I shall write letters, a chore I have, I confess, avoided until now. The pen may indeed be mightier than the sword, but I find it considerably more tedious to wield."

And wasn't that the truth. It wasn't until they were living under the same roof on a semiformal basis that Sharon had discovered that there was more to being a swordsman than just owning a sword. Or, even, a couple of swords. Ruy's career had seen fashions in dress and military swords change several times. He had kept up with fashion, but seemed unable to bear to part with old weaponry. Racks of the things, and other weapons besides. Had Sharon not known that Ruy hailed from a rural region, she'd have pegged him for a hillbilly from that alone. His collection of lethal hardware was eye-popping stuff that was cousin in spirit to the racks of guns one still saw in the backs of trucks around Grantville and the arsenals many of the townsfolk maintained beyond anything they could ever actually use.

And all of Ruy's weaponry, apart from a few collectors' pieces, was used, some of it to the point of near collapse and most with at least one outrageous story attached. A fair bit of it was for ornamental as well as lethal purposes, too. He had more dress swords than Sharon had dresses, although she was working on remedying that condition now that the actual cash from the previous year's trading successes in Venice was starting to filter through.

"I think," she said after they had strolled along in companionable silence for a while, enjoying the sunshine and the street bustle of Rome in the spring, "I'll see what the hired staff at the embassy know about whatever the local version of wedding planners might be."

"Most excellent, my heart. You may approach the day of our nuptials knowing that matters are in professional hands, and I in the sure and certain knowledge that I merely need stand in place and recite my lines in order to have my heart's desire."

Sharon decided on a change of subject. "We've not heard back from the Vatican about a proper meeting, yet," she said.

"I misdoubt you will, my lady. His Holiness could not refuse to receive your credentials as ambassador, but more would be inopportune."

"Mike and Don Francisco warned me as much. Not that we've a lot to talk about with the pope, as it happens. It'd just be nice to do some proper ambassadoring to go with all the other work we're doing here."

"If I may make the pretense of being a judge of diplomatic skill, your other work is no cause for modesty, Sharon." He wagged a finger at her. "Let it not be said that the ties you make and break in this city do less than the utmost good for your country."

"Flatterer."

"Deserved flattery, for your modesty, becoming as it is, ill serves your talents and finer qualities. I, Ruy Sanchez de Casador y Ortiz, say it is true."

She slapped his arm. "Enough, already," she said. "I'll get a swelled head."

"Ah," he said, after a few moments' more stroll. "Here is a contact that, if it is offered, you should cultivate."

They were passing the Palazzo Barberini, much of which was shrouded in scaffolding and busy with workmen. It was a constant reproach to the Barberini pope Urban VIII that his relatives were leeching on the church's revenues for projects such as the grandification of their house in Rome, a project that would result, according to Larry—now Cardinal—Mazzare, Grantville's former catholic parish priest, in the place having been one of Rome's foremost art museums outside the Vatican when the then Father Mazzare visited it in the twentieth century.

"I've thought about trying to get a foot in that door, yes," Sharon said.

"Most astute," Ruy said, "indeed—"

Sharon cut him off before he could deliver another dump-truck load of praise. "—as I was saying, I was thinking about getting a foot in that door, but I figure that whatever's holding the pope back's got to be holding his relations back as well."

"True. Although I suspect that there are younger members of the family—Antonio Barberini, for example—who might be less constrained. A matter, of course, for your judgment."

For a wonder, he seemed to be offering plain and simple advice, not heaping on the praise and flattery that Sharon, for all her protests, secretly rather enjoyed. Perhaps he genuinely was trying to hint that she *could* make an end run around the official attitude of noncommittal that the Vatican's equivalent of the State Department was maintaining.

The year before, when there had only been a consulate relaying radio messages from Magdeburg and the Low Countries, there had been messengers to and from the Vatican the whole time. Of course, between the business with Don Fernando and the pope's refusal to help Spain by interfering in Naples, Spain was profoundly annoyed with the pope. Not least because of what it cost them to move as many troops as they had in to Naples and Calabria—and what it had cost them to get the duke of Osuna to desist from open rebellion was anyone's guess, as was how firm his newfound loyalty to Madrid might be. And what with all those troops in Naples right now, His Holiness was probably a little more nervous of Spanish displeasure than he'd been before he'd had a medium-sized army just across the border "suppressing internal dissent."

"Well, maybe," she said, as they came level with the grand entrance of the palazzo. "For the moment, I don't really have any reason to be urgent about cultivating any contacts there, so it can wait a while. Maybe we can invite this Antonio—he's a cardinal, isn't he?—to some function or other just to test the waters. Meantime, I've got other chickens to pluck. This stuff about Cardinal Borja, for one. And getting married to a disreputable old Catalan, for another."

"Ah, wounded to the quick," Ruy groaned.

The Piazza Barberini, as the guidebook named it—Sharon wasn't sure if it bore that name quite yet, although the palazzo had been there long enough that it might—gave on to several little side streets that looked as though they might prove to be a shortcut through to the neighborhood where the USE embassy now stood. The road that should have led directly there seemed not to have been built yet. According to the guidebook, Mussolini, Napoleon and Victor Emmanuel had remodeled large amounts of Rome among them. So the relationship between the street plan in the back of the guidebook and the streets Sharon and Ruy were actually walking was sketchy at best.

The attempt at a shortcut turned in to a rather confusing series of lefts and rights through increasingly narrow streets—alleys, to give them their right name—and it became obvious that even in the good parts of Rome there were places where the company was less than congenial. Sharon had no particular difficulty with that. While she had grown up in a nice part of town, her dad's ghetto clinic had been a place she'd gone with him from time to time. With him being so familiar with that kind of neighborhood Sharon had never really gotten the idea that the other side of the tracks was alien territory. So she wasn't more than mildly concerned—it being a bright morning, after all—until Ruy halted in mid-chat and stopped her with a hand on her arm.

"A moment, Sharon," he murmured, and then in two quick and surprisingly silent strides was at the mouth of a side-alley between two buildings, scarcely three feet wide. She just about caught the glint of his dagger and the blur of his arm reaching round the corner and suddenly Ruy was swinging around and bringing a roughly dressed individual with him into the middle of the narrow street they had been walking down.

He had one hand in the guy's collar and was jabbing the pommel of his dagger into the guy's arm just below the shoulder. "Good morning!" Ruy said, brightly, once the scream and the stream of Roman vernacular had subsided.

Another burst of obscenities.

"If you are going to follow us and work your way around to ambush, friend, be less clumsy, hey?" Ruy said, in Italian with a distinct flavor of gutter. Sharon had heard him address merchants and doctors and minor nobility in the floweriest formal phrases. She'd had no idea that he was also fluent in the kind of language she'd heard the stable hands at the embassy using.

"I wasn't doing—" The protestation was choked off in a strangulated squawk as Ruy flicked the tip of the dagger up the guy's face and held it, unwavering, maybe a quarter-inch from a wide, staring eye.

"Nothing?" Ruy finished for him. "Then why did I just have to make you drop that blade?"

Sure enough, there was a knife in the gutter. Maybe four inches of cheap metal, bright and worn-down from years of sharpening. With that, he had to have intended to simply stab Ruy straight from ambush—using it to merely threaten a man with three feet of Toledo steel on his hip would have been suicide.

"Nk," said the would-be mugger, who Sharon saw was probably only about fourteen or fifteen.

"Don't hurt him too badly, Ruy," Sharon said, "he's probably starving. In fact, here," she reached in to her purse and pulled out the little .38 she usually carried these days. "No, hold on—I—" She fished about again and came up with a few small coins. "Get yourself something to eat. You look like you could use it."

"Her copper or my steel," Ruy said in a mild tone, releasing him.

The mugger took the money and ran like hell.

"A nice touch," Ruy said, "with the pistol."

Sharon grinned back. "Would have been if it'd been intentional. It's just that I keep it on top of everything else."

"Also nice. Now, I believe that if we turn left at the end there, we will be back on the Via Veneto."

They passed the remaining half hour of their stroll with inconsequentialities and pastries they bought from a street vendor, and returned to the embassy in time for a mid-morning coffee.

Chapter 5

Rome

Franco was cooling his heels as usual in the mid-afternoon heat, savoring a bite of lunch—which was, in truth, his breakfast, the night before having been a busy one—when the money walked in. The guy was dressed down some, but it was clear that there was cash and to spare about him. A Spaniard, from the looks of the sword he'd got, and it was the sword that was the clue to the money. That and the knives that were just discreet enough not to attract attention, and just obvious enough to make sure any attention he got was polite. A lot of rich guys wore a sword just to let you know that they had the pull to make it worth your life to mess with them, but only the ones who really meant it carried knives as well. An older guy, some gray at the temples, dark longish hair and cavalier mustachios, neatly trimmed. The guy could afford a pretty decent barber. He carried himself like a well-trained swordsman, and that was another thing that took plenty of cash. Everything about him stank of money. You didn't even have to start making guesses about what he had hanging from his belt under that jacket to figure there was a useful amount of silver about his person.

So, some rich Spaniard, slumming on the wrong side of the Tiber. Franco looked around the taverna. It was Marco's place, and as usual was quiet around the middle of the day. It was kind of quiet in the evenings, too, which was why Franco generally took himself there just after he got out of his bed, because he was not generally at his best at that time. Still, if money walked into the place where he was breaking his fast, it was not for him to argue the matter. Nor, particularly, to wonder why the Spaniard was looking for entertainment at this hour, when most respectable folks had the business of the day to take care of before they thought about getting their ashes hauled. If Franco's luck was in—and assuming he could get either of the idle bitches awake to do business . . .

Still, time enough for that. There wasn't anyone else in the place who might steal a march on him, so he set about finishing his lunch while the Spaniard was getting himself a jug of wine. The guy was reasonably new in town, so he wouldn't be quite so likely as to give Franco the brush off straightaway. In his rare honest moments, Franco would be willing to admit that his girls were not exactly about to go off and make their fortune as high-class courtesans such as might be found in Venice. The pair of them were costing him a fortune in mercury salts, a fact that was widely known around Rome. So, until he could find something a little more valuable, Franco was reduced to hooking his girls up with out-of-towners and doing other odd little jobs on the side.

And that was another possibility to look out for, Franco decided, as he poured out the last of the wine he'd bought. A lot of rumor was flying about. One of Franco's more reliable sidelines was passing on information to people who might want to hear that there was a damned good reason there were a lot more Spaniards in town right now. They were pretty much all up to no good, one way or another, which meant that there was a certain amount of money floating about. Franco was currently not too proud to take that kind of money for pretty much anything.

He was just about ready to get up and go talk to the man when the real reason the Spaniard was drinking in a dive like Marco's turned up. A guy that Franco vaguely knew as a militia cavalry officer, a moneyed idiot who was occasionally seen looking for a whore but wasn't quite enough of an idiot not to know what he was in for if he approached Franco. The guy had a sergeant who, when he wasn't riding the horse his boss paid for, had an approach to most things that happened off the street and out of sight that was mediated by modest and regular payments, so it wasn't like there was a major problem there. They were mostly exactly the kind of town guards that Franco thought that a city should have, which was to say guys who liked getting about on horses and looking impressive for the girls and otherwise not bothering the citizens overmuch. The foot-constabulary were a lot more of a pain in the ass, since they knew pretty much who to lean on, and when and for how much. A sore trial in many respects. Still, Franco was in enough money right now that he was eating, so he didn't care to go looking for trouble. He got himself a little more wine while he waited for one or the other of them to leave so he could see about getting some cash from whichever remained behind. Fortunately, there was a fairly lazy, low-stakes dice game going on in one of the back corners. Franco could stand there and spectate with one eye on the money, so he didn't look too much like he was spying.

Why such a man as this militia officer would be consorting with the likes of this Spaniard, Franco had no idea. It was probably worth waiting to find out, though.

The two of them spoke for maybe half an hour or so. There was a lot of intensive gesturing. They stayed close together and the militia guy seemed to be concerned that he wasn't overheard. And was even a little nervous about being seen with the Spaniard. After a while he left, looking around him the whole time. The Spaniard leaned back in the chair he'd been occupying over on the other side of the room and stared right at Franco with a big grin on his face.

Franco knew when to take a cue, and so he sauntered over. "Looking for anything in particular, friend?" he asked, taking a seat uninvited.

The Spaniard shrugged and tilted his head to one side. "I just might be, at that," he said, his grasp of colloquial Roman quite good, "and I think you might be a fellow open to business propositions of one sort or another."

Franco gave his most engaging smile in return. "Well, now," he said, "it's early in the day, and not many could point you in the direction of a good time this early, but I think something might be arranged for the right sort of gentleman. Looking for anything in particular?"

"Well, probably not what you're thinking," the

Spaniard said, topping up his wine from the jug on the table, and most hospitably offering Franco a refill of his own cup.

Franco tried to keep his expression friendly. He hadn't figured the guy for a boy-lover, certainly not from his looks. And come right to it, Franco wasn't entirely sure how one went about catering for the likes of that. Oh, he knew it went on, but had never actually seen it going on, so to speak. "Ah, just what exactly were you thinking of, my friend?" Maybe now was the time to find out.

"Well, I need a few guys to do a little troublemaking. There's money in it, for maybe a couple of hours' effort." The Spaniard raised an eyebrow, waiting for an answer.

Franco tried not to let his relief show. When the Spaniard had started asking for a few guys he'd thought he was about to get asked to set something up that would ruin his good name in the city forever. "What kind of trouble, and how many guys do you need?" He was already mentally starting to draw up a list of fellows he could probably rely on to deliver at least a moderate beating, and a slightly longer list who would be good for standing around and looking threatening.

"Thirty, forty," the Spaniard said, rocking his hand from side to side. "And mostly it's standing around and shouting stuff outside one particular house. A popular protest, you could say."

"Popular protest?" Franco kept his face straight. This was *political*. Sure, he'd take the Spaniard's money, but he'd also make sure to have a prior engagement that would keep him somewhere other than where this "popular protest" was scheduled to happen. A lot of the time, if people got together and sounded off about whatever was riling them, none of the mucky-mucks cared that much. Every so often, though, someone would have a wild hair up his ass and then it was constables with billy clubs at the very least, and the likes of that militia guy ordering a saber-charge at worst. Sure, it was more than likely that there would be a bit of noise and everyone would go home, but—

"Yeah," the Spaniard said. "I've organized a few of these in the last few weeks. Just turn out where and when I say, shout a few things that some guys I'll send along will be there to pass around, get in the way and block the street for an hour or so, and that's all that's needed. It's been pretty trouble free so far. What it is, is the guy who's paying me wants a few other guys told that they're playing the wrong politics. And part of that is making 'em feel like the people of Rome don't exactly want them around. Everyone we've done this to has been an out-of-towner."

"We?" Franco said, curious and willing to at least find out how much the Spaniard was willing to spill.

"I've got a few other guys out looking for warm bodies, local guys. Truth be told, I wasn't expecting to be asking anyone myself, but after my old friend left I could see you were probably a fellow with connections of one sort or another, just getting by the best you could, and maybe you might know a thing or two about finding the kinds of guys we need. And, you know, there's a little consideration in it for you."

Franco grinned, suddenly taking a dislike to the Spaniard, although not to the money he'd mentioned. "Well, yes, a little consideration and I might just pass the word to some fellows I know."

With that money changed hands and the location of a taverna over by the Via Ripetto. Franco didn't like the fellow any better with his silver in his hands, but since it was only for talking to a few guys, it wasn't any great issue. And if he could talk a few of them into actually turning up, by no means an easy proposition if actual exertion was in the offing, so much the better.

But what really annoyed Franco about the Spaniard was the cheap joke about the cost of mercury salts he made when Franco suggested a little action for the afternoon. And Franco felt entirely justified. Anyone who could tumble to how shabby Franco's line of goods was when he was that new in town was clearly a smart-ass. And no one liked a smart-ass.

He especially didn't like the Spaniard when he saw the man later that same day, sitting earnestly discussing some proposition or other with Tomasso the Florentine, a man well known as one of the biggest assholes in Rome's underworld. Rumor had it that the guy had done three murders for pay, and had no qualms about a fourth. If he was getting that friendly with a moneyed Spaniard who was messing in political business, someone, somewhere, was going to get reamed.

Which made it all the stranger that, when everyone else was winding down after an evening's drinking, the Spaniard sat alone at a corner table, writing like he was some kind of damned clerk.

Chapter 6

Rome

Frank opened the door and looked inside. The building had looked ratty enough from the outside, although that was only to be expected when you considered the rest of the neighborhood. Inside, it looked like—

"What a fucking *dump*," said Dino from somewhere behind Frank and Maestro Bazzi, who had met them at the new place to hand over the keys and get Frank's signature on the lease.

"A real fixer-upper," Frank agreed, ambling inside and twirling the key ring on his finger. The place was a state, all right. From the looks of it, the ground floor had last seen its intended use as a taverna around twenty years before. The neighborhood looked like the better days it had seen had been in Caesar's time. Either prime Committee recruitment territory or a wretched hive of scum and villainy. Or, of course, both at the same time.

Maestro Bazzi, who was more or less the Cavriani office in Rome—truth be told, an attorney who handled the occasional bit of business for them, for Rome was not a major trading city—had come through exactly as asked. Cheap, low-rent neighborhood, something that could be opened as something like a taverna. To the letter, this place was. Although there was a definite smell of something here: sewage, and possibly something had died in the cellar.

Dino put down the box he'd carried in after Frank. "Where should we put our stuff, Frank?"

"Good question. I think maybe we should have a look around, first."

"Is all to your satisfaction, Signor Stone?" Bazzi asked.

Frank looked around at the lawyer, who had followed him in and appeared to be trying to keep from touching anything and getting a couple of decades' worth of dust and ratshit on his clearly expensive clothes. "Oh, certainly, Maestro, our requirements have been met exactly."

Bazzi's expression clearly showed he thought Frank wasn't playing with a full deck, but he was politeness itself. "I am grateful for your confidences, Signor Stone, and with your leave I shall proceed to other affairs. Please, do not hesitate to call on me if you have any further requirements, for it is an honor and a pleasure to serve a son of such a famous and illustrious house."

That confused Frank for a moment, and then he remembered that his dad and stepmom were well on their way to becoming some of the richest people in Europe. Sharon Nichols wasn't far behind, either. But, yes, it was just about possible to describe Frank Stone, former hippie kid from the Lothlorien Commune, as the son of a great house. If you squinted a bit. He tried to nod an acknowledgement in the best noble style—the little voice in the back of his mind sniggered uncontrollably—and replied in the floweriest formal Italian he could manage, "And thank you, Maestro Bazzi, for your most excellent service and please be assured we will not hesitate to recommend your services to all of our friends."

Frank decided he'd got it somewhere near right, for Bazzi gave a little bow. "I thank you, Signor Stone, and please, if you see Her Excellency Dottoressa Nichols before I next have that honor, do be so good as to remember me to her. She is a most charming lady as well as being one of my most valued clients." With an elaborate flourish of formal good-byes, took his leave.

"The dottoressa is still in Rome, then?" Dino asked.

"Guess so," Frank said. Sharon had been moved from the Venetian embassy to the Roman one by Mike Stearns, although Frank wasn't up on the why of it. "I wonder if she's okay about us dropping by to say hello?"

"Why wouldn't she be?" Dino asked. "You've known her for years, haven't you?"

"Yeah, but she's an ambassador now. I guess she's got to be careful about meeting"—Frank grinned—"us scary revolutionary types. I remember when we were first in Venice. They told us not to mix with the Committee."

Dino snickered. "Sure, and you ignored it then when you were a respectable diplomat; who says you gotta respect it now you're a wild-eyed revolutionary yourself?"

Frank chuckled. "Well, not a whole bunch. On the other hand, Sharon's pretty cool, she's a friend, and I for one don't want to give her any grief while she's working. I mean, she's the USE ambassador, right? I figure that means we're sort of on the same side, even if we gotta pretend like we're not. So play it cool, I guess. Maybe send her a letter saying hi, or something."

"I guess," Dino said, and Frank was relieved to hear that his cousin-in-law didn't sound too pissed at the thought of not making mischief. *Getting arrested will do that for a guy's sense of fun*, Frank thought.

"Anyway," Frank said, changing the subject, "what do we do about the luggage?"

"Well, I did ask you, *messer*," Dino said, grinning to show he was just kidding.

"Uh, yeah, right," Frank said, remembering. "I guess we should take a look around, see what's where and all, before we start piling things up. Maestro Bazzi sent us a floorplan, but I never looked too closely. Tell you what, go tell Piero to park the carriage in this yard thing here, while I try and get a handle on how this place is laid out. I figure he's going to want to stay overnight before he heads back to Padua with the carriage."

"Right," said Dino, putting the box he was carrying down where he stood. "He's going to ask when we eat—what'll I tell him?"

That was true enough, Frank realized. The coachmen who came with the carriages they'd hired in Padua seemed to have only two topics of conversation, which were how slow they were going, and how long it seemed to be between meals. Still, his own stomach was starting to rumble a bit.

"I figure if you ask Piero to find us a cookshop

or something where we can get dinner, it'll give him something to do while we unload the carriage."

"Sure," said Dino, and went outside.

The taverna was basically one big room with a big kitchen walled off at the back. The previous proprietor's living quarters were two floors above, if Frank remembered the plans right, with guest rooms on the floor in between. Servants got the attics and garrets. It had, in its day, been quite a decent place, judging by the trash. Sure, the furniture was only staying together because the woodworm was being careful not to breathe too hard, but it looked like it had been good stuff, once.

A quick look around confirmed that pretty much the whole building was in the same sort of condition. Four floors and a cellar, the bottom three the derelict taverna, the top two what could just about be called apartments.

The whole building was L-shaped, forming two sides of the coach yard with the stables at the back and the next-door building on the third side. The front of the courtyard was walled off with a high gate in the middle of it. A carriage would go through the gate, just, if everyone on top ducked. And what the building's contents consisted of mostly was pigeon-crap, broken furniture and trash. Cleaning up was going to be . . . interesting.

Still, there was a first job. From outside, he could hear the sound of the second carriage pulling up. And that meant—

He ran downstairs and outside, and there she was. There were some things that tradition just plain got right, and Frank had been looking forward to this.

He handed Giovanna down from the carriage seat

next to Niccolo, the other driver—the inside of the carriage was stuffed full of baggage, and the trip to Rome had been barely faster than the last fiasco—and kissed her hungrily. "Okay," he said, "I don't know if they do this in Venice, but—"

Giovanna squealed when he reached down and caught her up in his arms. As he got her to the taverna door Dino was just coming out and stopped to hold the door open. "Gotta carry you across the threshold," Frank said, trying hard not to show that carrying Giovanna was causing assorted muscles to protest.

Giovanna just giggled, and Frank stepped across the threshold with her in his arms. Only when they were inside did he put her down and kiss her again. *Damn,* Frank thought, *that felt good,* as he broke off to a chorus of cheers and whistles from the guys, who had all got down from the roof of the carriage to watch.

Meanwhile, Giovanna was looking around her at their new home, and her reaction was the same as her cousin's. *"Merda,"* she breathed. "Don't unpack yet! Get the carriages into that yard, we'll get some space cleared."

Frank turned around to where Dino, Fabrizio and Benito stood around the door, and shouted, "Guys, you heard Giovanna! Get the carriages squared away and we'll start clearing up."

Little Benito got moving, but Dino and Fabrizio just looked at each other. Frank could guess what was coming next. Time, he realized, to be distinctly firm with them. "Dino, Fabrizio," he said, sauntering over and putting a hand on each of their shoulders, "am I about to hear some reactionary crap about women's work? Surely not?"

The Marcolis looked confused.

"I really, really hope not," Frank said. "You see, we've got a lot to do here, and we're all part of the same revolution, and we're all the same when it comes to doing the work of the revolution, right? Equality and Fraternity, remember?"

"Sure, Frank, but—"

Frank clapped Dino on the shoulder. "Dino, I know, I know. You've been raised all your life among"— Frank stopped to look either way, and lowered his voice—"reactionary elements, right?"

Dino frowned. "Papa always said—"

"Oh, not Papa," Frank said. "Your neighbors. Everyone else on Murano. Shiftless idle guys who let their wives do all the work around the house, right?" Frank knew absolutely that there were plenty of guys like that on Murano, just as there were in pretty much every time and place. "Guys like that are part of what the Committee is trying to fight against. Oppressors. Exploiters. You know, reactionaries."

Frank couldn't quite pronounce the words the way Antonio and Massimo Marcoli did, with the capital letter, but he could see the buzzwords getting through. Frank always felt that doing it this way was a bit unfair, but there were definitely areas where the Marcoli boys were in need of reeducation and if there were shortcuts, Frank was going to take them.

Fabrizio was starting to nod. "You are saying that cleaning this new place is the work of the Revolution"— he had no trouble with the capital letters—"and not women's work?"

"That'll do for now," Frank said. "Get to it. Start clearing away the trash from this main room, hey? I guess we can stack it in the yard for now and figure out where we tip it later." He looked around. "Uh, I guess we can salvage some of this furniture, maybe, so put that in the stables that aren't being used for the horses."

"Okay, Messer Frank," Dino said, and began carrying stuff out.

Say what you liked about the Marcolis, they had no qualms about hard work, once they saw their way straight to it. By the time Piero and Niccolo returned from the cookshop Piero had found, bringing a couple of steaming pots of a soup they said was *stracciatella*, a big basket of *gnocchi* and another basket with cheese and bread, they had the main room cleared and a table and a lot of mismatched chairs set up.

Giovanna sat down to eat with her sleeves rolled up, soot smudged on her cheeks and her hands red from scrubbing. Dino had gotten the ancient brick range working—Frank wouldn't have been surprised to learn that the thing had been installed in Caesar's time and the rest of the building progressively rebuilt around it over the years—and she'd been using the resulting hot water to good effect. The kitchen was now just filthy rather than the total gross-out it had been when they arrived.

Fabrizio had been going around with the DDT sprayer giving the place a good fumigating. Frank doubted whether a building uninhabited this long would have any lice in it, but the cockroaches would be suffering. They might, he figured, get as much as a whole day free of roaches before their cousins moved in from the buildings on either side to replace their dead relatives. It kind of reminded him of the Freak Brothers cartoon—Dad had been a fan, naturally—where the cockroach king dismissed the millions slaughtered by Fat Freddy's cat by saying "plenty more where they came from." Frank made a mental note to write off for more DDT, and to get everyone alongside the idea of food hygiene.

Dino and Benito had been with Frank, shifting the trash out into the yard and, once they had a couple of rooms upstairs clear, fetching the first of their stuff inside. They'd made a priority out of cleaning gear. Giovanna's insistence on having a full set of that, along with a complete set of cooking utensils, was looking more and more like outright prophecy by the minute.

Frank had been making a mental checklist of everything they'd need to get fixed about the place. While Dino and Fabrizio were pretty useful handymen in all sorts of ways, they were going to need to hire some guys to get it all done in any reasonable time. Again, it was lucky Frank had a rich dad, or this revolution would be going on without any home comforts at all. Not that they couldn't do that, Frank thought as he spooned the soup up, but they'd be a lot less likely to get grief off the Roman authorities if they at least *looked* respectable.

They all ate in silence. It had been a long day, and was starting to get dark outside, and everyone had worked up a good appetite. Except for the coachmen, who just seemed to start with a good appetite and get hungrier as the day went on. "I figure," Frank said, "we should maybe concentrate on getting beds made up for the night, and then unload in the morning?"

That got a round of assent. Grinning, Piero produced a couple of jugs of wine that he'd got while he'd been out.

Later, sipping what wasn't bad wine by candlelight, and sitting with Giovanna on a blanket by a fire made of retired furniture, Frank reflected that this wasn't a bad start on the Committee's work in Rome. He figured that it'd take no more than a couple of weeks to get a Freedom Arches open, although using that name openly in Rome—much less the well-known golden arches insignia—would probably not be a smart move. They'd start by running the place like a social club, and see what they could do about getting a soccer league going. He was actually looking forward to doing a bit of coaching and spending the evenings in the bar, amiably spreading the good word about freedom and justice and generally being the good-natured kind of revolutionary. He'd had a bellyful lately of the other kind in the shape of his father-in-law, who'd had four guys beaten up and their ears cut off—one each, no one could say Messer Marcoli wasn't merciful—only the third time Frank had met him.

Not that Marcoli senior wasn't, for the most part, a great guy and as pleasant a father-in-law as a man could wish for, especially from the perspective of a couple of hundred miles. It was just that when he was thinking inside the box marked "Revolution" he got a little . . . scary.

Frank could see the point of that, in places where things got rough. On the other hand, a lot of Italy wasn't what you'd call a bad neighborhood, not these days, so Frank figured they could do it with food, drink, sports and a lot of social organization.

"Frank," said Giovanna, after a long and comfortable time spent staring into the fire and musing in this way.

"Hmmm?" he replied, not really being up to much

else after horsing heavy furniture and making makeshift beds on top of a long half-day's travel.

"I think I'm going to have a baby."

That stopped Frank's train of thought. Derailed it completely, rather. "Baby?" he said, weakly, unable to think of anything else.

"Yes. I'm fairly certain. Two months, now." She looked up at him. "I think. It's hard to be sure."

"Uh," he said. And then, collecting himself, "Well, I guess there's one way to know for certain and that's wait and see if you *are* pregnant."

"Are you happy, Frank?" she asked.

Frank paused a moment. How *did* he feel about it? After a moment he realized that what he felt was pretty good. Very, very good, in fact. He looked down at her upturned face, paused a moment to fall in love all over again, and let his grin do all the talking.

She smiled back, and it was pure sunshine. "Frank!" she chided him. "Don't tease me like that." Then she reached up and dragged him down for a heart-stopper of a kiss.

When she let him up for air, he chuckled. "Giovanna, darling, it's great news. We'd better start making sure you ain't doing any of the heavy work, though."

She frowned and wagged a finger. "Oh no, you don't! My mamma never stopped working, and none of the other women back on Murano ever stopped working. I am not some stupid noblewoman, finding excuses to lie about all day with the vapors, Frank, and don't say I should."

"Whoa, don't bite my head off. All I'm saying is take it easy for a bit, we're not in any great hurry here, and you've got someone else to think of now."

He looked down at her hand, with the wineglass in it. "Speaking of which," he said, and reached down to take her glass away.

"Hey, I hadn't done with that," she protested.

"Yes you have," Frank said. "Drinking while you're pregnant is bad for the baby. I don't know much about pregnancy, but I do know that."

Giovanna's eyes narrowed. "Who told you that?"

"It's common knowledge in the twentieth century," he said. "No drinking or smoking while you're carrying a baby."

"No wine?" There was a hurt tone in her voice. "I always learnt it was best for a pregnant woman to be happy, so the baby will be happy. No wine with food?"

"Well, you can be happy without wine, Giovanna." Frank could see that this idea wasn't going over so well, even though Giovanna never usually had more than a glass or two of wine with meals, and that watered. "Tell you what, Sharon's in Rome at the moment; we can go see her and she'll tell you. Wine, beer, grappa. It's all bad for a baby if an expectant mother drinks."

"I'll believe it if the dottoressa says it. Meantime, give me that back." She took the wineglass back from him.

Frank didn't protest further. Thinking about it, if pretty much everyone drank and they still managed to have babies, it was probably one of those things that was only bad if the mother did too much of it. When all was said and done, Giovanna didn't drink much by anyone's standards. Certainly not by seventeenth-century standards, and especially not by seventeenth-century German standards. It could probably keep until Sharon gave Giovanna the straight dope.

Besides, Frank realized a little later at bedtime,

the state of mind his mother almost certainly spent most of her pregnancy in didn't seem to have done *him* any harm. So far as he could tell, anyway.

The next morning, after breakfast and after an hour or so getting the carriages unloaded and Piero and Niccolo on their way home, Frank took a moment to check out the neighborhood. They were on the northern fringe of the Borgo, which was apparently one of Rome's roughest neighborhoods.

Frank could well believe it. Half of the neighborhood, even though it was right between the Vatican and Castel Sant'Angelo—you could just about see the dome of St. Peter's from an upper-story window—was in outright ruins. The rest would need a lick of paint and a good sweep just to look shabby.

Even mid-morning, there was hardly anyone about, just a few samples of street-life, a couple of stray dogs and a whole bunch of cats. Frank wondered, at first, where everyone was, but then remembered that Maestro Bazzi had told him it was one of the poorest quarters of Rome, that only the truly desperate lived there, and on no account to go south of the street called Borgo Angelico during the hours of darkness, unless he took several heavily armed friends with him.

Frank could believe that, too, and Borgo Angelico was a whole block over from where he stood surveying the street scene. Still, staying out of the genteel neighborhoods would keep them away from the attention of the authorities until they got established. Hopefully they'd be set up and running smoothly by the time they got their printing press, because that'd be a sure signal for Massimo to come visit, and if there was a man with a talent for putting out propaganda by the ton, it was Uncle Massimo. It would be about then that trouble might start.

It was while he was musing in this way that he felt a pair of slim arms go around his waist from behind. "Slacking, husband?" said Giovanna.

He laughed. "For a couple of minutes. Just thinking about all we've got to do here."

"Oh, yes. A crib to make, and baby clothes to make, and Dottoressa Sharon to see. You have responsibilities, now."

He turned around in her grasp. "You too," he said. "Mind what I said about the wine, hey? One glass, watered, with dinner, and if Sharon tells you to stop, stop."

She nodded, solemn for a moment. Then the smile came back. "It's a nice neighborhood, isn't it? So much space and sunlight."

Frank chuckled. "I guess it would look that way after Murano. I was just thinking it was a bit run-down around here."

"All the better!" For a moment Giovanna was all Revolutionary and a hundred percent Marcoli. "If we are to bring the news of Freedom and Justice to the oppressed, we must go where they are, no?"

"True. But we'll start with the social side of things. Maybe run a school, like Uncle Massimo does, hey?"

"Sure," Giovanna said, not sounding very convinced. "Meantime, we got work to do, husband."

They went back inside and got on with scrubbing their new home.

Chapter 7

Rome

When Sharon came in to her office after breakfast there was, as usual, a stack of paperwork waiting with Adolf Kohl, her German chief of staff, clucking over it.

"This uppermost packet, Fräulein Nichols," he said, tapping a bundle of papers wrapped in ribbon and sealed with a blank seal, "was brought to our door by a street-boy who says he was given a few coins to deliver it by a man he did not know. The boy demanded an assurance that it be given into your hands directly after you had finished breaking fast before he would leave, Fräulein. The remainder is invitations and routine correspondence from yesterday's deliveries and mails, for which I have taken the liberty of having draft replies prepared."

He hovered, plainly intrigued by the mystery. Before he'd been hired by the USE's infant State Department he'd been a foreign-correspondence clerk for some middle-ranking noble or other. The novelty of dealing with actual matters of an actual state still hadn't worn

off, quite, and years of a light and boring workload
had left the gangling, nervous Saxon with a tendency
to cluck like a mother hen when business departed
from the utterly routine. It was a mark of the man
that while Sharon had managed to get him, in private,
at least, to unbend a little as to the Your Excellencies,
he couldn't seem to bring himself to address her as
informally as by her first name.

"You haven't looked to see what it is?"

"Fräulein Nichols!" he exclaimed in genteel horror.
"This packet is most clearly marked private and for
the attention of the ambassador."

Sharon kept her face as straight as she could and
picked up her letter-knife to open the seal. "Well," she
said, "let's see what was so all-fired mysterious it couldn't
have been delivered by a proper messenger."

Pretty much everything else that came arrived with
either a liveried man carrying it or one of the more-
or-less professional messengers who carried things
around any town of any size. So that much about this
packet was unusual. Sharon unfolded the wrapper and
noted that it contained a couple of dozen sheets of
high-quality paper, closely covered in an elegant pen-
manship. She looked closer. It was all in Latin. She
sighed. That wasn't a language she had a good grasp
of, although a year spent speaking almost nothing but
one dialect of Italian or another had given her a leg
up on learning it. She sat forward at her desk and
began puzzling it out to see if it was worth getting
a better translation.

By about halfway down the first page, she realized
that it almost certainly was. And that the radio guys up
in the attic were going to be damned busy tonight.

Magdeburg

Don Francisco Nasi waited on the sofa in Mike Stearns' office for the report he had prepared to have the impact he was predicting. It had been something of an effort for him to get an unscheduled meeting with Stearns, as the increasing pressure on the office of the Prime Minister of the United States of Europe was filling the man's day from end to end and frequently had him burning the midnight oil. The appearance of free time in the prime minister's daily schedule of meetings was a rare event, and it was only the sheer unwontedness of Nasi needing more than his usual twice-a-week briefing session that had persuaded Stearns' secretary to squeeze him in between one meeting and the next.

They were not in the usual conference room—the office staff was taking the opportunity to get that cleaned out and ready for the next session—but in Stearns' actual working office, which had come to remind Nasi of the kind of room his relatives in commerce and legal practice tended to inhabit: filing and paperwork on every surface, and a complete nightmare for the cleaning staff wherever you looked. The office of a man, in short, who toiled hard at important work and was usually too busy to pay much mind to the details, and furthermore did not make life any easier for his staff.

Even so, Stearns managed to be more effective in his role than most of his equivalents. A willingness to work hard—the contrast with Sultan Murad IV of Nasi's own personal acquaintance was striking, and Murad had the entire Ottoman Empire to run—and to get much of the work done himself set him so far apart from other rulers as to defy comparison. It also made Nasi worry, for he had come to think of Stearns as a friend and, in the two years of their acquaintance, Stearns had visibly aged.

Which made bringing him this latest piece of information something of a trial for Nasi's conscience. Although a sly grin seemed to be—

Mike Stearns chuckled. "You know, Francisco, there are some aspects of twentieth-century spy mastering you've missed."

Don Francisco Nasi raised an eyebrow and tilted his head to one side. He recognized that tone. Mike Stearns, prime minister of the United States of Europe, had a decidedly odd sense of humor. He waited for the punch line.

"Well," said Stearns, leaning back from the report—a report that, by rights, should have been still smoking, so fast had it come from the Secret Service Cipher Office via Don Francisco's own team of analysts— "seems to me there's one thing about this source that's missing."

"And?" Francisco saw no reason to uncrook the eyebrow.

"Needs a codename. Something with a hint of mystery about it, something that sounds like it belongs in a Len Deighton thriller."

"Let us by all means call him Harry Palmer, then," Francisco said, pleased that he hadn't missed a beat.

"Truce," Stearns said, holding up his hands. "This time, you were ready for me. Still, a name would be good."

"I prefer not, Michael, truly I do. While a codename

is a useful administrative convenience within my office, I prefer the reports that come outside that office not to have any identifier on them beyond what is in the product itself."

Stearns gave a low whistle. "Every time I think I've reached the limits of your paranoia, Francisco, you still manage to surprise me. Still, your department. What do we know about this source?"

"Well, he has sent us one message so far, sent anonymously to our embassy at Rome. A plain packet, according to the description, handwritten in Latin. The contents are all about church politics, and he seems to have gotten us the outcome of a *curia* session a day or two ahead of our regular channel, and a lot faster since that channel sends his dispatches by courier rather than straight to the embassy."

"Well, that's helpful, I suppose."

Francisco pinched the bridge of his nose for a moment. "I can't help thinking, Mike, that whoever it is knows about how radio works."

"Hmmm. I wouldn't worry about that too much, Francisco. I think it's past time we started assuming that was a blown secret. We've used it too much in ways that give the game away. Tell the truth, I wish I'd sat on Sharon Nichols and her schemes in Venice, except they were doing us so much short-term good that I didn't think about the long-term security risk. And I should imagine that the Vatican and Don Fernando's people have leaked like crazy."

Francisco gave a loud and theatrical sigh, and said nothing.

Stearns snorted. "Can it, Francisco. All we really needed was a head start, and the giant stone towers bought us one. Even now that they've figured out radio is portable, they've still got to reverse-engineer it. You've seen the reports, only a handful of spark stations on the air yet, and most of those not very good. Don't forget the other part. We can hear their radios, but they can't hear ours. We've still got an edge, just not a secret edge. Anyway, back to this guy in Rome. When I get to the bit of your report headed 'Analysis,' what am I going to find?"

"We think it should be treated cautiously." Francisco decided he should accompany that with a grin.

Sure enough, Stearns rewarded him with The Look. "Our taxpayers fund your salary for *what*, exactly?"

Francisco chuckled. "Oh, all right. There are a lot of reasons to treat this with suspicion, frankly. A source that simply walks in off the street and assists us without asking for reward? Baffling, at best, since treason is never undertaken lightly."

"Treason?" It was Stearns' turn to raise his eyebrows.

"Treason," Nasi affirmed. "Our best guess is that the author of this packet, and by all means let us call him Señor Palmer, is Spanish. And since the Spaniards are the strongest national grouping in Rome if one treats the Italians as a lot of disparate subgroups, that makes the giving of insights into their thinking and perceptions to us treason. Information to the enemy. Also, he seems to be hinting that he is both inside Borja's confidences *and* working for Osuna. Since as far as we know Osuna is barely a hair's breadth short of open rebellion, it seems that our man is at least twice a traitor and since he has not asked us for money, I have to wonder why it is he is doing this."

"You think that a traitor's motives have to be clear and comprehensible, and preferably base and dishonest, before you'll trust them?" Stearns' smile was growing wryer by the second.

Nasi nodded. "Actually, that is a good, if cynical, way to put it. I would not say it was always required, though. It is just that this is either the clumsiest piece of disinformation I have received in my office in months or we are dealing with a man of genuine principle. And those, as we both know, are deadly dangerous creatures."

"True. You can always trust a dishonest man, where you can never tell what an honest man will do."

"Virtue is messy stuff, Mike," Francisco said. "If Señor Palmer can bring himself to treason for the greater good, what else will he stoop to?"

"I see your point. So you don't trust him when he says that Borja means to do something bad in Rome?"

"Actually, that's an area where I do trust him. As much as I'd trust him if he had said the sun would rise in the east tomorrow. It's *obvious*, Mike. What concerns me is his hinting that Borja means to depose Urban VIII by some means."

"Is that even possible?"

"It might be. Popes have been deposed and have even abdicated. I took the liberty of having one of my people who happens to be Catholic consult Cardinal Mazzare yesterday. The cardinal is well up on his church history, and he says that there have been something like thirty antipopes, the last of them only two hundred years ago, and while in the history-that-was there never was another, there's no reason why there should not be. I understand the laws on papal elections were tightened some years ago so as to make disputed elections all but impossible, though, so we need not concern ourselves overmuch with the possibility of an antipope."

"Without killing Urban VIII, surely that's the best Borja can manage? I don't know much about the Catholic church, but I do know that popes reign until they die." Stearns was riffling the pages of the report as he spoke. "Do we really think that Borja means to have Urban assassinated?"

"Truly, I do not have enough information yet," Francisco said. "And it is not limited to assassination, I fear. Cardinal Mazzare was able to cite at least one papal abdication. Urban could be forced off his throne by some means."

"Impeachment?" Stearns began stroking his chin. "I know that was a live issue when we left the twentieth century—"

"Impeaching the pope?" Nasi frowned. "Cardinal Mazzare did not mention—"

Stearns waved his hands. "Sorry, no. The Clinton business, I meant."

"Ah, I do recall that, yes." Nasi had studied that part of the twentieth-century United States's political history with almost as much interest as he had Nixon. There were some remarkable parallels with events in his own homeland, with the exception that there impeachment resulted in the offending pasha or vizier feeding fishes in the Sea of Marmara. "How does it bear on the situation in Rome?" he asked.

"Well, it doesn't, really, except that it's sort of the first thing I thought of when you said the word 'impeachment.'" He snorted. "I guess there's sort of a parallel, though. If Borja's as peeved at the pope as this suggests, and God knows the man has been peeved at the pope before, and vice versa, he might be looking for something, anything, to get Urban out of office."

"You think he might be looking for a—what was her name—Monica Lewinsky?" Nasi found it an amusing thought, but the days of popes openly maintaining mistresses were long over. He couldn't be sure but that the last one hadn't actually been Alexander VI, who had been Cardinal Borja's ancestor, or a great-grand-whatever uncle.

That was good for another chuckle from Stearns. "Maybe. I think the real issue will be something a bit more theological, or possibly just plain failure to agree with the king of Spain. Or—I dunno. Any clues from Señor Palmer?"

"Not really. He hints at dark deeds afoot against the papacy, and also hints that Borja has bought Osuna off so as to have a free hand, but says nothing specific."

"Can we ask for more?"

"He gave us no means to get back in touch with him, alas. I have some good people in Rome, in the embassy and—elsewhere. We could run this one as quite a useful agent, on either side of the balance."

"With a pinch of salt for the moment, then?"

Nasi nodded. "I think so. It puts a name to our prediction of a backlash within the church after the Galileo affair, and as it happens that name was on the top of our shortlist."

Stearns nodded. "Consequences if he succeeds?"

"A papacy hostile to our interests. Almost what we expected to deal with when we were first beginning, until Urban began positioning himself as strictly neutral—which, as you have remarked before, says a great deal from a man who is technically supposed to be on one side of a conflict. Only slightly worse than we might have expected had Mazarini not intervened as he did, and so effectively. That was unexpected, and very fortuitous."

"Sure as hell was. Crowned heads of Europe with no figleaf. Heh. Still, what can Borja do against us?"

"'How many divisions has the pope?'" Nasi quoted. "In this day and age, several, but they are not first-rate troops and they are a long way away. Indeed, if it comes to the worst, not even well-positioned to defend Rome itself without several weeks' notice. The issue, I think, is a moral one. There are some rulers—none of the principals here in Europe, but a number in the second echelon and lower—for whom the backing or otherwise of the pope will weigh on their consciences heavily enough to provoke concrete action. And, of course, it will create problems here in the USE between the different confessions. If the Protestants can accuse the Catholics of divided loyalties—" Nasi left that hanging. There was a demarcation point beyond which problems ceased to be his responsibility and became somebody else's.

Stearns drummed his fingers on his desk. "Probably. Can't think of a damned thing we can do about it from here, though. Any suggestions?"

"Other than waiting for more messages from Señor Palmer? No." Nasi had been mulling it over all night, had finally slept on it, and woken none the wiser.

"Hmm. Need to think on it, then. While I have you here, the message which Sharon sent straight to me. Don't tell me you don't read them."

"It wasn't marked private, Mike," Nasi said, smiling.

"True. Seems our ambassador thinks her prime minister might stop some of her wedding guests going down there for the nuptials. Like I could stop Rita doing anything she set her mind to." Stearns snorted. "Sharon's not the only one does as she damn well pleases. Ain't no wonder those two got to be such friends at college. The pair of 'em are . . ." Stearns waved a hand, as if trying to grab the word out of the air.

"Ladies who know their own minds?" Nasi offered.

"Ornery cusses, is more what I was thinking. James says he figures the only way to get his daughter to do anything is to forbid her from it, and Rita's the same. How safe will they be, Francisco? Professional assessment?"

Nasi had already thought this one through. "On the journey? Just a matter of enough guards. Any one of seven mercenary companies locally would be trustworthy and adequate to the task. Exactly the kind of work they like, as well, since it pays them to avoid trouble. I can let Rita have a list of worthwhile captains to approach. I assume they will not travel on state business and permit you to send Marine horse with them?"

"It might be that there's something for them to do in that line, but I'd rather not. Rita needs a vacation—"

"As do you, Mike," Nasi put in.

"—I know, and I'll rest when I leave office," Stearns

went on. "I don't think they'll need diplomatic immunity. Unless you've got a different assessment?"

Nasi waved a hand in the air. "Three months ago, I would have put it at no foreseeable risk. Now? Rome's mob is a paltry thing, compared to the likes of the *arsenalotti*, but still capable of storming an embassy. That is the risk, you understand, for the persons and property of ambassadors still remain sacrosanct to official action. It remains to be seen whether what Borja is planning will stir up popular passion to the point of street violence. I personally doubt it, but it is not a point on which I count myself an expert."

"Borja himself?"

"Unlikely. On his record, he is not a clever man. He's impulsive, tactless, high-handed and with more *amour propre* than is good for a man in his position with his responsibilities. Whether he is stupid enough to include an assault on embassy property with his machinations, I very much doubt."

Stearns nodded. "So what you're telling me is that you don't have enough information to justify a decision to recall Sharon out of danger so she can get married in Grantville and incidentally keep my sister from traveling to the other end of Europe in the middle of a war?"

Nasi folded his hands and looked piously toward heaven. "Mike, I am sure she will be a good and dutiful woman and do as her husband commands her."

Nasi watched with satisfaction as his chief cracked up altogether for a few moments. "Seriously, Mike, my gut feeling is that there is less to the situation in Rome than meets the eye. There will be trouble in the church government, of that we may be certain. Urban's position may well become difficult, if not untenable, but that will take months, if not years. I feel sure that Olivares is making the opening moves in a game that will see his master in control of the papacy, but I cannot see any workable plan he might have made which would result in fighting in Rome within the next year. Our people there should be safe."

Stearns sighed. "Well, I guess that's as much reassurance as I'll get. If your people have the time, though, could you see that Frank Stone and the Marcolis get watched? They're a lot more vulnerable now that they've moved down there, and having someone who might warn 'em to get out ahead of trouble just might save their necks. And I really don't want to be the bearer of that bad news to Tom, really I don't."

"It should be simple enough to arrange. In truth, our people in Rome have precious little to report on much of the time in any event. I am sure they can spare a little time to report on the Committee of Correspondence there a little more closely."

"How are they doing, out of curiosity?"

"Well, as it happens. I shall have the reports collated for Friday morning to let you have a fuller picture. Now," Nasi said, rising, "I have intruded enough on what I am sure is a busy day. You have all the facts at our disposal on the situation in Rome ahead of your meeting with Wilhelm tomorrow, and I feel sure he will ask."

Stearns frowned. "You haven't . . . ?"

"Watergate? No. I have simply made a point of studying the man's political style, much as I have yours, and I feel there are some matters in which he is quite predictable."

Stearns' frown evaporated. "Reading up on your next boss, Francisco?"

Nasi wagged a finger. "Now, now, Mike. That is not guaranteed, and mine is a political appointment. I may well be unemployed soon after you are."

Stearns snorted. "Sure. He's got a lot of respect for your talents, as it happens, and is comfortable enough with the idea of court Jews that he'll almost certainly leave you where you are."

Nasi clapped a hand to his breast. "Such a relief. I fret at the thought of losing my munificent salary."

In truth, Nasi did not do his job for the money. He'd been a rich man when he came to head the USE secret service and would leave office just as rich. He kept enough of the salary he was paid to cover his expenses and used the rest as a discretionary fund for the more delicate operations whose appearance in a departmental budget report under their own names would be embarrassing at least and disastrous at worst. No one could accuse him of hiding expenditures, though. Think of it though he might as the government's money, he was legally and morally spending his own cash on government business. Sometimes he wondered how his successor would manage without that little extra to draw on. Between that dodge and a few others such as the Congden library, still going strong after nearly a year, he managed to spend his departmental budget several times over and still have a reserve arising when he made sure that he spent the official allotment to the cent.

Stearns knew it as well. He laughed out loud. "Be off, go do something nefarious and I'll see you on Friday morning. I have a small pack of aggrieved noblemen to either appease or stomp on, I forget which."

Nasi took his leave and returned to, as it happened, arrange the subornment of a Saxon quartermaster. Quite nefarious enough to fulfill the letter and spirit of his orders, he felt, and it gave him plenty of appetite for supper.

Chapter 8

Rome

Frank was beginning to think that whatever he managed to do as a revolutionary, he always had a career ahead of him in the restaurant trade. Within a week—a week of chaos and backbreaking work—they had had the Freedom Arches end of the operation open for business. Benito was a natural with flyers, a form of advertising that hadn't apparently been a major feature of Roman commercial life until now, and they'd started getting good crowds within a couple of days.

They didn't *call* it the Freedom Arches, though. It was just "Frank's Place" for the time being. Frank had decided right off, even before they got to Rome, that they'd do the political stuff quietly and without fuss. Concentrate on substance, not form, to put it another way. He thought waving red banners and engaging in firebrand street oratory in the same city as—in fact, no more than a couple of hundred yards from—World Inquisition HQ was just plain stupid. Not to mention being a good way to get tossed into a cell. He'd had all of three nights in prison in his entire life and didn't want any more of that than he could possibly avoid, thank you very much.

Besides, it seemed to fit the Roman style. Frank had the impression even before moving to Rome—which had since been pretty well confirmed—that the Church and city authorities, at least with the current pope in power, were inclined to look the other way as long as you didn't insist on rubbing their noses in your activities.

There were only a few flies in the ointment, the main one being the *lefferti*. Naturally, Benito had mentioned that the place was run by Americans, and that had attracted the guys Harry Lefferts had hung around with during his time in the city, along with people with an actual interest in political issues. At least, they claimed Harry had hung around with them.

Harry had been more or less okay for a jock, as far as Frank could remember. He hadn't even been a real "jock" in the first place, in the sense of those mindless high school athletes who honestly thought that winning a football game was something you needed to pray to God for, because God actually gave a flying damn whether the guys in blue and white or the guys in red and gold got a ball across an arbitrary line more often than the other ones did. Harry had been one of the tough kids who were often enough in trouble. No high school letters for him, no sirree. He'd just been a "jock" in the operative sense that the real jocks stayed away from him because he'd beat the crap out of them if they tried to pick on him the way they did on Frank and his brothers. But really not a bad guy, in Frank's experience, as long as you didn't mess with him.

Some of these *lefferti*, though, were mean. Well-dressed mean, like the kind of guys who, when you saw them in a Western, you just knew were going to turn out to be called "Doc" or something similar.

Oh, sure, polite and friendly enough, and they all wanted to practice their English. A couple of them were looking Giovanna over, too, although there wasn't much Frank could do or say about that unless one of them stepped over the line. Not much he could do after, either, unless he was willing to shoot them. All of them had some sort of weapon on their belts. None of them had guns, but there were certainly swords and a couple of bowie knives. They were consciously trying to ape Harry Lefferts, and Frank hoped like hell they'd picked up on Harry's good nature.

On the positive side, at least some of the *lefferti* were reading the literature that could always be found in "Frank's Place."

Frank was taken from his reverie by a customer waving for service.

And one of the kind Frank was less than happy about, to be honest. One of the *lefferti*. "Signor?" Frank asked, going over with pencil and notepad.

"Signor?" the fellow said, swinging his boots off the table, which Frank noted with a small degree of satisfaction had a stack of pamphlets on it from the literature table. "Please, I am Piero."

Frank heaved a mental sigh of relief. This was one of the amiable ones, it seemed. "What can I get you, Piero? I'm Frank, by the way."

Piero touched a finger to the brim of his hat—a wide-brimmed number, naturally. "A pleasure to meet you, Frank. I should like a jug of wine and a pizza, if you please."

"Certainly," he said. "Be maybe half an hour before we have another batch of pizzas out the oven, though."

Piero nodded. "In the meantime, the wine. And when, pray, does the revolution begin?" Piero garnished that one with a big smile.

"Revolution? Not on the menu here, Piero." Frank's instincts started to murmur a gentle warning. He knew the term *agent provocateur*, after all—having been made a fool of by one only the year before. He'd damned near gotten killed because of it.

Piero shrugged. "Harry said something about revolution, I think." He'd dropped into English. Pretty good English, at that.

"Sounds like Harry. You knew him, while he was in Rome?"

"Who didn't? Harry was popular. Some nights, it was hard to get the attention of any girl in Rome, truly it was, but it was hard to resent him for it."

Frank smiled. "Harry, to the life." He found himself warming to Piero. "Say, mind if I join you in that jug of wine? Sounds very much like we have a friend in common, hey?"

That was overdoing it a bit. Frank had barely known Harry back in Grantville. After the Ring of Fire, Frank had seen Harry a few times in the Thuringen Gardens and spoken briefly to him when he showed up at Lothlorien now and then—sometimes on government business and a couple of times to quietly transact his own. Some of Dad's plants didn't turn out to be *quite* medical grade, and he didn't mind the occasional discreet recreational sale, provided the boys didn't make too flagrant a business of it. Although the War on Drugs had ended with the Ring of Fire, there were still some people with distinctly modern attitudes on that score.

However, part of what Frank had been doing since he got to Rome was making as many friends as possible. Contacts and allies and establishing a reputation as easy to get on with were as good a protection as Frank could think of in this time and place. So he went and got a jug of wine and a couple of glasses, letting Dino know that he was taking a few minutes out for political work.

"So, Piero," he said when he got back from the bar and sat down. "How long did you know Harry? He was here, what, six months?"

"About that, yes. Truth be told, I only got to know him later in that time, but as I am sure you can imagine he made something of an impression."

"Well, I guessed that from the clothes," Frank said.

Piero laughed. "Harry certainly changed fashion in Rome, that I can attest. I hear they're calling anyone dressed like this a *lefferto*."

"Seems to me there's quite a lot of you guys?" Frank had actually been wondering about that. Surely, not even Harry could have converted every single male between twenty and twenty-five in the city into an extra from a bad western.

"In truth, not many. A lot of us seem to come here, though. At least, those of us for whom it is not just fashionable dress."

Frank thought that one over. It figured. The ones who'd gotten a taste for Harry's American values would naturally find their way to the Committee of Correspondence's first establishment in Rome, even if it was just called "Frank's Place."

But then—

"You say there are some of you guys who it's just clothes with?"

"Sure. There are always plenty of people with enough money to be idle but not enough influence to have anything to do. Well, I am sure I need venture no lecture on politics, yes?" Piero took a gulp of his wine. "We would, after all, be wise not to incur any more Inquisition attention. I think you are not a popular man in that quarter, whatever His Holiness might say."

"Really, you don't say?" Frank grinned. "And here I was thinking that the pope had told them to play nice."

Piero threw back his head and laughed. "You intervene in their show-trial of the decade, and your punishment is a wedding in the Sistine Chapel? The chances of the Inquisition 'playing nice' after that are remote at best, Frank. Anyone could tell you that."

"Well, yes." Frank spotted the hint. "You can tell me more?"

Piero shrugged, but there was a smile on his face. "A little, as it happens. I have, ah, a cousin?"

Frank nodded. "A cousin, yes. Not necessarily implying any degree of relationship in particular?"

"Indeed not. But what I will imply is that he is from a branch of the family that is not perhaps as well-off as mine, and so must work for his living."

"With the Inquisition?" Frank frowned. This could be—but he resisted the urge to jump to a conclusion.

He'd made that mistake before and ended up in seriously hot water.

"Sure. As a servant, yes? Family pride would have me add as a fairly senior and honored servant, but still a servant."

"Nothing wrong with waiting tables and serving drinks, Piero." Frank grinned. "You want to get involved here, we kind of like it if you take a turn at it yourself."

Piero shuffled through the pamphlets. "So I understand. This is how it is done in Germany, yes?"

"Is indeed," Frank affirmed. "Value of work and the worth of workers is one of the points of our program, and doing a bit yourself is a way of learning that lesson. But about your cousin?"

"I do apologize," Piero said. "My cousin was, I should say, favorably impressed by your performance at Galileo's trial. So he asked me to pass on that your presence in Rome is not passing unnoticed."

"Oh?" Frank raised his eyebrows.

"Oh, indeed. You're safe for the time being, though. The Holy Office will not act against you so soon after that visible demonstration of His Holiness' support."

Frank thought about that for a moment. It was more or less what they'd been counting on, because even though he was a little hazy on the details himself he had managed to grasp that the pope's intervention had been very direct, very personal and very clear. The Galileo affair was very much *closed*, with no reopening possible by, for example, imprisoning and trying the perpetrators on any account.

Of course, none of the perpetrators had wanted to push their luck at first. Galileo had retired to his home, living near the abbey in which his daughter was a nun and probably working on his diplomatic skills for when he published his next paper, which Frank suspected would be a lot more polite than his last one. Most of the Americans had gone back to Germany, and the Marcolis—until Frank and Giovanna and her two cousins returned—had gone back to Venice. Even Mazarini had disappeared, Frank had no idea where.

"Safe?" he asked, after taking that moment to think.

"Within reason, I should say. They have other things to do, I don't doubt." Piero waved a hand in the air. "Oppression of the masses, lying propaganda, show-trials of men in the vanguard of Truth and Progress."

Frank laughed. "Yeah, the usual."

Piero grinned back. "I have a friend in Venice who sent me some of the Committee broadsides your friend Marcoli prints. It is not difficult to mock, I regret to say."

Frank grimaced. "I know. Massimo means well, but I wish he'd stick to actually doing some good rather than just flaming away the way he does."

Piero raised an eyebrow. "He does some good?"

Frank nodded. "Sure. You'll see Benito about the place, he learned to read from Massimo. He teaches street kids their letters."

"What good does that do?"

"Well, the idea is that as they grow up they're capable of more than just grunt labor or enforced idleness. With a bit of education, they figure out how to do things better. Not all of them, just the ones who really were being held back for lack of opportunity." Frank mentally summoned up Committee

Propaganda 101. "You see, the way a lot of folks end up going nowhere just because they're peasants or whatever is a real waste of talent. Give those people some education and the means to use it, and everyone ends up better off. We're trying to make all of Europe a land of opportunity."

"So I've read. For the time being I'll help by buying a meal, hey?"

"Right you are," said Frank, "every little bit helps. You want to get more involved some time, just ask anyone here. We've always got work for willing hands."

Frank took the order back to the bar. Before he got there, though, he heard a commotion and he turned around.

It was two guys over by the door, another couple of *lefferti*, albeit low-budget ones who could only afford the jacket and hat. Both were on their feet, stools overturned on the floor behind them. Neither had his weapon out quite yet, but there was a definite hovering of hands in the general vicinity of belts. The room was starting to go quiet, and the sounds of stool and chair legs scraping as the other customers turned to watch the action was, Frank had learned in only a few weeks' experience, a Bad Sign.

He dropped his notepad and began to amble over. A quiet word might help, and certainly couldn't do any harm. Hopefully, someone was pulling a gun out from under the counter to back him up if it turned ugly. He was careful to look as unthreatening as possible, and pasted a large smile on his face.

"Guys, guys," he said. "How's about being friendly about this, hey."

"Mind your own business," the taller of the two

growled, not taking his eyes off the other guy, who was a short, wide, villainous-looking customer with several days' growth of stubble and caterpillar eyebrows.

"You guys break any furniture, it's my business. My business if there's bloodstains to clean up, too." Frank kept his tone light and pleasant. "Now, I could say take it outside, round the back some place, but maybe you guys can talk about this, hey? Try and get along peaceful-like?"

That provoked a stream of very colloquial Roman dialect from both of them, and hands to clench around the knives—big knives, Frank noted—at their belts. He raised his hands, making placating motions. "Guys? Calm down, please, or take it outside. Neither of you has any quarrel with me, and I'd rather not have to clean up."

Glowering at each other, they did. Frank hoped they'd be able to sort it out without bloodshed, but from the way the crowd of spectators gathered to follow them out—including Piero, he saw—he didn't think it likely.

Chapter 9

Rome

Sharon and Ruy heard the ruckus from three blocks away—or what passed for blocks in a town that had grown, rather than being laid out in the manner Sharon was used to back up-time. As they rounded a corner, one of those tricks of big-city acoustics that Sharon had found were amplified by the lack of automobiles brought the sound of an uproar and what seemed like chanting. The part of town they were in was a little bit run-down, and so the streets were not busy. Such people as there were, however, seemed more than a little nervous, and were looking toward the source of the sound.

"What's that, I wonder?" Sharon asked.

"Trouble," Ruy said, and then, after a moment, smiled wryly. "I predict it will be futile of me to suggest that I am loath to take my lady to a place where there may be trouble, however curious she may be to see the cause of it."

Sharon grinned right back. "Ruy Sanchez, you have got precisely no room to talk about people who don't take care to avoid trouble."

Ruy sketched a small bow. "The chastisement of my intended, however mild, suffices to reform me forever. I, Ruy Sanchez de Casador y Ortiz, shall henceforth be the very model of circumspection. Come, my lady," he said, offering her his arm, "let us go by way of some more refined quarter of the city, even if we are on our way to the Borgo to meet a pack of revolutionary firebrands."

"Oh, phooey, Ruy," she said. "You don't get around me that way. Since we're heading this way anyway, let's go see what's happening. We don't have to go close, but if it's real trouble we ought to take a look firsthand to go with whatever our informants give us to send back to Magdeburg. Besides, we're heading for a worse neighborhood than this one."

Ruy dropped the smile. "Permit me a moment of gravity, my heart. I do not doubt that your Señor Stearns and Don Francisco have spies and informants enough. If I judge the sound of this aright, it is trouble that might well become a brawl, if not a riot, and in such anything might happen. We are heading into the Borgo, a rough quarter, and even I may be overwhelmed by a sufficient multitude. For that matter, a blade is scant defense if cobblestones are being hurled."

Sharon heard the concern in his tone, and realized that if Ruy, a superbly skilled soldier, was concerned, then things might just be a bit too rough for comfort. She'd seen him in action, once. Six armed assailants had only just been enough to take him down that time—and he'd faced those odds with a smile and a stream of witty remarks. If he thought going to take a look at the street theatre was risky, it was probably suicidally dangerous by anyone else's standards. Or could be, at any rate.

Or, and this piqued her a little, he was still operating on that hidalgo spinal reflex that reacted to women as—reality be damned!—frail creatures to be cosseted from even the chance of harm. Strange how a man who had been raised by tough Catalan peasant women could have internalized that damned myth so well.

A moment's reflection, and she decided to try compromise. "Okay. Close enough to get a sense of what's happening. The other end of the nearest street, maybe. We can always skedaddle if it looks like it's coming our way."

Ruy nodded. "My lady's desire is my command." He held up an admonitory finger. "But I shall decide what is a safe distance, and I shall hear no argument about when to withdraw, Sharon. I shall one day be your husband: cultivate now the habit of obedience."

Sharon was quite proud of her Old-Fashioned Looks. On her personal scale, the one she gave Ruy was about an eight, edging up to nine. Even that took thirty seconds to crack him up.

Five minutes' walk brought them to a corner where they could look down the street. It didn't look like much, Sharon thought. A smallish crowd, at most a hundred or so, gathered outside a building she didn't recognize and shouting. "Can you tell what they're saying?" she asked.

"That they are angry?" Ruy hazarded. "Actually, probably more like that they have been paid to come there and shout, or at least some of them have."

"You reckon? I don't know that I could tell a rented mob from the real thing."

"I do not see the kind of thing that real mobs do—you may recall I have been the recipient of the attention of street ruffians before. They are not pressing forward, for one thing, just standing around and shouting. And all shouting the same thing, what is more. Someone has told them what to chant."

Sharon looked again at the crowd. There did seem to be a distinct lack of unruliness about it, although as she watched a fistfight broke out on the fringes, distracting a couple of dozen of the protesters to watch the fun. "You're right, it doesn't look like their hearts are really in it. They're getting distract—Oooh," she said, as one of the combatants took a kick where it counted, "his heart's not going to be in anything for a while."

"Truly not," Ruy said, smiling. "Ah, we spoke too soon—"

Sharon nodded. It looked like the guy hadn't been caught square in the family jewels, and had come back up holding a knife. Not a big one, but enough to raise the stakes. The ring around the two who were fighting finally closed up, hiding the action, but jeers and shouting followed the action.

Behind them, a clatter of hooves on cobbles became audible over the hooting and jeering. "Militia," Ruy remarked, without turning around. "About five minutes too late, if my humble opinion is worth anything."

Sharon chuckled. "Can an opinion informed by forty years of soldiering be called humble?"

Ruy raised an eyebrow and flared his mustachios magnificently. "Humility is a thing of the spirit, woman. The mere possession of uncommon skill and discernment boots nothing to the pride I take in my humility."

Absolutely deadpan, save for the slight twitch of the left moustache, that anyone who did not know him would miss.

Sharon chuckled. "Why late?" she asked.

"Because five minutes ago they were simply a crowd of street-trash hired to be noisy. Now, they are minded to see a little blood. A sensible militiaman will simply chivvy them along to disperse into the taverns such normally haunt. What will you wager me that those eager hoofbeats are marshaled by someone who lacks experience?"

Just then the militia came in to view, wheeling prettily into the street Sharon and Ruy were on. They looked, to Sharon, like they were a cut above the usual seventeenth-century soldier—well turned-out, wearing something that came close to uniforms, their backswords held at the ready and gleaming in the spring sunshine. "They look okay to me," Sharon said.

Ruy's sneer was a pale thing compared to what he was capable of. A demonstration, in truth, of the contempt he had in mind—*not even worth the breath to call them dogs*, was one phrase she'd heard Ruy use a few months before. "Well drilled, well provided for, and badly led. Observe as the cretin on the lead horse—clearly, the horse has the brains and he has the money in that partnership—forms his men up for a saber-charge."

"How can you tell?" Clearly, Sharon thought, Ruy could see more than she could in the details. A lot more. They looked prettified, certainly, and not like the kind of riot police she was used to seeing on the TV news, but there didn't seem to be any obvious reason why they'd not be able to get the job done.

The sabers were, perhaps, a bit nastier than she'd have expected from twentieth-century cops, but then these were rougher times.

Ruy sniffed. "Town guards, militia. You can spot the ones who know their trade by the fact that they look as little like soldiers as they can. The ones who break up a tavern fight, rather than making it worse, tend to look little smarter than the participants—ah, did I, Ruy Sanchez de Casador y Ortiz, not predict this?"

The militia horsemen were lining up for a charge in the street out of sight of the rioters, just around the corner Ruy and Sharon were standing on. The officer on the lead horse—Ruy had picked him out correctly, for all he was attired similarly to his men—leaned down. "Signora, signor, move aside, if it please you. We shall clear this riffraff from the street directly."

"Come, Doña Sharon," Ruy said, adopting the form of address she had never been comfortable with. "Let us move to a less insecure vantage point."

"I thank you, signor. It would grieve me most greatly if the dottoressa was hurt in the unpleasantness to follow." The officer touched the hilt of his sword to the brim of his hat as he spoke, while behind him his men chivvied out into a column of fours. *At least he's up on current gossip in this town*, Sharon thought. As the wealthiest and most prominent black woman in Rome, she was distinctive enough that pretty much everyone recognized her on sight.

Before she'd arrived in Rome, Sharon had assumed that she'd be the only black woman in the city. But, to her surprise, she'd discovered there were a considerable number of black people living in several cities in the peninsula. Having black servants was considered fashionable by wealthy Italians. The same was true in southern France. There were a lot of African women in Marseilles, for instance. In fact, there was a subspecies of charity in France that consisted of orphanages for the out-of-wedlock children of African domestic servants whose masters would not allow the kids to be reared in the household, along with an order of nuns who ran them. In due time, she imagined, these children—or their children—would just merge into the general population.

But few if any of them looked the way *she* did— wearing very well-made and expensive down-time garments and accompanied by an armed caballero. She also knew that her bearing and comportment would be quite different. She still found the idea peculiar—downright bizarre, in fact. But she'd eventually accepted what Ruy and every down-timer told her, that she *acted* as if she were nobility, and high-ranked at that. A veritable Queen of Sheba, as Ruy had once put it.

Ruy took Sharon's elbow and urged her back down the street. "This should be amusing to listen to," he said, irritation coming through the veneer of good humor he usually projected. "And if we retire a little I shall be able to fight down the urge to call out that—" Ruy trailed off in a low, monotone stream of obscenities. Sharon's own grasp of Spanish—still less Catalan dialect—didn't let her follow more than a few words past the pithy description of what the officer's mother had done for a living.

"Calm, Ruy dear. Getting annoyed with stupid people for being stupid really does no one any good."

"Ha! Did not your up-time Charles Darwin say

it? Survival of the fittest? Did I not have clear duty here and now I should improve the next generation of Italians out of all recognition. I pray only that he did not breed before today."

"You think he's going to die?"

"May God grant in his infinite mercy that he should, Sharon." Ruy's tone was suddenly quite grim. "Forty years of military experience, ha!"

Sharon leaned in to Ruy, holding his arm tight. "Bad memories, love?"

"Yes. Of serving under officers like that fatuous, incompetent, deluded dullard." He sighed. "Oh, for a certainty more of his men will survive this day than not, but that will be in spite of him. He has orders to clear a disturbance from the home of some notable, and thinks to make a bold gesture. Ah, here it comes—"

A hunting horn blew from where the head of the cavalry column—thirty or forty mounted men, Sharon guessed—had turned the corner.

"It is as if the Sight were on me, Sharon." He cast his eyes heavenward. "No warning to the crowd to begin dispersing. An advance too rapid to let them disperse, but, since he bids them charge around the corner and left them too little street to achieve a gallop, not fast enough for true cavalry shock."

The sound of clattering hooves from the corner, building to a brief thunder overlaid with wild yells and screams. Then, a sound of a general melee.

Ruy covered his face with his hands. His voice, muffled: "Now, we hear the sound of horsemen in among a crowd. Some have been trampled, of course, but those who remain are frightened, angry and are carrying knives. The horses"—Sharon shuddered as she heard one of the animals scream—"cannot use their strength, and are crowded by people with knives. The rear ranks of the cavalry are pressing in, some of the horsemen broke through the crowd."

"Is there anything we can do?" Sharon asked, hearing another horse scream in pain, a noise that cut through what she knew must be the sound of sabers coming down on flesh. Screams, shouts, the clatter of hooves. And, to the ears of a trained nurse—trauma surgeon, rather, by any standard that mattered, these days—the sound of lacerations, fractures and God alone knew what-all other butcheries.

Ruy's face was bleak. "Does my lady have a preference in prayers for the dying?"

"How did you see this coming?"

Ruy waved a hand. "Rome is a town full of priests. Well-behaved. One might expect the militia to be less than brilliant. But it was when I saw that—" He stopped and took a breath. "No, I shall forego the curses for the moment. When I heard that fool give orders for a charge in column I knew there would be a disaster. There are orders one gives to disperse rioters, Sharon, and there are orders one gives to instigate a massacre. That idiot picked the wrong orders for either."

Ruy's tone had been blunt and professional. Sharon had a suspicion that Ruy had, in his time, taken part in both sorts of military action. The suave hidalgo gentleman's airs he affected had been earned on dozens of battlefields on more than one continent.

"I guess you'd know if anyone would. Say, it sounds like the fighting's over." She felt for her medical bag, which now went everywhere with her; she'd been caught with insufficient supplies once before. "I think it's time to go check on the wounded. Detour on the way to the committee place, I think."

"There is nothing I can do to dissuade you?" Ruy hardly paused for an answer before looking up to check where the sun was. "There is a bright side, by all the saints. We shall arrive at the Freedom Arches in time for lunch, and I shall finally discover what a pizza might be."

Sharon wiped her hands on the last of the boiled rags that a nearby taverna owner had provided to make up the stock she'd carried. "I guess this dress is ruined," she said. She looked down. Both sleeves were soaked in blood, and the bodice was just as plastered. The condition her skirt was in didn't bear thinking about.

The results of the riot were even grimmer. Six horses were dead, two in the fighting and the other four so badly hamstrung that they had had to be shot where they lay. Out of thirty militia soldiers, fourteen were hurt and four were dead. Including, fortunately, their commander, which saved Sharon from having to drag Ruy away from a duel. From the looks, he had been pulled down and then trampled by his own horse. He would have had a chance to escape if part of his troop had not gotten around the crowd and penned them in for a short time.

Ruy laid a hand on her shoulder. "The only order the fool gave was to charge," he said, in a soft voice. "And his men were not so well trained that they left the crowd a way out."

The crowd had suffered worse. The only soldiers they had hurt badly were the ones whose momentum had carried them into the midst of the riot. The rest had surrounded the crowd and hacked away with sabers. With the flats, at first, until they had been forced to fight in earnest. Sharon hadn't even tried to count how many were dead, but out of maybe a hundred who had been here, there were at least forty lying in the street. She'd been able to patch up half a dozen, others had rendered some assistance, but she would not be surprised by a final death-toll of thirty.

The rest had fled, for most of the troopers had been backed up behind their fellows at the tail end of the charge. The few who had gotten around the rioters had penned them in for only a few moments, and when one was pulled down the pressure had been relieved. Like lancing a boil. The troopers left behind, finally under the command of sergeants with some sense, had begun gathering up their wounded and dead. One of those sergeants had offered a sword-salute, but had said nothing. Now, he came over.

"Dottoressa," he said. "I thank you for your assistance. I fear the magistrate will wish to hear your witness of today's work." His face was grim. Sharon wondered if he had known, before the order was given, that he had been ordered to commit an atrocity?

"I can be contacted at the embassy of the United States of Europe," she said. "I shall be back there this afternoon, after I complete the business which this interrupted."

The sergeant nodded. "My thanks," he said. "For what it is worth, Dottoressa, if I had known before the order was given—" he spread his hands.

He had known, Sharon realized, but too late. Somehow she couldn't bring herself to feel sympathy for him. "I hope for your sake," she said, after a long pause, "that the death of your officer is enough to absorb all the blame."

He nodded, gloomily, and thanked her again before turning away to organize his troop's return to barracks.

"It will not suffice," said Ruy. "Like every militia, they are officered by gentry, and such as they do not allow their own to be blamed."

Sharon snorted her agreement. "Not my problem." Then, after a moment's thought, "What is my problem is what the hell started this lot off, Ruy."

Ruy smiled. "Your perceptiveness is yet another of your fine qualities. It is clear even to a simple Catalan soldier such as myself, the very byword of rusticity."

"Knock it off, Ruy," she said. "A rented crowd is one thing we need to look into. Everything in this town is political in some way or other. The fact that it turned into a massacre only adds to the mayhem. We've been here less than a month, and things are—might be, at any rate—turning ugly. I want to know what it means for the USE."

"If it means anything at all," Ruy chided. "You are not a Castilian, to be seeing plots in every shadow, Sharon."

"No, I'm not. But we've got powerful friends in this town, the USE has at any rate, and if things are changing around here it could affect us." She chuckled. "I'm stating the obvious, aren't I?"

"Most insightfully, my love."

"We'll see what the spooks have turned up when we get back. If anything. It all seems to be Cardinal

Whatshisface says this, and Monsignor Whoozit is maneuvering for the other."

Ruy cocked his head on one side. "In truth, these things are the very life of politics in Rome," he said.

"I think I may have heard a trace of sarcasm there, Ruy," Sharon said, looking down ruefully at her ruined dress. "And I'm wearing the reason I think they're missing something."

Ruy nodded. "Although I could wish that you had not rushed on to this scene so quickly, it speaks in a voice like thunder of the finest qualities my intended possesses," he said. "But, indeed, this is an unusual political maneuver for Rome. Did we not have a report that Borja is just outside the city, receiving a stream of distinguished guests?"

"We did. You think there's a connection?" It was Sharon's turn to raise her eyebrows.

Ruy shrugged, an expression into which he could put more meaning than most people Sharon knew could manage in an hour-long PowerPoint presentation. This time he was giving off *I am hypothesizing wildly* with overtones of *But I wouldn't be surprised* with a side order of *I really think we should gather more information.*

"In an infinite universe, Sharon, all things are possible. Even the possibility that I am mistaken. I would wager my three most expensive swords that that display was called for the precincts of some notable who has not curried sufficient favor with Cardinal Borja."

Sharon saw the sense in that. Borja was plainly, even blatantly, Up To Something. The USE's intelligence apparatus was expertly wielded, but still very much under construction. The best that they'd been able to turn up was the possibility that he was seeking to undermine the pope. Turn him, for at least some time, into a "lame duck" pontiff. A low trick, and a traitorous one, but all too common in politics down the ages.

Still, if the USE's newest and most surprising not-quite-ally was under attack in his own capital city, it would be purely negligent not to try to find out what was going on. And the fact that Sharon had had no advance warning that this sort of thing was to happen—assuming that this was only the first incident, or just the first to have such unhappy consequences—meant that there wasn't anyone covering this end of the problem.

That was, she felt, typical of the way they thought in this day and age. Maneuver, infight, factionalize, go to war. No one stopped to think about what the hell happened to the ordinary folks. Armies were sent to "live off the land" as a matter of course, a polite way of saying *go rob the peasants blind, we don't care about them.* She looked around her. There were, even this shortly after the killing and with the soldiers only just about to depart, people about on the street.

Mostly people who wouldn't ever count for much in an account of the Great and the Good, except by implication. When "the mob" was mentioned. Or "popular discontent." Or "civilian casualties." When those even got mentioned in these times.

They were, of course, looking at Sharon in a way she'd gotten kind of used to. First of all, she could afford good clothing, so they assumed she was some kind of nobility, even without the exotic appearance she had for this time and place.

But then they saw her getting down in the street and helping people. They called people like that saints, in this time, instead of—as Sharon thought of herself—simple working stiffs with the training to help.

The fact that she provided medical assistance was just the icing on the cake. Most of them probably had never even seen knowledgeable medical personnel, let alone professionals. That was something she genuinely liked about the Committees. They were trying to make that kind of attitude a thing of the past. People mattered. And that reminded her of why they were out in the first place.

"Right," she said. "Let's go see how Frank's getting on. I think it might do some good to go just as I am, as well. That boy's landed himself right in the thick of this, and I can't think of a better way to warn him to be careful."

"Indeed."

"And on the way," Sharon said on impulse, "we can discuss your new job. Spymaster."

Ruy halted. "Spymaster?"

"Spymaster. Well, intelligence analyst, if you prefer. I want some holes filled in the information I'm getting. I want to know who's hiring rented mobs, Ruy."

"This may be a little more difficult than you imagine, Sharon," Ruy said, his tone unusually serious.

"Surely not," Sharon said, teasing him. "I thought cloak-and-dagger stuff was most of your career?"

"Oh, the skills I have in abundance, let no man say he is the better of Ruy Sanchez de Casador y Ortiz in that regard. But there is the small matter of my being a subject of His Most Catholic Majesty, as is Cardinal Borja. I foresee difficulty with Don Francisco, supple-minded as that man is by reputation, and no end of difficulty if the authorities of my own country hear about it."

"Well, collecting a little local color for your intended can't hurt, surely? Speaking to people in bars and so on. I just want to know what the common folk are hearing and thinking. Gossip. Rumor. Surely no one who'd care about what you get up to would care about what people like that think?"

Ruy laughed, gently. "And to think I joked about your tepidity, woman. There are some subjects on which you wax positively Catalan. I assure you, the more intelligent of the servants of the princes and kings of Europe do concern themselves very much with popular sentiment. Alfonso in particular, since he was very much on the receiving end of it once."

Sharon nodded. Ruy had been Cardinal Alfonso Bedmar's right-hand man, back when he was plain old Marquis of Bedmar and intriguing in Venice. The pair of them had gotten out of Venice just ahead of a mob of *arsenalotti* who'd have had tar and feathers handy if they'd heard of the practice. And been willing to get that much closer to civilized behavior than what they'd actually intended to do to the members of that conspiracy.

"Still," she said. "You could maybe write the cardinal and ask to be formally released from service, and get on with laying the groundwork in the meantime."

"Your very whims are as the commands of God Most High, Doña Sharon. I, Ruy Sanchez de Casador y Ortiz, shall spare no effort in this matter."

He paused a moment as they strolled off toward the Borgo. "Did I mention, earlier, something about habits of obedience?"

Chapter 10

Rome

Frank groaned to himself. The two idiots who were insisting on a fight were heading for the door. He heard Giovanna's voice at his shoulder. "Can you stop them?"

"Don't think I can," Frank said, without taking his eyes off them for a second. "They seem to be dead set on a fight."

"This is the third time since we opened," Giovanna hissed. "Someone is bound to notice, and there will be trouble."

Frank nodded. "I just don't think I can stop these guys short of picking a fight myself." The pair were edging toward the door, neither willing to turn his back on the other. Frank had a vague notion that duels were supposed to be more formal than this, with seconds and meeting places to go to at dawn. Just taking it outside seemed to be a bit informal to Frank. Although taking it outside proved to be a bit difficult with neither guy willing to turn away from the other for even a split second. And that door was none too wide—Frank wondered how they'd negotiate that one. Maybe they'd have the fight right in his doorway.

Just then the door opened. There were two figures silhouetted against the early afternoon sunlight. One man, one woman, which calmed Frank's fears of a watch raid. The man stepped inside first, followed by the woman, and Frank's guts solidified and sank. Ruy and Sharon. Somehow, his instincts for when he was well and truly busted started screaming. He was not supposed to be running a wild-west saloon. *Pull yourself together,* he said to himself, *this is your place, not theirs.*

Ruy looked from one side to the other, taking in the two *lefferti* and their crowd of onlookers, and then settling on Frank. "Trouble, Señor Stone?" he asked, his gravelly voice even and calm.

"Couple of guys got a problem. They were taking it outside," Frank said, trying to sound nonchalant.

One of the would-be combatants seemed to take offense at the interruption, and let out a few choice Italian oaths. "Mind your own business, old man," he snarled.

Oops, Frank thought, with a slight buzz of guilty pleasure. He'd never seen Ruy in action, but he'd heard the story.

Ruy's face broke into a grin. "But I am minding my own business, signor," he said, in fluent Italian. "There seems to be a problem in the place of business of a man my intended is pleased to call a friend. This makes him my friend also, and a friend of Ruy Sanchez de Casador y Ortiz shall have no problem without my utmost efforts to solve it."

The other *lefferto*, apparently forgetting his quarrel for a minute, turned to point his knife at Ruy. "Butt out, old man, or your business will be imitating a gutted fish."

Ruy sighed deeply, converting the movement into a smooth draw of a sword and dagger. Both of them very, very sharp and, for all the golden curlicues about the hilts, very efficient looking. "It may be," he said, "that you are skilled enough to gut me like a fish."

There was a flash of a blade through the air between Ruy and the *lefferto* who had spoken, and Frank could have sworn Ruy—a man in his fifties at least—had blurred as he moved. Ruy was back on his spot, the tips of his blades rock-steady, before the *lefferto* yelped and dropped his knife to grab his hand and clutch it in pain. Frank could see blood already starting to seep between the fingers of the gripping hand.

"But I doubt it," Ruy continued. "And even if you did, my intended is here. I have been present when she totally disemboweled a man. And you can see that she has already been busy today."

Frank looked. Sharon's dress wasn't just in some dark pattern. There were definite bloodstains all down her front. Frank hoped, fervently, that she'd been rendering emergency medical assistance. He'd heard what she'd done in Venice, too.

The *lefferti* clearly got the message. The one Ruy hadn't stabbed in the hand very slowly and carefully sheathed his knife. "Signor," he said, "if I have caused offense to you, I most humbly apologize. I shall go elsewhere and await the man with whom I truly do have a quarrel." With which he went to the door, giving Ruy and Sharon—especially Sharon—an ostentatiously wide berth. The other guy snatched up his knife and scuttled after him.

The rest of the room let out the breath they had all been holding. It came out as a collective sigh. Ruy sheathed his dagger, flourished a handkerchief to wipe his sword point and sheathed that weapon as well. Frank couldn't help seeing a big, mad, feral tomcat, preening after a victory over some lesser moggy.

"So," said Ruy Sanchez, grinning and swaggering in a way that Frank thought was indecent in a man older than his father, "who do I have to kill to get lunch?"

"Man, that's gruesome," Frank said, once Sharon had told the full story of her events of the morning and gotten on the outside of a pizza. Not that the bloodstains down her dress hadn't told a tale all by themselves. Benito had been sent over to the embassy to get her a change of clothes. While she could get away with walking around the Borgo filthy with someone else's dried blood, she had to go through a whole other class of neighborhood to get back to her embassy and the stains would cause comment at the very least.

"It might so easily have been worse," Ruy said over his wineglass. "Fortunately, their commanding officer was killed quickly, before he could compound his errors."

"Frank," Sharon said, "were you involved?"

Frank shook his head.

Sharon gave him a hard stare for a couple of seconds. "Frank Stone," she said at length, "if I find out that there's even the slightest hint of you even stretching the truth on this one—"

Frank held up his hands. "No, scout's honor, I swear. For crying out loud, Ms. Nichols, we're less than a quarter-mile from the Vatican here. It ain't much further to Inquisition headquarters. My record isn't exactly spotless, but jeez, give me some credit for not being totally retarded, hey?"

Sharon seemed to accept that. "I don't want to see you get in trouble, Frank. Not again. And I don't want to see you mess things up for anyone else around here, least of all me. I'm supposed to be an ambassador, and I really don't want to have to explain away another serious incident."

"Not on my account, you won't," Frank said. "Look, we serve meals, we serve drinks. We have a singers' night every Tuesday, and Dino and Fabrizio are organizing a soccer league. We're getting a free school organized. We've got pamphlets on hygiene, basic medical care and technology as well as political affairs—and I make sure to keep those a little on the vague side. Stress on Italian unification, run pretty lightly when it comes to the role of Vatican."

He decided to leave unsaid the fact that Massimo's pamphlets ran a lot more toward the inflammatory side. *Frank* didn't write those himself, after all. Nor did he see any point in dwelling on the minor absurdity involved in stressing Italian unification while not directly attacking the Vatican, seeing as how Frank knew and the pope knew and three out of four urchins in the streets in any town in Italy knew perfectly well that uniting Italy would require dismantling the Papal States. Life was full of quirks.

He didn't think Sharon was really fooled by the act. But then, Frank didn't think the pope was, either—yet;

so far at least, Urban VIII had chosen to look the other way. Frank was pretty sure that as long as he kept the appearance of the Committee of Correspondence in Rome reasonably mild mannered, Urban would figure that the benefit of having them active in the city outweighed the disadvantages. That was a tactic Mike Stearns had recommended to him, in one of the letters he'd sent Frank.

. . . as long as you don't rile them too much, in ways they can't ignore, it's often handy for an establishment caught in the middle to have a devil to counterbalance the deep blue sea—"deep blue sea," as in "Spanish Armada." Just don't be stupidly provocative, and remember that time is on our side.

Frank had been much impressed by the letters. Partly, because it had never really occurred to him that somebody like President Stearns actually *thought* about these things. Mostly, though, simply because Mike had taken the time to write them in the first place. That was as good a reminder as any that "Mr. President," under the fancy suit and the slick manners, was undoubtedly the most radical politician in Europe. Mike Stearns just wasn't dumb about it, the way Giovanna's father and uncle were.

So, he plowed on stoutly, doing his level best to exude the aura of *responsible reformer* rather than *wild-eyed radical*. "When we get a bit of a stake together we're going to start a credit union, maybe a groceries co-op. I *know* the Inquisition's looking for any excuse to land on us, and I'm not going to give 'em one. I've had quite enough time in Inquisition jail cells for one lifetime, thanks."

."Most wise, Señor Stone," Ruy said, "but you are

still at risk. It will be said that you were responsible for the bravos we saw today."

"I can't much help that," Frank said. "Thing is, I've spent as much time as I can hereabouts making as many friends as I can. We get a good crowd in here most of the time. Those two idiots you saw weren't typical by any means. I reckon we've got a couple of dozen character witnesses any day of the week, if we need 'em."

"Not of so much use in a political trial," Ruy said. "But you say you know the Inquisition is looking for an excuse? How do you know, if I might inquire?"

Frank grinned. "Told you, we've got a lot of friends here. One of those friends has a relation who's on the staff with the Inquisition, a clerk or something, and we get passed a warning. They don't want to do anything this soon after the pope made it clear he wanted us left alone. I figure as long as we keep our noses reasonably clean, they'll keep their hands off."

Ruy turned to Sharon. "You remarked earlier that we might have been looking at only one end of the problem? It is my opinion, my dearest, that young Señor Stone is looking at the other end, and possibly also missing something."

"Well," said Frank, mildly annoyed that Ruy was talking about him like he wasn't there, "I figure since lunch is on the house anyway, you might as well fill me in on what I'm missing, hey? And maybe there's something I've heard down here on the wrong side of the tracks that you'll find useful."

Ruy nodded. "An offer most nobly made, Señor Stone. Perhaps there may be some useful exchange to be made. With your leave, Sharon?"

"Unless there's some reason why the Committee can't help the USE's intelligence network, go right ahead, Ruy."

"The first thing," Ruy said, refilling his wineglass, "is that I will warn you to be circumspect. It may be that this warning is not needed, for you have already been the victim of an agent provocateur and seen the chicanery of a true master of the art of deception. But I will repeat it: spycraft is not a trade easily or quickly learnt and you should not attempt more than you are confident is within your skills."

"I'd figured as much," Frank said. "So far it's just been listening to gossip and making sure folks know there's a drink on the house if they've got news for us. Nothing much, really."

"Most wise, if I may make so bold. However, you will not have heard that Cardinal Borja has returned to Rome?"

"I hadn't," said Frank, puzzling for a moment to remember who that one was, and then—"Spanish cardinal, right? He was at Galileo's trial. He's an Inquisitor, no?"

"He is indeed. And he was ordered out of Rome last year but came back. Your local gossip will not have heard that he is in his villa outside Rome receiving a great many visitors, including many high-ranking priests, bishops and cardinals."

"You got a handle on what he's up to?" Frank asked.

"Not as yet," Ruy said, gesturing with his wineglass. "It may be that the worst he can do is to frustrate and thwart His Holiness in revenge for the slights he suffered and the See of Rome's refusal to obstruct

Don Fernando's marriage. That is, as you may imagine, causing consternation among the Catholic powers."

"I can see that. But why would he be hiring mobs to cause trouble in the street?"

"I'm guessing," Sharon said, "because someone didn't want to play ball with him. So he organized that little party just to let 'em know what's what—and if you guys get blamed after last year's fiasco, so much the better."

"Just so," said Ruy. "I have agreed, if permission may be obtained from my former master, to look into the matter as it appears on the streets, as all our existing sources and spies are concentrated among the notables and prelates of Rome. So if there is anything you might hear, Frank, about who is hiring mobs, and on behalf of whom they might be doing it, that information would be most welcome. For our part, it may well be that we will hear sooner than you might if the Inquisition is in danger of growing a pair of *cojones*. You might need warning to leave town in a hurry, eh?"

Frank nodded. "I'll keep an ear out. Just don't expect anything spectacular, okay? I get what comes in the door and what Giovanna picks up when she's out buying groceries and such. We're not really professional spies, you know?"

"True," Ruy nodded. "But on occasion the kind of thing you hear will be of more use than what the professionals gather. Do not underestimate your worth, Señor Stone."

Frank grinned. He could recognize flattery when it came his way, but since he figured he was getting the better end of this deal, in the shape of a possible warning if things were going to go horribly wrong, he didn't mind. A warning, he realized, he might well need quicker than he would otherwise. Sharon and Ruy coming in all bloody had clean driven it out of his mind, but now was as good a moment as any to crack the good news.

"Well, thanks for the compliments, Señor Sanchez," he said, "but there's something else involved, another reason why I can't exactly go haring off being a spy and all, and why I've really, really got to be careful about staying out of trouble. You see, I'm going to be a daddy."

"Bravo!" Ruy beamed, leaning over to clap him on the shoulder. "Let me be the first, Señor Stone, to wish you every joy of this happy event. But where is your beautiful wife? I, Ruy Sanchez de Casador y Ortiz, must not be found wanting when there is a lady to be congratulated!"

Sharon was slower off the mark. "Frank . . . I mean, when? How soon? Where's Giovanna?"

"Here, Dottoressa Nichols," Giovanna said, coming over with a plate of pastries. "I see my husband has finally remembered that we have some slight news to tell." She gave Frank a friendly poke in the ribs. "I think perhaps three months? So six to go."

"You're looking well on it," Sharon said. "Any sickness? You don't seem to be starting to show yet."

"No, I seem to be lucky with the sickness. I felt a little ill in the mornings at first, but not recently. And it is showing, a little, but not in this dress. My tits, though!"

If there was one truly disconcerting thing about having married a working-class Italian girl, it was the utterly straightforward way she spoke about—

"—and when Frank tried to squeeze them, I nearly punched him. I think I did deafen him, I screamed. So *tender*."

"Well, that's normal," said Sharon.

Frank almost cringed. Across the table, Ruy shrugged and gave him a look that, in international cross-time Guy Code said, *women, eh?*

Giovanna nodded. "I thought so, I spoke to some of the other ladies around here. But I would know one thing, Dottoressa." A note of suspicion crept into her voice. "Frank tells me that the up-time doctors say that a pregnant woman must have no wine. Is this true?" She made it sound like they'd recommended she stop breathing.

"Well . . ." Frank guessed immediately that Sharon had run into this particular piece of stunned disbelief before. "Strong drink isn't good for your baby, no. On the other hand, there's not much else that's safe to drink, and a dose of flux will be worse. How much do you drink, normally?"

"Normally? Watered wine when I eat. From time to time, beer."

"You shouldn't be doing too much harm, then. Try drinking cool boiled water instead, though, when you can have that in place of wine." Sharon pursed her lips a moment, then went on. "If we were somewhere with a good, clean, water supply, I'd say leave the wine out altogether, but around here you're probably better off with wine in your water if you can't get boiled. But definitely stay off the grappa, you hear?"

"Yes, Dottoressa," Giovanna said.

"When you've got a moment, drop by the embassy and I'll give you a checkup. I've usually got some spare time in the mornings. Shall we say Friday, about nine? We can arrange regular checkups after that. Make sure you're coming along well, and all."

"I could not impose, Dottoressa."

Sharon held up a hand. "No, Giovanna, it's not an imposition. I've been meaning to hold some free clinics anyway, build up some good will. You can be my first patient."

"If you're sure . . ." Frank said, although it was purely for form's sake. Despite Giovanna's insistence that she was from tough stock and wouldn't "faint like some useless noblewoman," he got the cold sweats sometimes, watching her carry on working. And proper up-time medical care was beyond price, as far as he was concerned. He'd had to live without medical insurance for most of his life, and had discreetly found out what doctors in seventeenth-century Rome charged. The prospect of getting an up-time trained nurse for free was too good to pass up. And it meant they had a regular contact with the embassy as well.

"I'm sure," said Sharon, in a tone that permitted no further protests.

Just then Benito came in, breathless. It looked like he'd run all the way to the other side of town and back. "Hi Frank, Giovanna, Dottoressa, Señor Sanchez," he said, trotting up to their table with a parcel done up in muslin under his arm. "I got the signora's fresh clothes."

"Thanks, Benito," said Sharon. "Frank, if I can have the use of somewhere to change?"

"Sure. Go out back of the bar and pick a room. Giovanna'll give you a hand if you need it."

"Thanks." Sharon got up and left for the back rooms.

"The dress was not all I got," Benito said. "See!"

He held out a piece of paper. "Someone gave me a flyer. I couldn't read all of it, but it looks like someone else is starting a Committee."

"Thanks, Benito," Frank said, taking the paper. "Where'd you get it?"

"Some kid was handing them out on the Via Crescenzio. I took one as I went past." Benito shrugged. "I didn't recognize the guy, though. Just some kid, probably handing them out for a mouthful of bread." A year ago, Benito had been that kid, or very much like him.

Frank nodded. "Thanks again. Go get yourself a cold drink, you look like you could use it." As Benito excused himself, Frank turned the paper over a couple of times—cheap rag paper, smeary printing—looked at the text and whistled. Then, grimaced.

This had the authentic smell of *Problem*. "Well, here's your first piece of intelligence from the Committee, Señor Sanchez," he said, handing the handbill over.

Ruy looked at it, holding the paper at arm's length. "I take it you did not print this?"

"Nope. Although some of the quotes on there are from Massimo's early stuff. Back before we persuaded him to tone it down a little."

Ruy chuckled, but there wasn't much humor in the sound. "Tell me, Frank, how would you go about proving you did not print this?"

Frank had been annoyed. Edging toward angry, even. Ruy's question made him realize that he might have, all unknowing, ended up in serious trouble. "My word of honor?" he tried.

Ruy had the grace not to laugh out loud. "That

might actually work, you know. The standards of proof before the Inquisition are quite high, and they have strong rules of evidence. One of which, alas, is putting you to the question to see if you stick to your story under threat of torture."

"Can we complain that someone's passing themselves off as us? Protest now that that stuff—" Frank waved his hand at the leaflet, which had taken all of Massimo's more inflammatory stuff and combined them into one absolute scorcher of a broadside "—is nothing to do with us?" A thought came to him. "Maybe if we demand they do something about these frauds?"

Ruy threw back his head and laughed. "Truly, that would be a rare jest! Who knows? It might even work."

Frank grinned back. "Hey, don't knock it. If it's dumb but it works, it ain't dumb." Then he pulled his face straight. "Seriously, Señor Sanchez, I think the main thing in our favor at the moment is that we don't have a printing press yet. It's due to arrive soon, I'm told, but for the time being all the propaganda we've got is what we brought with us, and we've had to pay printers to get flyers done for this place."

"I hope for your sake you are right, Frank. For now, perhaps you might try an indignant protest to the authorities. If nothing else, they will not be expecting that. Although whoever produced this also knows about the efforts of Messer Marcoli in Venice, and can readily send in a few samples for them to compare with." Ruy's tone was serious, too. It looked like he had recognized some of Massimo's choicer phrases right off the bat, which left Frank with the uneasy feeling that some bright guy at the Inquisition could easily do the same thing.

Frank nodded, and picked the leaflet back up. "Well, maybe I can talk us out of that situation. After all, this stuff is mixed and matched from a lot of different broadsides and pamphlets, you know. If I point out that whoever prepared this edited it to distort our message, we might be able to get away with it. I dunno, though. Massimo's pretty fiery in the original Venetian as well."

Sharon came back just then. "Ruy, if you guys are finished, I'd like to get back to the embassy. I've got some meetings in the later part of this afternoon, and I'd like to see what we've got on file that we might have missed about what happened today."

"The most pleasurable of duties calls me away, Señor Stone," Ruy said, rising to his feet. "Perhaps I might visit you again in a few days and we can compare notes over a convivial glass of wine?"

"Sure thing, Señor Sanchez. Don't be a stranger, by any means."

"Thanks for lunch, Frank," Sharon said. "Come on, Ruy."

After they had gone, Frank rounded up the others from their various chores. "Guys," he said, "Committee meeting. We have a problem . . ."

Chapter 11

Rome

"The immediate problem is Quevedo," Vitelleschi said.

That, thought Barberini, was the father-general of the Society of Jesus to the life. Straight to the point, not a word wasted. Still, there were drawbacks.

"How is he the problem?" Barberini asked. He'd heard of Quevedo, of course. The man's poetry was well worth the reading, if one took the trouble to learn Spanish. And he had a history that was equal parts pure romance and pure picaresque. The man's capacity for getting involved in the hairiest and most alarming scrapes Europe had had to offer for the last twenty years was, to say the least, prodigious.

"Ha." Vitelleschi came as close to laughing as the man ever did. One short, sharp, bark, accompanied by the flash of a smile breaking through the icy clerical reserve that was the man's defining demeanor. "My agents have nothing but contempt for the man. Flashy, spectacular, prone to overcomplication, and bent on intrigue for intrigue's sake."

"Well," Barberini said, deciding to offer at least

some apologia for the man, "He is a poet and philosopher by trade."

"Philosopher?" His Holiness interjected, turning
away from a shrub just beginning to put forth the
first buds of spring flower. This audience was taking
place, as Barberini's uncle, His Holiness Pope Urban
VIII, was wont to have them lately, in the newly laid
gardens of Castel Gandolfo. They were looking a lot
less rough-and-ready than they had the year before,
that was for certain.

"Oh, yes," Barberini said. "His latest work is on the
proper conduct of Christian monarchs, and most interesting. If Your Holiness takes a fancy to Spanish poetry
I can recommend his work in that line as well."

"Christian monarchs, you say?" Vitelleschi said, in
a musing tone.

"Indeed." Barberini wondered what train of thought
he had sparked.

"Perhaps, Father-General," His Holiness said, "you
would venture to define exactly what the problem with
Quevedo might actually be?"

Vitelleschi coughed, returning from whatever realm
of pure reason he had set out to conquer. "My apologies, Your Holiness. I became momentarily absorbed
in a line of reasoning I might develop further directly.
Quevedo has been retained by Borja in furtherance of
whatever scheme he is currently engaged in. Quevedo
has a reputation, well deserved, for at once being
effective in such schemes and also being prone to
provoke absolute chaos. Until today, I considered the
most probable aim in Borja's schemes to be to provoke
such chaos in Rome in order to prevent any interfer-
ence by Your Holiness in His Most Catholic Majesty's

schemes for Europe. There is also the interesting datum that Quevedo joined Borja's service immediately after Borja bought off Osuna earlier this year. There is no discernible connection between the two events, but the possibility that whatever price Osuna received included the requirement that he assist in Borja's scheme is one that deserves consideration. There was some suggestion that after Quevedo fled Madrid in disgrace some months ago he took service with Osuna, much as he had with Osuna's father."

Barberini felt his eyebrows raising. Vitelleschi appeared to be actually growing loquacious. Clearly, he was utterly entranced by the problem presenting itself to him. Still, the man was staying somewhat in character; he had fallen silent again. His Holiness appeared content to wait for the next communication from the deeps that were the leader of the Jesuits, but Barberini could not resist the urge to prod. "And the Father-General has changed his mind because?"

"Your Eminence reminded me of Quevedo's philosophical treatise. And, necessarily, his other works. I am reminded that the man focuses in no small measure on Brutus as a means of examining the proper duties of ruler and subject."

His Holiness' eyebrows shot up. "Surely he cannot have been ordered to—"

"I would counsel Your Holiness to at least consider the possibility." Even by his usual standards, Vitelleschi had turned grave.

That earned a papal snort. "I doubt it. We are still receiving protests from Naples over Brancaccio, and over Naples from Madrid, but no sign of the military action they threatened, for all the movement of troops to Naples. And, further, if the man was recommended to Borja by Osuna, we need worry less, not more. It was to Osuna's advantage that we refused the requests of his Most Catholic Majesty last year."

"Brancaccio is still in Rome?" Barberini asked. Brancaccio had been a Neapolitan cardinal, and in one of the more delicious scandals of the last few years had had to flee across the border to the Papal States to escape the displeasure of the Viceroy of Naples. They had loudly and blusteringly demanded his extradition, but the See of Rome had flatly refused. So far, nothing had come of it.

"Indeed he is," said Urban, "and mildly embarrassing it is, too. However, handing over cardinals to secular princes for judgment is a precedent I do not wish to set. For now, at least, they do no more than bluster. Reasonably politely, as these things go. However, Father-General, you were suggesting that Borja might have turned Brutus?"

"I speculate only, Your Holiness. The most likely course of events remains that Borja seeks to disrupt the business of the See of Rome. Your Holiness will recall that Spain was most displeased that you stated that you were to take no further part in secular disputes in the Germanies. Since Olivares is sufficiently simpleminded to reason that he who is not with his king is against him, disruption of anything you might do in support of Protestant arms in those wars will be an obvious maneuver for him."

"But you still think there is a risk to Our person?"

"Inevitably. Your Holiness would not be the first pope to be arrested or even assassinated."

Barberini coughed politely. "If I might suggest

that there is no need to plan against one eventuality exclusively? Your Holiness has guards, after all."

"Indeed," said Urban, beaming at Barberini as at a bright schoolboy who had mastered a basic point. "Not all assassination plots are as feeble-witted as Camillo's."

"Indeed not," Barberini agreed. Camillo had tried to kill the pope with sympathetic magic, sticking pins into a doll. He had been tried and found guilty and thoroughly laughed at.

"There is more, however," Vitelleschi said. "The Committee of Correspondence has become active in Rome. Quevedo is using them."

Barberini had heard about that, and could not suppress a chuckle. "So' that was Quevedo?" Barberini was, technically, an Inquisition cardinal these days, and so received reports. "That young revolutionary whom Your Holiness ordered me to marry off to his inamorata was most incensed about the false broadsides that have begun to circulate in Rome. He had to be escorted out of San Mateo, I understand. He demanded an investigation and the perpetrators be punished. It, ah, was what brought those broadsides to the Holy Office's attention in the first place. There is some confusion as a result."

"Ha." Vitelleschi laughed for the second time in that meeting. Barberini began to wonder if the old Jesuit was not becoming addled in his old age: the man appeared to be in danger of developing a sense of humor. "Indeed it was Quevedo," he went on. "The printer he went to is one of our informants."

"And the substance of the printing?" Urban asked.

"A pastiche of revolutionary propaganda, anticlerical

and rabble-rousing. Of a piece with the mobs he has been organizing, to whom his agents have claimed to represent the Committee," Vitelleschi answered.

"Even if it was the Committee," Urban said, "I doubt We have anything to fear from that direction. I have met most of them, and they seem quite ineffectual."

Barberini could see where it was going, however. "I would predict, Your Holiness, that within a few days Borja's tame preachers will be viewing all this with alarm from Rome's pulpits. It would not be the first time that more nefarious elements have used the Committees of Correspondence as a cat's-paw."

"My assessment also," said Vitelleschi. "However, almost certainly a pure distraction."

"How so?" Barberini asked. It had certainly seemed to him, and to his staff, that an accusation that the pontiff was not in control of Rome would be a serious stick with which to beat on His Holiness. Whatever could be turned to reducing the esteem in which the pope was held would be of use to Borja, if he truly wanted to cripple the papacy for a time, or even pending a new incumbent.

"While attention is elsewhere, more useful measures will be taken. It might also be of use in securing wavering cardinals in a vote in consistory."

"Yet His Holiness may override consistory votes—" Barberini began.

"Not without political costs, my dear nephew," Urban said. "It is already said that I am a nepotist and a bloodsucker. If it were added that I am a tyrant also, I should come to find it difficult to have my orders carried out. I have spent much of my political capital in this past year, I must needs husband what I have most carefully. Father-General," he said, turning to Vitelleschi, "there is a service which I would have the *Societas Jesu* perform for me."

"Your Holiness," Vitelleschi nodded.

"I need travel arrangements in hand, discreetly as may be, for every sympathetic cardinal within two weeks' travel of Rome, and men on hand to get them here at the highest speed possible. I think I should like to force a vote in consistory and demonstrate I still have a clear majority of opinion in my pocket."

"As you wish, Your Holiness."

"It only remains to determine the issue. And to ensure that we have a majority on the day of the vote. I think we can summon a majority, yes?" Urban sat down on a stone bench.

Vitelleschi pondered a moment. "Even with the Spanish cardinals all come to Rome, Your Holiness, it can be done. Unfortunately, several of your partisans are outside Italy at this time, so it will be a close vote."

"The Borghese," Barberini said.

"Indeed," said Vitelleschi.

"We will have trouble wooing them away from the Spanish party if they have already defected," Urban said. "There is no love lost between Borghese and Barberini. One wonders whether Borja has promised them anything?"

"I have no information on that matter, Your Holiness," said Vitelleschi.

"Any intelligence you can develop will be warmly received, Father-General."

"No effort will be spared."

There were occasions when Vitelleschi outright frightened Barberini. Somehow, a simple promise of diligence gave him the impression of cardinals hauled in to lightless rooms and the truth beaten out of them. Of course, the society was—usually—a little more refined than that. "I note," Barberini said when the shudder had passed, "that the esteemed ambassador from the United States of Europe was present for one of the incidents in the last week."

"At Monsignor Grazzi's lodgings? Yes, she was. Witnesses spoke warmly of her care for the wounded. Most warmly."

"Grazzi is one of yours, I recall," said Barberini.

"Indeed. Cardinal Borja is not well disposed toward me lately. Or any Jesuit." Vitelleschi's tone made Barberini wonder whether Borja was not biting off more than he could chew. More than one cardinal thought the Jesuits over-mighty, and the fear that motivated those thoughts—and the occasional calls for suppression of the order—was well founded. There were limits to Jesuit influence, but within those limits no pains were spared if the father-general gave orders. "I note that he has not ordered action taken against any USE interest in Rome, however."

"An attempt to divert suspicion?" Urban said from his seat.

"Indeed, albeit only in the minds of the common people. Those of us with access to proper intelligence have quite current knowledge of where Quevedo is and what he is doing," Vitelleschi said.

"But no clue as to his ultimate goal?" Barberini asked.

"No. Quevedo and Borja surely know that there are very few secrets in this city, and keep their own counsel about what their ends might be. It must be soon, however. Troop movements to Naples appear to be nearing completion. My most recent intelligence in that matter is two weeks old."

"Troops?" Urban asked.

"Troops, Your Holiness," Barberini said. "It, along with the movements of all of Spain's senior churchmen, was the first clue we had that the game was afoot. Our initial speculation was that it was simply a measure to crush unrest. Then, the numbers rose beyond any reasonable need for such, and we received reports that troops were being positioned for a movement against France, the movements to Naples being largely a sideshow. However, movements to Naples have gone beyond what might merely be overspill from winter quartering in Northern Italy. They mean, I most respectfully suggest, to threaten the Papal States."

Vitelleschi nodded. "Against that analysis is the fact that everything to our north is fully marshaled as well, and spending on *condottieri* has been liberal in that quarter. It may be that the movement in contemplation is simply too large to be mustered wholly in Milan and Genoa. It may also be that similar concentrations are occurring on France's southern borders."

"If my nephew is correct, why the efforts in Rome itself? No amount of political maneuvering will serve half so well as a tercio in St. Peter's square."

"With the greatest of respect to His Eminence," said Vitelleschi, and to Barberini's mild surprise he spoke the formula as though he actually meant it, "I incline to the view that the political maneuvering in Rome is evidence that an invasion is not intended, at least in the short to medium term. Against that, one might suppose that disorder in Rome could be taken as a pretext for invasion, but such would take considerably longer at the present rate of Quevedo's operations than that number of troops can be quartered in readiness."

"And if your various sources are missing something?" Urban asked.

"Then there is a risk of invasion. The best estimates of my brethren are that any such invasion would take place at the earliest next year, once the business in France is well in hand, using some reserve of troops retained from this larger movement."

Barberini realized that he and his own staff had been over these points before. "Could it be that we are simply not seeing what is here because we think the idea of Borja trying to depose His Holiness is unthinkable even for the likes of that man?"

"Possible." Vitelleschi barked the word out. "But unlikely."

"Even with Quevedo assisting Borja?" Barberini pressed. "The man is fond of high-stakes games. He was at Venice, remember."

"My dear nephew," said His Holiness, "remember that Rome is not Venice. This game is not for the rulership of one merchant state, however rich. We already hear that Our new insistence on neutrality in secular disputes has troubled the consciences of some of the Habsburgs' adherents. How much more troubled will their consciences be if Spain places an antipope on Our throne? Or worse, deposes Us by force?"

"Counterproductive," Vitelleschi added in a return to laconic form. "Olivares knows this."

"It would not be the first time that Borja went beyond his orders." Barberini remembered Borja's last appearance at consistory. The king of Spain had had to send a personal letter of apology.

"That apology was for form's sake," Vitelleschi said. "Borja did his master's bidding, depend on it."

"If only we could be sure who his master was in this matter."

His Holiness chuckled. "If only we could remind him who his master truly *is*." He slapped his thigh. "But we are distracted. The ambassador from the United States. My esteemed nephew raised her presence in all this a few moments ago. Pray continue, Antonio."

Barberini said "I did?" And then, recovering a train of thought abandoned moments before, "I did. Yes. I think the presence of that embassy, and the prospect of its reception by Your Holiness beyond the formality of her presenting her credentials, may do much to exacerbate matters. The Spanish have had many smarts to their pride inflicted by that new nation, I fear, and the novelty of their ways is a theme which recurs in much of what they are saying. More than one of my acquaintances has been invited to sup with one Spanish churchman or another and all have mentioned this."

"I have noted it also," Vitelleschi said. "Has Your Holiness' secretary of state fixed a date for a meeting with the dottoressa?"

"As I am sure the Father-General is aware, there is no meeting currently planned." Urban smiled to show he did not disapprove of Vitelleschi's almost certain knowledge of the matter through unofficial channels. "Assorted clerks and functionaries have met, you understand, and I believe that the United States is most gracious in recognizing that it would be politically inconvenient for the time being for there to be discussions as between heads of state. The impression I gather is that they feel that what has been done to their advantage thus far is quite sufficient, and they are not such ingrates as to press for more."

Barberini nodded. "Does Your Holiness want me to make any kind of contact? My youth and inexperience and reputation for flightiness have proven valuable in such contexts before."

Both his uncle and the father-general frowned and looked at each other. Barberini could almost hear the churning of ideas, sense the crackle of intellects that routinely thought four, five and six moves ahead. *One day*, he thought, *I shall have to play at this same table*. It was a daunting thought.

After a while, His Holiness nodded. "Make no business contact," he said. "I am sure, however, that there are innovations in the arts in Thuringia these days. By all means, receive Her Excellency and see what luminaries you can patronize."

Barberini nodded. "There are occasions, Your Holiness, when a reputation for interior design is of great advantage."

"Interior design?" Vitelleschi asked, clearly able to understand the individual words but not knowing what the phrase signified.

"An expression for all the arts of beautification of indoor places," Barberini said. "Brought to our times by the Americans. You see, I have already been in correspondence with acquaintances of Cardinal Mazzare for the very purpose His Holiness suggested."

"Ah," Vitelleschi said, understanding immediately.

"Although," Barberini went on, "I am less than impressed with their Martha Stewart."

Chapter 12

Naples

Don Vincente found himself missing his company's pikes and halberds sorely. The newfangled bayonets that had been promised, the ones that did not plug the muskets, had simply not been provided; the output of the Toledo factory had gone to the units heading directly for France first. Many of the men had knives or short swords or other close weapons, but they were going to be of limited use.

The crowd that gathered in the piazza whatever— Don Vincente hadn't been here long enough to learn the names, although he could find his way about—was certainly excitable and unruly but those present weren't actually rioting yet. A firm and resolute advance with cold steel would dampen their enthusiasm without anyone getting hurt. And people getting hurt would be sure to make the *next* mob that little bit angrier and harder for him, Don Vincente, to deal with.

He swore under his breath.

"The men are forming up, Don Vincente," Ezquerra said, quietly, from behind him.

"I could wish we did not have to open fire," Don Vincente said, just as quietly. There had been trouble before this in Naples, but now it was Don Vincente's company's turn. He wondered if any of the other captains had had to lead a musket-only company against people expressing their anger? Probably not, or the grapevine that Ezquerra seemed to be at the root of would have carried the news to him already. There were agitators galore all over the kingdom of Naples, and they were thick as lice in the city of Naples itself. The place was as ready to explode as Vesuvius, whose glow lit the night sky outside Don Vincente's billet window.

If there were anything that might be called a massacre, they would have word of it to every corner of the kingdom faster than lightning. And Don Vincente truly, truly did not want to spend the next few years of his career acting as a glorified constable if the trouble flared up. If nothing else, the opportunities for loot would be terrible. "Go and bring the men up, Sergeant. We should get this over with."

Ezquerra nodded and ambled off to carry out the order. Doubtless he would break in to a jog the moment he was certain his captain's back was turned.

Don Vincente had left the company a little way back down the street and come ahead alone to assess the situation. There were perhaps four or five hundred people, mostly men of the rougher sort, gathered in the piazza and shouting slogans. There were a few women, possibly whores looking for business, but Don Vincente did not know what Naples' required dress for such women was. Don Vincente's command of Italian—a necessity for any professional soldier—did not include much in the way of the local dialect of the language beyond what he needed to order servants about and other small matters. However, the tone was clear enough. These people were unhappy about something, and were demanding to know what the officials and notables in the huge and gaudy confection of a building in front of them were going to do about it.

"Disgusting," came a prissy and slightly sibilant voice, and Don Vincente's heart sank.

"Indeed, Father Gonzalez," he said, as smoothly as he could manage, mentally adding the words "you pious prick" as he did to everything he said to the man. After trying to police the morals of the soldiers, Gonzalez had returned to his campaign to find evidence of secret Jewry among the soldiers. Thus far, he had managed to completely miss the two actual Jewish veterans in the company. Their comrades had covered for them completely, and in any event the pair of them were sufficiently unobservant of their religion that a hypothetical Jewish Inquisition would probably suspect them of being secret Christians. He'd also ignored the openly Jewish surgeon who accompanied the tercio. He had, instead, given Don Vincente himself a hard time over sleeping late the Saturday after their two weeks of enforced training had ended.

Apparently, not working on a Saturday was evidence of a secret conversion to Judaism, Don Vincente's certificate of *limpieza* notwithstanding, and not simply the consequence of having indulged a little too heavily with his fellow officers at a small party the night before. Fortunately, the other two inquisitors who were assigned to the tercio seemed to dislike Gonzalez just as much as everyone else did, and had smirked and overruled him when Don Vincente had sent runners to them to come at their earliest convenience and pointedly eaten a large portion of the local ham in front of them. Also fortunately, all three inquisitors had been out of sight when the thick, rich, salty fat on the ham—which ordinarily Don Vincente was rather partial to—had hit his stomach. When this mixed with the remains of the previous night's drinking, he had become copiously ill. The experience had not made him any better disposed toward the good father.

"—and, of course, you will open fire immediately to suppress this ungodly disorder." Don Vincente realized that the memory of throwing up an otherwise perfectly good portion of ham had distracted him from whatever the obnoxious priest was bleating about this time.

"I shall, of course, take all proper military measures, Father Gonzalez," Don Vincente said as smoothly as he could manage. "And now if you would be so good as to retire, I believe my men are commencing to advance."

"I am not afraid to be in the forefront of God's work against those stirred to impious revolt by—"

"Indeed not, Father Gonzalez," Don Vincente interrupted, over the sound of his men's booted feet and of shouldered muskets clanging on gorgets, "and if my words have suggested as much then I, Don Vincente Jose-Maria Castro y Papas, most humbly apologize. But the good father is standing in the way of what will likely be my men's first volley of musket fire."

"Ah." Gonzalez tried to scurry to the rear without appearing to hurry.

Don Vincente savagely suppressed the wish that he

could have left Gonzalez directly in front of a hundred soldiers with loaded muskets while he gave the order to fire. Certainly, the sight of an inquisitor being riddled with bullets would have placated the crowd like little else; the Holy Office was no more popular in Italy than it was in Spain. But the wretched man's death would doubtless have created yet more paperwork. Don Vincente sighed, and turned to watch his men approach along the street from where he had had them form up out of sight of the crowd. "Sergeant," he called. "Are the men loaded?"

"They are, Captain," Ezquerra called back.

"Musician!" Ezquerra called, "A march, if you please."

Diaz, the company's trumpeter, and the drummer boys struck up something suitably martial, and the men's pace quickened as they approached where Don Vincente was waiting. The company standard was drooping in the airless spring sunshine, but otherwise the company made a fine sight as they came in sight of the crowd. The music got their attention and there were a number of faces turned away from the building they were protesting outside, which Don Vincente vaguely recognized as the palace of someone in the city's administration, rather than that of the viceroy. It was good to see that the crowd had noticed the company early, as it would give them more time to think.

As, indeed, Don Vincente had taken time to think. "Sergeant Ezquerra," he called. "Extend to line of four ranks."

Ezquerra gave his captain an odd look, as did Lieutenant Rojas as he came from his proper position in the rear of the company. Six ranks was considered to be the shallowest that gunners could be ranked, giving each rank time to reload while the others took their turn to shoot. Don Vincente knew that he was taking a chance, but he suspected that reloading would not be an issue today. In any event with the new light muskets and the drill he had had the men engage in, he was seeing nearly two shots a minute from many of his men, and three shots every two minutes from all of them. Despite the doubt written in their faces, Ezquerra and Rojas began ordering the men into the required ranks as they fanned out in to the piazza.

"Front rank, level arms!" Ezquerra bellowed, not waiting for the order. Don Vincente stole a glance, and saw that true to form the man was leaning on his halberd even as he readied the men for action. To the company's front, no more than thirty yards away, the nearest members of the crowd had shifted from stupefied curiosity at the interruption to their afternoon's entertainment sounding off at their city's notables, and were now looking nervous. More than nervous, in fact.

Don Vincente crossed himself, kissed the rosary he wore at his belt, and offered a silent prayer that the threat would be enough. Honorable deeds on the field of battle were all very well, and there was loot to hope for there besides. Giving fire, twenty-five muskets at a time, into a piazza crowded with civilians, was most definitely not what he had followed His Most Catholic Majesty's colors for.

"Why do you not give the order to fire?" The voice came from behind him. Gonzalez had come back.

He paused a moment before turning to address the

pompous little—*most holy inquisitor.* "Because, good Father, we must permit some little time for the crowd to realize the error of their ways and repent."

He hoped that putting it that way would get the wretched priest off his back. For a man supposedly forbidden the profession of arms, Father Gonzalez was a bloodthirsty little bastard. And doubtless he was a bastard in all ways that counted. Not even the most loving of mothers would wish to be associated with the squinty-eyed little runt. The man managed to be as scrawny as a gypsy's donkey while still having the piggy little eyes and puffy face of a glutton long since run to seed. Those eyes were unsettlingly close together and the straggly hair around the priestly tonsure made the effect more that of a rabid polecat than anything which might one day be something as useful as a ham.

Don Vincente's belly rumbled at the thought of ham. This fiasco had come hard on the heels of morning drill and he, and all his men, were missing lunch.

Gonzalez appeared to consider Don Vincente's words for a moment. While the crab-ridden priest was dithering, Don Vincente decided to dispense with good manners and returned his regard to the crowd. The initial shuffle away from the soldiers had ended with the near edge of the crowd some ten yards farther away, at the edge of practical musket range although the balls would still have killing force at that distance. There was an ugly murmur now coming from them instead of the roar of protest they had been making before.

The near edge of the crowd seemed to roil like a simmering stockpot as the fainter spirits retired into the

safety of numbers and the bolder souls came forward
to glare at the soldiers. Some of them looked like they
were weighing the odds, and Don Vincente hoped
there weren't enough experienced soldiers among them
to come to the correct conclusion. Outnumbering the
soldiers who faced them more than four to one, if the
crowd charged with any real spirit, they would run
over the company like a wave over beach sand, with
only a few losses. Don Vincente began to regret that
he had been so vigorous in arranging that his men
should drill and train. Had he not been in possession
of the only company mustered and equipped today, he
might have escaped having to do this. And the risk of
seeing his command come to a messy end.

Movement beside him caught his eye. When he saw
what it was, he groaned aloud. Gonzalez was striding forward, in that stupid ass-out, leaning forward
waddle he had among his only-slightly-less irritating
characteristics, and hectoring the crowd. Worse, the
man wasn't even bothering to address them in their
native tongue, but was haranguing them in Spanish.

Another groan, this one very loud and theatrical,
came from Sergeant Ezquerra.

As Gonzalez was winding up to "—and there is
a place appointed for you, a place of torment and,
and, and"—and otherwise becoming too excited to
speak properly, Don Vincente realized that he had to
act quickly. If he held fire to keep the odious little
ti—*the most holy inquisitor* from getting hurt, he would
give the more militant members of the crowd ample
time to overrun his company and then dismember
the inquisitor at their leisure, proving that it was an
ill wind that blew no one any good. Don Vincente

considered simply drawing his pistol and shooting the man down in mid-expostulation, but even though that would save his men from the suggestion that they had killed the priest, it would not solve the current problem. There was nothing else for it.

"Lieutenant! Be ready to give the command for a front rank volley," he shouted, and strode out to grab the ranting idiot and haul him bodily out of the line of fire.

"And did not Saint Paul say—what?" Gonzalez halted in mid-diatribe as Don Vincente seized him by the shoulder.

"Time to go, Father." Don Vincente was unable to keep the nasty tone out of his voice. "My men are about to begin shooting."

"They are?" Father Gonzalez looked around. "They *are*." He turned his back on the crowd. "As you can see, Captain, there was no point waiting. They have not dispersed, no matter the exhortation. Too steeped in Sin."

Don Vincente took Gonzalez by the elbow and began to lead him to one side, much as one would an elderly and rather confused relative. The crowd was still tense, not coming closer to the guns, but the nearer members were watching them intently. Don Vincente could smell the crowd, the unwashed clothes, the smells of cheap cooking and cheaper drink and the nervous sweat of people who have realized that the situation has escalated. More than one had a billet of wood, a knife, or some other simple weapon. Quite enough to deal with a company of musketeers at three or four to one odds.

The front rows of the crowd now consisted entirely

of men, the women having filtered away to the back. That would be a load off the conscience, at least. There was precious little to be proud of in firing into a crowd of civilians, but at least there would be no women hurt.

He got Father Gonzalez back to the edge of the square. It was a standoff, now. The crowd was hushed and murmuring their discontent. There was no movement toward his men, but likewise no movement to disperse. Had there been just *one* more company, preferably a pike company, present to assist, there would be no problem. A volley into the air, and the pikes would advance and the crowd would *have* to run away. A volley into the air now would achieve nothing. A few faint hearts would run, but the rest would know that that meant a quarter of the musketeers were unloaded.

Something was needed to break the moment. Don Vincente very slowly and deliberately drew his saber, and held it, low and loose by his side. Several of the people in the crowd were watching him, not the musketeers. He began looking for eye contact, staring hard at each man in turn.

Suddenly, with hardly even time for the eye to register it, there was a surge from behind the crowd. Some of the men at the front nearest Don Vincente staggered forward a few paces as the people behind pushed into them, but did not come any closer than that. Some of them were nervously looking behind them, and those not directly in the front row were facing away from the musketeers and craning their necks, some on tiptoes, to see what was going on.

"Captain?" Lieutenant Rojas called.

"A moment!" Don Vincente called back. He could just about see over the heads of the crowd and—yes! there seemed to be some mounted troops. There were some local mercenaries who were a cavalry outfit who might well have been turned out as well for this business; Don Vincente did not recall hearing of any Spanish cavalry arriving in Naples. There was no sound of screaming, yet. If the moment was to be broken, now was the time. "Lieutenant! Prepare to fire!"

The front rank of musketeers leveled their weapons in cadence with the shouted commands of the cabos. They awaited Don Vincente's command.

Lord God Almighty, forgive me this—

Behind the crowd, the cavalry were forcing their way into the square. They seemed to be just using the weight of their horses, but the sounds of shouting could be heard, and it was surely only a matter of time before someone was hurt. Don Vincente raised his sword, the reflection from the blade scattering sunlight across the faces of the crowd. One or two of them flinched.

He dared to breathe again after a moment, when some of the crowd began filtering away. Between the musketeers here and the cavalry there, many of the Neapolitans present were beginning to feel less enthusiastic about protest than they had only a few minutes ago. And there were several routes out of the square, none of which were blocked.

And then the screams started. *Oh, shit*—the thought was followed swiftly by the realization that the crowd was about to surge toward his men. Without taking further thought, he flashed his sword down.

As the powder-smoke and ball belched out and the

crowd began falling and dying and milling and running and trampling its weaker members underfoot, Don Vincente looked on, numbly listening to his NCOs and Lieutenant Rojas barking the orders for the continuing volleys that flayed and hammered the nearest face of the crowd and drove the survivors away to the other exits. He told himself, over and over, that it had been the only action he could take. That not to act would have seen all his men dead. That the cavalry had been sent to the other side of the square had been sheerest bad luck. That surely it had been the hand of the Devil that caused some poor soul to be trampled by a horse at *just* that moment.

It was over in minutes. Any thought the crowd might have had of escaping through Don Vincente's company died under the constant hail of bullets, each volley more ragged than the last as men reloaded at different rates. Any thought that they might have resisted died as the cavalry brought their sabers in to play. Some few might have had the courage and the will to stand, but they were tossed on a storm of panic. The shooting had prevented them acting as a coherent mob, and had turned them into a crowd of frightened individuals. An ounce of leadership and they would have torn the soldiers apart, but that ounce was lacking.

When the crowd had cleared, the ground was littered with bodies. Don Vincente's men had, between them, discharged perhaps three hundred rounds. Many—most, even—would have done little damage. Missed, or done no more than cause a mild scratch. Of the ones that remained, a musket ball two-thirds of an inch wide did terrible injury to flesh. The cavalry had accounted for far fewer, the horsemen being limited to what was within reach of their arms. But for those first few seconds, the first fifty or so bullets, the crowd had been packed tight together, twenty yards away at their nearest. And at that range, a musket ball is accurate and deadly. Some would have wounded two or more. There was a ring of bodies around Don Vincente, and all of them seemed to accuse him of murder.

"Most commendable," Father Gonzales said, a note of warm approval in his voice.

Slowly, carefully, not making any sudden movements, Don Vincente Jose-Maria Castro y Papas sheathed his sword without turning on the priest and hacking him into bloody hunks of tainted flesh. It was, he found, the hardest thing he had ever done in his life.

Part Three

April 1635

Chapter 13

Rome

The mid-morning sun was making the paperwork on Sharon's desk glow in a way that was getting close to inducing eyestrain. Most of it was tedious stuff, but while she would have been happy to delegate, Adolf was not very good at accepting delegation. Preparing drafts for her approval or signature was as close as he was prepared to get. She wondered whether she should just start signing things without reading them—approvals of accounts, bread-and-butter correspondence with the embassy's suppliers and responses to invitations. Nothing earth-shattering. That gave her a slightly guilty start, though, and to be fair to her chief of staff he did manage to whittle the admin down to, on the worst days, about an hour. She sighed, and reflected that if she'd ever actually qualified as a nurse back up-time she'd have had more paperwork than this to reckon with.

The state papers, the copies of the intelligence briefings that had come in via radio overnight and from the few USE agents in Rome who actually reported direct to the embassy via various channels, had been brief today. The twenty minutes of interest they generated hadn't been enough to sustain Sharon through an uncommonly large stack of, well, crap.

There had been a couple more near-riots. Nasty things were being said in Rome's tavernas about the way that second one had been handled. More than one informant had heard rumors that the slaughter had been deliberate, rather than the result of outrageous stupidity.

And rent-a-mobs were turning up elsewhere as well. Information on those was starting to trickle in as well, and whoever was organizing them—three different descriptions so far—was claiming to be either with the Committee of Correspondence or the Sons of Joe Buckley, a group apparently devoted to avenging Buckley's death at the hands of the Inquisition. That had caused Sharon a moment of grim amusement. The man who had almost certainly murdered poor Joe had, at the time, been a member in good standing of the Venice Committee of Correspondence. If they were a real group—and so far no one could say for certain that there wasn't a genuine protest or two happening among the hired demonstrations—then they were wildly misguided.

And, of course, the references to the Committee were bringing exasperated notes from Magdeburg, notes that had Don Francisco's style all over them. Sharon had sent back that she had Frank's personal assurance that he had nothing to do with the disturbances. Even if Frank had wanted to engage in that kind of shenanigans, he didn't have the cash, with his restaurant-cum-social club not yet breaking even, let alone turning a profit. Whoever was running these sideshows was spending money like water to get groups of several dozen out to each event, gathered in knots of half a dozen or so from across Rome. That suggested that there were whole teams of agitators at work, although there were bound to be a few genuinely aggrieved folks joining in the fun by now.

She realized with a guilty start that she was woolgathering, and not getting through the day's paperwork. She was just signing the last letter when Ruy came in, not bothering to knock, and grinning with his usual swagger. He was, of course, indecently cheerful in the mornings, alert before his first coffee and usually up an hour before Sharon to perform a vigorous workout with the Marines in the embassy's ballroom. He was more-or-less fully recovered from the surgery Sharon had performed on him the year before, and determined to get, and stay, in shape. As his doctor, Sharon wholeheartedly approved, of course. And as an unexpected benefit, he was taking the embassy's Marine guard in sword drill, being as proficient with the saber as he was with his usual rapier. The sight of fit soldiers in their twenties emerging red-faced and blowing from a training session with a man old enough to be their father was entertainment all by itself, and apparently Ruy relished it.

"Good training session, you old goat?"

Ruy stroked his mustachios. "Excellent. The woeful lack of stamina of the youth of today was once again made manifest to my entire satisfaction. Although I will say that one or two of them show promising signs of future accomplishment in *la destreza*, Sharon. The Scots and Germans are hardy and courageous breeds. Once schooled in finesse and good footwork they have every promise of being fine swordsmen. I declare myself pleased with my new pupils."

"Well, try not to break any of them while you do it. I have enough paperwork as it is," she said, ringing the bell on her desk. Adolf came in and took the finished work away for dispatch to its various destinations, and reminded her she had an appointment with representatives of Rome's College of Physicians later that afternoon.

"Anything in particular you wanted to talk about, Ruy?" she said, stretching in her chair now that Adolf had gone.

"Indeed, Doña Ambassadora." Ruy's face was still cheerful, but he had assumed a position of attention by her desk. She noticed he had a letter in his hand.

She sat up straight. "In my official capacity? And you're carrying a letter? May I presume you've heard from Alfonso?"

"I have, indeed. His response was as we both predicted, once one disregards the feeble attempts at wit and pallid attempts at invective and sarcasm."

Sharon raised an eyebrow. Ruy Sanchez de Casador y Ortiz had served many years as first retainer to the marquis of Bedmar, and later as gentiluomo to the cardinal Bedmar. She'd seen the close relationship the two had, marked as it was by constant mockery and barbed insults, while Ruy had first been convalescing under her care in Venice. "I seem to recall a certain short fat cardinal who gave as good as he got from a certain uppity Catalan ruffian," she said.

"Faugh," Ruy waved the criticism away. "What can a woman know of such manly pursuits as persiflage and insult? Besides, the fellow is Andalusian, so what can he possibly know of proper wordplay? The import of his message is that he bids me remain in touch, but recognizes that a man should be with his wife and being there, make himself useful. Once we disregard the vile calumny that I never made myself useful in his service, it seems uncommonly gracious for the canting little bullfrog."

"Miss him, don't you?" Sharon realized she was getting quite good at seeing through the front Ruy kept up.

He sighed. "Indeed I do. It takes years of friendship to learn what an insufferable, gluttonous prick Alfonso can be. But the winds of war and the tides of politics mean we must needs insult each other at one remove for the nonce. Somehow, it is not the same." Another sigh.

"You think he'll be able to come to the wedding? Only we're going to need a—"

"No!" Ruy roared, clapping a hand to his forehead and crumpling the letter in his hand. "A thousand times no! I, Ruy Sanchez de Casador y Ortiz, would sooner slit my own throat than hand Alfonso that much ammunition. Not all the torments of all the sinners in Hell would match the insufferability of that pompous buffoon if I once let him perform the sacrament of marriage over me. I say again, No! And thrice! No!"

"So that's settled, then," Sharon said. "I'll write and ask him if he can attend and officiate."

Ruy collapsed in to a chair. "Doomed! I am doomed! Twenty years and more I have had the upper hand! Undone by a woman! It is to weep for the glory that will be lost!" He made as if to rend his clothes.

Sharon lost it, badly. It was a minute or more

before she stopped laughing, not helped, in any way, by Ruy reinforcing success with yet more weeping, wailing and gnashing of teeth.

When she'd gotten control, she asked, "So, did you make a head start on your new job?" This, she thought, would be interesting. Europe in the seventeenth century was full of spymasters and intelligence chiefs, most of them very, very good at their jobs. One of the things the modern age had got in hand very early on was skullduggery.

It was like flipping a switch. Ruy was suddenly all business. "Alas, Your Excellency Doña Ambassadora"— he clearly had the thing neatly compartmentalized in his mind—"I have little progress to report. I beg your forgiveness in this matter, and would say that it is as yet early and my ability to pass for an Italian is not great. I inevitably hear the story that the people tell a man from out of town. Thus far, my reasoning is that we are dealing with someone who is trying to provoke civil disorder. Rome is not entirely ripe for such, but there are always a few layabouts who can be paid to make small mischiefs. Whoever is doing this declares his allegiance openly, at least, by masquerading as the Committee of Correspondence. All I know of them is that there are at least four men involved, and that they recruit their idlers and vagabonds around the Borgo and other low neighborhoods, such as the Ripetto. I mean to go there on the morrow, and see for myself."

"Won't you be recognized?" Sharon asked.

"Almost certainly," Ruy said, smiling. "And if I am recognized by the perpetrators, it is the most certain proof that Borja is responsible."

"You suspect Borja?"

"Naturally. He has motive and is close by Rome. Don Francisco's analysis was most cogent, Doña. I would also add that the most recent disturbance was outside the premises of the Lyncaean Institute, which also tends to suggest Borja. He was, after all, most embarrassed by the Galileo affair, and as such would want to see everything associated with the man harmed by this trouble he is causing. The only such target within reach is the college of natural philosophers that Galileo helped found. The evidence is most compelling, and I expect to find only confirmation tomorrow, not surprises."

"Well, don't provoke anything worse than what's happening. I want to get approval from Magdeburg before we act, if it turns out we can do anything."

Ruy frowned. "If we are not directly at risk—and I think Borja is not so great a fool as to attack an embassy directly—what ought we to do? My humble understanding is that His Holiness is not an ally of the United States of Europe. Meddling in his affairs might be counted an affront."

"Maybe, but he's done us at least two big favors so far," said Sharon. "I'll find out what the administration thinks about doing him one in return if we can. It isn't like we could piss off the Spanish government any more than we already have."

"There is truth in that last. Castilians and Aragonese," Ruy sneered. "Even when offered no offense, they are a sour and crabbed lot at the best of times."

Sharon chuckled. "Tell me, Ruy, is there anyone in Spain other than the Catalans you have time for?"

Ruy shrugged. "On their better days, the Andalusians. Not that I would not swear on Holy Writ to Alfonso that I never said any such thing."

"Of course. Well, I'm about done here, and I've a couple of hours to kill. Suggestions?"

"Luncheon," Ruy said, with a definite air. "I must fortify myself. I am forced, once again, unwontedly, to work for a living. I, Ruy Sanchez de Casador y Ortiz, am driven under the lash of a hard taskmistress."

So to lunch they went.

Chapter 14

Magdeburg

"This has to be the most modest cardinal's palace anywhere," Mike muttered to Don Francisco as he got out of the carriage. Lawrence Cardinal Mazzare, otherwise known as Larry, newly promoted the year before, was a cardinal without a cathedral as yet. Magdeburg, the capital of the USE with its policy of freedom of religion, had several new Catholic churches for the city's Catholic minority, but no grandiose cathedral, just an ordinary parish church that served the function when needed. A proper cathedral, apparently, took more time.

Lacking a cathedral, Mazzare had apparently decided to do without a palace as well. He was using his cardinal's stipend—which was, Don Francisco understood, substantial—to rent two fine, but not too grand, townhouses in the middle of the city, one of which he had had fitted out as offices.

They were, however, heading for the one Mazzare lived in, since this was purely a social call. Or, at least, as social as the prime minister of the USE and his

chief spymaster could ever get with the head of the
Catholic church in their nation. Which, Don Francisco
reflected as they mounted the steps to the front door,
was not very social at all. There was a substantial
Protestant propaganda mill—now much more above-
board and respectable than it had been—which would
make a great deal out of the prime minister formally
receiving the cardinal or vice versa. Not to mention the
USE's Catholic propaganda mill, a sizeable minority of
which wasn't happy at all with the latest pronouncements from Rome, still less with the appointment of
an up-timer as cardinal over them all.

"Modest? Compared with a prime minister who
works in an office that would humiliate a senior clerk
in the Ottoman Empire?" Francisco had initially found
the Americans' unpretentious ways amusing, but lately
more than a bit exasperating as the shock of their
arrival wore off and Europe's power-brokers lapsed back
into old habits of confusing ostentation with authority.
Being underestimated was all very well, when it came
to military strategy, but in diplomacy and espionage
an ounce of bluff was worth a pound of credibility,
to paraphrase one of Mike's sayings.

The staff was efficient, mostly lay personnel, and
they hardly had to wait at all for Mazzare to see
them. Long enough, Nasi judged, that there would
be small wait for coffee and pastries and, indeed, this
was the case. "Good evening, Mike, Don Francisco,"
Mazzare said when he came to sit with them. "Thank
you, Dieter," he said to the servant who brought the
tray, "that will be all for the time being."

Once the coffee had been poured—excellent stuff,
Nasi found, to his surprise, it seemed there was at

least one American who didn't like his coffee weaker than a schoolboy's excuses—Mazzare came straight to the point. "Well, Mike? What exactly about the situation in Rome seems to be the problem?"

Stearns chuckled. "What isn't?" He waved a hand. "Oh, it's not that it affects us much one way or the other. Papal neutrality is a bit of a help but we managed without it before and no doubt we will again, and the political hay Wilhelm is going to make over it makes no odds either. It's just, well, predicting what Borja might do and how the college of cardinals is going to react to it. Since you're the nearest cardinal, I figured I'd come right out and ask."

It was Mazzare's turn to chuckle. "Second newest cardinal, as it happens. Father Joseph got his hat and ring shortly after I did, since my appointment made His Holiness' excuses for not elevating the man look pretty thin, and it wasn't like an extra French cardinal more or less makes much difference these days. And probably about to be the third newest, if rumors about Giulio Mazarini being appointed *in pectore* have any truth to them. And what I know about the internal workings of the cardinals in Rome, frankly, you could fit on the head of a pin and still have room for a troupe of dancing angels doing a Busby Berkeley number. You see, I'm not really much of a political cardinal. There are a few of us like that, you know."

"Yeah," said Stearns, "I figured you wouldn't be much for the machinations of the fancified folks in Rome. By the way, where's Father Scheiner?"

Nasi took a moment to ensure that his face was fully under control. The barb was a true one. His last update to Mike Stearns had been on the whereabouts of the

Jesuit astronomer-priest whom Mazzare had asked for as his senior scientific advisor when he had been appointed cardinal. The man didn't spend all of his time with his eyes on the stars, however. His travels around the various archbishops and secular nobility on the fringes of the USE were an itinerary that made interesting reading. Mazzare was, in his own quiet and understated way, doing some hard politicking of his own.

If nothing else, ensuring that all of those prelates and princes, weaned on the principle of *cuius regio, eius religio*, got regular updates on how well the Catholic church—as distinct from the Catholic powers—could do in an area where there was freedom of religion. Mazzare was meeting regularly with the upper levels of the German Jesuit hierarchy—Scheiner's influence again—to direct efforts to proselytize the Catholic religion. Nasi had been including that in his reports on the "good news" side of the balance sheet, not least because the Jesuits' efforts to get as many schools open as possible in as many places as possible were saving the USE a tidy sum in education spending. There were public order problems as well—there were plenty of places where riots against "popery" were easy to provoke, and would be, if Nasi was any judge of how Christians behaved, for many years to come.

Mazzare grinned disarmingly. "Fine, you've got me on that one. But there's a world of difference between smoothing the ruffled feathers of a lot of bishops who think they're about to be forced to turn Lutheran and knowing what Borja's playing at."

"So you think it is Borja, then?" Nasi asked. "I don't have any hard information on that myself. I have, shall we say, limits on how much information I can gather on the internal workings of the Catholic Church. Or any Christian institution, to be completely candid." It was a blind spot in Nasi's otherwise—false modesty aside—excellent espionage organization. Commercial and political rumor he could have for the asking; the correspondents he had already had before working for the USE had been collecting that kind of information for years for their own business. Mailing it to a new address represented no great change. Developing contacts within the religious institutions was going to take time and effort that Nasi simply had not been able to expend, thus far. Nasi was hoping for something to come of his contact with Mazzare on that account; an exchange of intelligence with someone who was developing his own contacts within the Catholic church from a position of near-supreme advantage would be invaluable, given how much stock Europeans had in their competing theologies.

Mazzare nodded. "I do think it's Borja. And you may be assured that my sources are of the best. What I get, I get a few weeks behind the times, but all the thinking as of the last report was that Borja was up to no good, and almost certainly behind the attempts to foment civil disorder. I guess you've had reports on that business already?"

Stearns said, "Yeah, we have. Sharon saw one incident right up close, as it happens. Ended up having to help the wounded."

Mazzare frowned. "She wasn't hurt? Everyone at the embassy is fine? Any word on Frank and Giovanna?"

"All unharmed as at my last report, Your Eminence," Nasi said hastily. "That was last night, from Ms. Nichols."

"Oh, good." Mazzare's relief was palpable. "All too many of the people I have to deal with either don't know that their little games get people killed, or simply don't care. You will, of course, remind Sharon from me, and ask her to tell Frank from me as well, to be careful? From what I gather Borja's trying to revive an old family tradition."

"He wants to be pope?" Stearns asked.

"What cardinal doesn't?" Mazzare shot back, smiling. "Seriously, though, I was talking more about the way the Italian branch of his family carried on back in the day. You might remember that they were a byword for lying, scheming, treacherous manipulators as late as the twentieth century."

"Figures," Stearns said. "So you don't think he's trying to make himself pope?"

"Doubt it," Mazzare said.

"You have intelligence on that as well?" Nasi asked, intrigued.

"Not really. It's just that Borja can do the math as well as His Holiness can. There are only so many cardinals who can get to Rome for a vote in consistory, even now that Borja's called in every Spanish cardinal he can scrape up from every backwoods cathedral in Spain. Of those, neither the Spanish nor the Barberini party—of whom I'm pretty much one, by the way, since I really don't like any of the alternatives, and I like what Urban's doing—can really force an issue by themselves."

"The college of cardinals is tied, then?" Mike asked.

Mazzare rocked a hand back and forth. "On the raw numbers, yes. Normally, though, most of the other cardinals are out of town and His Holiness can get his way, with only a minimum of horse-trading. He only really has to persuade the cardinals that're in town—"

Stearns held up a hand. "Isn't the pope the supreme authority? I thought it was his way or the highway, and that was what infallibility actually meant? Did I misunderstand?"

Mazzare chuckled. "Well, that's closer than most misconceptions about what infallibility means. But the doctrine's purely for matters of faith and teaching, not the government of the church, and even then it only applies if the pope says it applies to something he's said. And when it comes to running the church, the pope's word is law, except for where it isn't, if you take my meaning. The cardinals are the governing body of the church. They were originally the principal priests of Rome's parish churches, you see, and selected their bishop from among their number. Whoever was bishop of Rome was also the pope as a sort of side benefit. Anyway, the pope rules but by law some things require the consent of the cardinals. It's a system that seems to work in spite of the rules, if anyone's asking me. Sorry, I seem to be lecturing."

"Most absorbing, Your Eminence," Nasi said. "Do go on." Behind his polite face, Nasi was trying not to laugh out loud. Mazzare had ceased to be a simple parochial priest some years ago, but he still maintained the act. When it slipped, it turned out that there was a shrewd mind behind the facade, a mind that could claim all day long to be politically naive, but the reality was, well—

Nasi realized he could almost come to believe in

the Christian doctrine of the Holy Spirit from watching Mazzare rise to each new challenge.

"Thank you, Don Francisco," Mazzare said. "As I was saying, before I so rudely interrupted myself, the pope does need the cardinals to run the church, and the cardinals are definitely needed if there's an election for a new pope. Now, if it just comes to throwing a spoke into Urban's government, that's easy enough for Borja to do. Some of the bribes will be enormous, but certainly not beyond the means of the king of Spain. The disruption to civil life in Rome seems to me to be just a pretext to let Borja frustrate the pope. Plus I know someone who knows someone who thinks he's getting the straight dope from Madrid, and that's as far as Borja's orders went."

Stearns was frowning. "You mentioned needing the cardinals to elect a new pope. You think that's a possibility?"

"Unless Urban dies a lot earlier this time around than he did on the historical record, no. I think we can assume that his state of health remains the same, so the old boy's got a few years left in him yet, God willing."

Nasi couldn't resist the obvious question. "And if Borja brings about a worsening in the state of the pope's health? Under cover of rioting, say?"

"No."

Mazzare was firm about that, at any rate. Nasi hoped that whoever Mazzare's source was had that right. That started Nasi wondering who that source was. In a way, Nasi hoped it was Vitelleschi: *there* was a mind worth having on one's side. The actions of the Jesuits in response to the new opportunity the USE presented indicated that Vitelleschi was one of those prepared minds whom fortune was said to favor.

Mazzare went on. "As I said before, Borja can do the same math His Holiness can, that anyone can do. There are two big parties in Rome right now, and one small group who might go either way. There are the cardinals who'll not stand with Spain, and the ones who will. If Spain tries to put their own man in, they'll need the unaligned cardinals, which basically means the Borghese, to do it. And since the currently most *papabile* cardinal is a Borghese, and he can read the encyclopedias as well as the next man and see who was supposed to replace Urban VIII in a few years' time, they're not likely to help anyone into the Vatican other than one of their own."

"So it's a competition between two factions as to who can promise the most to the Borghese in return for loyalty after the event?" Stearns asked.

"Well, yes, but Spain pretty much has to lose that one. Most of the Spanish cardinals are going to have to return to Spain eventually, while everyone else remains in Rome. Able to help the new pope a lot more. Pretty much the only way that Borja would be able to ensure a Borghese cat's-paw kept his end of the bargain would be to leave troops there. And people remember the Avignon captivity. I don't think having the pope leaned on to change policy will play that well with a lot of the kings and princes and archdukes and what-not."

Mazzare took a sip of his coffee. "Same goes if Borja makes His Holiness change policy at the point of a pike. He's got to leave troops there to keep Urban's nose to the grindstone, and still a lot of people are going to think their consciences are free of any kind of obedience. Me, for one."

"So all he can really do is bring Urban's government to a halt and hope Urban sees reason convincingly enough to keep his word after Borja stops?" Stearns sounded skeptical.

"No, I think Borja means to keep this up until the papacy is unable to affect anything. It reinforces the primacy of the king of Spain within the church. Whoever's the next pope will have the awful example of Urban to look back to. If Urban changes policy, then that's a useful bonus, but I don't think that's what he's really looking for. He wants a lame-duck pope. Politically, at least."

Stearns sat quietly for a little while. Nasi didn't think there was anything he could add, and Mazzare seemed content to let him ruminate.

After a while, and after draining his coffee cup, Stearns said, "There's absolutely nothing we can do to affect this one way or the other, is there?"

"Not that I can think of," said Mazzare.

So you've been thinking about it too, Nasi thought to himself. "I must also wonder what we might gain from intervening, if there was some way we might?"

"Well, there is the safety of our people in Rome," Mazzare said, looking Nasi straight in the eye. "And the fact that if you help, and you're seen to help, then there's a very real political benefit. Especially if you're helping prevent the kind of mess that Borja seems to be hell-bent on making."

"Cardinal Mazzare is right, Francisco," Stearns said, sighing wearily. "Trouble is, there's not a damn thing I can think of to do to help. All the USE has is one embassy with a dozen or so Marines out at the end of the longest communications link we have. And even then, we'd have to know where and how to act, and I ain't got clue one. And I'm prepared to guarantee you that neither Gustav Adolf nor Wilhelm Wettin does, either. And your 'simple parish priest, no knowledge of politics' act aside, Cardinal," he went on, and Nasi could hear the testiness building in Stearns' voice despite the fact that he used the same stratagem himself, "you haven't got the know-how either. More than I've got, for sure, but still not enough."

"True," Mazzare said.

"You could maybe ask the father-general?" Stearns asked, hopefully.

"I could, at that," Mazzare said, and Nasi couldn't keep himself from opening his eyes wider and jerking a little. *Surely that was deliberate,* he thought. *Revealing that his source in Rome is Vitelleschi cannot have been an accident.* And Stearns had primed him for it by simply asking the question outright. Truly, when the simple hillbilly union organizer and the naive parish priest sat down together, what a wealth of subtlety was unleashed!

Mazzare was continuing, "Look, if you tell the embassy folks to stand by to be of assistance, I'll let Vitelleschi know that he's got help in that quarter. It'll raise both our stocks there and maybe do some good."

"I will see to it, Mike," Nasi said. "And pass the word to my own people in Rome to take whatever action they can without compromising their own cover."

"Please, Don Francisco," Mazzare said, "I don't want any more risks run than have to be."

"I can assure Your Eminence," Nasi said, "that I will order no one to run any extraordinary risks. I value these people highly, and even were that not the case, there is the future to think of. I will need agents in Rome when this is all done."

"Good," Mazzare said, in the tones of a man who had gotten thoroughly used to being obeyed. "Although perhaps your people could keep an eye out for Frank Stone? He doesn't have a platoon of Marines to get him out of town if things get rougher. And from what I hear, someone's trying to pin the blame on him. It could get very nasty, and he's really not much more than a kid."

Stearns held up a hand. "Already in hand, Cardinal. And try to remember that that 'not much more than a kid' managed to achieve some quite useful things last year."

"By accident," Mazzare said, his tone growing waspish. "Although, yes, from what I hear he does seem to be doing things sensibly down there."

"Yep." Stearns grinned. "I'd had a notion to get someone down there and teach that boy some tactics, but it looks like he figured out a few things by himself, once he got settled down. I reckon that girl civilized him some."

That produced a reaction. Mazzare's eyes widened and his jaw dropped. "Giovanna? Giovanna *Marcoli*? Civilized?" Mazzare paused and coughed. "Well, I suppose it ill behooves me of all people to deny the possibility of miracles."

Chapter 15

Rome

The affable smile he had painted on his face was starting to make his cheeks hurt. He had to force himself to remember that only those of a proper rank could be called out to a duel. If he was to pick a fight with any of the idiots he'd had to deal with this evening, it would simply be a common tavern brawl.

That thought was a cheering one. Ruy Sanchez de Casador y Ortiz, brawling like a vulgar ruffian in a tavern. It would be far from the first time. And it just might prevent this expedition from being—what was that phrase Sharon used?—a "total bust." And that started another chain of happy thoughts. The English language had some truly *excellent* synonyms for the dedicated punster.

Ruy picked up a glass of wine—on the better side of mediocre, and he'd paid a little extra to get it out of the proprietor of this particular pesthole of a taverna—and looked around again. It was the third watering hole he'd visited this evening, and like the others it was a noisy and boisterous place. Staying in the middle of the room where everyone could see you meant you got jostled. A lot. Which meant that every time he recovered his good humor, some idiot would barge past and annoy him again.

It would be different if he had come out in his own proper person, of course. No one would dare provoke Ruy Sanchez de Casador y Ortiz. That was half the reason for the finery. It kept the idiots at bay. Tonight, though, he was simply Manuel, in town because he'd hired on with the traveling arrangements of cardinal thus-and-so. He'd got away with not being specific so far and meant to continue in that vein. A simple porter, at a loose end until his master decided to go back to Spain, out for a few drinks and to see the sights. A complete and utter hayseed who would want anything and everything explained to him in short words. For the first time in years, he felt severely underdressed. And no one seemed to give a crap about offending Manuel, no matter how impressive the set of knives he had at his belt. He might not be able to arm himself as a gentleman, but without weapons he felt not just underdressed, but *naked*.

While he mused, someone was jabbering at him. "*Que?*" he asked. Manuel, he had decided, didn't speak Italian well, and was a bit simple.

"I said, you're not from around here, are you?" The speaker was an oily looking, pinched-faced fellow with pox scars on his cheeks who had come and sat on the bench beside Ruy at the scarred, scorched and splintered table. Ruy made a small wager with himself that he was about to be offered the services of whatever tired and ugly drab the wretch was pimping tonight.

"No," Ruy replied, downgrading his command of Italian a good few notches, "I from Barcelona. Just came to Roma, yes?" He gave the fellow his best friendly-country-idiot grin.

"Know your way around the city, yet?" There was a calculating light in the man's eyes, and Ruy shortened the odds on him being a pimp considerably.

"No' really," Ruy said. "Mostly I just shift boxes and things for cardinal." He shrugged. "First time off I get in two weeks. All done now, though, till we go back to Barcelona. Getting paid to do nothing." Ruy made his friendly-idiot grin good and ingratiating. However odious this fellow was, pimps, being idle, usually had good gossip.

"'S that right? You know, if you're looking for a little fun, I might know someone who can help you." The fellow's leer got so broad Ruy began to imagine it falling off one side of his face. And, of course, he mentally handed himself a large bag of gold in satisfaction of the wager.

Try the obvious approach first, then. "I don't know," he said, frowning a bit as if worried. "I hear of trouble in Rome right now, lots of riots and disorder and things. I figure maybe there's constables working extra-hard, eh?"

The pimp—Ruy noted that like many such, he wasn't going to give his name to anyone he wasn't sure was a customer—waved a hand in idle dismissal. "Naw, don' worry about nothin' like that. Ain't any real riots, except maybe one or two. Most of it's just guys turning out to cause a little ruckus and run away before the militia come. 'S a couple of guys organizing it, got a whole bunch of money to spend, too."

"Why?" Ruy felt quite proud of the puzzled frown

he now wore. He felt that anyone seeing him would expect him to start grazing. And, of course, the effort of pretending to be this stupid was helping cover the fact that he was delighted to have hit paydirt so quickly. Only four hours of damnably awful wine and worse tavernas. Just this pox-rotted pimp to endure, and he could call it a night and get back to civilized company such as he had grown used to over the years.

The pimp shrugged. "Who knows? They say they're Committee of Correspondence, but they ain't. *Those* guys are all over by the Borgo, at Frank's Place, and they don't want no trouble, whatever they say about those crazy folks up in Germany and Venice. Me, I'm in eating money, mostly, so I don't bother with 'em. Don't go looking for trouble, that's my motto. And the militia caught one lot of guys went out for these other guys, y'know? Some guys got hurt."

"Bad?" Ruy tried his best to get his eyebrows into his hat, made his eyes go big and round. *Stop overacting, Sanchez,* he told himself.

The pimp didn't notice. "Some guys got killed. A few more didn't make it after they got hurt. That American *moro* from Germany, the one they say is such a miracle-working *dottoressa,* she was there and helped some guys. I figure if that's what these folks from the future do, they're okay with me."

It was intriguing that the fellow had dropped an American term into the flow of Roman dialect, but Ruy cautioned himself not to make too much of it. He'd already concluded that whatever other changes the up-timers were making to history, "okay" seemed certain to infect every language in Europe. The pestiferous word seemed as contagious as the plague.

"But they are witches!" Ruy expostulated.

Pimp blew a raspberry. "*Merda*. Good doctors. Good cooks. Run a clean and sensible tavern, man. Stuck it to the great and good last year, stuck it to them right in the ass. That makes 'em *okay* by me. Nobody believes they're witches, 'cept maybe a lot of excitable priests. They should get laid, y'know?"

Ruy chuckled. "True, they should. But I keep hearing where they do all kinds of magic, and burn people alive." He realized as he said it that he'd let his Italian improve, but it didn't look like the pimp was noticing.

"Burn people alive? I heard the same about your Inquisition, friend." There was a slightly wary look appearing in the pimp's eyes now.

Ruy realized he was probably pushing too hard for a reaction from this fellow, especially if he wanted to stay in character. He held up his hands, spread. "Hey, I'm from Catalonia. The Inquisition's a lot of damned Castilians, humiliating decent people. I know plenty of good folks who're shamed by their family names being hung up in the church as *marranos* and *moriscos*. They complain but nothing is done."

"That's the same all over, man," pimp said, shrugging. "Now, about that good time?"

"What kind of good time?" Ruy wondered how he was going to wriggle out of this one. It had never been his idea of fun to spend money that way, never mind that there was Sharon to think about. Some fellows he'd known had had no other idea of pleasure, and in a way he pitied them more than the poor souls rotted by drink. And since he'd taken that fateful decision that there was more to life than was traditionally offered to country boys from Catalonia, he'd learned that there were ways of getting laid that were a hell of a lot more fun, too. He'd never wanted for that kind of action, and the pleasures of romance and seduction were more lasting and more real.

The pimp laughed aloud. "What kind of town is Barcelona anyway?" he asked, sneering the question. "What you do for entertainment there? Goats? What kind of good time, Christ have mercy, man, what kind d'you think? Pussy, man, pussy!"

"Oh," Ruy said, "Look, I'm sorry and all, but I've got a wife, you know?"

The knowing leer he got back for that one was pure pimp. "Yeah, sure, man. And where is she tonight?"

"Uh, Barcelona," Ruy said. "But I never told her a lie yet, you know?"

The pimp's face was a picture of a building rant. Ruy had the gloomy suspicion that he was going to have to hit him to get him to shut up, and that was going to fix him in this man's memory. And that he'd pumped the man, none too subtly, for information about "those guys" who were paying for the riots. If he wouldn't sell that information, first chance he got, Ruy Sanchez de Casador y Ortiz was no judge of the breed.

Fortunately, just at that moment, someone jostled past. Ruy let the slight nudge spill his drink, then rose to his feet and roared *"Watch what you are about, you dog-fucked son of an Italian whore!"* He stuck his face right into that of the fellow who'd jostled him, trusting that the sentiment he'd expressed in Catalan would carry over into Italian.

Truth be told, the fellow wasn't much of a threat to

anyone. Weedy, at best. But Ruy needed a distraction to get him out of the place with everyone remembering him as an obnoxious drunken out-of-towner rather than anything more noteworthy. "I—I'm sorry, friend," the fellow stammered, flinching back.

"Sorry?" Ruy shouted, switching to Italian, "I make you sorry, shit-britches!" Under the bluster and fury he was cool and calm and noticed that the taverna had gone gratifyingly quiet. It had been so long since he'd done this that he'd forgotten how much *fun* a good bar-fight could be.

"Look, if I spilt your wine, I'll get you more," the fellow said, already looking pale and nervous. Ruy realized he'd not picked a very good target for this, but then he'd been improvising as he went along. Clearly this fellow didn't know how to stand up to a bully.

"Damn right you'll get me more, you fucking coward," Ruy shouted. "Same as all Italians, no fucking *cojones*!" He made the filthiest gesture he could think of, hoping it meant the same here as it did back home. The circles he'd moved in every other time he'd been in Rome, no one made gestures like that. Not out in front where they could be seen, anyway.

Amid the silence, there was the scrape of stools on the floor as—he counted the sounds, two of them were behind him—four men got up. From somewhere over his right shoulder, he heard "Watch your fucking mouth, Spaniard."

Ruy turned nice and slowly around. "Going to make me, cat-eater?"

This was more like it. This fellow almost certainly did something that involved lifting and moving heavy things. And obviously liked a good fight just as much as Ruy did. He was taller than Ruy by half a head, a good deal wider, and was built like an ox. And plainly wasn't even thinking about buying him a drink.

Beside him, he heard the pimp draw a blade. Something short. Ruy hadn't lived to his mature years by being slow, however. Without really thinking about it or doing more than glance to his side, he had a stiletto against the fellow's scrawny throat. "Put it away, little pimp, or I shave you real fucking close."

He pressed the edge of the blade against the man's Adam's apple. It was a stabbing weapon, with no edge to speak of, but where he was holding it the pimp couldn't see that. The pimp's knife went back into its sheath, which it had hardly cleared.

Ruy looked back at the big guy. "You want to make something of it?" he said, ostentatiously returning his stiletto to his belt. He didn't want anyone to get the idea this was a knife-fight. A few bruises and broken furniture was no one's concern, but if there were dead bodies it would be an effort to clear up.

There was doubt in the big man's eyes now. Ruy knew his speed had that effect on many people. Nevertheless, and credit the fellow for courage, he took a step forward, curling up his fists. "I got no knife, Spaniard," he said. "You man enough to face me without?"

Ruy spat in front of his new opponent. Behind him, he heard the fellow he had originally challenged backing away and getting the hell out. *Good*, he thought, *fighting the likes of that milksop would be no fun at all*. He heard the others who'd stood up resume their seats, and around the place there were knowing grins. Clearly this fellow was the local hero. Best to get him good and mad. "I'd face you without hands, you fat fuck, and beat you with my cock. You ever seen a real cock, bitch?"

That did it. Elegant and flowery insults were wasted in a place like this. The fellow charged. Ruy's sidestep would have done a matador proud, and it was hardly any effort at all to trip the lumbering mass so he went into a table full of revelers, scattering their drinks and spilling the two whores who were with them to the floor. That got them up and advancing on Ruy with blood in their eyes, while Big Fellow got to his feet, shaking his head to clear it.

A quick step forward, and a couple of punches rocked one of them back on his heels. A space cleared, Ruy stepped back, grabbed a vacant stool and threw it at the others. The rebound cleared another table, they barged two more tables, and suddenly—the speed at which these things happened was too fast for even Ruy to follow—everyone in the taverna was on their feet jostling and shoving and shouting and in the ruckus, and the original cause of the disturbance was starting to feel quite surplus to requirements.

It was still a good imitation of pandemonium. Fighting his way to the door, Ruy had to hit another guy with a stool, then two more with the leg of the stool that had somehow come apart in his hand—damned shoddy Italian carpentry—and finally kicked a fourth in the crotch and whacked him in the ass with the makeshift club as he doubled over.

He paused at the door, waiting his turn in the stream of people leaving before knives came out, and looked back to survey his handiwork. Complete chaos and mayhem, he felt, quite compensating for the tedium of the evening so far. And, yes, the pimp was on the floor with blood running from his head. Accident, or a score settled in the confusion, Ruy didn't care. Couldn't happen to a nicer fellow. He took one last look around before dodging out, and froze. Then, he uttered a whole stream of swearwords under his breath.

"Not *him*," he murmured, "anyone but *him*."

There, across the room, flanked by a couple of bravos, holding off the swirling brawl from their corner table with stools and chairs with unmistakable whores cowering behind him for protection, was Francisco de Quevedo y Villega, in the flesh. Ruy Sanchez had sat in plain view in the same tavern for nearly an hour before standing up and picking a fight.

"Fuck," he said, and left.

"So why's this guy such a problem?" Sharon asked.

"Gah!" Ruy was pacing back and forth like an agitated cat. "Say better how is Francisco de Quevedo y Villega *not* a problem! Say, rather, is there any way in which his presence is not an omen of the direst deeds, the most ridiculous catastrophes, the follies most lacking in sanity! The man is born to make trouble!"

Sharon's mockery was well placed in reply. "Sounds like a fellow you'd get on with then, Ruy Sanchez de Casador y Ortiz."

"The difference, *mi corazon*, to use your charming American phrase, is that I know my ass from my elbow. I am not, to pick just one example of many, away abasing myself in a Venetian whorehouse when I ought to be organizing a *coup d'etat*, thus leaving my compatriots to get out of town one step ahead of an angry mob."

"Oh," Sharon said, catching the reference. "You think Borja's using this guy?"

"There is nothing more certain save my love for you," Ruy said. Then, feeling more amplification was called for, went on. "I was once pleased to count him as a friend. A younger fellow, just starting in the service of His Most Catholic Majesty, with a slight taint of disreputability but a man with fire and soul nonetheless, forced to be abroad after an unfortunate duel. I taught him much, but he learned rather less. Since those days, there has not been a botched plot or a bungled maneuver anywhere in Spain's dominions in Italy that that whore-hopping drunkard has not had a full hand in making into a worse disaster than it need have been."

"So this is good news, right?" Sharon asked, "I mean, if they've put a complete idiot in charge?"

"Would that it were so! God grant that he were simply an idiot. It is worse, Sharon, so much worse. Not only is he stupid, he is indefatigable, a force of nature! He has skills, skills that I, to my shame, taught to him. He has resources, furnished by that child of a diseased donkey and a dockside whore Borja. He will mean to achieve great things, Sharon, and the result will be tragic farce such as Cervantes himself could not have compassed. I, Ruy Sanchez de Casador y Ortiz, and as God is my witness I am no coward, I tremble at the thought of what he might do."

"Oh," Sharon said again, this time quietly. "Do you think he recognized you?"

Ruy shrugged. He had had time to think about that on his way through Rome's nighttime streets. "It may be so," he said, "but I was disguised somewhat. Nothing of great invention, but I was doing my best not to look or sound like my inimitable self, you understand?"

Sharon just grinned.

"And I think the years have changed him less than they have me. He is, as I recall, some years younger than I and is not yet embarked upon the full maturity of manhood." He drew himself up. He knew he was an old man, of course, but he was in much better shape than many men half his age. Activity had been the key, constant training and living well. But a little self-mockery seemed to amuse Sharon far more than anything else he essayed by way of humor, and so it pleased him to indulge for her sake.

"I figure you're about to say we should plan on the basis he did recognize you, I think," Sharon said, grinning at his comedic posturing, "since you are so astonishingly well preserved. Why, you might pass for a man of sixty."

Ruy gave her his best bristling affront. "Why, I am not a day over, well, ah"—he made great play of counting on his fingers—"Fifty-three. I think."

Truth be told, Ruy was not exactly sure how old he was. All he was truly certain of from his mother was that he had been born on the day after Ash Wednesday, a fact that did nothing to help fix his birthdate, and if his mother had told him what year that had been, or ever made any mention of precisely how old he was, he could not now remember. And it was thirty-eight years since he could have gone back and asked her. Nearly that long, he realized with a start, since he had last visited her grave. A practice that would have immediately exploded his pretense to gentility.

Sharon noticed his sudden shift of mood. "Bad memories, Ruy?" she asked, gently.

He shook his head. "A melancholy moment. God did not grant that I retain much from—from my earlier life. And what little there was I had to abandon to make my way in the world on the best terms I could secure. That the path led to my present happiness does not prevent me recalling what was lost along the way." He sighed, deeply. "For now, though, I have you, my love," he said, and took her in his arms.

Chapter 16

Rome

"Your Eminence," Quevedo said, bowing fulsomely.

Borja choked down the first retort that came to mind, which would have been an ungracious comment that the man was at once late and improperly attired. Instead, he nodded in return, proffering his ring for the formal kiss. "Señor Quevedo y Villega," he said, "what have you to report?"

Quevedo took a seat a moment after Borja did— *without being invited!*—and cleared his throat. Ferrigno poised his pen. The matter had now gone beyond maintaining full and formal confidence, and Borja had taken to admitting Ferrigno into his meetings simply in order to have notes of what was going on. It was becoming fearfully complicated, between the dealing with the cardinals and other notables of Rome, receiving updates on His Majesty's forces in the kingdom of Naples, the reports from the spies with which Rome was now liberally infested, even more so than usual, and keeping track of Quevedo's machinations. There was nothing for it but to bear the load, however. Above all else, he was a Borja, and that was a line that had never been found wanting where scheme and maneuver had been at issue. Still less could he flinch from the work where, as here, the work in hand was clearly God's.

He fixed Quevedo with his best glare. "Pray continue."

"As the Cardinal wishes." Quevedo bore the cardinal's regard without so much as a flinch. "During the course of the last week we have instigated three incidents of a serious nature, at the Lyncaean Institute, the Palazzo Borghese and the Palazzo Barberini. Efforts to suborn captains of militia continue and we hope to provoke another massacre soon. Also in hand is the production of broadsides and handbills linking the incidents to the Committee of Correspondence. We also seek to start rumors that the Committee is linked to the USE embassy and further that they are also provoking the militia massacres in order to destabilize Rome and the Church."

"The militia business is new," Borja said. He still maintained his suspicions of Quevedo, even though over the last few weeks he had done all that was asked of him. There was always the danger, however, that the man would develop an uncomfortable amount of initiative at some inopportune moment.

"Indeed, Your Eminence," Quevedo said, "but the discontent that the fortuitous actions outside Grassi's house provoked was most useful. We had volunteers for several incidents thereafter, and we hope to capitalize on that reaction. In the event that we can provoke full-scale disorder, popular hatred of the militia will be to Your Eminence's advantage."

"And the prospect of full-scale disorder?" Borja was, he would admit to himself, impatient to have the business done with. If for no other reason, the amount of money that Quevedo had spent thus far on hiring ruffians for his business was eye watering.

"Thus far, Your Eminence, not much greater than when we began. We face a situation where the populace was laboring under no great burden of discontent, although the usual seasonal rise in food prices at this time of year will undoubtedly help us for a few weeks. Bringing them to a mood of insurrection by spending money on them, Your Eminence, represents an exercise in futility. What we hope to achieve is a sufficiently bad reaction from the civil authorities that popular discontent will develop naturally."

"And the chances of that?" Borja asked, resisting the impulse to remind Quevedo that he had not asked for a lecture.

"The same as the chances of the civil government of Rome doing something remarkably stupid, Your Eminence. I fear that Your Eminence's best chance will be to pay for sufficient public disorder, which I must remind Your Eminence is very much not the same thing as popular discontent, that Your Eminence will have a pretext for the intervention Your Eminence has in prospect."

"I thank you for your most cogent analysis, señor," Borja said, fighting to keep sarcasm out of his voice. He had been resigned for some weeks to the fact that simply spending money on agitators would not produce the anarchy he was hoping for. His instructions from the count-duke were simply to hamstring the Barberini pope and ensure he could do nothing more to harm the interests of Spain. The promise of troops from Naples had been extracted by his own efforts, and could not be fulfilled easily beyond a few months away.

Once matters proceeded against France, Spain's strategic bases in Spain and Italy would be all but uncovered save for what was needed to suppress revolt. Troops would be hard to come by for any purpose, no matter how high and holy. Not to mention that what troops were left in Naples would more than likely have their hands full; discontent there was genuine and naturally occurring and the agitators of it were of a far more sincere character than Quevedo was ever likely to be. Even now that he had managed to quiet Osuna for a while with promises of future preferment and a few trifles in earnest of that preferment, there remained a most pestiferous infestation of malcontents.

"Your Eminence is most welcome," Quevedo said. "And I also am most pleased to be able to report that the prospects of an intervention by the United States of Europe are now much improved."

"What?" The involvement of the heretics from Germany had been no part of his plans, other than as a target of mob violence if the providence of the Holy Spirit should be generous. Borja would take a frank and unalloyed pleasure in the sight of *that* den of vipers being made to scatter with a swarm of enraged ruffians on their heels.

"The people of Rome are, like common folk everywhere, suspicious and untrusting of foreigners, Your Eminence. The sight of them meddling in the politics of Rome will provoke them, I am sure of it."

"And what have you done to bring the United States of Europe into the play?" Borja asked, almost dreading the answer.

"Nothing, Your Eminence. It appears that Sanchez has involved himself of his own accord. I saw him questioning a pimp last night."

"A pimp?" Borja was now prepared to admit to himself that he was completely baffled by this turn of events.

"A procurer of women for the purposes of prostitution, Your Eminence. Please accept my apologies for presuming that a churchman of your standing would be aware of the existence of such men."

Borja stared hard at Quevedo, but could detect no trace of sarcasm. "I am not so unworldly that I do not know what a pimp is, or what one does, Señor Quevedo. I requested enlightenment as to how it is we know Sanchez is involved from his conversation with a pimp. How do we know, for instance, that he was not transacting the ordinary business of such a fellow?"

"If Your Eminence will forgive me, I have some prior knowledge of the character of Ruy Sanchez de Casador y Ortiz. It is the defining character of the man that he is honorable, almost to excess in certain matters, and he is engaged to be married to the American moor. If there is one thing he was *not* doing, it was engaging the services of a prostitute."

"And do we have information as to why he was *actually* speaking to this pimp?" Borja asked. "Did we, for example, overhear the conversation?"

"I must ask Your Eminence's forgiveness," Quevedo said, "but my surmises are based on observations of Sanchez's character and habits, and of his actions during the time I saw him. He was affecting some rudiments of disguise, sufficient that he would not be

readily recognized at a distance by anyone who did
not know him well. I myself did not pick him out
for some considerable time, and was not certain of
my identification of him until he called attention to
himself. His voice, Your Eminence, is quite distinctive. His actions, insofar as I observed them, were
that he was haunting a popular taverna close to the
church of San Gioacchino, engaging the patrons in
conversation. The taverna was too crowded for me to
overhear every conversation, and as I have adverted
to Your Eminence, I did not at first notice Sanchez's
arrival."

Too busy drinking and whoring, Borja thought, but
kept the spiteful remark to himself. This was shaping
up to be interesting. Sanchez was Bedmar's creature,
and Borja had a personal dislike for the sarcastic
little Andalusian cardinal. Anything that redounded
to Bedmar's potential embarrassment was worth the
listening for entertainment value alone.

"Sanchez spent some time in conversation with
a pimp known to me as a regular in that taverna,"
Quevedo continued.

*And you known to him as a regular customer no
doubt*, Borja silently added.

"The pimp in question is a low and uncouth fellow
even by the standards of such," Quevedo said, oblivious to Borja's silent commentary, "and is apt to grow
insistent on the subject of his business. I gather that
when he did so, Sanchez picked a fight with another
patron in order to divert attention from his departure. The manner in which he did so was typically
flamboyant, I must inform Your Eminence, and it was
at this point that my identification was certain. The

resulting disturbance embroiled the entire taverna, and Sanchez made his exit under cover of the fighting. I did not discern the moment at which he made good his escape, as the fighting spilled over into the part of the taverna where I was sitting and I was forced to defend myself."

"Am I to presume you spoke to this pimp after the event?" Borja asked, picking up on Quevedo's obvious inference.

Quevedo smiled slightly, in a smug manner that Borja found even more irritating than usual. "Your Eminence is most astute. The fellow was stunned in the fighting. It was a simple matter to pick him up from the floor after the brawl had subsided, revive him with cold water and ply him with strong drink. I received a full account. Sanchez was posing as a porter from Barcelona, in Rome with the retinue of one of the cardinals Your Eminence has summoned on his own business. I identified Sanchez to the man as an agent of the United States of Europe, and enough people saw the disguised Sanchez that when the rumor spreads, the sight of him in the company of Dottoressa Nichols will confirm the rumor that the United States is fomenting discord in Rome in an attempt to suborn the See of Rome for their own nefarious purposes. I suggested as much to the pimp, and I have no doubt that the rumor is already beginning to spread. Your Eminence may depend upon it that I made much of Sanchez's hand in the Venetian conspiracy."

Borja realized that it would be ungenerous to begrudge Quevedo his smug expression, not least because there was a delicious irony in him, of all people, exploiting Sanchez's involvement in Bedmar's attempt to take Venice: Quevedo had been Osuna's man on the inside of that plot and had done just as much as Sanchez had, if not more. Irony aside, Quevedo had exploited a providential opportunity in a manner that would undoubtedly open up further opportunities to profit. If it became a matter of general gossip in Rome that the pope was somehow under the sway of the United States of Europe, for preference at the hands of that scheming Jew Nasi that styled himself a Don, much could be done to undo the harm that the Barberini had done to Spain's cause by publicly withdrawing his support. If, after all, he had been induced to do so by the machinations of a sinister Byzantine Jew . . .

Borja returned from his musings to ask Quevedo, "And what do you propose to do to further exploit this opportunity?"

"For the moment, Your Eminence, I will, with your permission, observe closely and react to whatever actions Sanchez undertakes. I would remind Your Eminence of my earlier remarks regarding the natural development of popular dissent. It is seldom that attempts to force such matters past their proper pace prove fruitful. The disorder we are provoking will create a soil in which any seed of genuine dissent may prove fruitful, but it is in God's hands whether any such seeds fall on the ground we have prepared, Your Eminence."

Borja nodded. It was as well to trust in Providence in such matters, for there was little that the agency of one man, or even a whole combination of men, could achieve. "I shall pray for the success of your efforts," he said, and realized that there was more. "I shall also thank God," he said, "for His having placed this opportunity in your path."

"Your Eminence is most kind," Quevedo said. "I only hope that the Lord God Almighty saw fit to direct Sanchez's eye to where I sat."

"Truly?" Borja said, intrigued, "Why so?"

Quevedo's smile was impish in the extreme. "The man bears a grudge like no one else I have ever known, Your Eminence. If he believes me to be involved in Your Eminence's business, he will stop at nothing to intervene and foil me. It is his rather rustic notion of hidalgo honor. As well the fact that he is a Catalan, a breed notorious for their touchiness. I feel we may depend on Sanchez to worsen his own party's position quite unintentionally."

Borja allowed himself a smile. "And, of course, he is Bedmar's man. And Bedmar is now firmly aligned with Flanders, and they in turn are making overtures to the United States of Europe. The opportunities for placing the blame do rather multiply." He savored the thoughts, for a moment.

"Señor Quevedo y Villega, your work goes well, and I am indeed pleased. I thank you for your efforts, and shall indeed pray most earnestly that God grant you further successes. You may go."

"Thank you, Your Eminence," Quevedo said, and with the proper formalities, left.

Chapter 17

Rome

"Well, this *is* a grand house," Giovanna remarked.

"All of 'em are, around here," Frank said. And it was true. The USE embassy was in a very nice neighborhood indeed, on the outskirts of the huge Borghese estate. That said, there did seem to be a lot of people just . . . hanging around. That wouldn't have been much out of the ordinary down toward the Borgo on the other side of the river. Frank was pretty much used to the sight of the street-life being seasoned with a fair few of what you could only call "colorful characters"—assuming, that is, you didn't want to call them bums and petty criminals. He had the feeling that seeing more than one around here would be a little odd. Come right to it, a few streets away there hadn't been quite so many specimens of the local wildlife mixed in among the well-to-do.

It was . . . odd.

That said, there were guards at the door of the embassy, a couple of big Marine cavalrymen looking relaxed but alert, and generally very smart and military.

"'Ow do, Mister Stone," one of them said as he and Giovanna mounted the steps.

Frank puzzled a moment to place the face under the helmet. "Private Ritson?" he guessed after a moment. He'd last seen the guy a year ago at the embassy in Venice. Looked like he'd been assigned here now. Ritson was one of the Englishmen in the nominally Scots cavalry regiment that had become the Grantville Marine Cavalry, a reminder that the regiment were borderers and that the border they came from had two sides.

"Aye, but it's Corporal Ritson now, thank you." Ritson grinned, pointing at the stripe on his arm.

"Oh, right, I didn't notice," Frank said, feeling a bit foolish. "Congratulations."

"Cheers," Ritson said. "Mistress Nichols is expecting you and the lady, go right on in."

"Thanks," said Frank, nodding to the other Marine—whom he didn't recognize at all—on the way in.

Inside, it was plain that whatever the USE's other budget problems, they weren't stinting on the rent. The place was, if anything, even gaudier than the palazzo they'd rented in Venice. In this case, Roman standards being a bit different from Venetian ones—they had more space, for one thing—the place was only accounted a large house, not a palace. Inside, though, there was marble and carven cherubs and gilt and a general air of *real freakin' expensive* about the place. Frank found himself looking for somewhere to wipe his feet.

Giovanna didn't seem fazed by it one bit. She was halfway to the reception desk before Frank was done gawking. A few quick words with the clerk there—Frank noticed that the seventeenth century had had its say and there wasn't a female receptionist, but a guy who'd been stuffed into smart clothes and given a quill and ledger to sign folks in and out—and she was back. "The dottoressa will be told we are here, someone will tell us when it is time to go in." Sure enough, Frank could see a messenger trotting off, some kid who looked maybe fourteen. The seventeenth century was getting its way on that score as well, whatever the folks back in Grantville might have had to say about child labor.

"Hey, guys!" Sharon's voice called from the turn of the magnificent marble staircase at the other end of the entrance hall. Frank sneaked a look and saw the receptionist wearing a pained expression at the manner in which Sharon was trampling over the right way of doing things as he saw it. And then Sharon came into view, trailed by the slightly sheepish-looking messenger.

"Hi, Sharon. Are we early?" Frank wasn't entirely sure. The battery in his watch had finally run out the year before. The timekeeping you got from Rome's church bells was only good to within ten minutes or so and varied from street to street depending on which church you could hear best.

Sharon waved it aside. "Close enough guys, come on up. I've got an examination room up here at the back where the light's good."

The way to the examination room took them past a door from behind which could be heard the sounds of a full-on sword fight. Sharon must have seen the looks on Frank and Giovanna's faces, because she laughed. "Ruy's putting the Marines through their morning sword-drill. Some days you can see the testosterone seeping under the door."

"Figures," Frank said, and chuckled. "Jocks, eh?"

"Thing is," Sharon said, "Ruy would agree with you. It's just that his notion of how a jock ought to behave would probably astonish most of the guys on your high school football team."

Sharon opened the door to a room that was, if anything, grander than the entrance hall had been. Big, and open, and with huge mullioned windows that looked out over a big garden that was all straight lines and angles, the kind Frank had only ever seen in movies. "Nice place you got here, by the way."

"Ain't it?" Sharon said, with a wry grin. "We pretty much have to spend all this money just to get taken seriously. Even as a doctor." She snorted her contempt for the idea. "Not that there weren't plenty of people in the twentieth century who had the same fool idea, mind."

Frank decided to take her word for it. "So, uh, I should go amuse myself while you and Giovanna, uh—"

Actually, Frank wasn't at all sure what the hell was going to happen and, really, didn't want to. Giovanna and Sharon were exchanging a look that simply said: "*Men.*" "I'll, uh, go look in on Ruy and the guys, doing, uh, guy stuff, okay?" He beat it before they could mock him any more.

When he opened the door to the training room— apparently a ballroom the rest of the time—it looked like the whole room had been turned into a gigantic human-powered mincing machine. There were about twenty guys in Marine uniforms with cuirasses over them paired off around the room and, as far as Frank could tell, fighting. And in the middle, his back to Frank and glaring at one pair who had apparently stopped for a breather, was Ruy Sanchez.

"Señor Faul!" He was bellowing. "The rapier for honor, the back-sword for duty, your countrymen say! Pray you remember it! If Señor Crombie should open himself to a kick in the crotch as he has just done, you will administer him one, with great force! Duty is to kill the enemy, not treat with him as a gentleman! Now, again! And this time, Crombie, close your stance because if Faul doesn't smash your balls for you, I, Ruy Sanchez de Casador y Ortiz, most surely will!"

The two Marines came to guard positions. Frank thought that was the right word, anyway, although what he knew about fencing pretty much stopped at knowing the pointy end went toward your opponent. There was a blur of steel. Clearly Crombie didn't make the same mistake again because the exchange ended with Faul yelping, saying something that was almost certainly filthy in Gaelic, and clutching his forearm.

"Better," Sanchez shouted. Without turning around: "Señor Stone! So good to see you! Will you join us?"

Frank looked around—*like there's another Señor Stone in here, dummy,* he thought. "I, uh, don't have a sword."

"A lack we can remedy," Sanchez said. "You will find a box of practice sabers to your right, and a cuirass which will fit you there also."

Frank began to think he should have hung around for the gynecological exam.

Forty-five minutes later he had a fine set of bruises, was gasping for breath, sweating like a boar hog and knew how to take guard, stand, advance, retreat, sidestep, parry to *quarte* and *sixte* and could perform two simple cuts and a lunge. All of them badly. But

Sanchez grudgingly allowed that he might survive as much as thirty seconds of a real fight. On a good day. Against an opponent who was profoundly drunk.

After dismissing the Marines, all of whom seemed indecently fresh after their own training session, Sanchez came over to where Frank was trying to summon the energy to get out of his gear. His thighs were burning, both arms ached, his stomach muscles were just on the good side of a cramp and his entire right side and arm seemed to be one big bruise.

"Thanks, Señor Sanchez," Frank gasped, pulling at the buckles of the cuirass that had saved him from being turned into low-grade hamburger meat, "Maybe I should get me a sword."

"Perhaps, Señor Stone," Sanchez said, "But do you have a gun?"

"Yeah, a revolver, six-shooter. One of the ones they're making in the USE these days. I really should practice with it more, but I just don't get the time."

"Find the time, señor."

"Please, call me Frank."

"Thank you, and, outside the training room, you may also address me with familiarity as a friend of my intended. As I was saying, find the time to practice. You performed well for a first lesson, for you are a sportsman, yes?"

"Soccer. Lot of running in the game, for ninety minutes."

"Indeed. It serves you well, and I worked you harder than I would have otherwise. Harder than I did the Marines, Frank."

"Yeah? You kind of caught me by surprise asking me to join in, actually," Frank was starting to get his breath back, but a couple of gallons of ice-cold water were starting to seem like a really good idea about now. "Why'd you do that?"

"Doña Sharon asked me to. Not the instruction specifically, but among the matters she has tasked me with is the safety of the Committee. The opportunity to instill some rudimentary skills presented itself, and I took it as furthering the desires of the woman I love."

Frank nodded. "Makes sense. By the way, can you teach me to do the thing with the eyes in the back of your head?"

"When you came in to the room?" Sanchez was chuckling. "Frank, the first lesson of the *destreza*, the one that is never taught but must be learned most well, is to pay attention and *observe*. And the uniform of the Marines, and I insist they train as they would fight, includes a cuirass. A very bright, shiny, polished cuirass."

Frank grinned back. "And there I was thinking you were pulling some kind of Obi-Wan Kenobi schtick on me."

"Who is Obi-Wan Kenobi?" Sanchez asked, frowning. "A real person of the future or a fictional character?"

Frank grinned. "Fictional, as it happens. A Jedi knight, a warrior and I guess you'd call him a wizard. If you ever go back to Grantville, ask Sharon to see that you get to see *Star Wars*; I reckon you'd like it."

"Ah, the television I have heard so much about? I shall make careful note of your recommendation, Frank. But likewise make note of mine. Practice with your gun, please. Be ready to use it, as well. You have more skill with the sword now than the common run of ruffian, but that will avail you nothing against a man who has been fighting since childhood, however unschooled he may be."

Frank felt a slight chill, and not a welcome one, however sweaty he might be. He'd seen fencing on the TV one time, and it looked like quite a silly sport—two guys in metal masks playing tag with car aerials. Suddenly he didn't see the training session he'd just been shanghaied into as having anything to do with that game. It was about kill or be killed. And he still got nightmares about the sight of Marius Pontigrazzi's head bursting from where Gerry had shot him in the face. That episode had calmed Gerry himself right down from his hillbilly-hardass pose, and sent him clear back to Grantville, with side trips to Rudolstadt and Jena, to rethink his life in major ways. "Right," he said, when he'd fought down the shudder. "More range time. I can use the cellar, put some targets up in there."

"You do that. Practice at short ranges, point and shoot. Those weapons are excellent devices, Frank, as good as having six pistols in one hand." Sanchez's usual good-natured grin was nowhere in evidence now. Frank felt the conversation was being altogether too serious for his taste. Sanchez wasn't letting up, though. "Practice with your left hand as well. Practice reloading as swiftly as you may."

"You really think there will be trouble?" Frank asked.

"There will always be trouble, Frank. And there is seldom any easy way in which to predict where and when it will come to you. For now, I suspect there are those who will use your presence and activities for their own ends, and while they care little enough to order your death, I feel sure that they would issue no tears were it to happen. And I, Ruy Sanchez de Casador y Ortiz, say that the way of honor is to prepare to flee, and cover your retreat with gunfire. Honor lies in doing one's duty, not throwing your life away."

Frank felt certain that Sanchez was hinting at something, but he couldn't tell what it was. "Understood, Ruy. I've had my taste of stand-up fighting and I guess I'm not the kind of guy that enjoys it. If it can be avoided, I'm out of there. I, uh, guess I'm a lover, not a fighter."

"Exactly my point, and as you—Ah!" Ruy straightened in order to deliver a sweeping bow. "Señora Stone, it is a pleasure and an honor to see you again. I regret, most sincerely, that I have caused your husband some shortness of breath, but it is certain to pass before you require him for anything."

Frank grinned ruefully and hauled himself to his feet. "Señor Sanchez let me try out with the saber. He recommends I practice my shooting."

"Oh, now, with much study, you would become a fine and competent swordsman, Señor Stone," Sanchez insisted. Then, to Sharon: "I felt it would be worthwhile to equip the young caballero with the rudiments of self-defense. If worse comes to worst, he should be able to hold off ordinary ruffians. With your permission, Doña Ambassadora, if he will again accompany his most beautiful wife on her next visit, I will endeavor to impart some more training?"

"By all means, Ruy. Giovanna and I went and had a coffee and a chat after we were done precisely to let you get on with that." Sharon turned to Frank.

"Giovanna's in fine form, nothing to worry about. I've suggested she start taking it easy as she gets toward her third trimester, just light work from then on. She's a healthy girl and a hard worker, and she complained about it, but those are doctor's orders. No sense in unnecessary risks, I say. See she doesn't take 'em."

Frank sketched a salute. "Ma'am," he said, "exactly what I was saying. Between me and her family, we should be able to keep her from doing anything too strenuous."

After Frank had gotten the long cool drink he was gasping for, Sharon made another suggestion. "Would you like Ruy to come over and check out your place to advise on things like defenses and routes out in a hurry?"

"Well, sure," Frank said, frowning. "Señor Sanchez is welcome any time. But, uh, between you and Señor Sanchez that's the second warning of trouble I've had today. You think there's more to it than leaflets and rent-a-crowds?"

"Well, we do and we don't," Sharon said, her face a perfect deadpan. "On the one hand, we can't see where everything we're seeing is leading except for trouble for the Vatican. On the other hand, there's trouble in the streets as well. And Ruy's seen at least one guy he knows is a real nasty customer, and apparently he's capable of anything."

Ruy barked a laugh. "Say rather, he will attempt anything, and the results are usually disastrous for many. Capable, outside of doggerel and philosophical musings, he is not. But in bungling whatever business he is about, he is sure to cause trouble. I have had one of my own operations ruined by Francisco de

Quevedo y Villega, and been one step ahead of an angry mob as a result."

"How will I know this guy if I see him?" Frank asked, visions of some sinister Spanish agent haunting his club flitting through his mind.

"Likely, you will not," Sanchez said. "It was purely good fortune that I spotted him when and where I did, and it beggars belief that he is not working for Cardinal Borja, if the evidence of the past few weeks' deeds is of any worth. It is precisely the manner of foolishness that he would attempt."

"So, Frank," Sharon said, "we're taking precautions just in case. And you have responsibilities, not just to the Committee."

"*Dottora!*" Giovanna said, her voice sharp, "Do not suggest that I will shirk any danger!"

Frank stifled a groan. Sharon had unwittingly pressed the Revolution Button in Giovanna's brain. "Giovanna," he said, "look at it this way. We don't have enough to face these guys in a straight fight. If we have to, we simply melt away, and come back when their attention moves on. We don't play the game by their rules, Giovanna, because if we do, we lose. We stay until it gets hot, and then we get our heads down until the trouble passes."

"*Frank*—" Giovanna began, her eyes starting to flash. On this subject, she wouldn't even think about hesitating to pick a fight right in front of Ruy and Ms. Nichols.

Nothing for it, Frank thought, and drew himself up. "Enough!" he said, looking her straight in the eye. "I decide the tactics. When we cannot win, we bug *out*. No one's going to be a martyr. No one."

Giovanna plainly didn't like it, but she had very strong reflexes where some things were concerned. She'd been raised to be a dutiful daughter and someday a dutiful wife. Frank hated using that against her, but on some issues—like her probable willingness to stand on a barricade and defy a regiment of cavalry with nothing but cobblestones and raw courage so as to be a Martyr of the Revolution—he figured the payoff was worth acting like some domineering asshole. Raised as a commune hippie he might have been, but if it came to a choice between dumping his dad's principles in the crapper or letting Giovanna get shot, he didn't really have to think too hard.

Giovanna subsided from the rant she had been building up to. But Frank could tell, from the way her lips thinned and she glared at him, that he hadn't heard the last of this. He'd deal with it later. Although, from the looks, he'd gone up in Sanchez's opinion.

"Señora Stone," Sanchez said, "your husband's thinking is in accord with that of a professional soldier. I can find no fault in his reasoning. Duty is not always both honorable and pleasant, and is frequently neither."

That didn't go over too well with Giovanna either, Frank noticed, but decided that pressing it now wasn't such a good idea. "We should get back," he said to Giovanna. "We need to make sure the guys are ready for the lunchtime rush."

They said their good-byes to Sharon, and Sanchez agreed to come over and make a start on the defenses of the Committee and have lunch with them. On the way out, as they turned along the street to head for the bridge that would take them to their own side of the river, Sanchez leaned over, and in conversational tones, said, "Our movements are being reported. One of the people who have been watching the embassy building for the last few days just ran away, doubtless to deliver tidings of your departure."

"You saw?" Frank fought the urge to turn around. He didn't know much about this sort of thing, but he figured letting on that they knew was a wrong move.

"A small boy, who was standing with a group of ruffians. Who, I might add, did not accord well with the character of this quarter of Rome."

"Did you see where he went?" Giovanna asked.

"The opposite way from our present direction," Sanchez said, pausing a moment to tip his hat to a lady passing them, "running fast. A risk of using street urchins in this kind of business, they do not know how to be inconspicuous."

"What do we do?" Frank asked, trying hard to give an air of *just chatting with an old friend as we stroll along*.

"Nothing, Señor Stone," Sanchez said. "Let them believe we do not know we are being watched."

The rest of the walk back passed without incident.

Chapter 18

Rome

Cardinal Antonio Barberini was not, in any measure, a happy man. He stood at the window overlooking the square where, money permitting, he would be wheedling his uncle to commission a new fountain. The piazza needed it, frankly. Something by Bernini, if the man had time to work on it before he died. The trouble with Bernini, of course, was that he was so good, he had more commissions than he could truly keep up with.

Right now though, the problem with the piazza was not so much the absence of fountain, but the very real and present presence of what looked like a couple of hundred people. Not, if one were to be truly pedantic, a mob. They didn't seem to have a great deal to say for themselves, and while there would certainly be pockets being picked and minor scuffles, the whole scene didn't look criminal. Or, at least, not from this elevated and removed vantage.

It was just—untidy. Badly composed. An eyesore. A little while ago, he'd asked that someone be sent to wander through the crowd and see what had drawn them. Idle curiosity, really. The fellow who'd gone out—someone had picked out one of the below-stairs porters as being most likely to blend in, and Barberini could see the point, the man looked quite charmingly villainous—had come back a few moments ago saying that the crowd wasn't really there for much. A couple of the fellows Barberini's man had talked to had been paid to turn up and the rest had hung around to see if anything was going to happen. That alone would just have been an amusing oddity of idleness and the beginnings of a long, hot summer.

It was not alone. There was the paper. *That* had been handed to the porter, he said, within minutes of him setting foot in the square. There were street-boys down there giving them to anyone with hands to hold them. The porter could not read it, but had kept it to show his boss. Barberini had it in his hand now, read once and then gripped tightly. Naturally, the thing was scurrilous beyond belief. No one who actually knew him would believe a word of it. Not least because the author had at one and the same time accused him of sins against nature and of patronizing Gentileschi simply in order to fornicate with her. In its way, it was quite amusing. And damnably infuriating.

"Your Eminence is . . ." A long pause. "Angered?"

"Father-General," Barberini said, not turning away from the window, "I did not hear you enter."

Vitelleschi moved over by Barberini, but did not, the younger cardinal noted, stand in the window. "Your Eminence's majordomo vouchsafed that you seemed ill at ease. I took the liberty of entering unannounced."

"To be sure of seeing me helpless in fury? Knowing my weakness?" Barberini drew on every drachm of civility and manners at his command not to snarl at the father-general. It would not do for the pope's nephew to lose his temper with his uncle's most dependable ally. And most useful one, at a time like this.

"Your Eminence recognizes it for the temptation it is. Wrath is a deadly sin." Vitelleschi's dry rasp had softened somewhat, Barberini noted, and he found himself all the more angry with the old man.

"I need no catechism from you, Father-General." Barberini took pride in the fact that his voice was icy calm. Another deadly sin.

"It is a provocation, nothing more." For a wonder, Vitelleschi said it without sounding patronising. "Similar things have been written about your uncle. Many times, over the years since he was elected."

"I also need no schooling in such footling tricks as this," Barberini said, snapping at last. "Did I need such, there would already be squadrons of horse in the square, slaking my wounded name in blood." He realized as he said it that he was losing his white-knuckled grip on his self-control, and had brandished the paper at Vitelleschi.

"I doubt they seek to provoke anything so crude." Barberini noticed for the first time that Vitelleschi had brought a slim brief-wallet, and took from it other handbills like the one that was passing in the square below. Barberini could see that the ones from the case were different, for all that he could not read the contents from where he was standing. Vitelleschi was silent for a long moment, before he went on. "Your Eminence might perhaps consider the possibility of other hasty reactions which those responsible for this libel might have sought to provoke."

What little patience Barberini retained was barely a shred. "Such as?"

Vitelleschi's glare was as baleful as the basilisk of legend. "What did Your Eminence think to do after dismissing the thought of ordering a massacre of innocents?"

Barberini's urgent desire to slap the father-general across the face parsed the full measure of the insults in that question faster than his sentient mind could. He actually raised his hand before realizing that the barb had been a deliberate goad. The sharp sting of the schoolmaster's cane. *Never forget that the Jesuits are educators as much as they are anything*, he told himself and lowered his hand. "Father-General," he said, bowing his head and folding his hands together, "I must apologize most humbly for my unseemly and unwarranted action," he said.

"It is nothing, and still less to forgive. Your Eminence will please remember that I am your uncle's most obedient servant, and he and I have grown old in the service of Christ. Yet neither of us has forgotten what it was to be a young man, with a young man's passion and impulses." There was the faintest ghost of a smile about the Jesuit's lips.

Realizing how thoroughly he had been stung, Barberini could not help but smile himself. "I confess, Father-General, that I had not as yet passed beyond the thought of horses stampeding through the piazza. Except, and I offer this in the most desperate mitigation, that when you entered I was musing on the possible themes for a new fountain in the square."

He smiled again, a more amiable smile this time. "It does so need it. Far more than it does a carpet of libelous handbills."

Vitelleschi's smile became almost discernible. "Come, Your Eminence. We must discuss more constructive suggestions."

"I fear the Father-General will be far ahead of me," Barberini said, still rueful at having been chided like a slow-witted schoolboy. "We have confidence in our estimates of what mischief Borja intends to work, and I have considerable confidence that the Father-General's subordinates have done excellent work in securing that the cardinals who will vote in His Holiness' favor will be present in Rome at or before the critical juncture."

Vitelleschi's smile faded to a mere spectral hint of earthly pleasure. "The Society attempts as ever to repay the confidence Your Eminence and, through Your Eminence, His Holiness places in us. I have every expectation that on this occasion the account will be paid in full measure."

Barberini felt genuine amusement at that. Vitelleschi must be well pleased in his people's efforts if he was prepared to be that flowery in his description of their success. Barberini clapped his hands together. If Vitelleschi was prepared to be mildly pleased, it behooved lesser mortals to be demonstrative. "Excellent," he cried, "and therefore it only remains to ensure that there is nothing lurking beneath the surface of Borja's plot?"

"There's the rub, Your Eminence." The smile was gone, now.

"No further success?" Barberini asked, turning

away from the window at last. "Maddening, to lack definite answers."

"Normal," Vitelleschi corrected him.

"For the Father-General, perhaps." Barberini looked about for a chair. "And, please, rest those bones that have grown old in the service of Christ. I find my fit of childish pique is quite past, now."

"Very good, Your Eminence."

"Now," Barberini said, when they were both seated and he had rung for a servant to bring refreshments, "we may be no more certain beyond our educated guesses as to what Borja is about, but what is Quevedo doing?"

"Printing handbills," Vitelleschi said promptly, and Barberini could have sworn there was an impish tone in his voice as he said it.

Barberini refused to be baited, suspecting the while that he was being taught a lesson thereby. "I presume that there are more handbills than simply these that slur what there is of my good name?"

"Your Eminence presumes correctly. We have identified twelve distinct ones, in the course of the last week alone. Each framed so as to be as barely coherent as the one which I note Your Eminence still has in his hand."

"I do? I do." Barberini put the offending paper down on the table, grateful for the moment of levity. "It is as if Quevedo does not care what rumor he starts, so long as he starts some rumor to the general disorder of Rome."

"Just so, Your Eminence."

"What is to be done?" Barberini asked. "What can be answered in the one about myself does not merit the dignity of a response, I feel."

"Your Eminence's considered response is commendably temperate. It is usual for the populace to be restive at this time of year when the price of bread is at its highest, seemingly each year higher than the year before. Quevedo seems, in our estimation, to be casting as many seeds as possible on the ground."

Barberini caught the biblical metaphor. "And he hopes for fruit from the stoniest of ground?"

"He does not act alone. Borja, directly and indirectly, can exert control over what is preached from a number of Rome's pulpits. Things are being said from those pulpits, Your Eminence."

Barberini thought about that for a moment. In the course of analyzing what Borja was up to, he'd had to review the control of all of Rome's churches. "I do not believe the Spanish party controls any churches in the poorer quarters. Those that are in the localities frequented by the common folk of Rome are all in the gift of the old families of Rome."

"The Borghese."

That was a connection that shed a great deal of light, Barberini realized. The Borghese were among the oldest of Rome's nobility and controlled the benefices of some of Rome's oldest parishes. And the older parishes tended to be the poorer neighborhoods. And if they were preaching Spain's interest—"The Borghese are definitely against us?" he asked.

"Subtly so. Their more popular pulpits speak against the malign influence of the United States of Europe. Sermons against the *Strega* Nichols have been preached in at least two churches in the last week, and much is being said about foreign plots against the Church of Rome. In the more affluent neighborhoods, they are viewing the discontent of the people with great alarm."

"Stirring up class against class?" That was the very definition of sedition, Barberini realized, and if the Borghese had gone that far, then whatever efforts had been made to ensure the Borghese remained at least loyal to Italian interests over foreign ones had been in vain. Barberini had not personally been involved. Discussions between the noble houses of Rome were delicate business at the best of times, and never left to men in their twenties, however dizzyingly they had been promoted. "This grows grave."

Vitelleschi made no reply.

Barberini thought further. Nothing suggested itself. The report he would give to his uncle would be an uncomfortable one. He tried to anticipate the course of that audience. His Holiness would almost certainly suggest that approaching the problem from its fundamentals would yield results; the schools of philosophy and theology he had adhered to all his life left clear imprints on the way he thought. So, what was at the root of Borja's stratagem?

"They are making allegations about the influence of the United States of Europe on His Holiness, yes?"

"Yes, Your Eminence." Vitelleschi's face betrayed nothing.

Vitelleschi had received his education, if not at the same time then at least from teachers trained in the same tradition as Pope Urban VIII. Their generation was the last of the medievals, in truth, where that of Cardinal Antonio Barberini the Younger was really the first to be untouched by that old way of thinking. It could make for conversations at uncomfortable cross-purposes, especially when the older man was bound and determined to make a Socratic dialogue of it. *Very well—*

"And it remains the case that the contact between His Holiness and the United States of Europe since the conclusion of the Galileo affair has been only of the most perfunctory and formal kind, not such as to permit any opportunity of influence? And that their time in Rome has been spent making and maintaining contacts with merchants on the one hand, and learned men and doctors of physic and natural philosophy on the other, to the almost total exclusion of anyone with real political influence?"

"So far as I am aware, Your Eminence."

"And that has not prevented Quevedo's busy printers from nevertheless telling anyone who will listen that His Holiness is wholly under the spell of these wonder-workers from the future?"

"It has not, Your Eminence."

Barberini searched the older man's face. There was not a clue to be read there. Nary a twitch nor crease out of imperturbable place. "It therefore follows that there is no harm to be done by opening informal, social contact with the Dottoressa Nichols?"

"None that is not already being done in the fullest measure within our opponents' power, Your Eminence," Vitelleschi said.

"But why would I do such a thing? I confess I have not taken any steps since my uncle last spoke to me of the matter."

Vitelleschi avoided the trap of Barberini's rapid-fire question by mis-parsing it. "Your Eminence needs no excuse to invite a notable lady of high repute in the medical arts and sciences to one of his salons. Your Eminence already cultivates several doctors of natural philosophy."

"I would have us drop the pretense, Father-General," Barberini said after a short pause. "While your efforts to educate me in matters perquisite to my position are greatly appreciated, in this matter I must ask that you advise me."

Vitelleschi's smile returned, for the merest *scintilla temporis*. The blink of an insect would have sufficed to miss it. "On Friday last in the forenoon Frank and Giovanna Stone, at whose wedding Your Eminence was pleased to administer the sacrament, attended the embassy of the United States of Europe in the first of what will be regular meetings. Giovanna Stone is under the medical care of the Dottoressa Nichols."

"Is she ill?" Barberini's concern was genuine. While he had been scared out of his wits by the gunplay at Galileo's trial-that-was-not-a-trial, he had found them to be a pleasant young couple, only a few years younger than he was himself, for whom he had heartfelt wishes of every happiness.

"On the contrary. The marriage Your Eminence performed is to be fruitful in the latter part of this year, if God grant there be no complications. The girl is young and healthy, so as these things go the prospects must be accounted good."

"Excellent!" Barberini cried aloud, thinking *at least someone is getting good news*. "And this bears on my contact with the dottoressa—oh." Now he said it aloud, it seemed obvious. Vitelleschi had scored against him again. Which was, given the man's age and formidable learning, only to be expected. "The Committee of

Correspondence is dedicated to organizing mass action. You believe they . . . ?"

"Almost certainly not in our direct interests. But they have a laudable commitment to honesty in their dealings, or so I understand from my brethren in the Germanies. We would find them foes, but honorable foes," Vitelleschi said.

"I understand, though, that Stone is, as far as the activities of the Committee of Correspondence in Rome are concerned, careful to undertake his organizational work patiently. Given his history with the Inquisition, it seems wise of him."

"True. But we face many months of Borja's actions, and given time, the presence of an organization which concentrates the minds of the mob on ills which can be remedied will prove useful. In the longer term, we would have to deal with them more directly."

"Surely such things take time? The reports I have seen on the Committee—"

"We should have time. The present unrest is sporadic, and small. There has been little call for the militia. It will take time to build to a serious problem. By then, with a guarantee of the Inquisition's restraint, it may be that the Committee will be working against the machinations of Quevedo's agitators. They do something very much like it in the Germanies."

"I am unconvinced of the value of such a stratagem, Father-General."

"I would ask Your Eminence to cultivate the contact nevertheless. It will be some time before I can meet with His Holiness without attracting comment. Please pass to him that this is my recommendation also."

Barberini sighed. "I feel sure that he, too, will not

think well of a plan that involves inviting revolutionaries, anticlerical revolutionaries at that, into Rome.
But, be that as it may, I shall speak with Dottoressa
Nichols in any event. Her presence at my salon will
be stimulating."

"I thank Your Eminence for the consideration."

Barberini reached for his drink again, and saw the
handbill on the table. "Of course, I will be accused
in print of inviting her in order to fornicate with her.
I had better invite Bedmar's man as well. He is her
intended, and I have heard *stories* about that man."

Chapter 19

Rome

Frank wasn't liking the atmosphere in his club one little bit. It wasn't that the place was rowdy, at all. If anything, the number of people in the place was a bit light for a Saturday night. It was quiet, too. The usual pick-up band—some combination of French André, Martino, Andreas and Fabrizio plus whoever wanted to join them—weren't in and no one seemed to be ready to take up the slack. And the people who were in were largely sitting quietly and talking well below the usual drunken Italian volume.

"Anyone saying what's up?" he asked Benito when he came back to the bar. "Seems quiet tonight."

Benito shrugged. "Looks like we only got the real regulars, Frank. I'll ask Piero, he usually knows what's going down."

Frank looked over, and indeed Piero was there. Usually he had a girl with him—and usually a different one each week and one or two of them obviously hookers, but Frank figured that wasn't any of his business. "I'll go over and have a chat, actually," he said. "Mind the bar for me."

Piero nodded as Frank dragged up a stool. "You've heard, then?" the *lefferto* said.

"Heard what? I was kind of wondering what was up, like, where is everybody?"

Piero heaved a deep sigh, and shrugged. "You haven't seen the handbills, then?"

"Well, I've seen a couple—" Frank began, and then stopped. "There's another one out today?"

"Yesterday, actually. I figured it was false, since you denied the earlier one and it just plain doesn't sound like you."

"Don't leave a guy in suspense, Piero, what does it say?" Frank had a sinking feeling in his guts. He'd thought that whoever was printing the things was trying to get him in trouble with the Inquisition, and he'd been going in and making a nuisance of himself denouncing whoever it was to the Inquisition himself.

Sharon and Ruy Sanchez were certain it was the Spanish but Frank didn't know enough to be sure. So he'd been going back and writing letters demanding to know if they'd caught the guy, which he'd thought was a nice touch, to the point where the junior priest who met him whenever he went over there looked visibly alarmed whenever Frank showed up. Frank liked that. Turnabout was fair play, after all.

"I can do better," Piero said. "I kept mine." He dug inside his jacket somewhere and brought out a rumpled and stained piece of cheap rag paper.

Frank looked at it. It was badly printed, and the type looked as if it had slipped a bit, blurring the letters. He read it closely. It started with the usual stuff ripped off from old broadsides by Massimo—who would probably be pleased to hear that he'd made at least that much impact. Then it went on to—Frank groaned. "We'd never say any of this stuff, Piero."

"That's what I thought," Piero agreed. "I mean, you don't want to end up in jail, right? I figure you don't want to die either. I mean, we're allowed to make nasty cracks about the city, but you're still a foreigner. As for the suggestion we all hold our women in common, well, you could maybe say I don't get too attached to any particular one, but I—Frank?" Piero looked concerned.

"Sorry, I was just reading some more of this. It makes it look like I wanted to insult everyone I know around here. About the only thing I left out, according to this, is that I think everyone in Rome is fucking his own sister and killed his mother."

Piero chuckled. "Well, if you read it one way, it's like you asked everyone to whore his sister out."

"It ain't funny, Piero. We got to do something about this, man."

Piero cleared his throat. "Well, actually, *you've* got to do something about it. Only reason I'm here is, ah, I'm avoiding someone." He flashed a grin. "I kind of made a start on the whole holding women in common thing last week, and I figured no one was going to come looking here. Maybe things'll blow over, though."

"I don't see how they will. Whoever's printing these things still has a printing press and no one seems to know who it is. Benito's been asking the street kids, but you know how they are if you ask them questions."

"I was thinking more about the husband I pissed

off, but you have a point. Anyway, I heard where the one thing the Committee of Correspondence always has is a printing press. So why don't you just get your own word out there?"

"We don't have our press yet. We've only been here a couple of months, and it takes time to get the things shipped from where they're made in Germany."

"All right, why not use a press in Rome?" Piero's tone was of a man explaining things to an idiot.

"I would, but all the legal ones get watched by the Inquisition. All of the ones we spoke to flat told us they wouldn't do any propaganda. They only print stuff for us if it doesn't mention the Committee and isn't political in any way. Kind of narrow-minded of them, and we sneak some stuff in anyway, changing-attitudes kind of stuff that doesn't look like politics unless you know what you're looking for, but—" Frank realized he was babbling. "Look, it's just impossible right now."

Piero shrugged. "I figure it's not so bad, though. Get around and tell people it wasn't you. Get the word spread. Maybe bribe one of those street kids to rat out the guy who gives them the handbills. How much damage can they do before you start answering them?"

"Plenty," Frank said. "And I don't like the idea that someone's going to see this as a good tactic; it could get used against the Committee elsewhere. Oh, not back in the USE, I figure. They do nasty things to people who pull shit like this back there."

Frank was interrupted by the sound of breaking glass and a bellow of alarm and rage. He spun around and leapt to his feet. "What the—?"

It looked like someone had thrown a brick through the window. Frank saw it bounce and tumble to a halt on the floor. He found himself, absurdly, staring hard to see if it had a message tied to it. There didn't need to be. Another window went, and this time it didn't just *nearly* hit someone, and the roar was of alarm, rage, and pain. Frank winced. The guy it had hit was a big, usually amiable guy name of Giulio, a teamster from just outside Rome who had moved to the city a few years before. He was a real nice guy with hardly a bad word for anyone, right down to the bottom of his third glass of wine, at which point he started getting rattier and rattier until he was a first-class mean drunk. And he'd had a few tonight.

Frank figured he had a few seconds before Giulio ran out of swearwords and did something everyone'd regret, and still less before the place went into a complete uproar. "Benito!" he yelled. "Get the guys down here, I'll get the shutters."

He grabbed the shutters for the nearest window and got them closed just as a brick hurtled through the glass—he sure as hell wasn't going to lean out and close the outer shutters—and banged into the wood, slapping it painfully against his hands. Whoever had thrown that had meant it. From the brief glance he'd gotten out in to the street, there wasn't a crowd there, but there was a sizeable gang of what looked like drunks.

"Frank!" Giovanna shouted. She wasn't a shrinking violet, either. Frank could hear her over even the sudden uproar the place was in. She'd obviously passed Benito on the stairs, and seemed to be in that state of general anger she sometimes got in where it could

strike to earth anywhere, like lightning. One time it
had been Frank in the way, but more usually it was
her brothers. Tonight it looked like being Frank's turn,
although he didn't have time. He dashed to the next
window, and swerved as another brick came through.
This time he didn't get a whack on the hands as he
shut the thing up, and he got to the third one and
shut it without any trouble. A couple of the regulars
had gotten the idea and the other windows were
shuttered before Frank could make another move.
Everyone else was either on their feet and shouting or crouching under a table and shouting. Dino
and Fabrizio and Benito were back in the room and
shouting, and Giovanna and Giulio were squared off
and shouting at each other. That was kind of funny,
if everything else weren't so freaking serious, Frank
thought. Giovanna, five-five in her working shoes, and
Giulio, six-three and the best part of two hundred
and fifty pounds. Not big muscles, but the kind of
fat you get on guys who load carts and wrestle with
balky mules for a living. Giovanna was actually doing
her best to get in the guy's face, which given that she
had to crane her neck took some doing. And Giulio
had that ability to bellow back at a woman that comes
with a guy who knows he's not going to haul off and
belt a girl no matter what.

Frank could only catch bits. It sounded like he
was going to have to calm things down. "Dino, Fabrizio, hold the door closed!" he bellowed. Once he
was certain they were heading that way he ducked
through the now-milling crowd to get Giulio and
Giovanna apart.

When he got there she was yelling that he was

a big dumb ox who should've ducked, and he was letting her know that if she ran a decent house this sort of thing wouldn't happen. Better, Frank figured, than Giulio running outside to take 'em all on, but still not helping any.

"Sorry to interrupt this conversation!" he yelled over the noise. The pair of them weren't even a half of one percent of the racket in the room, and conversation was putting it a bit too gently for the business of the pair of them yelling at each other at the top of their lungs. Neither of them was listening to the other or, for that matter, Frank.

There was a hammering at the door. Dino and Fabrizio were holding it shut, and were getting the bolts in. Frank began to wish he'd gotten around to fixing those old and balky fasteners a bit sooner, but it'd been easier to persist with a few seconds swearing and jiggling every morning and night.

There was a bright side, though. Everyone shut up.

At the same time. In a room full of Romans, that was a miracle in itself.

Bang, bang, bang. There was shouting in the street outside, but no way to tell about what.

Frank figured he had to take charge somehow. "Giulio, come with me."

He had no idea whether or not the big guy was any use in a fight, and had no idea how to tell. Once upon a time, he'd thought big and strong was the way to tell, but then the one guy he knew who *was* good in a fight—he'd gotten the story from Billy Trumble—was a short, wiry Catalan who was older than Frank's dad. Still, having a big guy standing behind him would help.

And now he had backup. He hoped that would keep there from being any trouble. "Open the door, guys."

Dino and Fabrizio looked at each other and looked at Frank. Frank saw that both of them had brought the cudgels that were kept behind the bar. Maybe that'd help, too, although the two Venetian boys weren't anyone's idea of hulking goons. Scrawny little guys from the wrong side of the tracks, those two. Not that they didn't know a thing about street-fighting, being from Murano, where it was the local sport. And Frank had seen them pile into a gang of muggers with a will, that first night he'd visited them at home. It's just that you wouldn't know it to look at them, and that meant someone might try something, not knowing that the pair of them were pretty handy with those clubs.

They shot the bolts and opened the big double door wide in front of Frank. He stepped out, not letting himself have any time to chicken out. The street was dark, apart from where light spilled out from the couple of other buildings that were occupied around here. Frank's first guess had been off. There were maybe a dozen guys out there. All of them at least half drunk, if not more. A couple had been standing right by the door, and having it open in front of them had clearly come as a surprise. *Well,* Frank thought, *don't waste it.*

"What are you doing, you sons of whores?" he roared, stepping right up to the nearest drunk. The guy looked like he'd been stunned. Certainly not about to call Frank's bluff.

Some of the others weren't so taken aback. "Whore-monger!" "Pimp!" and "Pervert!" were the few cries

Frank could pick out. His grasp of Roman idiom wasn't good enough for more than the basics of the local swearing.

"Yeah, says who?" Giulio shouted. Bellowed, rather.

"Yeah, show yourself!" Frank shouted.

He really wasn't happy about this. The whole stand-up-to-a-bully thing just wasn't his scene. Back down and take elaborate comedy revenge later, that was his style, but it just wasn't going to work here and now. Time to find out if confrontation worked.

A moment's tense silence . . . *Not right away, it doesn't,* Frank thought to himself. Aloud, "Come on! You got a problem with me, step right the fuck up." He pointed at the ground in front of him. He wasn't sure why, he just thought he'd seen it on TV one time.

More silence, a couple more shouts from the back of the crowd, calling him a pimp and a few other things. He looked around. Most of them had drifted closer, and enough windows were opening that Frank was starting to see faces instead of just pale, unshaven blobs. He didn't recognize *any* of them, and a dark suspicion began to form.

Behind him, he heard Dino say, "You want we should break some heads, Frank?"

"Yeah, say the word," Giulio added.

"I shall probably regret this," came Piero's voice, and the sound of something steely slipping out of a scabbard, "but I do not feel that I can let this pass without intervening."

Something about that last bugged Frank a little, but he wasn't going to worry about it now. "No, guys," he said, doing his best to imitate his father-in-law doing the mafia-don act he put on for Murano's low-life. He held up a hand. "I see how this is. You guys," he said, waving a hand at the gang in the street, "I see how it is. You got your money, you did what you came for, go collect your pay. It's over. And next time, you take the money, you come here and have a quiet drink, and go back and just say you did it, okay?"

There was a pause. "What about all that stuff you wrote?" came a voice from the back.

There was always one, Frank figured. "I never wrote it," he said. "And I wouldn't. Only guy gets to fuck my wife is me, you hear?" he shouted, grinning. "If you saw her, you'd understand why I feel real strongly about that."

That got a few grins. *Hey, it's working.* He decided he'd strike while the iron was hot. "I figure you all got someone you feel that way about too, and I ain't going to mess with that."

"But you wrote—" said the heckler, and Frank noted that he was staying in back.

"I—WROTE—NO—SUCH—THING!" he roared at the top of his lungs. "The bastards are trying to get you angry at your best hope of getting what's coming you, is all. They've seen what the Committee's done in Germany and they don't want it happening here! You think some stinking Spanish nobleman wants to see you doing well? When he's getting fat off your hard work?"

There was a round of muttered noes, although Frank would have guessed that most of these guys hadn't done a day's work in their lives.

"Right!" he pressed on. "So maybe they want to tell you a few lies and get you mad at us over bullshit!

That's what it is. Nothing but fucking bullshit. Now, you guys going to go home, or come in for a drink, or what?"

In the end, most of them drifted off. A couple of them came in for a couple of drinks, but seemed kind of embarrassed, and the regulars didn't exactly make them feel welcome. Frank wished he could fix that. If he could just get a few of these fellows on his side he'd have someone who could tell him what the hell was going on with all this rent-a-mob stuff. It wasn't like it was even doing much harm, apart from the odd rock getting thrown and Frank having a hell of a repair bill. As it was, all he could get out of them was that some guy had offered them a bit of money and a skinful of drink to turn out and throw rocks at Frank's Place, and some guy had passed around the handbills and gotten quite irate about the whole sharing-of-women thing. And that was it, apparently. Two of them had "worked" for these guys before, and they were usually in one of the taverns on the Via Ripetto picking up warm bodies for this kind of thing. There were some guys all but making a living at it.

Still, it was more than he'd got up to now, through Benito asking street kids. And he wondered if they'd be dumb enough to let, say, Dino or Fabrizio join one of their hired crowds. That would get them a lot more information, assuming he could drill the Marcoli boys with the absolute necessity of keeping their yaps shut and not arguing with whatever bullshit they were asked to shout or hand around.

He decided he'd sleep on it.

Chapter 20

Rome

Sharon had been in the Palazzo Barberini for less than an hour, and was already feeling under siege. Ruy had wandered off to discuss poetry with someone or other—Sharon suspected that he almost certainly had the poor fellow completely confused by now—and she had been, well, mobbed was the only word for it, by every single one of the physicists, physicians, astronomers and in a couple of cases outright charlatans that His Eminence Cardinal Antonio Barberini seemed to have surrounded himself with.

She'd exchanged maybe ten words with the cardinal, a short, slightly pudgy, bright-eyed little fellow who, whatever his priestly vows, came off as gay as the eighteen-nineties. Which was some achievement for a man born in the early seventeenth century. Doubtless he'd be around again later; it beggared belief that this invitation had turned up for no good reason after nearly three months of very polite cold shoulder from his uncle the pope. For now, though, she was having trouble keeping the names straight of the dozen or so guys who were literally hanging on her every word. She'd managed to get through a blow-by-blow account of the operation she'd done on her fiancé, and made a list of the mistakes she'd made for them to learn from.

That seemed to puzzle them. She'd read up on the way science operated in this time after the business with Galileo. Half of what would be peer-reviewed journals, in later times, was filled with outright bragging. That was a good part of the reason that scientific controversy reached the levels of venom that had got Galileo in trouble. Not that, judging from some of the stories her dad told about getting papers published, it was much different in the twentieth century. It was just that the backbiting and nastiness tended not to end up mixed in with the science.

So when she pointed out that her dad had explained that getting direct sunlight on Ruy's innards was a bad idea, and that he'd listed a whole lot of other mistakes she'd made, they seemed to decide that as well as knowing a great deal more than they did, she was capable of saintly forbearance as well. As for the rest of it, she was trotting out high-school science, and they were hanging on every word.

That was what was so damn exhausting. Individually, they were charming, wouldn't let her move a muscle to call for more food or drink, and were solicitous of her every want and need. She just found it hard work to carry the entire load of the discussion, when what she really wanted was whatever gossip they had about Rome and its notables. On the other hand, she wished it was this easy to get people to listen elsewhere. Of course, elsewhere, she didn't usually have an audience that consisted entirely of the most forward-thinking minds in the neighborhood. Lots of other people considered themselves too hardheaded and practical to believe in something that they could neither see nor read about in the Bible. How Stoner got the results he did when he lectured, she'd love to know. It wasn't like she said anything different. She supposed it was because where she was simply exotic, where Stoner was otherworldly to these people. There was the air of alien wizardry about him, which just seemed to establish confidence and credibility the way that the charlatans of alchemy and magic did.

As she was winding up an explanation of the difference between bacterial and viral infection, Cardinal Antonio Barberini finally returned.

"Signori," he said, cutting in smoothly as Sharon wound down, "you monopolize the dottoressa, for shame!" He wagged a finger around at the assembled scientific talent of Rome. "My salon is for the sciences *and* the arts, doctors. So let me show the dottoressa some of the finer things we have here, eh?"

There were a few rueful grins and flowery apologies.

"Really," she said, getting in to the spirit of the thing, "it is no trouble at all. I wish every audience I had was this appreciative."

Barberini's grin was impish. "And in some quarters, getting an audience at all would have been a help, perhaps?"

Here it comes, she thought. She and Ruy had discussed the matter, and there had been a couple of hours of back-and-forth radio traffic with the State Department over it. No one really had a clue why

Barberini had invited her to her salon, except to manage the stunningly obvious conclusion that the pope's nephew was hardly likely to invite her over to the family *palazzo* for an afternoon of wine and chit-chat in learned company if there wasn't some deeper purpose. If it was purely for the sake of her scientific knowledge, entirely practical and rule-of-thumb by the standards of the twentieth century but cutting-edge theory here and now, why not earlier?

There had been some change, and she was probably about to find out what. "Your Eminence need not worry," she said, uncomfortable at how stilted she sounded in the more formal Italian they used hereabouts. "The doctors have been most kind, and I in turn have learned far more about their own fields of expertise than I have been pleased to help with from my own small knowledge."

Of course, that brought a round of flowery protests from the doctors—why, their own arts were nearly medieval—the new learning far outstripped their own—the dottoressa was a legend, and deservedly so. Polite fictions, all of it, and Sharon realized there was a huge difference between the way in which polite society functioned and the cut-and-thrust of scientific debate. The conversation she'd had had up to now had been far more colloquial and informal, more near to what she'd been used to back home. Earlier, they had, to their credit, been challenging what she'd said and taken notes when she'd described high-school lab experiments they could do to verify some of it. Not that they needed scientific method explained, though. That was familiar to all of these good Lyncaeans, in its practical terms if not as a formal methodology.

The flowery protests ran down, and Barberini beamed. "Nevertheless, doctors, I shall claim the privilege of rank and steal the dottoressa away from you for a time. Doubtless you will seek to recapture her later, but for the time being let me show her that this symposium is not of natural philosophers alone?"

Well, Sharon thought, *it's his party.* And, truth to tell, she was dying of curiosity as well. She got to her feet. "Thank you, Your Eminence. I should like that very much, if only to repay your generosity as host in some small way."

Barberini offered her his arm. "Let me show you around some of the things we have here, Dottoressa. Doubtless you have heard the stories of Barberini peculation?" Not waiting for her to acknowledge the reference to the principal charge against his family's tenure in the papacy, he added, with a sly smile, "I should like to show you what it has bought."

"I should like that very much indeed, Your Eminence," she said, and that was the plain truth. The place had more art about the place than any museum she'd been in back in the up-time U.S., although her experience in that line hadn't been much. She wasn't a great connoisseur of art, really, but she'd tried not to be a complete philistine. And Cardinal Mazzare had told her that the collection that this man had assembled was, in the twentieth-century Rome that Mazzare had worked in as a young priest, the nucleus of the Italian state's national art collection, in a museum housed in this very *palazzo.* So she was getting a tour of one of Europe's better art collections conducted by one of Europe's leading patrons of the arts who was also, despite being only three or four years older than Sharon herself, recognized as one of the leading experts in the field as well.

Indeed, it soon became apparent the man was encyclopedic on just about everything in the place, and there were dozens of rooms packed with beautiful things. The rest of the salon was taking place in the huge hall on the ground floor that still looked a little bare. Apparently Cortona was due to begin work on it soon, although Sharon hadn't a clue who he might be. But the Palazzo Barberini was a huge building with a dozen or more rooms on each floor and even the parts that were still under construction were breathtaking.

At length, she could resist no longer. "Your Eminence," she said, "I love what you've done with the place."

He creased up at that. "Yes, it is a little overwhelming all in one go, isn't it? I confess, I am a thieving magpie."

He was looking at her expectantly, and she realized there was a reference she wasn't getting here. And there was no guarantee it was even one she could ask about. From what she'd heard, he'd had a lot brought from Grantville and there was every possibility he knew more about twentieth-century art and literature and music than she did. She decided to brush past it if she could. "Who wouldn't be, if they could?"

"True. It does not stop my family's enemies upbraiding us for it." His face twisted up in a sour expression for a moment. "Horseflies, they call us. Still, Cardinal Mazzare tells me that one day all this will edify the multitudes." He waved a hand around.

"He told me that, as well," Sharon agreed. "He said

he found it strange to be staying here in what he last came to as a museum." She paused a moment to take in the profusion. The décor was remarkable in every detail, the themes varying from room to room in wild profusion without ever clashing, and almost completely hidden with every square inch covered in art and sculpture. You could, she realized, lose days in here. It was a wonder that this Barberini, whose enthusiasm seeped out of every pore, ever left the place.

As it was, he was ranging his eyes over the collection. "Mazzare," he said, after a moment, "is a man who is destined either for great things or to be remembered by history as the worst disaster ever to befall the Church."

"How so?" Sharon asked. "The disaster part, that is."

"It is . . . hard to explain," Barberini said, after another long stare at the paintings. "I do not, you understand, pretend to understand all of the politics. Or the theology. Or how the two go together."

Sharon looked around, and realized that, for the first time since they had started on this little tour, they were alone. Barberini had stopped in a spot where, with only a little effort, easily covered as contemplation of the surrounding artwork, he could see for quite some distance into the adjoining rooms whose doors had been thrown open. They would not be easily overheard by anyone. After Barberini's pause had grown uncomfortably long, she said, "I don't really understand all of it myself. Really, I just wanted to be a nurse. It wasn't my fault I ended up a politician. As for theology, well, I went to church on Sundays and that was it." She refrained from mentioning which church, since the African Methodist Episcopal church didn't even exist in this time and place. Not that Barberini wouldn't have had full reports on her accompanying Ruy to Mass on Sunday.

"There are those that do, Dottoressa. And they have taken decisions I do not pretend to understand, and cannot see the wisdom of. There are times when I wonder whether we would not be better simply to denounce everything from your time as witchcraft as some of the older generation want to." He sounded weary. "It would spare us all so many complications. After all, everyone *understood* the world before the Ring of Fire came, even though some of us affected a certain skepticism. Cynicism, even. Now? My esteemed uncle seems to have an idea fixed in his mind that God himself is speaking to him in this matter but is not yet convinced he knows what he is being told."

Sharon didn't know what to say to that. And so the uncomfortable pause stretched even longer than the one before it. She said nothing, and just waited. What was up with the man? Either he thought she was going to be offended or he wasn't happy with what he'd been ordered to say to her.

She hoped—no, she wasn't sure what she hoped. She could take offense in stride, she figured. It wasn't like most of what she saw around here wasn't offensive in some way or other, and after a while she'd stopped noticing, most of the time. If he was unhappy about what he had to say, what was the worst of it? Business as usual, the pope carefully pretending he didn't have one more ambassador in his city, one who wasn't getting invited to his court. Something that, between any other nations not actually at war, would be an insult but which the USE was being very forbearing about since they'd had the bare minimum recognition that protocol required. So either way there was no need to worry.

Barberini was making it look like there was, though. After a moment or too more, he turned back to her. "I must apologize, Dottoressa. I am being most unmannerly with you. I am uncharacteristically unsure of how to phrase what I would ask of you."

Well, that was easy enough to deal with. It wasn't like a bashful patient wasn't something she had the training and experience to handle. She shrugged, and summoned up her best bedside manner. "So begin at the beginning. I promise I won't hit you."

He smiled a small, sad, smile. "For all that I would extend you every courtesy, Dottoressa, it is not for your sake that I hesitate. I am unconvinced of the wisdom of what must follow as it affects the interests of the Church, or as it affects the interests of the Papal States. I am, I confess, no diplomat, nor yet much of a politician, measured against those who instruct me. So perhaps I am naive."

Sharon decided to try firmness. "Please, Your Eminence, stop beating about the bush. I'm a doctor, for goodness' sake. You can *bet* I've heard much weirder things than you have in store. And it might be that I'll have to say no, and you can heave a sigh of relief."

"I must apologize once again. So, I screw up my meager courage. *Dottora Ambassadora*," he said, and she caught that he had suddenly started using her other title, which couldn't have been idly done since he'd completely left it out so far, "I must ask what contact you have with the Committee of Correspondence in Rome? And whether they would follow directions if you were to communicate them?"

Well, that was unexpected. "Officially," she said, "I don't have any contact with the Committee of Correspondence anywhere. Unofficially, Frank Stone is a friend of mine. His stepmother is a very close friend and business partner. His wife is one of my patients. So if you want a message passed, I have plenty of opportunity, although I can't promise anything. I suppose that ethically I have to pass on any message you want me to pass. Although Frank's his own man these days, not just a kid, and it's him in charge of the Committee, not me. And if you want to hold a discussion, I'd rather not act as your messenger-girl. I can ask Frank to come talk to you. I'm guessing you can't go haunting low tavernas like the one he runs, right?"

"Not that my reputation could get any lower, if the handbills are to be believed," he said. "But the Ambassadora is most generous and gracious. A message is, indeed, what I would have passed. What, rather, those instructing me would have passed."

"I guess I ought to mention that even though you married Frank and Giovanna, neither of them is really likely to take any message from any part of the Church on trust. Not after their last experience of you included a spell in one of your jails."

Barberini laughed aloud. "And ours of them included them shooting up one of our churches in the middle of a most solemn occasion! Monsignor Mazarini might have bent his considerable talents to making that particular outrage disappear, but I need hardly say that such things are not readily forgotten, whatever the public appearance."

Sharon shrugged. "Well, with bad blood on both

sides I guess asking a diplomat to act as go-between makes sense, then. What's the message, Your Eminence?" Truth be told, she was getting a little impatient with Barberini's constant dodging around the point.

"We would prefer they were less solicitous of official concerns," he said, flatly and without intonation.

"You want them to start being more—" she groped for the right word "—revolutionary?"

"Just so, Ambassadora."

"Forgive me for saying it, Your Eminence, but that sounds like a trap. What's to say that they won't find the Inquisition landing on them and getting a little payback for, as you say, shooting up one of your churches?" She figured a little annoyance was safe to show. There had to be more to this, since surely an institution as long-lived and subtle as the Catholic church wouldn't be *that* simple-minded?

"A promise, which His Holiness instructed me to make on his behalf." He winced, and Sharon got a feeling that the meeting at which Barberini had been told what to say by his uncle had not been an easy one for him. "The Inquisition will be restrained. We make no promises in respect of other methods of opposition. Counterpropaganda, other methods. But the persons of the Committee themselves will not be molested."

"I have to ask why," she said flatly.

"Because my masters would rather the Committee fought back openly than let themselves be used as a tool against us. If people were not being duped about the Committee, it is felt that they might not be so ready to create disorder in the streets." He sighed deeply. "The disorder they would create if some of their firebrands from the Germanies come here is quite overlooked. But I am a man under authority."

Sharon felt quite sorry for the little cardinal, then. Well, almost sorry. He might be wearing a priest's robes, but he was really every inch the consummate nobleman. A plot by other nobles, he was comfortable with, and if he lost, well, there was no great shaking of the world order as a result. If Sharon had to guess, this particular idea came straight from the Jesuits, who were making great strides back in the USE. Their reasoning was that freedom of religion was freedom to convert the Protestants, one at a time if they had to. They were doing a lot of good educational work, and leave it to the Committees of Correspondence to be brutally pragmatic about working with them on things like setting up schools. Or, at least, to leave them alone. An organization mentally supple enough to make as many converts as they had in Japan, of all places, would regard the USE as easy pickings. And the Committees of Correspondence as no particular obstacle. Allies, even, in some matters.

Barberini, on the other hand, saw the social and economic consequences for his own class first and foremost. And if there was one thing Sharon had no sympathy for, it was the nobility clinging to their power and wealth, no matter the consequences.

But she was enough of an ambassador to realize that rubbing it in wouldn't be a good thing to do, just now. "You can pass the message back that I'll speak to Frank. I can't speak for his response, and I've no idea what good it'll do you if he starts doing what you want, but I will tell him."

"I thank you, Ambassadora."

"If there's anything further the USE can do to help, again, I can't guarantee what my instructions from Magdeburg will be, but feel free to ask. And I'm always happy to come to your salon, Your Eminence. The company is excellent, and your home is a pleasure to visit."

"And for my part, Ambassadora, if there is any service I can perform in a purely personal capacity, you have only to ask. Your presence in my home is a pleasure and a privilege, and"—the impish grin came back in full force—"too much of a social *coup* for me to resist, when so graciously offered."

"Well," she said, "we should be getting back, or people will talk." She realized it was a feeble joke, but she felt she had to lighten the young cardinal's mood.

It seemed to work. "They already do, Dottoressa," he said, giggling a little. "Mostly they say that your honor is quite safe from the likes of me, I am afraid, except when they denounce me as a fornicator."

Sharon couldn't help chuckling. "I could help with that first one," she said, "I could claim you tried to press your attentions, and I had to fight you off . . ."

He wagged a finger. "Not even in jest," he said, mock-serious. "I have heard stories of your intended, Señor Sanchez. A most bloodthirsty devil, it is said, who has left corpses on dueling fields from here to America. Deadly with any weapon and completely without compunction in killing on the slightest provocation."

"Oh, true," Sharon said, "but how well squashed those rumors will be! Who could think a man slain by a jealous fiancé was anything other than red-blooded?"

"Enough! Before you tempt me, woman. Sanchez de Casador y Ortiz is a lucky man, and I would not deprive anyone of such happiness."

Chapter 21

Rome

"Well, that could've gone better," Sharon said to Ruy after seeing Frank and Giovanna out.

"Frank is not so young a man as he once was, Sharon," Ruy said, in that rumbling he-man voice he put on when he thought she wasn't being too smart.

"I know, I know." She sighed. "And if I was to be honest I'd say I pretty much expected him not to buy it. He was pretty okay about it otherwise, though." Actually, Frank had doubled up laughing when Sharon had told him what Barberini had said. At first, anyway. And then he'd pointed out that even if Barberini was serious, he knew from his own sources that the Inquisition was a power in its own right and while the pope could restrain them for a time, they were waiting for an opportunity. And since he'd already made himself a pain in the ass by regularly denouncing the fake propaganda—Sharon had chuckled herself when Frank described the reaction of the junior priests there whenever he walked through the door—he wasn't going to put himself where the pope couldn't save him, not for anybody. And if these people really were plotting against the pope, where was the pope's guarantee if he lost?

Frank was quite happy to just keep his toehold in Rome and make sure there was a core of support that would discount the bullshit that was going around. They had a soccer league going, running more or less without their help, and numbers had picked up a bit at the club he was running. Soon enough, he'd said, he'd have a press of his own and he sure as hell wasn't going to use it to put himself or anyone from his organization in jail. And if he had to bug out if the pope lost, he'd do it, too. They could always come back when the heat died down.

And Sharon couldn't disagree with any of it. She wondered, idly, for a moment, how Barberini was going to react at the salon she'd been invited to in two weeks' time. Would he be disappointed, or relieved? She'd find out soon enough, of course. Enough daydreaming; she had an appointment, right after lunch.

"I shall go out and make more enquiries in the afternoon," Ruy was saying. "It may be that I can find out more of what Quevedo is doing. Two of his demonstrations in the last week have resulted in small riots. The militia grow heavy-handed, I fear. On which line of enquiry I shall be purchasing drinks for a sergeant of horse tomorrow, as I believe that the orders being given arise from more than the usual incompetence. Furthermore, there is the matter of the teams of recruiters he is now using to hire lay-abouts for—"

Sharon leaned in close and put a finger over his lips. "Not this afternoon, you're not, Ruy Sanchez de

Casador y Ortiz. Father Maratta and Signora Fontana will be here for a meeting. It's not going to be a big society wedding, but we are going to make a party of it and we ought to have the planning in hand before Tom and Rita and my dad arrive."

"Ah," Ruy said, when she let him speak. "Truly, my love, I cannot let you face such things alone. Never let it be said that Ruy Sanchez de Casador y Ortiz flinched from the horrors of matrimonial strategy. Far be it from me to take the coward's route of espionage and spycraft! I put aside all thoughts of going forth and risking mere death and disgrace! I shall face the dangers of floral arrangement! I shall brave the terrors of banquet menus! I shall—what?"

Sharon was going weak-kneed with laughter. He was funny enough, but the heroic posturing that went with it was too much. *God,* she thought, *but I love this man.* "Stop it," she snorted, "just stop, all right? It'll take an hour or so, and then you can go lurk in seedy bars and beat up on people—"

"It was only one man, and him a pimp," Ruy said, suddenly all affronted dignity, "hardly a person at all."

"Whatever," she said. "Just try not to make me have to come bail you out of somewhere, okay? Bad enough at the best of times, but my dad's going to arrive tomorrow or the day after, and that'd be all I need, him growling about what a no-good bum his daughter is marrying."

Ruy shrugged and smiled. "But Sharon, he would be right. Never let it be said that Ruy Sanchez de Casador y Ortiz is not honest, nor that he believes that confession is not good for the soul. I have broken every commandment save the first and the last. The first, because I am no sculptor, whatever my other talents. The last . . . ?" he let it trail off, and shrugged.

"Why not the last?" she asked, trying to remember what it was, and then realizing she'd given him the straight line.

He grabbed and squeezed. "Why covet my *neighbor's* ass?"

"Ruy!" she squealed, sounding like a schoolgirl to herself, and swatting his hand away. "Not here!"

She glared around at the staff who were in the main hallway, daring any of them to laugh. To their credit, none of them were. Although every last one had a big grin in evidence, even the normally straitlaced Adolf. Oh, well, fair was fair. They were all looking forward to the wedding too, and the searching for the right people to get the wedding organized had all been done without Sharon having to lift a finger. By all accounts, Signora Fontana was a battleaxe to beat them all, and Father Maratta was one of that large minority of Catholic priests who looked like he enjoyed a good party. If he had heard of the ascetic traditions within Christianity, he wanted no part of them. He even had a list of caterers he could recommend from personal experience, and seemed to want more input into the reception afterwards than he did into the liturgy of the nuptial mass.

Ruy was giving off his best sweet-and-innocent look—about as convincing as a party hat on a tiger—and his eyes were twinkling.

"If you've quite done embarrassing me in front of *everyone*," she said, trying to get a mad on and failing, "let's get lunch."

✧   ✧   ✧

But no sooner did they reach the front door to the embassy than their plans got scrambled. The big double doors were yawning wide before the servant who was preparing to open it for them got within ten feet.

Through it came Sharon's father, Melissa Mailey, and Tom and Rita Simpson. Behind them Sharon could see a few members of the military escort that would have shepherded them to Rome.

"You bums!" Sharon wailed. "You're not supposed to be arriving yet!"

Dr. Nichols smiled at her. If she looked really close and squinted, Sharon could possibly argue than it was an "apologetic" smile. It'd be a stretch, though.

Rita grinned. "You idiot. Don't you remember the time, roomie, when you and I sat up half the night in college and figured out the Three Laws of the Universe. The ultimate ones, not that silly thermo-dynamics business."

Sharon stared at her. Rita clucked her tongue.

"Poor girl's mind is going already. Repeat after me: The First Law is that you will always be late when it's critical to be on time. The Second Law is that—"

Sharon laughed. "—everyone else will always be early when you don't want them to be."

Then the hugs started.

Rita's was the first, and wildly enthusiastic. Her father's was heartfelt and paternal. Tom Simpson's was the genuine but slightly careful embrace a young man gives a young woman to whom he is neither married nor related and who possesses a very voluptuous figure.

Melissa's was complex. The sort of hug a woman gives who is, first, not temperamentally given to hugging; but, second, went through a prolonged period in her radical and semi-hippie youth where hugging was more or less a Social Mandate and thereby learned the art, however reluctantly; and, third, happened to genuinely like the young woman whom she sometimes described as her "common law step-daughter."

The last one done, and still holding Melissa by the shoulders, Sharon grinned at her and said: "So. Are you and Dad still shacking up, or have you finally decided to make him an honest man?"

"He's starting to pester me about it," Melissa growled, "but I got my principles."

Dr. Nichols snorted. "Principles! What she actually said was: 'if it ain't broke, don't fix it.' And then added—unkindest cut of all—that it wasn't as if I had any Social Security she could collect as my widow when I croaked, so why bother?"

And now, it was time. Sharon had spent months wondering and worrying about how she would handle the situation. But, in the event, it all came quite easily and naturally.

She turned and placed a hand on Ruy's arm, to bring him forward and to her side. "I'd like all of you to meet my fiancé, Ruy Sanchez de Casador y Ortiz."

Ruy immediately bestowed a bow on the new arrivals. No courtier in Madrid could have done it better, even one whose pedigree was genuine. Actually, they couldn't have done it as well, because they wouldn't have known how to keep it from being too elaborate. Ruy had now been around Americans long enough to know that the more ornate flourishes of seventeenth-century punctilio were not only wasted on them but would be viewed as slightly ridiculous in any event.

Sharon *still* didn't know Ruy's real last name. But

she'd stopped nagging him about it after he'd told her, in a tone of voice that was genuinely sad, that he would not impart the information until the time came—if the time came—that he could visit his mother's grave. Openly, and in broad daylight.

Her father's reaction would be the critical one, so Sharon eyed him a bit nervously. Leaving aside the normal tension that automatically existed whenever a man was introduced for the first time to his future son-in-law, there was the added factor of Ruy's age. Sharon was pretty sure that Ruy was a bit younger than her father, but "a bit" was the operative term. A few years, no more—and he could conceivably even be as old as Dr. Nichols.

And . . .

It was weird. Her father wasn't even looking at Ruy's face, after an initial glance. He was studying the costume, most of his attention on the sword.

Sharon herself hadn't even noticed that Ruy was armed. Or hadn't thought about it, at least. Being armed in public was such an ingrained part of Ruy Sanchez—his persona, for lack of a better term—that she'd long since stopped giving it any thought at all.

She couldn't help it. She burst out laughing, covering her mouth with her hand.

Her father cocked an inquisitive eye at her.

"Sorry," she half-choked. "I was just remembering the time I introduced Leroy to you for the first time. You gave him that very same scrutiny."

Dr. Nichols chuckled. "No, not really. That time, I was trying to figure out where the bum might be hiding some drug paraphernalia."

Then he smiled at Ruy and extended his hand.

"A pleasure to meet you, Señor Sanchez. I will say you don't quite match Sharon's depictions of you in her letters."

"Her very long and fulsome depictions," Melissa added dryly.

"Sure don't," added Rita, who was back to grinning.

Now it was Ruy who was cocking an inquisitive eye at her.

"It's not fair," Sharon whined. "You weren't supposed to be here yet. I'm not ready for this."

"Yup," said Rita smugly. "And there's the Third Law. 'No good deed shall go unwhined about.'"

James Nichols was trying to hide his genuine surprise at finally seeing Ruy Sanchez in the flesh. Surprise so great that it bordered on outright shock. The man didn't look *at all* the way he'd thought he would, from Sharon's letters.

He realized now, in retrospect, that he should have been prepared. His daughter was the sort of person who always responded to problems of a personal nature by what he'd come to think of as the "Sharon preemptive strike."

And if you think THAT's bad, Daddy dearest, lemme tell you what else—

So, naturally, her letters had emphasized all the possible drawbacks to Ruy Sanchez, as a husband. Among those, pride of place had been given to the fact that he was a generation older than she was. By the time she was done, Nichols had been stoically prepared to greet an ancient mariner, painfully hobbling about and breathing wheezily.

Instead . . .

James Nichols no longer wondered how a man of such an advanced and decrepit age could have not only challenged six men to a swordfight, but pretty much *won* the thing. If you ignored Sanchez's face, with its lines and its gray hairs, you'd swear you were looking at a man in his physical prime. Somewhere in his mid-thirties—no older than his early forties—and in superb condition. Not tall, and with a wiry build, except for very broad shoulders. A waist that would be the envy of most teenagers.

From time to time, as a doctor, Nichols had examined both amateur and professional athletes, including one memorable instance where a well-known major league baseball player had suffered a car accident nearby and been brought into the hospital. The man had been an outfielder through most of his career, and then once he reached his mid-thirties brought in to play first base to extend his longevity. He'd lost a bit of his running speed, but his reflexes were so superb that the team wanted him in the lineup. Batting clean-up, in fact. At the age of thirty-nine, he was still averaging thirty to forty home runs a year, with a .300-plus batting average.

Nichols was quite sure that if he gave Sanchez the sort of examination he'd given that athlete, he'd find the same thing. Some men are simply blessed with a physique so hardy and top-notch that, provided they maintain a decent diet and a rigorous exercise regimen, they really don't lose all that much physically even after they're well into middle age.

As for the man's face, Sharon's letters had done the same. *Gray hair. Lines all over. Weather-beaten. Etc., etc., etc.*

The man was *handsome,* for Pete's sake! The sort

of Latin male who could age with immense grace and dignity, the way men of any other ethnic lineages had a hard time managing. He reminded Nichols, more than anything else, of some Italian and Mexican movie stars once they reached their fifties. Giancarlo Giannini, for instance, or Ricardo Montalban.

Well, not *that* handsome. But certainly a lot closer than the wizened old geezer Nichols had braced himself for.

It remained to be seen, of course, whether Nichols thought Sharon's assessment of her fiancé's other qualities was on the mark. Her letters had been considerably more expansive in their praise of Sanchez's character and intelligence, and positively enthusiastic—very unusual, for Sharon—about his sense of humor.

But, whatever else, the basic mystery was solved. His daughter had gotten attracted to her future husband for the same reason women had done so for ages. She had the hots for him, simple as that.

Sanchez had a very good handshake. Nichols wasn't surprised at all, by then.

"Lunch!" Sharon exclaimed.

"Good move, girl," Rita approved. "Always a great sideslip."

On their way out, Sharon took Rita by the arm and murmured: "I missed you, a lot, all that time you were in the Tower. Now I'm half-wishing they'd kept you there."

"As if they had any choice! We woulda sprung ourselves anyway—don't think we wouldn't—but once Harry Lefferts and his wrecking crew got to England, it was a done deal."

"Not to mention Julie Sims," Melissa added, shaking her head. "Gawd, at my age, to be having such adventures."

"So what happened? I've never gotten any *details*, dammit!"

But before Rita had gotten out more than two sentences, the carriage had arrived.

"So it's a mess at both ends of Europe," her dad said. It was early evening, by then, and they were back at the embassy enjoying some glasses of wine at the big table in the formal dining room.

"Yes, but not so bad here," Ruy offered. "I think we will see some play made in the internal politics of the Holy See. I cannot believe that all of this agitation is an end in itself, Doctor Nichols. I believe that Borja seeks to destabilize the Barberini and their grip on the political workings of Rome to further his master's ends; we have had direct intelligence that this is the end they have in view. While I have taken steps to ensure that all here can get to safety at a moment's notice, and advised the Committee of Correspondence in the same way, this is merely a precaution which your daughter has most wisely ordered."

Her dad chuckled. "That's got to be the first time my daughter's ever been described as cautious by anyone," he said.

"Compared to him, anyone's cautious," Sharon said, grinning.

"Well, I figure he'd have to know no fear," her dad said, before she quelled him with a glare. "Peace. I'm proud of you, honey. You're a surgeon in your own right now, and—if you don't mind me saying so, Señor Sanchez—you've found yourself a good man."

He gave Ruy a sly little smile. "Not that I've not worried on that score, before now. Let me tell you about the time, while she was at college—"

Sharon groaned and put her head in her hands. There wasn't going to be any stopping him. She quietly thanked God that the album of baby photos hadn't come through the Ring of Fire.

Chapter 22

Rome

Frank stood behind the bar and moodily wiped at a glass. That morning's meeting with Sharon at the USE embassy had been an eye-opener. It hadn't been helped by the fact that he'd been tired and sweaty and aching from another punishing session of sword practice with Señor Sanchez.

The goddamn nerve of the bastards! They needed him, and claimed they would keep their inquisitors off their backs. They hadn't been able to do that for poor Galileo, and he had been one of the pope's oldest friends. What chance did a bunch of scruffy revolutionaries stand? He wasn't even that safe by being inconspicuous, and had to dance pretty damn fast to make sure the Inquisition didn't blame *him* for the crap that was going around with his name on it. Come right to it, they were all but admitting that even that pathetic little protection was about to dry up like spit on a hot stove.

And it was that last part that had Frank worried. It looked like it was going to be a long, hot summer, and he'd heard that there were always at least some riots when food prices went up. Apparently it was like summer storms, everyone expected it and provided it didn't go too far, there wasn't much official reaction. Except this year, Frank had heard of at least two groups getting attacked by militia horsemen, and some of them had been killed. That was pissing people off. And there was also the rumor that whoever it was that was claiming to be the Committee was being run by some Spaniard, and *that* was pissing people off even more. So, if there were riots, they were likely to be bad ones. And since riots tended not to happen in the nice parts of town, Frank's Place was at risk.

Señor Sanchez had been round and gone over how to defend the place, but he'd been more focused on the best ways out. He'd not been too reassuring about that, either. Frank's Place was backed in to blind walls on three sides. Pretty much the only ways out were into the street out front. Frank had been over the cellar as carefully as he could, and he thought that one bricked-up arch might lead somewhere. But he'd been afraid to knock it through in case it turned out that the folks next door had something in there that they'd be ticked about him getting in to. Like he'd be, if someone tunneled into the cellar he kept his stock in. Although, if there was any real trouble, he had a pick and a prybar down there and he reckoned he could be through any of those walls inside an hour or so.

Still, despite it being a hot, sticky night that might have seen everyone get irritable—more so since they'd stopped leaving the shutters open at night, to avoid repair bills if nothing else—the crowd in Frank's

Place seemed to be pretty good-natured. The soccer league had had its first five-a-side tournament, and the winners were drunk and singing while the losers were drunk and, well, singing too. Frank felt a bit peeved that he wasn't really able to get into the mood with everyone, although there was a rowdy edge that seemed to have everyone a little on edge, under the cheerful barracking and singing.

"Why so melancholy, husband?" Giovanna said, coming to stand behind him and wrapping her arms around him.

"Mmmm," he replied, as she began to nuzzle his neck. "Melancholy, me?"

"Melancholy, you," she said. "You've done nothing but mope since you got back this afternoon." She began rubbing his stomach in tight little circles. Fortunately, Dino was tending the bar, because Frank was beginning to think that stepping back from the counter to get anyone anything might suddenly not be so good an idea. And—he looked—a few of them could clearly see what was going on, and were smirking.

What the hell. He turned around and hugged her too. "Sorry," he said, "it's just all that crap about the Inquisition. And maybe it's going to come to us having to bug out. I mean leave, that is. Because it might come to the Inquisition having a free hand to act against us because Borja's taken him out."

"Borja's trying to assassinate the pope?" Giovanna said, her eyes going big and round. "The dottoressa didn't say that!"

"Not assassinate, maybe," Frank said, "but make him unable to act to protect us. Do something political, maybe, make him a lame duck or something."

"You said the pope is going to be assassinated?" The voice came from behind him. One of the regular barflies, a guy name of Giacometti, and Frank found it kind of surprising that he'd heard over the hubbub of a pretty raucous night in the club, or was sober enough to follow the conversation. Still less that he'd been able to say something relevant.

"No, Giacometti, I didn't say that. But all the crap you've been hearing about the Committee is part of a plot to make the pope look bad. It's Cardinal Borja, he's pissed at the pope."

"Not going to assassinate him?"

"No, Giacometti. Nobody thinks he'll do that. Well, he probably won't. He might, I guess." Frank realized that he probably ought to start a rumor that the fake Committee was part of a plot to assassinate the pope. That would piss people off with the rent-a-mob organizers, maybe make things more difficult for them. It was just that Frank was, deep down, too frigging honest. He heaved a deep sigh. "Mostly folks think he hasn't got the balls, you see."

"Cardinal Borja's got no balls?" Clearly that was getting through, although Frank wasn't sure what starting a rumor about Cardinal Borja's testicles was going to do to help.

"That's right, Giacometti," Giovanna added. "No balls at all. It's why he's got guys pretending to be Committee when they're not."

"So you don't really think the pope must die, then?" Giacometti frowned. "Everyone said that didn't sound like you."

Frank frowned back. "What didn't sound like me?"

"Was in a paper, going around. Heard it today while

I was toting some stuff over by Sant'Angelo. Committee paper, they said, but it sounded like it was a phony one. Everyone knows you folks got married in the Sistine chapel, like not even nobles get to do. You wouldn't want to kill the pope, not when he's your buddy."

"Not buddy, exactly," Frank said, "but we've met. And no, I don't want the pope dead. Freedom of religion and all that, y'know?"

"Right, let everyone be Catholic how they really want to be, not like these princes in Germany and England who make people be Protestant and spit on the body of Christ at mass."

"I don't think they do that, Giacometti," Frank said, not sure how to follow this turn in the conversation. For all he knew, spitting *was* part of it. He'd been raised—technically—in a religion that had smoking as a sacrament, so who knew? It still sounded unlikely.

"No, it's true." Giacometti leaned over the bar, swaying slightly, and attempted to bellow over the noise and music in a confidential manner. "They say they're Christians, but it's all devil-worship in disguise." Giacometti seemed pretty sure of his facts on this point, although Frank wasn't sure what he'd do if he was ever confronted with an actual Protestant. Stay out of spitting range, that seemed certain.

"I wouldn't know," Frank shrugged. "I've never been in a Protestant church." He tactfully omitted the information that his youngest brother had taken a notion to become a Protestant minister of the Lutheran variety. What Giacometti didn't know wasn't likely to hurt him. "But, you know, pass the word. It's not us saying the pope should be killed, it's these other guys. The Spanish."

"Eh? I thought you said they didn't want to kill the pope."

"No," Frank said, as Giovanna went off to serve another customer. "They're just saying that. I don't think they mean it."

Giacometti sneered. "Frank, you're too good a guy to see it. Not everyone's a nice fellow like you. Spaniards, hah! You watch, they wouldn't say a thing like that unless they meant it. No balls, Frank. They got no balls." He made a gesture of grabbing and squeezing a pair. "They ain't gonna just mess around when they can stab the Holy Father in the back, now." Giacometti sat back on his barstool with the air of a man who'd completed a logical proof.

"I, uh, guess that stands to reason," Frank said, although he wasn't sure exactly what Giacometti was saying. He'd only had one drink himself tonight, so he wasn't able to follow the beer logic.

"'S right, Frank, it does," Giacometti said, waving his glass for another drink.

He was just pouring Giacometti's drink and wondering where the man put it all—a bar could stay open just with him as a customer, and he'd never been in a condition where he'd plainly had enough—when there was an almighty crash from somewhere out in the main room. Frank winced.

The room went quiet, as usually happened, but the ironic cheers Frank was expecting as the usual response to someone going ass-over-teakettle didn't happen. Instead, there was a hiss of indrawn breath.

Oh, hell. He'd heard that before. It was the noise people made when a fight was kicking off, but it wasn't the sound you got when it was a kind-of-fun brawl.

This was the sort where people got badly hurt. Frank put a foot on the shelf under the bar and boosted himself up to take a better look.

It was pretty clear what the problem was. The two characters involved hadn't even bothered with the glare-and-insult stage, just gotten straight at it. One of them with a knife. "Oh, shit," Frank murmured. They had seconds before it spread, crowded as they were, and—he looked—Dino wasn't going to make it from his bouncer's station over by the door. The place was way too crowded.

Frank watched with a feeling of helplessness as the two combatants grappled and staggered out of the ring they were in. There was shoving and jostling and two more guys, their blood up from watching the first brawl, started yelling and shoving at each other. Someone shoved one of *those* guys from behind, and *he* turned and threw a punch, and—

It was like watching a slow reaction spread through a reaction vessel. Roiling a little at the interface where the reagent was titrated in, but it quickly diffused. Frank heard glass break, and then the first scream of pain, shrill over the roaring. "Get down!" he shouted at Giovanna. For a wonder, she did. *Probably seen more bar fights than I have*, he thought, and then there was a bright flash in his eyes and a shock ran through him and everything seemed to be red a moment and then black and then he was looking at the ceiling and couldn't get his breath.

And then he whooped air into his lungs and started hauling himself to his feet, taking a couple of tries at it because he suddenly had to think about moving his arms and legs instead of just doing it. He could sort of remember a bottle flying at his head. He must've fallen off the bar. Fallen right on his ass—nothing seemed to be broken, although his back, somewhere around his right shoulder blade, felt like one massive bruise. And the whole bar, it looked like, was throwing punches and swinging furniture. His vision blurred, steadied. Someone was pulling at him to get down, but he had to *see*, damn it.

"Fuck!" he shouted, if only to hear himself over the din. Everyone was shouting something, the sound of splintering furniture was punctuating it and glass was shattering everywhere. The doors had to be open, both to the street and to the yard; the place was emptying fast leaving only the hard core behind to duel on. It was emptying in front of Frank's eyes as people streamed out away from the mayhem.

Which was all they needed. A crowd of angry, frightened, half-drunk people in the street outside *his* place. Nothing he could do about—*oh, double shit.* There were bodies on the floor. Two—no, three. Frank hoped like hell they were just unconscious, the last thing he needed was some magistrate poking around the place. And—*oh, fuck!*—one of 'em was Benito. Dino had spotted him too and was cautiously making his way across to try and render some help.

Frank saw that his way across was clear, too, and began to make his way, grabbing one of the cudgels from behind the bar. It wasn't going to do much good—everyone left had either a knife or a broken bottle or a barstool. He felt a grab at his jacket—he turned, and Giovanna was there, her eyes angry, "Don't," she yelled, "let them finish."

"Benito's down," he yelled back, and she let him go.

Please, he thought, *don't let her try to follow me*. None of the dozen or so pairs now left grappling and thumping and trying to stab each other looked like they were in any condition to be chivalrous. Although even they seemed to be quieting down as their wind gave out. Twice in quick succession someone got hit hard enough to go down, was administered a quick couple of kicks for good measure and his opponent cleared out.

Dino was already with Benito when Frank got over there. The poor kid was conscious, but groggy, with a nasty red mark, probably going to be a bruise, around his left eye and what looked like it was going to be a broken nose. "Got hit," he said, now just about audible over the last of the racket, revealing that he was cut inside the mouth as well. Sure enough, his lip was swelling.

"Doesn't look serious," Frank said, and indeed it didn't. Maybe a punch to the face. In a way, Benito was lucky. He wasn't a big guy, and getting knocked down quickly had probably saved him from worse.

"*Momento*," Dino murmured and stood up. Frank carried on checking Benito over, and winced slightly when he heard a solid, wooden thump and Dino growl: "*Enough*. Now go."

Whoever it was didn't think it worth starting in on the guy who'd waded in on his side—Frank hoped like hell Dino was at least *trying* to bean the right guy in each fight, because there was another—and another again, someone had had a hard head—and Frank didn't like to think how it would be if they were just storing up trouble by cold-cocking people who might have helped if they hadn't been half-brained by Dino.

And then there were none.

"Last of 'em, Frank," Dino said, heading toward the door to see the last guy went out. He'd added two more forms to the ones on the floor, one out cold and the other one on his hands and knees and vomiting impressively. *Head injury*, Frank worried silently to himself and then, slightly sickened by his own callousness, *as long as he dies off the premises, we're golden*. Although it was more than likely just a great deal of drink catching up with the guy. Fabrizio had finally gotten downstairs—he must've heard the ruckus—and was starting to check the bodies for life-signs.

"Good work, guys," Frank said, helping Benito to a chair. His eyes looked okay, as near as Frank could tell in the lamplight—*oh damn, the lamps*—he checked around hurriedly but there didn't seem to be any broken lamps that were about to burn the place down. He'd noticed that the previous owner had hung the lamps and candles up near the ceiling, and now he saw why. When the customers wrecked the place, they were less likely to accidentally torch it as well. "Dino, get the door," he said, and then looked and saw Dino was ahead of him.

"Frank, you should see this," Dino said, standing with the door open only a crack and looking out in to the street.

Frank went over. A whole bunch of rowdy drunks had spilled into the street after a really savage brawl and hit the cool night air full of wine and hormones. There weren't many nice possibilities that suggested themselves to him.

He looked out through the gap. "Oh, fuck," he said when he saw what was coming up the street.

"What I thought," said Dino, from over Frank's shoulder. "Anything happens, we lock the door real quick, you hear me Frank?"

"Right," Frank said. Dino'd know, he reckoned. Guy had grown up in a rough neighborhood and must've seen this sort of thing before. A whole crowd of rowdies in the street and then a militia patrol—on foot, or this would've been really bad—just happened along. Frank couldn't see much—the moonlight was good right outside the club, but farther down the street was shadowed by taller buildings and the fact that the street crooked slightly there—but it seemed that they were forming up with halberds to clear the revelers away.

Since when did we get militia patrols around here? Frank had seen the like down toward the Vatican, quite close by, and a fair few across the river in the nicer parts of town. Here, on the edge of the Borgo? *Let the scum slaughter each other,* seemed to be the official attitude. Patrols *around* this neighborhood, maybe. Inside, there wasn't jack to protect or to serve, so keep 'em in to make sure they didn't come out to trouble the nice folks.

Frank snorted, softly. *Set up! Danger, Will Robinson!*

"Who called the militia, Frank? Any idea?" Dino asked. Sounded like he'd been thinking the same thing Frank had.

"Same guy egged on those guys to start the fighting," Frank said. "This could get ugly." Not that it was exactly pretty work right now. It'd only been a few minutes since the fight started, so most everyone was still milling about in the street outside wondering

whether to go back in, call it a night, or go somewhere else. A few people were squaring up to each
other, but the space and lower temperature out here
meant they were less forceful about it than they'd
been. And at the edge of the crowd there were guys
shouting things at the militiamen. Mostly, as near as
Frank could tell, about their mothers.

He got an impulse, and opened the door wide.
"Folks," he said, speaking calmly and evenly as he
stepped out. Behind him he could hear Dino mutter
something about damn-fool crazy Americans, but there
was a note of admiration in his voice.

"Folks," Frank repeated, and got some attention.
"Let's get inside, hey, before the militia come? They're
getting ready to oppress us all, let's go inside where
we're free, eh? Come in, Frank's Place welcomes
no militia, pass the word, come on inside, fighting's
over." And on and on, in a voice that he couldn't stop
from becoming sing-song. A few people went inside,
and then others. He wasn't trying too hard to get
everyone in. He didn't want to get too far from the
door himself, and he could see the militia dressing
out into an orderly line. Those halberds looked *sharp*,
and Frank really didn't want to be out in the street
when they charged.

Others noticed that people were going back in, and
followed along. The militia were advancing, now, at
a steady walk, halberds leveled. The wicked-looking
spikes and axe-blades glinted as they passed the beams
of light that stole through closed shutters. Some idiots
were still shouting insults, probably figuring they could
outrun a bunch of militia goons in breastplates.

They were probably right, too, but only if Frank

could get the street cleared behind them. More came inside, and a few drifted off into the night, or at least into alleys and sidestreets away from the main street.

Good, he thought, *since we ain't got too many stools left. Where'd they all sit?* He grinned a little. If he judged that heavy-footed march right, he'd have most everyone out of the way before they charged. He figured that was what the militia wanted, too. They probably didn't like the idea of chopping people down in the street much either.

And then someone threw a stone. One of the loose cobbles from Rome's badly maintained streets, it looked like. Frank never saw who did it, but then another cobble flew, and that one hit. A militiaman fell backward with a shout and a curse, and apparently without orders the halberdiers charged.

"Everyone inside NOW!" Frank roared and dived for the doorway himself. The charge had started from maybe thirty yards away, a long, long stone's throw with one of those cobbles, but even militiamen could cover that in seconds. There was a press around the doorway, and people tripping over each other in the street, and then screams. And then a frantic heave to get the door shut when the people wedged in it got themselves shaken through.

Frank winced at the sound of something—someone—being chopped with a leaden finality, and looked at Dino.

Dino stared back. "Oppression," he said, a slight quaver in his voice.

The sounds outside went on for maybe a minute. Everyone inside Frank's Place was deathly silent. Just standing there, looking shocked. A few of them were putting two and two together, as well. No way in hell did those halberds just happen to be in the area. And they'd arrived too quickly to have been called out to the disturbance. Even if they had, they'd never have come until the morning, any other time.

When it got quiet again, he opened the door a crack and looked out. He could see two bodies in the street in just the thin slice he could see. He'd no idea how many they'd killed or maimed, and wasn't about to go out and see. He could hear orders being barked. He shut the door and, with Dino's help, barred it. This time, the bolts went home quickly and easily.

Right, Frank thought. *They want agitation? I'll give 'em fucking agitation.*

He got up on a table—one of the few still unbroken and on its feet. "People," he said, into an expectant silence. "I think we're safe for now. The militia are just clearing the streets of some people they think don't matter. People like you and me. That's all they think they're doing. I want to tell you what *really* went down tonight. Why we've got people—people you all know, people from this neighborhood—lying *dead* out in that street. And I'm going to tell you why it happened. Let me tell you about Cardinal Borja . . ."

He spoke for a good long while, it felt like. And it was a long, long night.

Chapter 23

Rome

It *had* been an evening for everyone to go out and hear some music. One of the minor Colonnas was hosting an evening of string recitals by someone who, as far as anyone could remember, was destined to be thoroughly forgotten by history.

A hired carriage had been booked and Sharon was busy getting ready. She'd been uncomfortable at first with the idea of having a maid to help, but Gavriella and Maria, whom Adolf Kohl had hired as part of the housekeeping staff for the embassy, had gotten to be friends and insisted on helping her get ready for the various functions she held and got invited to as ambassador. And, truth be told, it was kind of fun to have a bit of a girls' pre-party, especially given the fussiness of some of the dresses that were fashionable hereabouts. A girl *needed* help. Not that they weren't, sometimes, gorgeous, and Sharon had enjoyed playing dress-up as a kid as much as anyone.

And, of course, now that Rita and Melissa were

here, there was every possibility of their being ever-so-slightly late. Not least because Melissa was approaching the whole thing with a determination to have fun that bordered on the grim. "Sharon," she'd said, "I spent all those months shut up in the Tower. You think I'm *not* going to make the most of every opportunity to go out, think again."

She, too, had been a bit chary of having maids to help. She hadn't said anything, but there was a faint aura of disapproval until she got into the spirit of the thing. It wasn't really part of either girl's job, just a bit of after-hours fun with the boss. Sometimes, Sharon wondered what the shock would be like for them if they went back to working for the usual run of Roman gentlefolk. Since Gavriella was engaged to be married, her prospects for remaining in work were pretty limited anyway. The USE might not follow the usual practice of not keeping any but the more senior servants on if they married, but her husband-to-be would have to be something out of the common run if he was going to tolerate having a working wife. Sharon had wondered how to approach the question of getting the guy—he did something with horses, she wasn't sure what—to take a job at the embassy in the hopes that with the pair of them sharing servants' quarters he'd not feel so publicly humiliated and just take the extra income. Gavriella was really good, and great fun to have around.

Still, it wasn't the evening to be fretting over the problems of being a boss. They were getting ready to go show the assembled minor nobility of Rome how three American gals could knock 'em dead, even if they did have to make do with down-time makeup these days. Thank God for Stoner, was all she could say. His dyes and pigments might not have been up to making lipstick to Revlon's standards, but compared with the poisons others used down-time, they were a godsend.

The clothes made up for it, though. Rita was quite vocal about dressing up as a fairy princess, and she wasn't far off the mark. Melissa might not be saying anything, but Sharon could tell she wasn't exactly protesting at the confections of, well, pretty much everything that the local seamstresses had turned out for them.

So it was that when Captain Taggart knocked and Sharon shouted out "Come in! We're decent—"

—and Rita had shouted "Speak for yourself, girl!"—

He put his head round the door to see a scene that looked like the aftermath of a twister in a cosmetics-and-lingerie warehouse. To his credit, other than his eyes widening briefly, he didn't seem fazed. "Mistress Nichols, you should see this, out the front."

Sharon's suite of rooms was at the back of the building. As they followed the Captain of Marine Horse toward the front of the building, she heard the commotion before they saw it. The ballroom-cum-exercise-hall had the best view of the street and it was there that he led them. Ruy and Tom and her dad were there, already ready to go out. In Dad's case, he'd probably been ready for a while and was all set to complain loudly and bitterly about female tardiness—not that that wouldn't stop him strutting once he had the results on his arm. The three men, along with one of the Marines, were peering out the window looking at whatever was making the racket in the street below.

Sharon went over and joined them. The twilit street outside was hardly crowded with the group who were doing all the shouting. They stood back a little from the entrance, no doubt because there was a constant two-Marine guard there with rifle, bayonet and saber. Other than that, they were gathered around the entrance, reached back maybe halfway across the street and a few yards either side. As mob protests went, pretty feeble stuff. At a rough guess, between the staff and the Marines, the crowd was outnumbered by the embassy they were picketing. Or, if Ruy was making the estimate, by him alone.

"They arrived all together a few minutes ago," Captain Taggart said.

"All together?" Sharon asked.

"Not even the pretence of spontaneous action," Ruy said, sounding amused.

"This one of the rent-a-crowds you've been telling us about?" Her father addressed his question to no one in particular.

Melissa sniffed. "I should go out and give them some pointers. In my day, we knew how to *protest*. I could start evening classes, I'd clean up."

Ruy chuckled. "Doña Melissa, it is certain that your skills in these matters would command a higher price than was spent on all of these poltroons together. I have made enquiries. This is work for those lacking the skill to shovel dung from the streets. I have spoken with some of the people who have been to such things, and wit was not much in evidence. I have not spoken to the teams of men Quevedo has organizing these little parties, but the practice seems to be that any warm body will do."

"Ha!" Melissa's laugh didn't have much humor in it. "Astroturf. Still, on the bright side, it'll be the first time the official estimate of the crowd will be more accurate than the protestors' one."

"Really?" Sharon's dad asked.

"Sure. We'd get a couple of hundred thousand marching through Washington. Next day, you'd read in the paper that 'official estimates'"—she pronounced the words the same way most people would *damned lies*—"would say that the demonstration consisted of a couple of thousand, most of who had been paid to be there. I wish we had been paid, I'd have had some money back in those days. Now here, we really have got, what, fifty? Sixty? And all paid to be here."

"Less than usual," Ruy said. "Perhaps they grow short of funds?" He didn't sound like he believed that.

"I've had t' lads stand to wi' billets, Cap'n, mistress," Corporal Ritson said, in his broad Cumberland accent, "behind t' door, like as we won't provoke yon shites, beggin' y'presence, mistresses."

"Thank you, and well done," Sharon said, absently, as she tried to figure out what to do next. Having the Marines pick a fight would probably be quite fun to watch, since they could probably clear the street without administering more than a few bruises and broken teeth. Brawling was second nature to most of them and they were a disciplined lot who'd follow orders. Trouble was, if there was the slightest accident, the propaganda value for someone would be very high indeed. No sort of official protest would do a blind bit of good, either.

"Has anyone called the militia?" she asked.

"No, mistress," Captain Taggart replied. "Yon's no job for halberdiers or horse. Shall I send a man anyway?"

"No, no," she said, taking the hint. "I can't say I was impressed last time."

"And some of them are suborned, I am certain of it," Ruy growled. There had been reports of militia turning out to demonstrations and overreacting, although it tended to be a bit murky who *exactly* had managed to call them in time to react so quickly. It was pretty much standard for seventeenth-century policing that when it went beyond local watch or constabulary—who pretty much couldn't handle riots worth a damn—then heads got broken, because the militias weren't cops as such but trained bands of men maintained by the gentry for local defense. Mostly, they were the military hobby of rich men who occasionally got used to preserve disorder, to borrow the old Mayor Daley line. Turning them out took time, though, because most of them had day jobs and didn't keep their equipment handy. Most of them mustered once a year, if that. That first militia squadron Sharon had seen had been, by a very unfortunate coincidence, preparing for its annual muster and close enough to get to the scene of the disturbance within half an hour.

"I think we're going to be late to the Colonna place," Rita said, into the slightly amused silence.

"Reckon so," said Sharon, following her gaze up the street and seeing what she'd seen. "If we get there at all."

"We will let this rabble get in our way?" Ruy said, incredulous. "If you do not desire blood on the street, Doña Ambassadora, bid the carriage come to another entrance."

"Maybe we can, Ruy, but it looks like they had enough money after all," Sharon said, pointing. A little way up the street, just about visible from where they stood, was another crowd. This one was quiet, and looked like it numbered a couple of hundred. They were gathered around someone who was talking to them. "Captain," Sharon said, "have you got a spyglass?"

"Aye, mistress," he said, handing it over.

She was about to open the window and lean out for a better view, but then realized there was a better way, one that wouldn't draw the earlier crowd's attention to the newcomers. She had a sneaking suspicion she knew who it was, and she didn't want to do anything that altered the situation until she was sure. "Upstairs," she said. "There's a balcony up there, right?"

One short climb later—*more of an effort in one of these skirts than is quite reasonable*, she thought—and a quick look through the good captain's spyglass confirmed it. "It's Frank," she said.

"Frank *Stone*?" Melissa's eyes widened. "He's got that many people following him? Tell me it's out of morbid curiosity, please."

"Not fair, Melissa. I don't know what he was like at school, although I can guess if last year was anything to go by. He's really steadied down since he got married and moved to Rome, though."

"Frank's *married*?" Melissa said. Then, pursing her lips a little: "Good for him. Those boys, frankly, needed some security in their lives and I'd been afraid they'd go off the rails completely."

Sharon's dad snorted. "Why, you, you . . . *bluenose*. Melissa Mailey, if I didn't know you better I'd swear that those were the words of a gen-you-wine *conservative*."

"Well, Tom Stone's a good man, but hardly what you'd call—"

"A good role model? Caring? Someone who'd put a roof over their heads and food on their table? Reckon I probably know Stoner a sight better than you do, Melissa. I figure those boys have had their fill of commune life, but I'm not even a little bit surprised they turned out to be decent young men. Now, me being such a pillar of the community, given where I grew up, *that's* a surprise."

"Well. Um. What I meant—"

"Leave it, Melissa," her dad said. "There's a difference between the wrong side of the tracks and wrong side of the law."

"It seems the young señor has marshaled his forces," Ruy said. "I have to agree here with Signor Nichols. There is a young man with a head on his shoulders."

The crowd Frank was leading had spread out to cover the street, and was walking slowly forward. The group at the front of the embassy hadn't noticed yet, being still too intent on their catcalls and jeering. Plus, Frank's people had been out of their sight from ground level, what with there still being a fair amount of traffic in the early evening. It was starting to clear, and carriage drivers and pedestrians and riders could see what was about to happen and turned down sidestreets and alleys and got into doorways.

"He's got them moving kind of slow," Rita remarked.

"Keeping them fresh if there is a fight," Ruy said.

"Or giving the other guys time to run away without one," Dr. Nichols said. "Given how Frank was raised, I'd put my money on that. And he'll not have guys with knives or swords in front, either. It'll be sticks and clubs."

Ruy nodded. "Also sensible decisions. Well, perhaps

not the clubs. I might have counseled the use of blades, the better to encourage the enemy to run."

James Nichols shook his head. "I don't think Frank thinks that way. He might not object to handing out a few lumps, but he's going to draw the line at killing."

Sharon couldn't tell who was right from the second floor, with the dusk gathering, but the folks out front were starting to spot the oncoming crowd. And the ones who saw what was coming were peeling off from the bunch they were with and getting away. None too slowly, either. In fact, as Frank's impromptu army got closer, the rest realized they were outnumbered and began to run. Some of the front rank from Frank's people dashed after them, but Sharon suspected they wouldn't chase far. Down in the street, lit by the light from the embassy's windows, Frank waved up at what, to him, must have been just silhouettes. Everyone else with him had stopped to shout insults and jeers after the running rent-a-crowd.

When Sharon went down, followed by Tom, Rita, Ruy and her dad, Frank was grinning. "Not bad, for my first night as a rabble-rouser," he said, once greetings had gone around. "Problem taken care of, and nobody hurt."

"You've come a long way since last we met," Dr. Nichols said. "You were having a beer in the Gardens, as I recall. What happened to that soldier you were with?"

"Aidan? He made sergeant. He's still posted in Venice, I think," Frank said.

Sharon remembered the serious-faced Englishman. He'd joined the USE forces after being taken captive at the Wartburg, learned to read and joined the

Marines. Since the Venice embassy was on pretty much friendly territory now, the guard there had been reduced and Sergeant Aidan Southworth was second-in-command after Lieutenant Trumble. Which was, unless Sharon missed her guess, doing a world of good for his career.

"So you're doing what Cardinal Barberini wants?" Sharon asked.

"Not from my point of view, no," Frank said, shaking his head. "Although I guess you could argue the matter either way. Somebody tried to organize a massacre at my place last night, and nearly did a real number on us. Four dead, maybe ten badly hurt but they'll make it. That kind of got me mad. So we figured we'd completely cover everywhere they were hiring rent-a-crowds, get someone on the inside, and pass the word that they were setting people up for militia massacres, which put a few people off. And I've got the word that those guys are working for Spain around most of Rome's worst gossips."

"Good work, señor," Ruy commented.

"Yeah, good. What're you planning from here on in?" Sharon asked. "If you can tell me, that is."

"We'll keep spoiling this rent-a-crowd crap, where we can. Can't do much about the fake propaganda for the time being, although between the fifty or so people who nearly got killed last night, we've now got a cousin's wife's brother or something like that in every printing shop in town. We'll find out what's going down there, too. I, uh, got a lot of new friends last night."

"Sounds like it," Sharon said. "Come by in the morning and tell us the whole story. Right now I've got to go and be an ambassador, but this has to be worth hearing."

"Sure is," Frank said. "Gist of it is that they got someone to start a bar fight in my place, and had militia ready to 'suppress the riot' when it spilled into the street. We got lucky, to be honest; their timing was a bit off. We saw it coming in time to get a lot of people inside and safe. Turns out they had some other guys on the street as a backstop. We'd have lost a lot more people if they'd been able to stop up all the little alleys and such."

"Why?" Rita asked.

"Disorder and riot, Doña Rita," Ruy said. "A pretext for political action against His Holiness. Señor Stone, ensure you have scouts to warn of militia movements. I would wager that Quevedo has suborned militia whom he positions to be ready. Many of their officers truly believe they are suppressing genuine insurrection, and harsh measures are required. They will not readily see the difference between your people and Quevedo's hirelings."

"I figured as much," Frank said. "I'm not going to do much beyond spoil this kind of crap. I saw how trigger-happy they were last night."

"Is there likely to be real rioting?" Dr. Nichols asked. "Way I heard it, it was just stuff like tonight. But from what you're saying, people are getting pretty pissed."

Frank rocked a hand. "Maybe. There's usually some, this time of year. But like you say, people are getting pissed. Now that we've got people finally listening to what we're saying about it being the Spanish, that's really got 'em going. What can I say? They don't cotton to foreigners much, when they look like they might invade. And, uh, no disrespect, Señor Sanchez, some of the older folks remember what you did in Venice and are saying something like that's going to happen here."

Ruy chuckled. "A shame, really, that the elder Osuna was executed. It would be such a pleasure for him to know that that scheme was still biting Spain in the ass fifteen years later. I shall tell Alfonso when I see him; he will be ecstatic. At the time, he truly believed it was a good plan."

Rita spoke up. "Sharon, can you explain all this on the way? We really should be going."

"Right," Sharon said. "Frank, can you be here at, say, ten tomorrow? We need to talk. I need to make a report back to Magdeburg about tonight, if nothing else, and your part of the story needs to go in it."

"Sure thing, Ms. Nichols," Frank said. "Meantime, I've got a bar to run."

The evening at the Palazzo Colonna was quite refreshingly dull.

Chapter 24

Rome

Frank returned from the embassy to find his place full of people, most of whom he'd never seen before. Pretty much all the regulars were in, though. And everyone wanted to know if it was true that the Spanish were about to invade. The best Frank could manage was "not right now." He could tell a lot of folks weren't believing him, but nobody seemed to be calling for barricades and the like yet. In fact, everyone seemed to have settled in for a goodly long evening of drinking, dancing and generally hanging out.

Dino, Fabrizio, Benito and Giovanna were moving quickly and dealing with the rush for beer and wine and pizza. Frank had a moment's unease about whether a crowd like this could drink his bar dry, and decided he was probably okay for stock—and it looked like some of the guys from the soccer league were starting to get down with the whole working-together thing they did in Germany's Freedom Arches and were helping out.

Frank had taken a flying leap earlier in the day.

Getting people to spread out in the right neighborhoods and find the guys hiring rent-a-mobs had been easy. Lots of his regulars didn't have day-jobs, as such, being hired by the day, and could afford to take the occasional day off. And, being as they were pretty pissed about the whole nearly getting killed thing, and Frank had goosed 'em up a bit by ranting about the Spanish—he was kind of pissed himself—they'd been pretty enthusiastic about getting themselves planted in today's faked demonstration to find out where it was.

What hadn't been quite so certain was that anyone would show, when he asked for volunteers to turn up and bring friends. He'd timed it for after the usual working hours, since the bad guys had done the same thing. They were having trouble recruiting, according to a couple of reports. The crowd he'd got was gratifyingly large, and not a penny spent. If anything, he'd had more trouble persuading them not to just charge in and rip the poor slobs who'd taken the money limb from limb. Frank had managed to bring them round to the idea that it wasn't right to beat up on someone for being so desperate he had to take Spanish money. And it'd all come off pretty sweetly, so now he'd just led maybe fifty guys—the others had peeled off into other tavernas on the way back—into a bar that was already crowded.

Giovanna took one look and just dealt with it. It was a warm night, the stable yard was clean and hadn't been used for stabling in a while, so she got a few of the soccer players to drag some tables out there and break the really old furniture out of storage in the stables. Then, with the musicians persuaded to play an outdoor gig and the dancing moved outside, it was all going smoothly again. Frank took a moment to open the yard gate as well. If he could turn this into a really good party, that was so many more people not off somewhere else rioting. And there was the local goodwill part to remember too.

Frank found himself playing politician, or at least as near to it as he got. Yes, they'd run those sorry fools off. No, this wasn't the revolution, not yet; it was a long way off still. Yes, the beer was good here; they tried their best. Yes, pizza was a good idea, wasn't it, and no, he didn't want a bite, he'd already eaten.

All in all, pretty good-natured, considering, but he'd seen how that could change in a minute. Wasn't like he could even spot the provocateurs, either. He had to force himself not to act suspicious, in case he set everyone else off. For all that everyone was eating and drinking and having fun, there was an undercurrent in the crowd.

Damned Spaniards!

It wasn't so much that the militia was breaking heads, although if it had been women and kids, that'd be different. A lot different. It was the fact that they were doing it at the bidding of *foreigners*. Being Romans, big-city folk from a very cosmopolitan city, they had a much suppler notion of what constituted "foreign" than you got out in the sticks. The year before, Frank had met one old guy who figured foreign parts started about ten miles from his house, any direction. Romans, though, while they preferred fellow Romans, were pretty much okay with most other Italians. So the Committee weren't foreigners, much. Venetians, to be sure, and apt to be a bit strange. Frank seemed to be either getting a bye as an honorary Venetian, or, as an American, they were assuming—until they met him—that he was too weird to count one way or the other. Foreign, but an okay kind of foreign. Not trying to be the boss of anyone. Looking back, Frank realized that he'd probably done himself good by starting out low-key. He'd done it to avoid the Inquisition, but it'd probably stood him in good stead with the people he was trying to reach. Let him earn some trust and credibility before he tried anything. So now, he had some to spend with his neighbors, when they were pissed off enough to be buying.

He probably still couldn't lead them to much of anything, mind. The folks who'd nearly gotten killed here last night had been royally ticked off and looking for someone to beat on good and hard. Frank had just directed them to the spot they wanted to go anyway. No biggie. Afterward, he hadn't even been able to lead them all to an open bar. Still, he'd work with what he'd got.

Then he heard the cheers. *Uh oh.*

Frank didn't know where he'd acquired his instinct for trouble, but his chicken-sense was tingling now. It didn't take long to find out why.

The news went through the place quickly:

They've gone to the Villa Borja.

Hundreds of guys.

Some of 'em got weapons.

They're going to run that fat son-of-a-bitch Spaniard out of town.

Frank pasted a smile on. Not a thing he could do about it, clear over the other side of the city. And trying to stop anything would just get him ignored.

Inside of five minutes, the place was nearly empty

again. Everyone had gone to the Villa Borja, to find the nearest Spaniard or just to look for trouble.

Frank sat down and wondered what tomorrow morning would look like.

Another long, long night.

"What are they chanting?" Borja asked Ferrigno. The cardinal and his secretary were standing halfway along the drive of the Villa Borja, just about able to see, at a hundred yards' distance, the crowd gathered about the iron gate. Enough of them had torches and lanterns that it was possible to see them, and the lanterns at the gatehouse made them quite acceptably visible. Borja's people had roused him at this late hour—certainly past midnight—in a state of near-panic about a mob at the gates. What was present certainly fit the description well enough. Borja could see, even at this distance and with his ageing eyes, that the assorted refuse who had come to his threshold were ill dressed and filthy looking. He offered a small prayer of thanks that he stood upwind.

"Insults to Your Eminence," Ferrigno said, without being specific. Roused from bed after midnight, disturbed at his rest by a mob of ruffians and jeered at and calumnied by utter scum? Not even the most forbearing master would be in a good humor, and at such times even the most obtuse servant walked with a nervous tread. How wrong Ferrigno was, this time, although Borja reflected that it was no great folly to decline to repeat the slur.

Borja smiled. It was being chanted clearly enough that he could determine exactly what the slander was. *Exactly* what he wanted, in general, dislike the specifics though he might. "And how many would you say there are?"

"Several hundred, Your Eminence." Ferrigno's tone remained nervous. The estimate seemed about right, although the company of mercenary musketeers Borja had kept on hand for just such an eventuality seemed, for the moment, to be sufficient threat to keep them from coming over the walls of the estate or trying to force the gate. Ferrigno seemed to find that nearly as alarming as the prospect of the cardinal's displeasure.

Of course, Ferrigno had not heard *everything* that had gone on. Nor was he privy to everything that Borja had compassed in his designs—much of *that* was kept only in the secret counsels of Borja's own heart. The orders he had received from Olivares—who was presumptious in the extreme to give such to a prince of the church—had encompassed particular ends purely to Spain's advantage. It was only with the guidance of the Holy Spirit that Borja had been able to see the best and most effective way to do that, and at the same time cut out the rot growing at the heart of Christ's Body on Earth. Ferrigno had been gifted with no such insight. Nor had he been present at Borja's meetings with Osuna, when the fullest possibilities of what might be achieved had been discussed between the two men.

Thus, his bearing of news of the mob at the very gate of the estate had been nervous. Fearful, even. He could not have known that Borja had prayed for just such as this for weeks. Perhaps he was nervous that the insults being chanted by the crude and ruffianly types at the gate would anger Borja? Not a bit. He welcomed it. Even the part about him having no *cojones* was, in its way, mortification of the spirit.

He could still feel nervousness streaming off Ferrigno like sweat from a lathered horse. The temptation to make sport of the frightened Italian was almost overwhelming. Almost. Borja heaved a deep and theatrical sigh. "So sad, that the Holy Father's misgovernment should come to this. Have you pencil and paper, Ferrigno?"

A sound of rummaging. Doubtless while Borja had been being dressed, Ferrigno had been arming himself for his professional offices. "Yes, Your Eminence."

"Then, to His Excellency The Viceroy of Naples—fill in the proper protocol and apologia when you prepare the dispatch for my signature, it is to go tonight—I have the misfortune to report disorder, unrest and revolution of the most serious kind, as I have seen with my own eyes at the very gates of my villa."

". . . at the very gates . . . of my villa," Ferrigno repeated, his pencil scratching away.

Borja paused for thought. He had, of course, made arrangements that a modest force, sufficient to every likely eventuality, had been reserved for just this occasion. They could be here in a week, ten days at the most. Any closer deployment than the closest anchorage to the border between Naples and the Papal States would have been a giveaway of the most disastrous kind.

At that moment of contemplation, a messenger boy ran up. "Your Eminence," the lad gasped. Borja was some little way along the driveway that led to the front gate, and the youngster had clearly hared about looking for the cardinal for some minutes. "Señor Quevedo y Villega attends Your Eminence at the house. He says he has most urgent news."

"Does he?" Borja mused aloud. "Preserve that draft, Ferrigno, I may find myself adding to it momentarily. Let us go indoors and learn what news Quevedo brings us of riot at our very gate. The boy will inform Captain Mancini at the gate that my orders are to fire upon the crowd. Scum such as that must not be gently handled."

Borja heard the first crackle of musketry just as he reached his front door, and smiled. He would have to task Mancini with finding more myrmidons of his own stripe to deal with the consequences. A single company would hardly suffice for the next such assault, although the preparations he had had the man make to resist an assault would help for the time being. The works Mancini had erected behind the walls had not been cheap—neither carpenters nor lumber were inexpensive—but Mancini had assured his master that the saving in the soldiers required to hold the wall would more than pay for it. Borja dismissed the matter from his mind; the diminishing sound of musketry, replaced as it was with the screams of wounded scum, told the tale of how successful the preparations had been.

Within, Quevedo had, to Borja's irritation, retained the street-ruffian attire in which he went about Rome doing Borja's bidding, and had his filthy clogs on the furniture. He made no effort whatsoever to rise on the cardinal's entrance being announced. "Well?" Borja asked, deciding that drawing attention to Quevedo's loutish behaviour would be undignified.

"Your Eminence ought to know that there was rioting at the embassy of the so-called United States of Europe earlier in the evening. Rival gangs brawled in the street outside." Quevedo smiled thinly. "It appears that the ambassador is fomenting unrest of her own, and the rivalry between the insurrectionary factions is spilling into the streets of Rome."

"Take note, Ferrigno," Borja said. "You will append a full report on this latest outrage to the dispatch to Naples."

"Yes, Your Eminence," Ferrigno said distractedly, his pencil scratching away.

"Is there more?" Borja asked.

"Much, Your Eminence, if I might anticipate the contents of Your Eminence's next dispatch to those set in authority over him."

"Do go on," Borja purred. *Truly,* he thought, *the providence of the Holy Spirit is in generous humor tonight.* It was humbling, truly humbling, to be the agent of God's will in the mortal world.

"Your Eminence is already aware from earlier reports that the ambassador from the United States of Europe is in communication with the anarchist elements of the Committees of Correspondence?"

Borja nodded. "Yes, yes."

"The ambassador of the United States of Europe and the sister of the prime minister of that nation were both seen in conversation with the ringleader of the Committee, following the disturbances outside the embassy. That it should be coincidence that there followed the unpleasantness at Your Eminence's very doorstep is to strain credulity, I most respectfully suggest. Furthermore, I have reports that a large party of ruffians departed the very nest of these vipers shortly before I set out to report to Your Eminence and warn him of the impending danger. I made haste to outpace those miscreants and bring advance warning. It seems, however, that these were but reinforcements for an assault already in hand, and for my failure to deliver warning of that, Your Eminence, I, Francisco de Quevedo y Villega, must most humbly apologize."

"And, in view of your most diligent and excellent work otherwise, Señor Quevedo y Villega," Borja said, amazed at the man's ability to keep his face straight, for the provocation of just such an assault had in no small measure been directed by the agent himself, "I can do no other than accept your most gracious apology in the spirit in which it was offered, and tender the forgiveness which is by Christ's law your merest due."

Quevedo sketched a bow of acknowledgement from where he sat, but did not trouble to disarrange his footwear from the chair on which his feet took their ease. "Your Eminence is most charitable in overlooking his most humble servant's many failings." It was all Borja could do not to strike his insolent face where he sat.

He took a deep breath. "Is there anything further that I should include in my dispatch?"

"Only, Your Eminence, that the Committee of Correspondence, as well as acts tending to the general disorder, are inducing the common citizenry of Rome to acts of immorality. I had agents present earlier in the evening at their principal den, and I grieve to report to Your Eminence that the place was the scene of the most lewd cavortings and intoxication. The corruption of the city's youth seemed to be their principal end, Your Eminence. Such lasciviousness and abandon must needs be stopped. I also have a full dossier of the material circulated about the city under this organization's aegis and name. Your Eminence, it is fomentation of the most disgusting sort, calling for revolution, brigandage and the atheistic folly of separation of church and state. Production is in the thousands, and naturally Your Eminence will be concerned about an attack on the morals and faith of the best-educated of the common folk—those who can and do read. Not least because the Inquisition appear to have been suborned by these wretches. The felon Stone visits there regularly, twice a week it is said, and not once have efforts been made to arrest him. The connection is obvious."

"I thank you, Señor Quevedo y Villega. Doubtless my secretary will take a full report from you in due course. Ferrigno?"

"Yes, Your Eminence?"

"Go and prepare the draft. I want a dispatch for my signature within the hour. Ensure His Excellency is asked to put in hand the measures already agreed with all possible haste, and encypher that part. Use your discretion as to what other parts must be encyphered, but have a mind that this matter is urgent, both here and in Naples."

"Yes, Your Eminence." Ferrigno was still scribbling as he left.

"So, Señor," Borja said when Ferrigno had shut the door, "was it the stupidity of the civil authorities?"

"Largely, no. The unpredictable nature of the common folk and a number of useful coincidences were among our principal advantages. That the matter worked on the first provocation was of great good fortune. The matter could so easily have died away to the status of street-gossip for the next week."

"The hand of the Holy Spirit!" Borja cried aloud. "I was surer of nothing else!"

"Your Eminence's insight into such matters is well known," Quevedo said gravely.

In the end, the dispatch went on a fast horse to Naples at two in the morning. The shooting at the gate had died down an hour before.

Chapter 25

Rome

The drive back from the Palazzo Colonna was anything but dull, Sharon noticed. Cities being what they were, preautomobile, sound carried. The cool that came with the Mediterranean spring night let it carry even further. Somewhere, there was trouble. The roaring of a crowd, somewhere, and the sound of shooting.

"Sounds like it's a long, hot, night," her father remarked as the carriage driver trotted his team along a broad street.

"It would appear that the disturbance earlier was not the last," Ruy added. "It is the time of year for it."

"Bread prices?" Rita asked.

"Indeed. This year's harvests are not yet in, and last year's are running low, and last year's was nothing special. If there is trouble, it spreads quickly." As if to underscore Ruy's words, a column of cavalry came along the street in the opposite direction, heading toward the river.

"Where will they be heading?" Melissa asked, craning her neck in the open-topped carriage as the horsemen went by.

"Probably to the rougher neighborhoods across the river," Sharon told her. That side of the river had become run-down during the years the papacy was in Avignon. Despite the fact that the pope had been back in the Vatican for decades, the area had never recovered. The neighborhood right under the Vatican's walls was the roughest of all, and the adjoining parish where Frank had sited the Committee's headquarters wasn't much better. There were tough neighborhoods on this side of the river, the area around the Ripetto docks for one, but for sheer nastiness the streets within the Leonine wall that was part of the Vatican's medieval defenses were Rome's low point.

Dr. Nichols harrumphed. "Always the same. Poor folks wreck their own neighborhood first."

"I wouldn't be so sure, Dad," Sharon said. "You hear gunfire too?"

"Isn't that part of it?" Dr. Nichols asked.

"The preferred weapons in those quarters are knives and cudgels, Señor Nichols," Ruy said. "I would wager that there are bodyguards and the better militia bands attempting to restore order."

"By killing everyone?" Melissa sneered.

"If their officers feel it necessary, yes," Ruy said, plainly not much more impressed than she was. Sharon was reminded of something Ruy had once said, shortly after she had met him. *If it was my duty, yes. Not simply because it was ordered.*

"We should be safe enough, right?" Rita asked. "If it's staying in the rougher neighborhoods, we should be okay, I mean. I'm supposed to be here on holiday."

Sharon laughed. "Rita, honey, if I'd known this was all going to break out, I wouldn't have invited you. Everything was quiet two months ago."

"Perhaps, Sharon," Ruy said, "if these disturbances go on past tomorrow night, we might consider postponing the wedding. I am uncomfortable with keeping the Doñas Melissa and Rita in a situation of danger, and I am certain Simpson and Doctor Nichols are being too polite to suggest we postpone our nuptials."

"I wouldn't say that, Señor Sanchez," Tom said, hurriedly. "But if you're offering to do that, I would like to see Rita safe. But let's wait a little longer than just tomorrow before you make that decision. After all, Rita and Melissa and I have been in stickier situations than this."

Sharon nodded, then grinned at Ruy. "You don't get out of standing at the altar that easy, Ruy Sanchez de Casador y Ortiz," she said, wagging a finger at him. "We're getting married even if we have to have the aisle cleared with grapeshot."

"She'd do it, too," her dad said.

"I well believe it, Doctor," Ruy said, "for did she not resort to disembowelling me to get me into her bed?"

Sharon groaned, and looked to Rita for support. "They're ganging up on me," she pleaded, "help me!" There was no help from that quarter. Rita was smirking.

"I suppose," Melissa said to no one in particular as they drew up to the embassy, "that it's too late to issue any warnings about men and their juvenile senses of humor?"

"Entirely," Sharon said.

They sat up talking a while. Tom and Rita finally had time to fill everyone in on the details of their frankly hair-raising escape from the Tower. Ruy said that he should very much like to meet Harry Lefferts, a notion that made Melissa go a little pale.

For her part, Sharon made sure her report had gone with the night's radio dispatches before settling down with the others. Once Tom and Rita had gotten through a blow-by-blow of the dash out of London and the wine was going around, Sharon realized she was pretty much bushed. "I'd tell you all what you're missing at the Palazzo Barberini," she said, "but I don't reckon I can stay up another minute."

"Now you mention it," Tom said, "beauty sleep is calling to me, too. And a guy like me needs all he can get."

Just then, Corporal Ritson stuck his head around the door. "Mistress? There's trouble out."

"What?" said everyone at once.

"Brawl in the street outside. Lads've barred t' door."

Sharon had to think about that for a moment. Ritson's accent was pretty thick—he pronounced door as "do-er." "Will we see from the windows?" she asked.

"Best not, mistress," Ritson said. "They're hoisting stones at one another. I've sent a lad to wake t' cap'n, mistress, and come t'tell you and the señor, mistress." He looked worried, which probably meant pretty much the same from the case-hardened borderer as it did from Ruy.

"I predict you will want to go and see in any event, Sharon," Ruy said, not bothering to embroider it with any weary tone of resignation. "I shall accompany you, and I would esteem it a great service if Captain Simpson came also. Your presence, señor, will do much to deter the common sort of ruffian and avoid the need for steel to be drawn."

"Be glad to oblige," Tom said.

The embassy fronted straight onto the street, so there was no easy way to defend the building and still have the door open. The Marines on guard had come inside and barred the big double-leaf main door, and one of them was looking out of the spy-hatch at the street outside. There were four of them, all with their carbines at the ready, and Sharon could hear booted feet jogging into other rooms. The windows were shuttered, but to a determined man with a prybar they were unlikely to be much defense.

"Let me see," said Sharon, already hearing the sounds of a commotion outside. The Marine at the hatch stood aside and let her peer through the little iron grille. With a four-inch square to look through, she couldn't see much other than a confusion of ragged clothes and flying fists. There were hoarse shouts, the sounds of blows landing and yells of pain, fear and anger. And, lying in the street, mostly clutching at parts of themselves but in one case ominously still, people who had been hurt.

"The scunners hae been at each other like that f'r a wee while, mistress," the Marine who'd been at the hatch said. "Two mobs ae 'em come at once, and fell tae blows. We came within doors, mistress, rather than be involved wi'oot the rest o' the lads, mistress."

Sharon had the feeling that that was out of an unselfish desire to ensure the fun was shared. "Did you hear them say anything about why they're fighting?"

"Some ae 'em're agin all foreign folk as they see it, mistress," he said, plainly doubtful that a Scotsman could be called a foreigner by anyone, least of all someone who was a foreigner himself, "and t'others are riled aboot yon Spaniard papist."

The Marines seemed to have a fair bit of Italian between them, Sharon had found. Every single one of them could order drink, and probably less savory pleasures, within hours of arriving in Rome, and most of them had a working vocabulary. Several of them had spent years, before the Ring of Fire, in the notoriously polyglot armies that fought the wars in Germany, and would have gone back and forth between the loosely defined sides as the tides of battle ebbed and flowed. Colonel Mackay, who had brought most of these cavalrymen to Grantville originally, had a distant cousin whose mercenary regiment, raised originally to fight for the Protestant powers, had been on each side at least twice. "Can you tell which gang is winning?"

"Them as is angry at all foreigners, I think, mistress," he said. "A' wouldnae go oot, mistress, 'tis awfy rough." Again, a slightly wistful tone that he was missing the fun.

Sharon had no intention of opening the door. There was at least one pair of fighters not three yards away, and between the knife one had and the cudgel the other one was swinging wildly, anyone who got near them was in as much danger as their mutual opponents. "Dad?" she said. "Can you have your emergency kit ready? Only I think we're going to have casualties. One of you Marines get word to Captain Taggart—"

"Here, mistress," the captain said, behind her.

"Oh. Well, we'll want an aid station set up. I think the ballroom will be best. It's at the back and there's plenty of space," she said.

"As many lanterns as you can find," Dr. Nicols added, "and at least two tables big enough for a man to lie on."

"Aye," Captain Taggart said, "we've a field manual for the such as that these days, and I've lads here who assisted the lady doctor in Venice when she mended the guts of the señor."

"Good," Sharon said. "Hopefully this will—"

Stars flashed before her eyes and she flung herself back from the grille. She felt, rather than heard, the resounding clang of a rock hitting it, and chips of stone stung her face and eyelids where they spattered.

Shouts of alarm, steadying hands, and she got her eyes open. "I'm okay, okay, really, I'm okay," she said, "more surprise than anything. Someone threw a rock at the door."

There was a volley of thuds and crashes as more and more rocks hit the front of the embassy.

"Permission to return fire, mistress?" Captain Taggart asked.

"No," Sharon said, hearing her dad, Melissa and Rita say it at the same time. "Not unless it looks like they might get in, please. I don't want any more casualties than we've already got. I don't think it's safe to bring in any of those wounded quite yet, but let's have that aid station anyway."

Another series of crashes. "Aye, mistress," the captain said, sounding dubious, and left to give the orders.

"Last thing we want's a massacre," Dr. Nichols growled. "Surest way to make this last longer than it has to. Eventually they'll get tired and go home to sleep it off."

"This is most likely," Ruy said.

It was the dawn of a sleepless night before the last of the hooligans began to drift away, not notably pursued by any militia presence. Sharon hoped that that was because they had been busy with worse trouble elsewhere. No one else on the same street had been much troubled, from the looks, and certainly the armed retainers in those houses would likely have a lot less compunction about firing into a crowd. The casualties were few in number, in the end, and if there had been fatalities, someone had removed the bodies under cover of darkness. Those that were left were being helped away by others by the time Ruy and Captain Taggart would let her or her dad open the door and go out, so in the end there was nothing to do. Sharon wondered if any of them would have refused treatment after a night spent hurling stones at her residence, and supposed she would never know.

Then she realized that the rioting had probably gone all through Frank's neighborhood, and she had no way of knowing whether he was even alive.

Frank shoved the broom across the floor with angry, bashing motions. They'd had maybe half an hour of quiet followed by the first sounds of trouble. The band had quit—half of them had gone off to join in the so-called fun—and when it was quiet, it was eerily quiet. Everyone who'd stayed behind had gotten a little bit subdued. Even the *lefferti*, normally a boisterous bunch, were hunched over their tables and conversing in low tones. Frank was making an early start on the cleaning once the patrons had been persuaded to shift in close to the bar. Some nights like this had been pleasant, convivial even. A few regulars, up half the night and putting the world to rights.

Tonight, it was small knots of people around the couple of tables nearest the bar. Frank figured he'd get the place near enough that it wouldn't be too much trouble in the morning and call it done. Then he'd pour one for himself, see that Giovanna was getting some rest, and see if he couldn't get the worry out of his head. He kind of wished he'd inherited more of his dad's calm approach. Or maybe it was something his dad had learned; there were a couple of incidents in the early seventies that his dad was pretty quiet about.

Benito wandered over with a dustpan just as Frank got the crap into one tidy heap. "It's not a good night," he remarked. Frank had been about to think of him as a kid, and then stopped for a moment. When he'd first met Benito, nearly a year and a half before, he'd been a snot-nosed little guy that Frank had taken for about eight, maybe nine. Since then, with a fair chunk of help from Frank's dad, who had remarked that you couldn't solve world hunger by buying everyone dinner but you could at least make a start, Benito and a fair few of the other youngsters whom Massimo was more or less bringing up as Committee cadets had gotten a good deal more feeding. Benito was now nearly as tall as Frank and occasionally his voice wobbled a bit. It would be easy enough to take him for a kind-of-short fifteen now.

Frank caught himself. "Sorry, Benito, I was daydreaming. I think I'm getting old."

Benito shrugged. "Kid on the way, I figure you are old, or will be soon." He stooped to hold the dustpan where Frank could make use of it. "Gonna be weird. You're the first guy I know to have a kid."

"Eh? Messer Marcoli's got—"

Benito stood up with the pan full of garbage. "You know what I mean. Regular guys. Guys I, like, *know* . . ." He trailed off, expecting Frank to get it.

He didn't, of course, and he was trying to think of something to say that would make any sense when there was a godalmighty bang from the shutters out front. "Shit!" he yelled as he flinched.

"What was that?" Benito said, and there was a chorus of scrapes as everyone in the barroom got to their feet.

Then the door flew open, banging back against the wall. Frank didn't get more than a split second to take in the sight of half-a-dozen guys bursting in through the door, before one of them yelled "There he is!—" The guy doing the shouting was a local, a short, wide guy who'd been in a couple of times maybe. Frank didn't know his name, he was just one of the neighborhood bums. Some kind of small-time criminal, if Frank was any judge. The mob with him—there were more coming in the door, maybe fifteen or twenty, started to move in on Frank.

"*Basta!*" Frank looked to his right when he heard the word snarled, and saw that Piero and a couple of his friends had stood up and come over by Frank. All three had the big knives, the nearest the local cutlers could get to Bowie knives from descriptions alone, that the *lefferti* tended to favor if they didn't carry rapiers. Piero, being a bit more of a high roller than the others, had a rapier as well and was using his bowie as a main gauche.

Frank hefted his broom, feeling more than a bit silly. The crowd came up short, the guys in front staggering a bit as the ones in back crowded up behind them. Frank saw clubs, a couple of lengths of chain and some knives in evidence. Piero and his friends—more were coming over to join them and they all looked like they were looking forward to a fight—certainly had them outclassed in the blade department.

That cheerful thought was followed by another that made his belly sink. *People are going to die, tonight. Right in my bar.* He took a deep breath. He wasn't going to let this happen without he at least *tried*—

"Everyone calm down!" he yelled, trying to keep his voice steady, hoping that the various noises behind him didn't include Giovanna getting tooled up. "Nobody needs to get hurt, just head back on out, okay?"

"Damned foreigner!" That was "Shorty"—as Frank found himself mentally naming the first guy to speak. "You think you can tell us what to do in our own neighborhood?"

Frank took a step forward. "No," he said. Then, with another deep breath and a step toward Shorty, he yelled, "But in my own damned bar I can! See if you get served another drink in here, asshole!"

Shorty seemed a bit nonplussed at that. So Frank decided to try and defuse it some more. He let the broom fall and leaned on it. "Anyone who wants a drink, take a seat. Except you, asshole," he said, pointing at Shorty. "Get out of my place."

That got a laugh. Frank let himself hope that the situation was about to defuse, when there was another crash and something smashed through the window and shutters both. A kerbstone, or something like it,

Frank thought, as he watched it come through and smash a chair to kindling.

And then the place just erupted. Frank never did figure out who started it, but there was a sudden swirl of bodies, he brought up the broom to fend someone off, gave him a faceful of bristles, swayed back as someone else slashed at him with a knife and missed, stumbled as someone else jostled in to him from behind, and flinched again as the first shot was fired.

Oh crap, he thought, *now it's really serious*. Except that the mob seemed to be retreating, and there were clouds of plaster dust in the air. Then he heard, slicing through the din, female shrieks. His heart tried to sink and soar at the same time, as *That's my girl!* tried to shout down *It's not safe!* in his mind. Still, he stood up straighter, and looked around. There were a couple of the crowd on the floor, mostly still moving, and clutching bits of themselves. And there, coming from behind the bar, eyes flaming and Venetian invective in full Marcoli flow, was Giovanna, working the slide on the shotgun.

"Who's next?" she shrieked. That was followed by comparisons between the crowd and various animals, all of them greatly to the disfavor of the crowd. But as far as Frank could see she'd only shot holes in the ceiling so far. "Come on? Lackeys of the exploiters! Class traitors! I'll give you a taste of what's waiting for your noble masters—"

She punctuated it with another round into the ceiling and the last few diehards turned and bolted for the door.

Frank let out a breath he hadn't realized he'd been holding.

Giovanna handed him the shotgun and a handful of shells from her apron pocket. The sound of the broom hitting the floor as he dropped it was the only sound. Into the silence, she said, "Next time, we have someone waiting for them."

Frank wondered what to say. What he *dared* say. In the end, like husbands since the dawn of time, he settled for "Yes, honey."

Ten minutes later and it was hard to tell whether or not there'd been a fight. The *lefferti* had ordered more drinks and were congratulating each other. None of them had had a chance to close in on anyone and hurt him; they were all too well armed for anyone to have tried anything in the few seconds the fight had lasted. A couple of the other regulars had been hit, and had bruises, and a couple of others had gotten in a few licks, and left some of the crowd limping as they left.

Benito was watching out of the door, occasionally orbiting the windows onto the street, and looking worried. After a while he came back over. "There are still some guys out in the street, Frank," he said.

"Doing what?" Frank asked, checking where his pistol was holstered across the back of his belt where he could get at it without looking too threatening.

"Just watching the place," Benito said, looking worried.

Frank remembered that Benito had grown up in a far, far rougher neighborhood than Grantville, West Virginia, which while not exactly high society had been a quiet and decent place. He pretty much ought to know what trouble in the offing would look like.

"Okay," Frank said, thinking about it. They'd been

driven out once, they were more than likely pissed about it, but most of them wouldn't want to come back in and get shot at. After a while, though, only the real diehards would still be out there. What would they do? A few unpleasant possibilities crossed Frank's mind. The building was brick, solid brick, but most of the internal floors and the furniture and fittings were wood. Extremely flammable wood. And all the lamps that made the place so bright and cheery at night were, from one point of view, simply fragile bottles of oil held up where they could shatter easily. "I figure we keep watches all night," he said after looking around the place. "Fire watches."

Benito nodded. He'd probably been thinking the same sort of thing.

It was a long, hot night. Uneventful, in the end, but long and hot.

Chapter 26

Rome

His Holiness stood at the open window. Very little of St. Peter's Square could be seen from that window—there was a builders' scaffold in the way—but the sounds of riot and disorder were very much to be heard. Much less than they had been in the hours after midnight, but still there.

Cardinal Antonio Barberini could just about hear the crackle of muskets, a sound he had only rarely heard before and never in Rome. Again, there was less than there had been the night before, when every militia commander and bodyguard captain in the city—and not a few concerned citizens—had shot at rioters in the streets. There would certainly have been fatalities, and it was too much to hope that all of them were of the blackest character and surely guilty of some heinous crime. Barberini had expressed that hope in the darkest hours, and been told by several of the gentlemen of his salon, more than one of whom had been *condottieri* in one small way or another in the course of their careers, that the chances of that were slim at best. Ringleaders in riots tended to lead from the rear; those at the forefront were the young, enthusiastic, stupid and drunk, and often all four in the same person.

He was not standing so close to the window—even if the pope is one's uncle there is a certain minimum level of etiquette to observe—as to see much other than sky. But there were columns of smoke visible, rising and spreading on the light breeze of early summer.

Barberini looked from the smoke to His Holiness and back again. Suddenly, the serene and dignified pontiff looked far more like his elderly Uncle Maffeo, who to a much younger Antonio had seemed like a kindly old man. And yet he had grown terribly old, without his nephew noticing, and seemed bowed this morning.

The night had been long and hot, and there had been rioting in the city. Antonio, who was no spymaster but had the native wit to recognize the need for a corps of paid informers and the contacts to find someone with the skills to run such a network, had had reports waiting for him before breakfast. And it had been an early breakfast. Cardinal Antonio Barberini was what a later age would call "Bohemian," for all that he was in theory a senior man in a hierarchy that vowed poverty, chastity and obedience. On an ordinary day, he would rise at a leisurely and civilized hour, on those nights when he took to his bed at all. This night past, he had retired late, slept little and risen early. The morning had an air of unreality about it.

Not least because the reports had been so conflicted,

so confused. The rioters were chanting, by Barberini's rough count, fourteen different sets of slogans, attacking three different groups and were coming from a dozen different parishes. It was almost as if the citizens of Rome were looking for *any* excuse to engage in disorder. It was surely too much to believe that so many disparate strands of disaffection had surfaced at the same time.

Barberini had made his way to the Vatican as soon as he had decently breakfasted, and found himself immediately admitted to His Holiness' presence. Of course, his uncle had always been an early riser of habit, but there was usually at least something of a wait before one might be seen. In fact, one almost expected—

But the pope was speaking. "My dear nephew," he said, "I presume your early appearance betokens information you have for me on this night's business?" His Holiness turned from the window and smiled at Barberini. It was the simple smile of an old man for a favored, if somewhat wayward, nephew.

"Your Holiness, it does. But I fear that what I have to report to you does not begin to plumb the depths of what is taking place outside—" Barberini began, before the pope waved him to silence.

"Peace, my boy, peace. I am not the first pope to arouse the ire of Rome's mob, nor will I be the last, I should imagine. Indeed, I can remember worse rioting than this, and over less. During the course of breakfast this morning some of the older of my retainers regaled me with tales of some of the disturbances they had seen, and assured me that nothing I could remember was more than a minor brawl by comparison."

The pope paused to chuckle. "Truly, I remember being your age and being irked beyond measure at the tendency of old men to reminisce about how everything was bigger and better in their day. Be assured, my boy, that the phenomenon does not disappear as one ages. There is always someone who can remember more than you can, and he will always assure you that what you see now is naught but a pale shadow of the glory that once was."

Barberini found himself smiling. "Your Holiness finds me too transparent."

The pope chuckled again. "Come, claim your cardinal's dignity and sit in my presence. Summarize for me what your spies tell you, and let us compare it with what my spies tell me. It will pass the time while we wait for a man who truly knows what is happening."

"The father-general?" Barberini realized as he said it that he was not surprised. The Society of Jesus was considerably less well represented in Rome than it was elsewhere, since the Jesuits were great believers in being out in the world doing their work rather than intriguing in Rome. It was nevertheless a body of men that did not stint in any aspect of information-gathering. That the pope should send for their leader at a time like this was only natural.

Barberini realized, as he gave a précis of the little he had learned, that it actually *would* be a surprise to see Vitelleschi here. It was, after all, civil disturbance. Criminality, albeit on a scale which was surprising to Barberini. Why was the Society involved? Were they involved? Barberini stuck to his report and resolved himself to patience.

Barberini had just completed listing the incidents which had come to his ears when Vitelleschi arrived. The formalities of greeting completed, the spare, ascetic old Jesuit came straight to the point. "Your Holiness, Borja sent a messenger south last night. A fast horse, and a rider with evident orders not to spare the animal."

His Holiness nodded, his gaze turned inward for a moment, reflecting on the news. "And the most recent news from Naples?"

"As it stood when last Your Holiness was apprised."

Barberini frowned. "The situation in Naples? It has worsened?" He had heard some few small things about the worsening politics south of the border with the king of Spain's Italian possessions, the part of Italy that Spain did not rule through local proxies. It had, of course, been news touching most directly on Barberini's own principal concerns, those of the arts, music and, recently, natural philosophy, but he had heard enough to know that matters were growing . . . restive there. Not that there weren't always at least some agitators; Campanella for one had been more-or-less constantly in jail for one sedition or another prior to his recent refuge in Paris.

"Your Eminence may recall that we discussed the reason for Spain's movement of troops to Naples some weeks ago," Vitelleschi said, the reproof in his tone being no more than mild. "It now appears to have been a measure with no small degree of foresight regarding the situation in Naples, not simply prepositioning for a movement toward France."

"So Borja will be refused any men he asks for?" Barberini asked. While Vitelleschi had not reported what dispatch that rider from Borja's estate had carried—doubtless even the Society of Jesus had limits to the information they could obtain—that Borja had reacted to Rome's troubles by asking for troops to "help quell the disorder" seemed obvious. The man had a hair-trigger temper and would not have given thought to the simple fact that a message would take at least two days to get to Naples and even troops stationed on the border would take weeks to move back. Bad as the rioting had been, only the incurably pessimistic would think that it would not have burned itself out before any "help" could arrive. It was, Barberini thought, another example of Borja acting before thinking, a habit of his that had caused Madrid to have to issue hasty apologies for his conduct during his last sojourn in Rome.

"I consider that likely, Your Eminence," Vitelleschi said.

"Unless the plans for this were laid ahead of time?" His Holiness suggested. "Borja knows that he ought properly to await a request before providing troops. Perhaps he knows that troops are already available, should he find some suitable pretext for summoning them?"

Barberini swallowed, hard. It was not unprecedented that kings should attempt to rewrite papal policy by simply strong-arming the reigning pope. He himself had spent time as legate at Avignon, a papal seat that existed principally because the king of France had compelled the pope to reside where he could be controlled. After bringing one pope to heel by force of arms, the kings of France found that the Frenchmen subsequently elected as popes were happy to reside at Avignon where, for decades, the papacy danced to the tune played by a piper paid in French money.

"Your Holiness is, perhaps, too cautious?" Vitelleschi ventured. "I would suggest that Borja's strategem remains primarily political. Such is the Society's understanding of his instructions from Madrid, and a military action would mean that the movement of every cardinal friendly to the Spanish party into Rome was no more than a diversion."

"Borja has gone beyond his brief before," Barberini interjected, "if the Father-General and Your Holiness will forgive the interruption. And he did stop in Naples before coming here."

The silence that followed that was long, deep, and embarrassing.

"Antonio," His Holiness said, "even Spain would balk at setting the precedent of impeaching a pope. They would certainly stop at ordering me openly killed to make way for a more compliant pope. And too many of Europe's Catholics already regard their consciences unbound by the See of Rome's political leadership for a new Captivity to be worth their while."

Vitelleschi nodded. "Perhaps a further embarrassment for Your Holiness is in view?"

His Holiness raised an eyebrow. "That I cannot control the city? Perhaps. How do we stand with arrangements to bring our party to Rome?"

"In hand, Your Holiness. You may depend on having every vote we can count on, enough at least for a bare majority, in Rome within two weeks of your order to begin, at the latest. You will force your opponents to ensure they have every cardinal present for every session within eight days."

Barberini could not resist the obvious question. "Why not bring them all in now? The Spaniards are."

"Better, Antonio, that they should try and fail than that they should be discouraged. I wish them to be seen to fail of their purpose." His Holiness had a smile that was not even faintly humorous. "I wish to make it plain what happens when overweening cardinals seek to frustrate the workings of Holy Mother Church. So we must await their first move before reacting swiftly."

Barberini frowned. It was all very well leading a debating opponent into a false position in order to expose his error, in the best Socratic tradition. But—

"Your Holiness, the risk—?" He saw no need to be articulate about what might happen. Even the most optimistic need spend only a single quiet afternoon with the histories of the Church to gain an inkling of *that*. After a night spent listening to Rome erupt in a criminal *carnevale*, Barberini was in no mood to be even slightly optimistic. Imagining grew more doleful by the hour.

"Is justified." It was Vitelleschi who had spoken, curt as usual. "If Borja intends misfeasance in the *curia*, a few days' delay in assembling the cardinals to defeat him will matter nothing. If he has truly taken leave of reason, and has engineered this strife in order to seek a new Captivity or even depose Your Holiness, the presence of the cardinals will make scant difference."

Barberini nodded. That made sense, at least. And then he caught up with parsing what Vitelleschi had said. "Trouble which *Borja* has engineered? How?"

"Quevedo." Vitelleschi said the name like it was sufficient explanation all by itself, and in a way it was. The Spanish soldier-poet was that most paradoxical of creatures, a notorious secret agent. There was little that Spain had done in the Italian peninsula for years past that had not had his name floating to the top like scum in a pond.

Oh, for certain the man's writing was excellent; he was truly an ornament of Spanish letters. But he had taken his several years' exile from Spain as license to stir Italy's constantly simmering stockpot of trouble whenever it took his fancy. A good many of Italy's politicians had heaved a sigh of relief when, only a few years previously, the man had returned to Spain. Barberini had mentioned Quevedo to Mazarini, very much the coming man in European diplomacy and every inch the peacemaker and conciliator. Mazarini had, in the few moments that followed, taught Barberini more obscenities in four different languages than he had learned in his entire life up to that point.

And yet that tirade of obscenity and vulgar abuse had been tinged with no small measure of respect. Fiascos like Osuna's plot against Venice apart, Quevedo did have a habit of delivering the goods, even if ordering them was usually something of a devil's bargain. They had known he was in the city, of course, but Barberini had assumed that he had been about the business of suborning senior clergymen. Guiltily he realized that he had not troubled to set his own people to tracking the Spanish troublemaker, but clearly the father-general had not been so remiss.

"How has he achieved . . . ?" Barberini waved an arm at the open window to indicate what he asked after. The sounds of trouble were still audible, the palls of smoke still smearing the sky.

"It is reported that he began by simply disbursing money to procure crowds at selected places. It may be that he suborned a militia officer to overreact, although that seems doubtful. Gulled him in some way, most likely, if ordinary stupidity does not suffice to explain the matter. Certainly the officer in question seems to have died in the melee. The resulting ill-feeling swelled some of his subsequent performances, and it appears he has taken pains to ensure a strong militia reaction at several of them. He maintained this activity for some time, until food prices rose, provoking further discontent, and Rome's Committee of Correspondence made the unwise move last night of breaking up one of the demonstrations."

Barberini caught the tone with which Vitelleschi had said the word "unwise." Almost . . . approving. He decided to ask—"Unwise how, Father-General?"

Vitelleschi smiled. Slightly, and one would have to know the man well to see it there, but he smiled. "Unwise, did they wish to continue with a policy of what the Americans call a 'low profile,' Your Eminence. A crowd, probably inspired by Quevedo even if not actually paid by him, attacked the hostelry they keep. The young Signor Stone, following the disturbance, grew . . . eloquent. A demonstration at the embassy of the United States of Europe last night was chased off without injury to any person, but the core members of the Committee have been spreading rumors through the Borgo and beyond that the troubles are Spain's doing. The worst of the disturbances last night were antiforeigner sentiment, I understand."

That accorded with the reports Barberini had had as well. The worst of the rioting—and the most shootings—had been at the gates of the Villa Borja. If Borja had paid for *that* mob, the implications were downright nasty. If it wasn't murder at law, it was certainly murder before God. Barberini shuddered again, as he had done when he had first heard about Borja's company of mercenary bodyguards pouring musket fire into that crowd. They'd even had a firing step erected under the estate wall, expecting to need it. There still wasn't a certain count of the number of dead, although reports ranged from twenty to two hundred. *One would be too many*, Barberini thought to himself. He realized he now understood all too well why Mazarini bent so much effort toward making peace wherever he could. He had seen two wars at close quarters, and the second of those, the war of the Mantuan succession, had included more than its fair share of atrocities.

And he found himself unable to share the comforting logic that his superiors were following. He'd met Borja. Had spent session after interminable session with him on the Galileo Commission. He knew, precisely, how self-righteous, arrogant and impenetrably stupid the man was. Whatever his orders from Madrid were, Borja could be relied on to do something spectacular. Even if he didn't intend it, he could easily bring about, if not the actual biblical apocalypse, a reasonable imitation of it. And in Naples he had hired Quevedo. And Quevedo had been trying to provoke disorder. Barberini realized that this particular recipe for disaster was already in the oven and the cooks had sent word to announce dinner.

"Has Your Holiness . . ." he began diffidently, and

stopped. While he had been musing, the father-general and his uncle had continued conferring, on the subject of what stratagems might be expected once Borja was in a position to begin his political assault.

They looked at him, both with a patient and forebearing expression on their faces. He felt himself color momentarily, then cleared his throat. "Please, excuse my impertinence in persisting with a subject which Your Holiness and the Father-General perhaps had deemed closed, but ought it not to be prudent to ensure that the See of Rome's military forces are called to their colors? And perhaps make preparations for a defense of the city?"

His Holiness nodded. "My dear nephew, your concern for Our safety is quite proper. Commendable, even. However, the prospects of Spain—whether His Most Catholic Majesty or his viceroy at Naples— undertaking anything so rash as to invade Rome at this time are remote. And the risk of that is as nothing compared to the certainty of worse disorder if word should spread among the people of Rome that we were calling out our troops."

"I see," said Barberini, "and should the worse come to the worst, does Your Holiness have plans for evacuation?"

"It will not come to that," His Holiness said, with a definite hint of closing the subject. "And if any such step should come to light, the political embarrassment would cause Us trouble elsewhere."

Barberini could not, however, stop worrying. He followed the discussion of possible schemes that Borja might have in hand, even offered some small suggestions, but could not shake the feeling that Borja really was about to attempt something that would leave Rome in flames. Surely he would not send for military assistance if he fully expected to be refused? Was even Borja that stupid? On reflection, Barberini realized, he was. On his worse days, at least.

It was that firing step, the waiting mercenaries, that were the worry. That betokened preparation. And that Borja had set Quevedo to work on the street disorder rather than the political maneuvers. His Holiness and the father-general might affect to have seen it all before when it came to fighting in the streets, but Barberini found it worrying. In and of itself, not just for what it provided outsiders with a pretext for doing. And while Borja might be a profoundly stupid and ignorant man, he could bring more brain-power to bear on being a fool than most men could exert in the profoundest philosophical inquiry.

As the meeting came to a close, Barberini realized that while His Holiness had denied the necessity of an escape plan, he had not forbidden his nephew from seeing that one was in place. Better that a little effort be wasted than that something so vital should not be in place at dire need.

Chapter 27

Rome

Sharon looked at the clock again. Still only half-past nine. Ruy had risen early and gone for a walk around town, to get a sense of what was happening. Talk to a few people, pick up on the gossip. He'd gone out in his other persona, the simple porter from Barcelona, and had promised to be back by lunchtime, or possibly a little earlier.

Frank would be along shortly, she hoped. The night had been broken more than once with the sound of gunfire, and not just the occasional shot, either. Volleys, such as Sharon hadn't heard since her first months after the Ring of Fire. She hadn't done much trauma medicine since those days, what with one thing and another, but the effects of a three-quarter-inch musket ball on a human body were hard to forget.

Again, the ballroom had the best view of the street. The usual swordplay session had been cancelled due to press of business, and all of the Marines were busy about the place. Captain Taggart was making preparations so he could rapidly fortify the house or organize an evacuation as the situation demanded. Although, looking out over the city and listening through the open windows, Sharon wondered whether or not either would be necessary. There was smoke rising over the river and in a few other places. Not just the usual fug of cooking fires, but the thick black columns of roiling smoke that came from burning buildings. A couple of them were in the general direction of the Vatican, which meant Frank's neighborhood, and she knew he'd been a target once already.

"Penny for your thoughts?" It was her dad.

She turned and smiled at him, suddenly realizing how tired she was. She'd tried hard to sleep, but she'd been woken three times that she could remember. Ruy, the rat bastard, had been fresh as a daisy at some ungodly hour. The side effects of a life spent soldiering, she supposed. "Just tired and wondering what the hell's going on," she said.

"Ruy's not back yet, then?"

"No, but he only promised to be back for lunch. I figure he'll hear a thing or two, one way or another. There's nothing in from any of Don Francisco's people either, yet, although I reckon they'll be looking after their own business first."

"I suppose so. Most of 'em are Jewish, aren't they?" He shrugged. "I figure that's going to be part of it."

Sharon shook her head. "Not here, no. The restrictions on Jews in Rome are among the worst in Italy. Most of our commercial contacts hereabouts are Cavriani affiliates of one sort or another, selling us commercial intelligence. I think Don Francisco maintains someone in the ghetto, but they don't get about much outside the rag trade. As for them being targets last night, I doubt it. They're locked in at night, and apart from some nasty rituals they used to do during *carnevale* they don't tend to get bothered much. Just a horrible example of what it's like not to be Catholic. A lot of Jim Crow, but no real popular feeling behind it."

Her father nodded. "You think Frank's okay?" He sounded more than a little worried.

"I don't honestly know, Dad," she said. "I think Ruy will have gone that way first to see what happened. If he went there, he got there early; he was out the door by half past seven. If everything was okay, he didn't think to send someone with a message. Frank's supposed to be coming by this morning to let me know what happened, but I keep seeing smoke from over that direction."

"Try not to worry, Sharon. Frank's got a sensible head on his shoulders, and isn't fool enough to go looking for trouble. If I'm any judge, he'll have buttoned up tight for the night and waited it out."

"That wasn't what I was worried about. I have visions of his place getting attacked and set on fire. You haven't been there, but it's got no back way out and it's in a real rough neighborhood. Ruy reckons they'd need a pickaxe to get out any way but the front."

"Oh." She could see her father deflating. He'd been trying to keep up a cheerful front, almost verging on his bedside manner, but the facts had punctured that.

Just then, there was a tap on the ballroom door. It was open, and Adolf was peering in. When Sharon smiled an acknowledgement of his presence, he said, "If you will forgive the interruption, Doctors, Señor Sanchez and young Herr Stone are here."

Both Sharon and her father heaved a sigh of relief. "He's early," Sharon remarked, to cover the slightly weak-kneed feeling she was experiencing. "Both of them, come right to it. Where have you put them, Adolf?"

"He has put us nowhere, Sharon," Ruy boomed, from behind him. "When foul deeds are afoot, I stand on no ceremony."

So saying, he came in to the ballroom with Frank in tow. Ruy looked furious, there was no other word for it, although his voice had not betrayed the emotion written in every quiver of his mustachios.

Frank, behind him, looked weary and generally pissed off. And smudged about the face in a manner that could only be soot.

"Frank?" she asked, not seeing any obvious place to begin.

"What Ruy said." Frank shrugged. "Everyone back at my place is okay, though. We had a little trouble, but it was just a few rowdies and Giovanna saw 'em off with the shotgun."

Ruy's face changed like spring weather, from thunderous to delighted. "Frank is a lucky man, Sharon. Such a one, ah, she bids fair to match your own marvelous spirit! A woman to daunt the mightiest, not even all the eloquence of all the poets could do justice—"

Frank was chuckling. "Give it a rest, Ruy. Sharon, he's been lecturing me on how I've got to do right by Giovanna ever since we left my place, like I couldn't figure out that part by myself."

Ruy was all affronted dignity in an instant. "It is the proper place for those wise in years to guard against the folly of youth."

"Damn straight," said Doctor Nichols, senior.

Sharon groaned. "I take it from this display of what passes for wit among the nearly senile that things aren't too bad?"

Ruy's fury was suddenly back in evidence. "The answer to that, *mi corazon*, is both yes and no. The trouble is subsided, Frank's Place and the embassy are secure and all seems quiet. But there is news of foul work, this night past. Frank, the rumors you have heard?"

"Right," said Frank. "First thing we heard after we got back last night was that there was a crowd going over to Borja's place. Word was they were going to storm it and run him out of town on a rail."

"It was not so," Ruy finished for him. "Frank and I went by the villa on our return here, hence our slight tardiness, for I was certain you would wish earlier news of Frank's well-being than you asked for last night."

"It was a massacre," Frank said. "Nothing but."

Sharon could suddenly see the reason for Frank's weary demeanor. She could guess that he'd been up all night keeping watch, but Frank was still, in all but name, a teenager. A missed night's sleep wouldn't leave him much out of sorts at all. When he'd trudged into the ballroom, he'd looked *beaten*.

"It is as Frank says," Ruy said, his face growing stonier with the recollection. "We arrived to find burial parties at work. We saw eight corpses, Sharon, and that after those poor souls had been at work for some time. We questioned bystanders, and heard of perhaps thirty. They also spoke of Borja sending a rider for Spanish tercios to suppress the populace, and the pope calling in his own forces for the same purpose. Such may be accounted wild rumors, but these people witnessed a slaughter last night."

"How many went there last night?" Sharon's dad asked.

"Fifty, sixty from my place alone," Frank said. "I don't know how many of them made it back. From what we heard, I'd be surprised if it was less than a couple hundred all told. Borja's goons just fired into the crowd, from what I hear."

Doctor Nichols nodded. "And you can figure on three times as many again wounded who got away in the night. Maybe half of those will die of their wounds, too." He shook his head.

"The only mercy, Doctor Nichols," Ruy said, "is that the crowd ran at the first shots, and were not so hemmed in that many would have been trampled."

"But it's worse," said Frank. "Tell 'em, Ruy. I never would've spotted it, not being a soldier and all."

"That—" Ruy broke off here to snarl a few choice phrases in broad, rural Catalan. "Quevedo. And his stinking swine of a master, Borja. It is almost certain that they enticed that crowd with the express purpose of firing into it."

"Surely you don't get that from just rumor," Sharon protested. While she was quite prepared to assume many bad things of the Spanish government, cynically engineering the murder of civilians was, she thought, something they'd left behind with the previous century.

"Not rumor, Sharon," Ruy said, the gravity of his tone not mellowing the fury in his eyes one bit. "Simple inference. I saw, with my own eyes, the firing platform which Borja had had built behind his wall. Right up to the gate, and still manned in broad daylight."

"Oh," Sharon said. *He'd been expecting the rioters.*

"Indeed," Ruy said. "I am no doctor of natural philosophy, no student of mathematics, but I can add two and two and reach the same conclusion as any peasant, haggling in the market. With your permission, Sharon, I will seek out Quevedo and deal with him. This cannot go on."

Sharon *knew*, without having to think about it, that right here and now she could order a man assassinated, and be sure it was going to be carried out. And, furthermore, that she could refrain from giving the order, and know that Quevedo would be safe from Ruy. She tried to think about it. Was there something to be—

She cut the thought off. Horrible as the man's actions had been the night before, the proper way to proceed was with an arrest and a trial. The fact that she didn't think they did things that way around here didn't affect, not one little bit, the fact that she knew what was right and what was wrong. Ruy's values were different, but bless him, he was making sure that he didn't do anything she wasn't happy with. "No," she said. "If you run into him and can't avoid it, and can't take him prisoner, then I figure he'll get what's coming to him. But I'm not going to order an assassination."

Ruy nodded, and behind her Sharon thought she could hear her dad letting out a soft sigh of relief. Somehow, that pleased her immensely.

"For now," she said, "Frank, we're going to get a hot meal inside you, and some coffee, and you can give me all the details. And Ruy, we need to get more information. I need to make a report to Magdeburg and take a decision on whether or not we should postpone the wedding. I want to hear a plan from you."

"And Sharon?" her dad said.

"Dad?"

"See if we can put out the word that there's free treatment here for anyone who got hurt last night. Maybe we can save a few lives, build up some goodwill. I brought plenty of supplies down from Germany, so I reckon we could do some serious good on both sides of the ledger."

Magdeburg

"My sister's in that mess." Mike Stearns' tone was quiet and understated.

"We cannot be sure it is a mess quite yet," Don Francisco said. This message had come in overnight in time for this morning's twice-weekly briefing, and Ed Piazza had joined them. By good fortune, the president of the State of Thuringia-Franconia happened to be in Magdeburg on a visit.

"From what I hear," Ed said, "the real mess is further south. Whatever Borja's up to, it'll be a sideshow to what's brewing in Naples. Or to whatever the Spanish are doing to stop it."

"Just so," Francisco agreed. "Mike, there is nothing unusual in there being rioting at this time of year anywhere in Europe. Borja seems to have made it a little worse, but truly, the political situation in Rome will not support sustained disorder. The people I have reporting to me are natives of the city, Mike, and they know how it goes."

"When you say natives, Francisco," Mike said, his tone level, even and, Francisco knew, very angry indeed, "you're talking about guys who work as lawyers and bankers and the like, aren't you?"

"With one exception, yes." Don Francisco was determined to stop this before it started. Mike Stearns was apt to grow increasingly testy of late, and small wonder. "Mike, I have worked for you for the best part of three years and I have learned a thing or two. Yes, the outlook of people in different social classes is different, and the view is indeed very different from the street. However, one of my informants is a distant cousin who makes his living in a small way in the ghetto, a saddler. And one of the things people do in a saddler's shop, Mike, is gossip. Artisans among themselves and the customers with the man himself. He is no maker of fine harness for the gentry, he makes work harness for other artisans. Well regarded for that sort of thing, he tells me. And what he heard was that the disturbances were all fomented by Spaniards with money. The talk was all over Rome. My last report from him—he sends his dispatches in the regular mails, not through the embassy—was dated two weeks ago. All was not quiet then, and he predicted some such outbreak as occurred last night. His assessment then was that it would come to nothing. Rome is not a city much given to civic disturbance, Mike."

Stearns held up his hands, his expression a little less icy. "All right, I surrender. So the Turkish nobleman is getting a little class-consciousness, good. Won't be the first time we've been caught on the wrong foot by a popular movement, though, Francisco."

Ed Piazza chuckled. "Mike, you're just jealous because there's a risk of an uprising you can't get up in front of, and that wasn't your idea."

"Hold on a minute," Mike said, "which is it? No popular uprising at all, or one I should be jealous of?" He was smiling as he said it.

"You know what I mean, Mike," Ed said. "Happens I think Francisco's right. We—that is, the State of Thuringia-Franconia—have our own sources—"

Don Francisco hazarded a guess—"The Cavrianis?"

Ed nodded. "Useful guys to have around, once you allow for the selection effect—they only report on what interests them. I suppose I could get them to do some more general reporting for us, but budgets are kind of tight. That wasn't a hint, by the way," he added hurriedly in Mike's direction.

"Money's tight all round," Mike said, "so it wouldn't have done any good if it was." His smile was a little rueful. What with trouble breaking out in all directions, the treasury of the USE was starting to look a little threadbare as the available credit began to run low. The deficits were a lot more manageable than those of other European powers, on the other hand. So when stability came to the USE, it would recover faster and harder than any of the other powers.

However, in the present, Ed was running through what Spain's major concerns in Italy really were. Nothing that was surprising to Don Francisco. He let himself muse over what *could* be happening in Rome. A coup? Unlikely. The Church hadn't had an antipope in over a hundred years and on the record of the future history had already got that particular disease out of its system. In any event, Francisco's own people had bought good information—confirmed from several sources—that Borja's instructions specified simply obstructing the pope's business, not deposing him, whatever that mysterious letter-writer had hinted at a few weeks ago. Likewise outright arrest. There were good reports on every major concentration of troops in Naples, which was all in all the only place Borja could get military help from. And it would take regiments to arrest the pope. The Swiss Guard were a serious fighting force all by themselves, and while the various regiments of Rome's nobility were not of the best in the military field—Italy's better soldiers tended to be *condottieri*—they would perform adequately in supporting the Swiss Guard and increase the troops needed for such an endeavour beyond what anyone thought Borja could shake loose from Naples, which was a tercio at most and more likely a couple of companies of musketeers.

The risks to the embassy at Rome were of the more ordinary kind. Riots were chancy things, especially if the sentiment against foreigners that Miss Nichols reported was a genuine popular feeling and not simply a slogan the crowds she had heard had been paid to chant.

"—and so while I'm sure the Spanish would like to be able to commit those troops further north, pretty much anyone with eyes to see can tell they're going to have a better use for them real soon now, Mike," Ed was finishing up.

Mike looked to Francisco, "And your assessment?"

"As I say, it is the season for domestic troubles. We have been seeing something like it here. It is simply that much of it is handled at a local level if it does not go beyond street-brawling. I think you have been spoilt by life in the twentieth century, Mike. The seventeenth century is what you would call a rough neighborhood."

"All right," Mike said, "so I needn't give them a recall order, then? Because that's what it'll take to shift Sharon away from the job she's doing."

"I reckon not, Mike. Or at least, not right now," Ed said. "Although I reckon she'll git if she has to, and she'll know way before you will when that time is."

Don Francisco frowned. "You think it will come to that?" He couldn't see it, himself. Rioting was one of those things that simply happened, and the options Borja had for action that was at least within shouting distance of rationality precluded anything worse. His actions so far were of a kind to make cardinals and senior churchmen and Rome's other notables a little more nervous than they might otherwise be, and demonstrated a certain looseness of grip on the part of Urban VIII, but as a prelude to something more serious?

"Just covering my ass, Francisco," Ed said. "You know and I know that there's probably nothing deeper to this. I just get the feeling that Borja's playing with fire and even if he doesn't mean to make everything blow up in everyone's face, well . . ."

"Yeah," Mike sighed, and rubbed a hand over his face. "Life would be so much simpler if we didn't have all these assholes who played games with other peoples' lives. On the other hand, we wouldn't have as much support as we do, either. For now, then, we'll leave things as they are. I want to hear about it if things really start boiling down there, though."

Chapter 28

Rome

"Your Excellency," Ruy said, coming into Sharon's office and dragging up a chair, in to which he flopped dramatically.

"It sounds weird when you call me that, Ruy," Sharon said. "I became an ambassador by accident, and it still feels a little unreal."

"It is a task you undertake well, and I find that remembering the correct title when we are working helps me to be clear as to the task in hand."

"And the news is?"

"There are some small changes." Ruy ran a hand through his hair. He'd been out nearly all day and Sharon could guess that getting around Rome on a warm spring day would have been more than a little wearying. "Quevedo has not been seen, or at least the men he had hired to gather his mobs have not been seen, since the night before last. There is much tension. I have heard no less than four rumors that the pope has summoned his papal regiments in order to suppress dissent in the bloodiest manner imaginable, and two other men I spoke with said they had heard, at fourth or fifth hand, that the papal troops are in a state of mutiny and refusing to muster."

"Did we get anything that sounds like it might be true?" Sharon asked. Similar rumors had gone around various parts of Germany while she'd been there; they always turned out to be so much wind.

"I spoke briefly with a constable on customs duty at the Ripetta. His view was that if there was to be a mobilization he would have heard of it, and that he had heard nothing. And that it would take weeks to organize the papal regiments to any kind of action, most of them last having seen action nearly ten years ago in the Valtelline. I think he had the right of it. Also, I learned that this morning's sermons were, by papal command, of the day of prayer and fasting which His Holiness has decreed, in the cause of civic peace, to be observed this Friday."

"Is that going to help?" Sharon had to wonder. The people most likely to riot were pretty poor folks, and asking people who were already a little hungry to go a little hungrier seemed like not much effort.

"It can do no harm, certainly," Ruy said. "And in truth, the other part of His Holiness' pastoral message was that there were proper means of airing grievances and that petitions would be received and considered on their merits. If the troubles are as entirely manufactured as I think we all suspect, this will be of some assistance. Since the alternative for His Holiness is the use of soldiers to quell disturbances, we may consider it a fairly enlightened approach."

Sharon nodded. Put that way, it did seem a little more sensible. "I guess getting people to concentrate on their religion and deal with the political stuff in a sensible way might well be the way to go about it." She thought for a moment. "I guess we might be able to do something to help. I'll get Adolf to put a notice up outside saying that the embassy will close that day out of respect for the occasion. As you say, it can't hurt."

"Just so. I also called upon young Señor Stone, although he was out taking the air when I was there. His most charming wife and her brother were there to tell me that matters seem more restful in that neighborhood, although there has been an ugly mood at some of the funerals. I also had the rumor about the papal regiments coming to slaughter everyone from there, and I am pleased to see that Frank is discounting it and counseling calm in all directions."

"That's good to hear," Sharon said, deflating a little in relief. Seeing Frank a couple of nights ago starting his career as a rabble-rouser had, once she'd had time to think about it, made her more than a little nervous. "In fact—"

There was a knock at the door. It was Adolf Kohl, sticking his head around the door in his usual apologetic fashion. "Your Excellency? I beg pardon for disturbing you with Herr Sanchez, but there is a visitor who makes much of his business being most urgent."

"Who?" Sharon was intrigued. If whoever it was had managed to get past Adolf's protective instincts regarding her schedule, he was pretty persuasive or had some genuinely impressive news to impart.

"A Jewish saddler, Your Excellency. A somewhat rough fellow, but he has presumed on the name of Don Francisco." There was a tone of distaste a mile wide in Adolf's voice. Not, Sharon suspected, because the man was Jewish, but because he was an artisan.

"Send him on up," she said. "If he's one of Don Francisco's relations he's probably got something relevant to say."

The fellow who came in shortly was a far cry from what Sharon had imagined when she'd heard he was a saddler and a relative of Don Francisco. For a start, he didn't look like he belonged in the needle trades of any kind at all. Had Sharon been asked to guess what he did for a living, she'd have said he was a blacksmith, maybe, or possibly a professional prizefighter. She knew quite a few big, powerful men. The man Adolf had announced as Isaac, no other name, was definitely among the top five. He had the big, scarred hands and rough knuckles of a man who did hard manual work and had grown up in a tough neighborhood, which by all accounts the Rome ghetto was. There was hardly a trace of the features Sharon had come to think of as Sephardic in his face. Had she not known the man was Jewish, she'd have simply taken him for an ordinary, if rather large, Roman. His face was one of those that, under the thick black hair, was always frowning with either worry or concentration. Right now, it seemed to be worry.

The other odd thing about him was that he wasn't wearing any of the clothing that was required by Roman civic law for Jews. Of course, with his size and appearance, he could clearly get away with not bothering to do so.

"Signora, Your Excellency," he said, clearly a little uncomfortable at the high-toned surroundings he found himself in. He was, Sharon guessed, rather used to coming to the tradesman's entrance and doing whatever it was saddlers did on a house call without getting farther than the stables. "I have had news that I think should come to you as well as going to Don Francisco."

That was immediately out of the ordinary. Don Francisco was usually extremely careful of his people's cover, and unless they had cast-iron cover for being at an embassy, like Ben Luzatto back in Venice, the embassy never even knew they were there. Even Don Francisco's digests were careful not to give away anything that might betray a source. Don Francisco advised on the running of the embassy's own network, but it was always kept separate from the deeper network of agents he maintained himself. Sharon suspected he planned for the eventual compromise and capture of every single embassy and assumed that at some point he would be left depending on only his own network.

"It must be serious, Isaac," Sharon said, after she realized he was waiting for permission to speak. She mentally chided herself. Just because all the members of the extended Abrabanel and Nasi families she'd met to date were highly educated people like Don Francisco and Rebecca, she shouldn't assume that there weren't also plenty of ordinary working stiffs like Isaac who wouldn't be entirely at their ease if they were invited above stairs.

"Please," she said, hoping her tone was putting him at his ease, "tell us. Señor Sanchez is my chief of intelligence at the embassy. Have a seat, would you? And if you'd like refreshments—"

"Thank you, no, Your Excellency Ambassadora," Isaac said, sitting and starting to gabble a little. "I have the contract for the repairs to the tack at the Villa Borja, Your Excellency, and this morning the boy who brings the repairs came to deliver this week's work. I saw to it that he took refreshments and talked a while. When I make my reports to Don Francisco, Your Excellency, I get most of it from such gossip. You see, when soldiers or politicians send messages, they always pass through the stables when the messenger rides, and so I get to hear much because I always have some wine, you see?"

"Yes, I see," Sharon said, trying not to smile. "Will you have some here?"

"Oh, no, Your Excellency, I wouldn't presume to—"

"Here," Ruy said, shoving a glass into the big man's hand. "Take a drink and slow down a little. You were talking to the guy from the Villa Borja? Good way to get news, that, by the way, well done."

Sharon noticed, as Isaac took a deep gulp of the watered wine—clearly, he was not as observant as Ben Luzzatto had been—that Ruy's accent and use of Roman local dialect had gotten almost comically broad as he spoke to the man. Doubtless Ruy hadn't even thought about it, he was just well practiced at putting informants at their ease. He'd probably never had to resort to beating information out of anyone in his entire career as a soldier-cum-spy. A couple of drinks and half an hour of casual bonhomie and Ruy could probably have cracked the head of the KGB, lack of common language notwithstanding.

And, indeed, Isaac seemed a little more relaxed. He no longer seemed to be trying to sit at attention, at least.

"Your Excellencies," he said, "I hear from the boy at the Villa Borja stables that on the night of the rioting and other disturbances, when all those poor people were killed outside the Borja's gate—"

His face screwed up in something very much like distress at that point. Sharon got the impression that Isaac was one of those big men who had a fundamentally gentle nature.

"—that on that night the cardinal sent a messenger riding fast to Naples."

"Did your man know what the message was?" Ruy asked, his tone gentle, almost casual.

"No, signor. But it was right after the shootings and there were messengers coming in from all over Rome. They were busy in those stables that night. And Don Francisco Quevedo was there as well, the boy remembered him particularly because he always brings a tip of a few bottles of grappa to make sure his horse is seen to well."

Ruy snorted. "I taught him that trick. Make sure the stable-hands like you, and your horse is always well cared-for and ready when you need him. It has saved my life more than once."

Isaac chuckled in his turn. "The same trick is also good for your saddler, signor. I speak as one who knows."

Ruy laughed out loud at that. "Here, have another drink," he said, holding out the decanter. "Did the stable boy have any idea what Quevedo was doing there? I can guess he was up to no good, I know him of old, but was the message from him or the cardinal?"

"From the cardinal, I think," Isaac said. "We talked

it over some and we think that the cardinal is sending for more troops, maybe mercenaries or maybe Spanish troops, to guard his villa better. Or that is what we thought at the time. After the boy left, and I was getting to work on parceling out the work to my own boys, I got to thinking and I wondered what if the cardinal was sending for a lot of troops. The Spanish sacked the city in my great-grandfather's time, you know."

Sharon looked at Ruy. "Does that sound likely to you?" she asked, and then realized how it must sound to Isaac. "Sorry, Isaac," she said, "but Signor Sanchez is a soldier and can probably make a better guess than either of us whether there might be that many soldiers who can come from Naples."

Ruy shrugged. "Maybe. I think they have more troubles of their own in Naples than to send the three or four tercios it would take to do anything worthwhile in Rome. In all likelihood your first thought was the right one."

"And if Borja really has called for an army?" Sharon asked, and she could see Isaac's face grow especially concerned at that.

Ruy shook his head. "Even Borja is not that stupid, I think. And if he is, unless the various rebellions that are threatening in Naples have suddenly given up the ghost, the viceroy at Naples is not so stupid that he might rob himself of his defensive strength voluntarily. I have not met Monterey myself, but I recall Alfonso thought him competent. A perfect bastard, but competent."

"Bastard? This is not the half of it," Isaac put in, and Sharon was pleased to see that the guy was unwinding a little. "I hear stories. Even for a viceroy of Naples the man is a bloodsucker."

"Such was Alfonso's opinion, too." Sharon noted that Ruy was carefully not saying to Isaac who Alfonso actually was. That was either part of his efforts to keep Isaac at ease or he was carefully not drawing attention to the fact that his last employer had been a Spanish cardinal.

"So he'll want all those troops down in Naples to guard his money, then?" Sharon ventured.

"In all likelihood. Unless there is something we are missing," Ruy said.

Sharon thought about that. What would they lose if they assumed that there was more to it than met the eye? If Borja was sending for troops to intervene in Rome, it would mean evacuating the embassy. And putting off her wedding, which was now less than a fortnight away. *Screw that*, she thought. On the other hand, having the embassy ready for an evacuation, quietly done, would do no harm. "Isaac," she said, "thank you for the information. If Borja does bring troops in force to Rome, will you and your family be safe? We can help if you need to evacuate—"

Isaac shook his head. "No, Your Excellency. The ghetto will survive, as it has always done. There will be looting, but little, as we are poor. What we have can and will be hidden."

"In the meantime, Signor Isaac," Ruy said, "I have some old tack you can take away for repair to cover your visit here, and perhaps the Marines need some small jobs done as well. I think perhaps it would be helpful if you also reported here from time to time, if it can be done without exposing you?"

Isaac agreed to that on his way out. A few minutes later, after seeing the man away, Ruy returned.

"You have a contingency plan, Your Excellency?" he asked. "Or do you wish one? On the one hand, we have the source who told us that Borja's plans were solely to destabilize the Holy See, and so far we have seen nothing that disagrees with this. Borja was almost certainly doing no more than report progress. On the other hand . . ." He left the question hanging.

"I think we ought to have one. Father Maratta and Signora Fontana are here this afternoon to go over the details for the wedding, so neither of us can make a start on it today. I think we should dump this one on Tom and Captain Taggart, since they're the nearest USE officers."

"Ah, less work for us? I like this plan already." Ruy grinned.

Naples

"We're going where?" Ezquerra's disbelief was written in every wrinkle of his gap-toothed face.

"Rome, Sergeant." Don Vincente could hardly believe it himself. "Apparently we are to take ship some time in the next few days, just as soon as the esteemed quartermasters remove the assorted sticks from up their asses, and sail to Rome. And, unless I miss my guess, we are to sack it."

"Sack *Rome*?" Ezquerra had clearly forgotten his every trick of concealing disrespect from officers. Not that Don Vincente could blame him. As orders went, these were more deranged than most.

"Well, I say *sack*," Don Vincente went on, looking again at the written order that was, in an example of undue haste on the part of the army, dated only the day before yesterday and had therefore reached company level with blistering speed. "But what it actually says is that following complete breakdown of civic order in Rome we are to advance on the city via Ostia and subjugate rebellion."

Ezquerra's face went blank at that, as well it might. As pretexts went, it was thinner than most. Especially since the actual disturbances in Rome had been news in Naples last week, with the renewed peace in that city the news *this* week. Order had, if the news was right, restored *itself*.

And even the plodding pace of army bureaucracy could reverse itself in that time. Especially if the reverse consisted of suddenly doing nothing, a maneuver that the army excelled in.

"When must we be ready by, Don Vincente?" Ezquerra asked at length.

"Tomorrow."

That, as it happened, was not what concerned him about this business. Ezquerra and Rojas would have the company ready, of that there was no doubt. Rojas had learned to stay the hell out of Ezquerra's way and let him work as well as Don Vincente had.

Ezquerra simply nodded. "We are expecting loot, then?"

"Possibly," Don Vincente said, spreading his hands and shrugging. "The rumor is that Ostia is already sold to us, and should fall with little resistance. Rome has no defenses, and will likely not resist. So a general sack? I doubt it." He decided not to mention that he had long since resigned himself to missing opportunities for plunder by sheer bad luck. It would be just his luck to get saddled with some fool mission that kept him away from the loot.

Part Four

May 1635

Chapter 29

Rome

Ruy reflected that he ought to be getting used to this by now. Signora Fontana and Father Maratta had planned—conspired would be as good a word—with Sharon to ensure that the nuptials he was now awaiting the commencement of were fully prepared for. And, like a well-drilled soldier, Ruy's job was to stand in line and advance on command.

The customs surrounding the ceremonial were a little different from what he was used to. Or, at least, had been used to recently. He had, after all, been married three times before, in three countries—counting Spain's overseas territories as different countries, which they were—on two continents. So the way in which Sharon had quietly insisted on some slight departures from what Father Maratta was expecting was not, in truth, that odd to him. Or, at least, it was odd, but he was comfortable with odd.

The custom of not seeing the bride in her wedding dress until she arrived at the church was odder than the others, though. The first time he had been

married his newfound in-laws had made sure he and
his intended had had a thoroughly good night according
to their own, pre-Christian standards before escorting
them all to the church in the morning. Indeed, he
had half suspected that many of the older members
of the family had regarded the pagan festivities as the
real marriage. In fact—

Ruy Sanchez de Casador y Ortiz, you are nervous.
He took a deep breath, held it, and exhaled it. Calm.
Nothing had shown on his face. That much was certain. *A lifetime of battles and fields of honor, and every
moment of near-unmanning has happened in the course
of getting married.* It was not even as if he had ever not
wanted to be there. There was probably some deeper
spiritual point to be made, but for now concentration
was certain to elude him.

He looked at the congregation. An unusual mixture,
certainly. Rome's notables were, in the main, not represented. The wedding of an unregarded ambassador
and her intended was not an occasion that would
cause them to turn out. From the Barberini, no one
save Giulio Mazarini the elder, Antonio Barberini's
majordomo. His son, who would doubtless have been
present had he not been in Paris about his masters'
business, was thus represented as well. More than
a few natural philosophers, acquaintances made by
Sharon at the Barberini salons, were present and,
indeed, bickering while they waited for the service
to begin.

Also, grinning and offering the thumbs-up gesture
that meant *good luck* among the Americans and *up
your ass* to just about everyone else, was Frank Stone.
He had, it turned out, enough money from his father

for a gentleman's outfit and wore a sword, even after only a few weeks' tuition, like he meant it. Today, for certain, purely because it was part of proper dress for a young gentleman, although Sanchez was pleased to see he had taken advice and obtained a rather heavier item than a rapier in the Italian pattern. A strong arm, the boy had. A back-sword might not be so suited to the swift kill of *la destreza* but it carried real authority in a close fight. As did, unless Sanchez missed his guess, the crowd of young near-gentlemen who were present as Rome's Committee of Correspondence. He'd heard the term *lefferti* going around. There were a lot more of them than turned out at Frank's Place, and the sight of them made him wonder about Harry Lefferts. Did the horde of imitators mean he was a fellow worth meeting or just another charlatan?

Mind wandering again, he thought. *I grow senile.* On which note, a sight appeared in the nave of the church that caused the years to fall away from him—Sharon, in a dress that, truly, he was glad he had not seen. *Nothing* should have been allowed to detract from the impact of this moment, and though he should live a thousand years he should never find the words to express it truly.

Some indeterminate time later, filled vaguely with the memories of a nuptial mass, Ruy Sanchez de Casador y Ortiz stepped in to the afternoon sunlight of a spring day in Rome with the most beautiful woman in the world on his arm and heard the pealing of bells.

Many bells.

Many, many bells.

In fact, the whole of Rome was being deafened with the pealing of bells.

Tocsin bells.

"*Mierda*," he said, with feeling.

Frank had the confetti improvised and ready to throw. He'd briefed the guys on the proper use of the stuff and given them positions to take. Distributed it freely. Damn it, his own wedding had been a truly strange affair, surrounded by Swiss Guards, in a world heritage monument, conducted by a bemused guy in cardinal's robes who wasn't much older than Frank.

This one, he'd decided, was going to go off just like the ones on TV, and the party that followed it was going to be a blast or he, and every other regular member of Rome's Committee of Correspondence, was going to die trying.

Just as he'd gotten the guys out in position, and just as Ruy and Sharon were heading down the aisle toward the door into the sunshine, the pealing bell of the church was joined by another bell, from a nearby church.

That's nice, Frank thought. *Perhaps they all join in when they hear good news*. And then some guy came running into the church, skidded through a hard left toward the belltower and was lost in the gloom inside the church porch. A few seconds after that, the bells of this church changed to a single, constant note.

Frank realized that the same sound was being repeated from every direction. He looked around at the other guys there. All of them were either native Romans or at least Italians, and all of them looked concerned. He realized that while he'd learned to recognize many of the other signals you got from church bells, from funeral-in-progress, as he thought of it, to the angelus, he'd never heard this one before. And it was making even the tough-but-cheerful Piero look a little worried.

Then Ruy and Sharon stepped into the sunlight and Ruy's face instantly went from beaming-fit-to-burst to an iron soldier's mask, the face of a man who's about to face death and doesn't want to betray any weakness. He was worried too.

The little voice at the back of Frank's mind said *the word you're looking for is "Tocsin."*

"Crap," he murmured.

She felt Ruy's arm on hers stiffen. She heard him mutter something, but couldn't tell what it was over the sound of the bells. Lots of bells. Sunday mornings could be good and loud in Rome, but at a little distance from the belltowers the noise was bearable. They were standing right under the belltower here, of course, and for some reason the whole of Rome seemed to be ringing its bells.

Sharon put two and two together. "Back to the embassy, everyone!" she said loudly, and tugged on Ruy's arm to get him moving again.

Beside her, Ruy called out to Frank. "Señor Stone, go by your place and see that it is secure. If you hear word of—"

He broke off as someone came out of the belltower behind them and dodged around to run into the street. Ruy's reflexes were simply unnatural for a man his age. Sharon had seen him with weapons in hand many times—once against armed opponents and repeatedly in training sessions with the embassy's

Marine guards. Reaching out to snag hold of the runner, he all but blurred.

"What news?" he barked as the guy was pulled up short. He was not much more than a teenager, now that Sharon got a look at him.

"Invasion!" the messenger panted. "Spanish troops at Ostia on this morning's tide. Signor, please, let me go, I must spread the word."

Ruy let him go. "Borja," he spat, "Quevedo. How stupid?"

"Very?" Sharon answered, trying to lighten his mood a little.

Ruy's laugh was little more than a bark. "There will be fighting, Sharon. Hard fighting. His Holiness may not command many troops, but there are militia troops all about Rome. If given time to organize, they may be able to mount a spirited defense."

"Should we evacuate?"

"For a certainty. Let Captain Taggart begin the preparations." Ruy turned back to Frank. "Signor Stone, see that all is secure with you and yours. I would counsel that you withdraw outside the city as soon as you may."

"Figures," Frank said. "I heard what the messenger said. Good luck, Ruy, Sharon." He set off at a fast walk, collecting Giovanna on his arm as he went and trailed by the small crowd of genial ruffians he'd brought along.

Tom, Sharon's dad, Rita and Melissa Mailey were next out of the church. Tom spoke first. "What's up, everyone? Why the long—oh," he trailed off, as he caught the sound of the bells.

"What *kind* of trouble?" Sharon's dad asked.

"Those bells are a tocsin, aren't they?" asked Melissa.

"You cut it too fine with the nuptials, girlfriend," Rita said, grinning. "Looks like neither of us could get married without trouble brewing."

Sharon chuckled. That was true enough. Rita had been married less than half a day before the Ring of Fire dumped them all in the middle of the Thirty Years War. "Yeah, well," she said, "this is one lot of trouble we can bug out of. Ruy and Captain Taggart are organizing the evacuation."

She turned to where those two were conferring. The Marines, who had been drawn up ready to form an arch of swords outside the church, had already spread out to form a watchful perimeter, and their captain nodded some final confirmation to Ruy and turned to Sharon. "The coaches are ready, mistress," he said, "and I've sent a lad back to the embassy at best speed to get things stirred about there. Happen we'll be ready to go before dusk."

"That's a relief," Tom said. "This all has the authentic feel of somebody else's problem."

"True enough," Sharon's dad said. "Glad to see there's some sense in that man of yours, Sharon," he said, smiling.

"Sense?" Ruy interjected with a wry smile, "I shall have you know that I have slain men for less offensive suggestions. Sense is for Castilians and other like dullards, Doctor Nichols."

"Whatever. We're getting out of town, then?" he replied.

"Certainly. I would propose that we withdraw into Lazio for the time being and seek lodgings in one of the smaller towns or villages. With those under our protection safe, we can assess the possibility of returning when the fighting has died down. For now, though, as Señor Simpson so aptly puts it, the fighting in this city is somebody else's problem."

Sharon saw the carriages pulling up, the Marines directing them into a line. "Well," she said, loudly, "it'll be our problem if we don't move. Everyone who wishes to join us on the road out of town, be at the embassy in two hours. We won't wait, but if you're there then, you're welcome to join us."

More than a few of the notables who had been following her and Ruy out of the church looked at her and gave noncommittal nods. Most of them, she suspected, would stay put, or would have places to go in the defense of the city.

Adolf was running around in a state of what looked like barely controlled panic. Captain Taggart and two of his men were out securing extra transport; the embassy had two carriages and a cart, but it was starting to look like the entire staff would want to come with the evacuation party.

Sharon suspected that most of them would be safer—far, far safer—to simply get to relatives' houses and hole up until the fighting was over. The USE nationals, on the other hand, had no such option. On the drive back to the embassy, she had thought for a minute about staying put and relying on diplomatic privilege. She'd tried the idea out on Ruy.

"No," he'd said. "Borja is plainly out of control. I cannot conceive of such as this being ordered, even by that pack of fools in Madrid. And where Borja has flouted authority in one way, he cannot be trusted to conform to it in another."

"And even if Señor Sanchez is wrong about Borja, which I doubt," Melissa said, "I've seen what diplomatic privilege amounts to in this day and age. One spell of house arrest is quite enough, at my age."

Tom Simpson chuckled. "And one Harry Lefferts rescue is quite enough for an entire lifetime."

"I desire to meet that young *caballero*," Ruy said. "Truly I do."

Now, though, the embassy looked like it was shaping up for a reasonably orderly departure, even with all the dependents they'd be taking.

"Lot of these folks are going to have to walk," her dad observed. The housekeeping staff had refused to let her help pack her own things. They had, quite sensibly, pointed out that the dottoressa should be overseeing, and if she was packing, then Gavriella and Maria were unable to take over the being-the-boss part.

"I don't see any alternative," she said. "None of them want to take the chance of staying in Rome, and they all figure we're a better bet for getting out of Dodge than just setting out and walking."

"It's going to slow us down, some," her dad had said. "Refugee columns aren't ever what you'd call fast-moving."

Sharon nodded. Her dad would know, of course. He almost never spoke about what he'd done and seen in Vietnam, but back up-time Sharon had been able to read a history book as well as anyone. And for this evacuation, they'd have no helicopters. Or motorized transport, even. The three sets of wheeled transport

they had would be just about enough to get a bare
minimum of baggage aboard, the classified stuff and
some supplies for the road. The Marines would have
their horses, but even without any military knowledge
at all, Sharon could see that burdening them with baggage when they might have to fight was a bad idea.
On the plus side, the Marines had two remounts each,
one of which wouldn't be needed for the journey. A
shame to use such pretty animals as pack beasts, but
it would spread the load even further.

Still, most of them would be walking.

"Dottoressa!" It was Carlo, one of the embassy's
resident runners. "You are wanted in the secret room,
please." He dashed off for whatever errand was next
on his list.

She mounted the stairs. Only the three radio guys,
all USE nationals, were allowed in there. Sharon figured it was probably pretty much an open secret by
now that messages came and went through the secret
room, but the local staff seemed to be pretty good
about at least keeping up the fiction that they didn't
know what went on in there.

The downside was that the housekeeping staff
never went in, and while Odo, Matthias and Jurgen
might have started out as apprentice boys from good
homes around Thuringia, they had become geeks with
a vengeance. The place smelt slightly of old socks
and stale toasted cheese—the down-time equivalent
of packet ramen—and until they came up with a new
word for it, "mess" would have to do.

Odo was sitting by the main radio set, a thing
cobbled together from spare parts that Grantville
had had. The electronics industry was primitive and

likely to stay so for years to come. He had earphones on—big, bulky, down-time manufactured things with curved trumpets in place of amplifiers—and was hunched in on himself, eyes screwed shut and plainly listening hard.

Matthias was coiling up the mess of wires and spares that had littered the place, and disassembling the assortment of bits they had been tinkering with when not occupied sending and receiving messages. Jurgen broke off from decanting the huge array of wet-cell batteries that powered the thing. "We think we had an acknowledgment, Your Excellency Mrs. Sanchez," he whispered.

Sharon got a little thrill from hearing that. "Any message?" she asked, whispering in turn.

"We think not." Jurgen shook his head. "This time of day? We might reach Basel, we might not. And maybe Odo was wrong about hearing a reply. And even so, we will do well just to send a code signal."

"Do what you can, but please try to be packed up within the hour," she said. "And don't forget to keep the classified stuff separate so we can burn it if we have to."

"*Kein problem*," Jurgen said, and returned to draining the batteries.

Back downstairs, Ruy was coming back in the front door, pulling off the battered felt hat and tatty old coat he wore for visiting low-life tavernas. She'd made him promise, when he got out of the carriage, that if he ran into Quevedo he would avoid the man. She'd been a little surprised when he'd agreed. "We have an evacuation to organize, wife," he'd growled, "and it is business before pleasure, duty before honor. But when the duty is done, I, Ruy Sanchez de Casador y Ortiz, swear that Francisco de Quevedo y Villega will rue his spoiling of our wedding day. Briefly."

"I'll hold your coat," Tom had added.

"Get in line," her dad had growled.

"Amazed we aren't passing out from the testosterone fumes," Melissa had said, although from her expression one might have thought she was about to grab a rapier and have after Quevedo and Borja herself.

Now, though, Ruy was wiping sweat from his brow and tossing the disguise into a corner, to be abandoned as no longer needed. It had been pretty threadbare today, anyway, as he'd not bothered to change out of his good breeches, which had been plainly visible over the battered boots he normally wore for training sessions.

"Bad," he growled, "and worse."

"The Spanish are already in the city?"

"Not yet," Ruy said, "although if rumor were right they were already firing the Vatican and molesting nuns. No, the one fellow I found who was not panicking had word that the Spanish had overrun Ostia and would be ready to march in the morning. For myself, I think they will attempt a night march, and be here late tomorrow after resting in the small hours. Otherwise, they will not arrive until the day after."

"So we can relax some, then?" Rita asked the question Sharon was already thinking.

"Perhaps," Ruy said. "Although, Your Excellency, there are arguments on each side of the scale."

"Why they pay me the big bucks, I reckon," Sharon said. "How far away is Ostia?"

"Fifteen, sixteen miles," Tom said. "I was here on vacation one time, back-when."

"A long day's march for any sizeable body of troops," Ruy said. "Let us presume that the man ordered to this folly is competent. More than likely an Italian, and it never pays to assume they do not know their trade as soldiers. He will allow two days for the movement, and if he has even the ordinary ration of *cojones* he will be beginning the march now with plans to march into the evening and begin early in the morning. We should not count on being able to depart safely for more than an hour past dawn on the morrow."

"We'll have to chance it." Sharon looked around her and casting her mind back to the scene of harried bustle and near-chaos that Ruy had missed out on. "We need more time to organize, damn it. We're picking up dependents every minute, it's already more than just the USE nationals taking it on the lam. Tom, go tell the guys upstairs to hold off on packing, they'll be able to send a message tonight. Melissa, calm the housekeepers down a little. I'll get with Adolf and revise the plans. Ruy, take charge of the Marines while Captain Taggart is gone and if anyone sees my dad tell him to take a moment to be sure he's happy with his traveling medical bag. If we're cutting it a little finer, we might be seeing wounded on our way out and we should at least be able to help if we get time. And we need to send someone over to Frank's Place. If he's not planning to leave, he damn well should be."

Everyone moved at once. And, while it was good to be the boss, Sharon decided she could wish it wasn't of a grade-A mess like this.

Chapter 30

Rome

"Your Holiness." Barberini presented himself, feeling again, despite the utter chaos he had come through to be here, like a naughty schoolboy summoned before a master for punishment.

"I trust," said His Holiness, "that you have made arrangements for our people at the *palazzo* to flee the city?"

Barberini caught the difference in inflection of that possessive determiner. His uncle was not speaking as Pope Urban VIII, but as the senior man of *Casa Barberini*. "Your Holiness, I have. Plans were in hand as much as two weeks ago, Your Holiness. I have given the order to prepare. Shall I give the order to flee? My elder brother will be leading an advance party in the morning come what may."

"You shall, my good nephew, you shall. I shall have to remain, of course. This will end badly, I have no doubt, but what chance there is of saving anything only remains while I am in Rome." His Holiness seemed serene as he spoke the words. "I shall withdraw to

Castel Sant'Angelo. It has resisted sack before, and will perhaps do so again."

Barberini looked his uncle squarely in the face. "Sooner, please, Uncle, rather than later, if only for the sake of your nephew's regard for you. Have we word of when the Spanish army will arrive? And in what numbers?"

A man in soldiers' apparel, someone Barberini vaguely recognized as a distant relation, said, "Twenty-five ships are reported at Ostia. As many as ten thousand soldiers, all or nearly all foot. We are not certain of those numbers; we have only one dispatch. We have no word of whether they have captured the guns at Ostia, or how they overran the garrison there. Treachery has been spoken of."

"Quevedo has not been sighted in Rome this past week." Those were the first words Vitelleschi had spoken since Barberini had arrived. Indeed, Barberini had barely noticed him until he spoke.

His Holiness drew the inference. "You suspect treachery?"

"Your Holiness finds me transparent," Vitelleschi said.

Barberini was gripped by the hysterical urge to giggle aloud. If there was one thing that Vitelleschi never was, it was transparent. Although, now that he looked hard at the elderly Jesuit, there seemed to be a lugubrious air about the man, replacing his usual icy taciturnity. Vitelleschi had, of course, counseled that what was manifestly happening was so improbable as to be discounted. It seemed that the old adage about the world's greatest swordsman only truly fearing the world's worst had some truth to it.

Barberini had heard the news over luncheon, and

had come close to choking on his food. That Borja could have demanded such an insane action be taken, and that his fantastic wish should be granted, was beyond belief! That the troops in Ostia, who would doubtless now be making ready for the march on Rome, could wreak havoc on a city unprepared for attack was beyond question. That they would kill hundreds, thousands even, doing so, was a certainty. Scarcely more than a hundred years before, Rome had been sacked for eight days by a combined Spanish and German army, with Italian mercenaries. One of the notables of the day had remarked that the Germans had been bad, the Italians worse, and the Spanish worst of all. Barberini could not stop himself from trying to remember who had said it, nor from churning his brain over and over trying to remember the precise Latin. All he could remember, as if he was compelled to repeat it over and over again in the silence of his mind, was *Hispani vero pessimi*, the Spanish were truly the worst.

Vitelleschi was speaking again, not heeding Barberini's frantic attempts to arrest his descent into unmanly panic. Barberini hoped that his condition was not visible, but he could readily imagine a stench of fear rising from him like steam from a winter dungheap. Everyone around him seemed so controlled, so sure, despite the disaster.

". . . and the principal papers of the Society were removed to separate caches in the small hours of this morning. Our agents reported the arrival of the last of Your Holiness' party of cardinals in the late hours of yesterday. Arrangements to evacuate them again are being made, although it grows difficult to find transport suiting their dignity."

His Holiness laughed once, and then smiled in the most sardonic manner Barberini had ever seen on the face of a living man. "Let them choose, then, between dignity and capture."

That confused Barberini. "Capture, Your Holiness? To what end?"

"Whatever that foul Spaniard has in mind. I do not doubt that we will see many martyrs from this business." His Holiness sighed. "Nor is it right to expect it. The governance of the church is more secular than divine, and in time Borja will feel his leash tighten about his throat. Madrid will not let this folly stand."

Barberini realized that he had heard that before. And it had been wrong before. And there was a clear and obvious way in which Borja could present Madrid with a *fait accompli* that none short of the Almighty himself could undo. "Your Holiness is assured of his bodily safety?" he ventured, diffidently.

"As sure as the walls of Castel Sant'Angelo and the prowess of my guard may make me," was the reply, His Holiness' gaze leveled at Barberini. "I hope to continue to be a troublesome priest for some time yet."

Barberini recognized the allusion, and smiled. Even Vitelleschi's pursed and narrow mouth twitched up slightly, at one corner. Did the Spanish government want to make a modern Saint Thomas out of the pope, they had picked the right method for it. For all that, much of the Castel Sant'Angelo had been built in Hadrian's time, little of the purely defensive works were of more recent vintage, and the Swiss Guard was only two hundred men. The Palatine guard would be mustering, but that took time for artisans, tradesmen and shopkeepers to gather their arms and report for duty. Those of them, that was, that did not elect to defend their own homes and places of business.

Any more military help would have to come from the militias, and they were a weak reed at best. Many of those would be neither use nor ornament against formed troops. The rest would simply remain in their homes.

There would be no assistance from any of the few papal troops that remained stationed near Rome. By the time they mustered and marched, the Spanish would be here and about their business. It went without saying that everyone expected there would be a sack. The last one was only just past living memory. There were ways and means of hiding what one had, of that Barberini had no doubt, but by far the simplest method of avoiding the horrors of a soldiery unleashed on a town was to pile belongings on whatever could be found with ·wheels and leave. Or simply carry it. Barberini had seen one family, every member of which from the grandmother to the toddlers had been carrying a bundle, heading north into the Lazio countryside.

The general who had spoken earlier—whatever his name was—had been speaking while Barberini had thus been moping quietly to himself, and was winding up his rather gloomy presentation. Spain had sent perhaps as many as ten thousand troops from Naples, and there were five hundred professional soldiers in Rome to resist them. The remainder of Rome's defense was whatever the citizens managed through their own unaided efforts. And they were fleeing.

Rome's fortifications were, for all practical purposes,

nonexistent. His Holiness had a program of construction in prospect, but very little of the work had been done. Indeed, the scaffolds around Castel Sant'Angelo would have to be brought down overnight lest they provide the Spaniards with ready-made scaling ladders.

Chapter 31

Rome

Frank heard Benito coughing in the dawn mist as he trudged along the street to get a look back at the night's work. He'd seen Piero handing around the handrolled cigarettes that Harry Lefferts had made popular, and had thought about trying to issue a health warning. The tobacco that they got down-time was way, way stronger and harsher than Frank remembered from back up-time. When he'd thought about it, it had seemed hypocritical. He'd been thinking wistfully about having a smoke himself to calm his nerves and settle his stomach.

Just not of tobacco.

He reached the corner of the next block down from the Committee building, about the farthest away you could stand and actually see it, given how crooked the streets were in Rome. If the rumors were right, he was standing about where a Spanish soldier would when he first caught sight of it.

So, he thought, *I've been marching all day. Maybe had to fight a couple of times getting here.* Imagining

being tired wasn't hard. He'd gotten an hour or so's nap
in just now, and it hadn't done him any good at all.
He'd been running himself ragged-assed since yesterday
afternoon. Which meant the footsore and pissed-off
part wasn't exactly tough to get into either.

Oh yeah, he thought, *I'm a jock, too.* He hunched
forward a little and let his arms hang loose. Knuckles
down, to drag on the floor. *Enough method acting,* he
thought, and chuckled to himself.

Right now, the light was in his eyes. The sun wasn't
over the roofline yet, but the sky was bright and the
morning mist that had come up off the river hadn't
burnt away yet. The diffuse and silvery light hurt his
eyes and made details hard to pick out. Later on,
there'd be early summer glare, and maybe smoke. *And
maybe we'll make sure there is smoke,* he thought.
*Bound to be someone who can tend a smudge. Me,
if no one else.* Not that he'd ever thought that the
gardening he'd picked up from his dad would find a
use in this kind of situation.

He closed his eyes, counted slowly to ten, and
then opened them and tried to make himself really
see what was in front of him. He'd tried to remember what the place had looked like when they'd first
moved in, all those months ago. They'd done a lot.
Frank couldn't remember sleeping much in those first
weeks, could remember spending money like water
and having workmen in every day. And with enough
hands the work had gone fast and come in less than
they'd guessed at.

Then we wrecked most of it in one night, he thought.
Looking at the facade of the building he could see
that they hadn't wasted their time. The yard gate

was nailed shut, a couple of baulks on the outside
for show and a much stronger reinforcement on the
inside. The windows had had all the outside shutters
replaced with boards nailed over them, and most of
the glass smashed. Soot had been smeared everywhere
they could reach—leaving Benito and a couple of guys
he'd gotten to help under firm orders from Giovanna
to get washed. Like chimney sweeps. Although that
was a real job here and now, even though the sight
of one walking down the street made Frank start
humming songs from *Mary Poppins*. The door was
ready to be nailed shut as well.

Inside, most of the stock had been hidden on the
still-mostly-derelict upper floors, and Dino had thought
for about two minutes about how to keep the Spanish from looting the booze and then ripped out the
staircase. It had taken him the best part of an hour
with a prybar and provided a lot of the scrap timber
for the frontage.

Basically, the place didn't look like it was worth looting at all, and inside they'd find pretty much nothing
where they could get at it easily. There were plenty of
more tempting targets, even if the soldiers strayed into
this neighborhood despite richer pickings elsewhere.
Hell, even after they'd vandalized it, Frank's Place was
still in better shape than most of the places around
it. A quarter of them were derelict for real.

Doing it had been the toughest call Frank had had
to make. The easy choice, the obvious choice, was
to take it on the lam and hide out in the sticks for
a week or so. That wouldn't have been hard. It was
what he'd meant to get everyone organized on when
he started back from Sharon's wedding, refusing to run

and strolling along with Giovanna on his arm and the rest of the guys trailing after him, taking their cue from him and chatting as they ambled along.

Probably no one had noticed, but Frank at least figured that anyone who looked would see the revolutionaries fearing nothing while the nobility scurried. When he'd gotten back, though, the reaction of the neighborhood had been weird. Benito and Roberto had been left minding the store, and they were swamped. The place was packed. Well, not packed, but definitely full. It wouldn't have surprised Frank to have everyone go quiet when he walked in and look at him expectantly.

They didn't. It took Frank a while to get around everyone who was there and figure out what was going on, but it boiled down to a fairly simple notion: these were the people who weren't leaving. A few, because it was sheer defiance. *Leave on account of a few fucking Spaniards? No way!*

For the rest, they simply couldn't leave. Or had no reason to. And they wanted to get together somewhere and try to stay safe. Frank would be the first to admit that he was far from being a highly experienced political organizer, but even he could see that bugging out right now would pretty much doom the Committee in Rome, and harm it everywhere else in Italy.

A straightforward defense—and some of the folks in there were already well into the wine and talking about barricades—would have been suicide, however. Frank had, precisely once, seen the results of a real battle up close, when he'd been running about as a medical orderly after the battle of Badenburg. And had seen that what it took to stop a tercio was a whole bunch of guys with rifles and a machine gun. And even then, from what he'd heard, they'd sucked it up and kept coming. The amount of firepower they had at the Committee was two pistols, the shotgun, a revolver and whatever collection of rusty antiques the neighborhood managed to turn up. Likely nothing. A decent pistol was pretty much no use at all in a street fight and could be sold for at least a week's food for a family. Or a couple of days' drinking, depending on who was doing the selling.

So a stand-up fight was out of the question. Some of the older folks in the neighborhood remembered stories their grandparents had told them about the last sack of Rome. Also by the Spanish, as it turned out, although that time they'd had Germans along to help. The town was going to be sacked, no question. Anything not nailed down was going to be stolen, because that was how soldiers got paid. And once the soldiers got good and drunk, or right away if they'd had to fight hard to get in and they were good and mad, the nasty stuff would start.

Rape, said a little voice in the back of Frank's mind. He'd tried, in the wee small hours of the morning, to persuade Giovanna to take some of the women and kids over to the embassy, to leave with the convoy they'd be getting ready to roll with right about now. He winced at the memory. They'd fought before. Blazing rows, fit to loosen plaster three streets away. In a way, those rows were kind of nice, they cleared the air. And often the prelude to some excellent make-up sex.

So having Giovanna ream him out in a low, sneering monotone had been pretty awful. She was, in some ways, a stereotypical Italian girl, raised to be feisty. Hot tempered. She'd defer to her husband, but would make sure her input into his decisions had been fully and clearly registered beforehand. This time, though, she'd come off as genuinely offended that he'd even considered the possibility. The idea of sending people to live on the charity of the USE embassy had pushed the Revolution Button.

He'd given ground as gracefully as he could, which wasn't very gracefully at all. The best he'd been able to manage was a promise that she'd stay on one of the upper floors, throwing firebombs if they had to defend themselves.

Would it come to that? Frank looked at the building again. Hopefully not. It looked like it had before they moved in, just another dilapidated wreck of a place, nothing valuable inside. Hopefully the Spaniards wouldn't get so stuck for billets that they'd try to move soldiers in. Hopefully they wouldn't just torch the entire neighborhood. Hopefully they'd stick with attacking the Vatican and Castel Sant'Angelo and the rich folks' houses, where the good pickings were.

Hopefully.

Frank was finding it hard to hold on to his hopes after a night without sleep.

A figure walking through the mist, silhouetted against the light that scattered from the eastern sky, resolved into Piero. "Does it look good?" the *lefferto* asked.

"See for yourself," Frank said, gesturing back up the street.

Piero gave it an appraising look. "Much the same as the other buildings around here. Which is to say, a shithole. I would not want to loot it. A Spaniard?

They say they would steal dogshit from the gutter, but there are better pickings in Rome. My own family's place, for one."

"Why aren't you there?" Frank asked. "Not that I'm not grateful you're helping, but won't your folks need the help?"

"I won't discount stupidity, Frank," Piero said, shrugging. "Truth be told, I asked myself what Harry would have done. I think here is where he would choose to be."

"True," Frank said, guessing as much as Piero was doing. He'd not really known Harry—the guy was a good few years older than him and had left high school just as Frank was starting.

"And," Piero went on, "my folks can afford a fast carriage and armed riders to remove my mother and sisters and the real valuables to safety. For the rest, a few barrels of wine on the ground floor will likely satisfy the Spaniards. Our real wealth is in land and buildings, Frank, which cannot readily be stolen. There will be some breakage, and my father will complain loudly about the loss, but my allowance will not dry up nor anyone who depends even on a *casa* as modest as my own go hungry."

"Still, they're family," Frank said, probing. "Surely they could use—"

Piero wagged a finger. "Yes, but there I make little difference, as one more guard among many. At worst, we lose a fraction and it is already well guarded. Here? These people came to you for the protection of everything they have. If they lose, they lose everything."

"Well, I can't fault your logic, and I'm grateful

as all get-out for you acting on it. Wish I could be certain I'd be as good as that in a pinch."

"You are, Frank," Piero said. "You could have left. I heard what that runner from the embassy said. Although you have a reputation as a tireless champion of the people to uphold. Me, I am a ruffian and a layabout and a philanderer. If word should get about that I engaged in—" he shuddered theatrically—"*altruism*, why, I should be *ruined*."

"My lips are sealed," Frank said, chuckling, "I'll tell everyone a jealous husband hit you over the head with a bottle while you were dead drunk, and your brains were scrambled."

"True," Piero said, grinning back. "Why, I hardly know what day it is. How many fingers am I holding up?"

"One," Frank said, dryly.

"See? I had to ask for help even with that. Must remember that gesture. If the Spaniards spot us, I shall need it again."

It was less than an hour before Ruy turned up. "I see you hope to hide, Frank," he said, dispensing with the pleasantries. His face was stern, and the effect over the rough traveling gear he was wearing in place of his usual peacock finery was more than a little scary. No one would think he was anything but a tough customer any other time, but dressed for a fight, he looked like a battle waiting to happen. The elegant rapier had been replaced with a much heavier weapon, he had a pair of down-time-made revolvers thrust through his waist-sash, two knives in each boot-top, and metal reinforcements glinted from the gauntlets he had tucked in his sword belt. There was also a small arsenal of lethal hardware neatly stowed around his horse's saddle.

He paused to look around the place. "Most sensible. I think that if it comes to a sack, you will likely be overlooked." Another fierce glare at the preparations still under way. "And your defensive works, within the limits you are under, are also practical and sensible. If misfortune should strike, you will buy time for many to escape. You have made preparations in the cellar?"

Frank nodded. "And we've cut through to the place out back and either side. It's vacant, mostly falling down inside. We can get out that way if we have to."

"Good," Ruy said. "More sensible still would be to bring your people out of the city. We aim to make a temporary place of safety, a refugee camp, on the outskirts of the city. You should come there, Frank. The army is a few hours away, if their commander knows his trade, but in that time you may cover far more distance than a marching army can." Something on his face seemed to have trouble with the words.

"I know it's sensible, Ruy. And believe me, I've tried to figure a way to get people out. It's just not something we can do." Which wasn't quite true. If it was just a case of finding enough handcarts and such to carry those who couldn't walk, and enough provisions, Frank reckoned he could probably organize a pretty fair refugee column. And an army that had to cover every mile on foot or horseback, and had to *work* to kill people, wasn't going to be massacring refugees. And they had enough people to make sure they wouldn't be casually robbed. The problem wasn't practical. It was that if he ran now, the Committee in Rome was *finished*. And, come right to it, Frank would have to spend the rest of his life not liking himself a whole lot.

Ruy nodded in turn. "I understand. Honor and duty compel you, just as duty compels that I should obey the order to ask. Your wife?"

Frank couldn't help rolling his eyes heavenward. "She feels the same way. Won't go. I tried."

Ruy's face was somber for a moment. Reflective even, seemingly lost in memory for a moment. "The best ones are ever thus, Frank," he said, and Frank wondered, for a moment, what story lay behind that remark. Ruy, in a sure sign that he was minded for serious business today, didn't go on to tell it. Or launch into some improbable—and hilarious—fiction.

Still, Frank had managed to find a few minutes to be ready for this. "Can I ask a favor, Ruy?"

"I am at your service to whatever extent my duties permit, Frank," he said. And not the usual flowery declamation of his public persona, either.

Frank realized that he'd just heard a man lay down his name's word on something, and mean it. That was good. He pulled out a small bundle of letters, scribbled on mismatched bits of paper, hastily sealed with candlewax and tied up with string. "I think we're probably going to be okay," he said, "but if things go badly wrong . . ."

Ruy nodded, and took the packet. "I will see your letters delivered. I shall return to the embassy now; our own convoy will be ready to leave soon. We are heading east into the countryside; there are villages there where we can find shelter and a defensible position until Rome is once more secure. I wish you good fortune, and a long life, Frank."

After that, there was little to do save wait.

Chapter 32

The countryside, near Rome

The heat of the Lazio countryside in late May was, after Naples and the never-sufficiently-damned ships he'd ridden here on, actually quite congenial. Captain Don Vincente Jose-Maria Castro y Papas was entirely used to hot summers, being from Andalusia.

He was still glad of the cool breeze and the thin cloud that granted a little shade, though it was small enough compensation for what was probably the most insane military operation of his life.

Insane, in its overall dimensions, he suspected—and certainly so, in the specific one to which he'd been assigned. No sooner had he and his men gotten ashore at Ostia, than an agent working for Cardinal Borja had accosted him. Quevedo, his name was. Don Vincente was not acquainted with the man personally, but he knew of him. More to the point, he knew that Quevedo spoke for the cardinal—and that this whole operation was being done at Borja's instigation and under his orders.

So, when Quevedo told him that there was special work for a small company—and, alas, his had been chosen—Don Vincente had not been able to refuse. He tried to find what little consolation there was in Quevedo's assurance that the work would bring an extra stipend, and first chance at the loot. Whatever "loot" might mean, in this case, which was probably very little.

Quevedo had also assured Don Vincente, with an air of great self-satisfaction, that there would be no questions asked or answered. As if the agent's attempts at secrecy meant anything! The real business they were about—twenty shiploads of mercenaries, no less—was an open secret. Cardinal Borja had been seen about Ostia throughout the day, once the fort had fallen, or been sold, depending on the version you preferred.

Not having any choice in the matter, Don Vincente and his company had pressed through the night on horses the cardinal's agent had had waiting for them when they got off the boat. There was a list of churchmen who had to be captured or killed. Preferably captured, but killed if it looked like they might escape. There was a party of men assigned to each name on the list and Quevedo had added a pair of local guides to each party.

Guides, Don Vincente thought, who might be able to guide a fellow to a dockside whorehouse but that was about it. Paid killers, every one, and not the genteel kind, either. The kind of men you sent along to make sure of the result after a platoon of soldiers had done the hard work.

These prelates, though, Quevedo was chasing personally: two of the pope's own relatives, Cardinals Francesco and Antonio Barberini. He'd shared the hard night's ride from Ostia. He'd had informants with fresh horses for Don Vincente's troops ready to let them know that the target was heading out of Rome already.

They'd missed Francesco, apparently, by less than an hour. Antonio, the younger Cardinal Barberini, had stayed behind in Rome for some unknown reason. The cardinal's agent thought about it for maybe half a minute, and led most of Don Vincente's troop in hot pursuit of Cardinal Francesco.

Hence Don Vincente being glad of the breeze. Somehow the heat was harder to bear, the sweat stickier and the saddle made a man's ass sorer when he hadn't had enough sleep. His mouth tasted foul, his clothes clung everywhere it was uncomfortable for them to cling and his teeth itched, of all things. And he was missing the first pick at the plunder he'd been promised for this fool chase across Rome's hinterland.

Now they could see another group of refugees on the road ahead. The first few they'd overtaken had been commoners, minor merchants and the like. No cardinals with them. Besides, unless Barberini was dawdling, he was likely farther along the road than this. But not too much farther. He surely wasn't simply riding down anyone who got in his way, as Quevedo was ordering. Twice, now, Don Vincente had been ordered to have his men clear the road with leveled carbines. Delays, but not as bad as if they'd detoured into the fields or tried to get through the parties of refugees without moving them aside. Four carts they'd driven into the roadside ditches were behind them now. Ahead, a plume of dust maybe a mile away. Don Vincente thought again of the loot he was missing back in Rome for this escapade. The extra pay had better be worth it.

They were in luck. Or so Don Vincente hoped. No one not seriously important had guards who were watching the back trail and who dismounted for a rearguard action.

"Loot in those carts," Quevedo growled. The man was middle-aged and carried himself like nobility, for all he reeked of strong drink. The weapons were expensive, even if the clothes were nondescript campaigning gear.

"Good," Don Vincente said, and rose in his stirrups to turn and address his men. "Hear that? This one's rich. He'll have his strongbox with him. Good pickings."

There was a growl of assent from the men. They, too, had been brooding on the plunder they were missing. There would be fortunes won this day in Rome, and every hour they were on the road outside the city the slimmer their chances were of getting their slice.

Don Vincente tried to get a count of the men facing them as they rode closer. A dozen, no more. Good. They'd brought forty-five, and these poor bastards ahead had had no time to manage even the hastiest of fortifications. Some of them had muskets, the old heavy kind, and were dismounted, taking aim over their saddles. Four muskets wouldn't matter worth a damn. The rest were still mounted and drawing swords.

"They'll not stand!" he yelled. "Horse-holders, Sergeant." Don Vincente himself could fight mounted, but he was probably the only one who could do so reliably. The rest of his men were musketeers, and only dragoons when need be. Fortunately, the new short muskets—carbines, they were called, a French innovation—were going down well, and getting them off their horses and shooting was the best option.

"They will escape," Quevedo said, but his tone made it a question.

Don Vincente silently thanked God and all his angels and saints for the minor miracle of a reasonable cardinal's agent. "I can put all forty muskets across this road in two ranks. Or I can charge six horse against twelve. Faster this way. More haste, less speed, yes?"

Quevedo nodded. "All possible speed, if you please," he said, and reined in as they came to a hundred yards.

Not wishing to waste the gift of the rationality of this man who accompanied them in the stead of their paymaster, Don Vincente sacrificed pretty drill and good order to get the men lined up. Only thirty-five, by the time all the horses were being held, but two well-dressed ranks that hardly wavered at all as his sergeants moved them forward. Cardinal Barberini's guard seemed pretty well schooled in what they were doing. Don Vincente peered to see if he recognized anyone. If they were contractors rather than household troops, he might know—but the moment was upon him.

"Halt," he said, idly flicking his sword side to side. He was conscious that this was highly irregular, but then he was away from anything he could have called a proper battle formation. He'd heard the Swedes were doing something like this with extended lines and many more muskets than pike. Doing it like this, with hardly any melee weapons at all—the sergeants' poleaxes, and the musketeers' knives and a few swords—was sheerest suicide on a real battlefield. But a stout volley before mixing in would make the odds even more favorable. And he was being paid to win, not piss about.

The cardinal's rearguard was looking more and more like household troops, now, and good ones. The sensible thing to do at this point was for them to run, for they had made Don Vincente's men dismount and bought time for their charge to get farther away. But they were going to buy every minute more they could. Don Vincente stared at the four musketeers opposing him, willing them to fire and get it over with. Four men, if they were lucky, at this range. Were they going to—?

Don Vincente couldn't keep himself from flinching as the ragged, four-shot volley came. He heard a grunt of pain, and felt his hat fly off. He could pick it up later. The man beside him was clutching at his belly with the hand that wasn't holding his musket. "Front rank, kneel!" he called out, and the sergeants repeated the command. A swift glance to see that all was ready, and then the guards ahead that remained mounted spurred forward, lowering their swords.

"Fire!" Don Vincente tried to bellow the command, half-swallowing the word in his surprise, and then "Fire!" again, this time with feeling. The volley was ragged, but at twenty paces, not a single horse and only two of the guardsmen were unhurt. "Forward!" he yelled, and the rest was a foregone conclusion.

For a wonder, the guards stood their ground. In some cases, they had no choice, and Don Vincente noted with approval that his men were granting them grace without needing an order. The rest were cut down where they stood, or knelt, or lay.

"We must be swift," Quevedo said, as Don Vincente's men finished their hurried searches of the bodies for any small valuables. Again, they were quick, being all seasoned professionals.

"As you command, signor." Don Vincente got his sergeants about the business of remounting the men. The cardinal had gained perhaps five minutes on him, and was almost out of sight over a low rise in the middle distance.

"At the canter, please," Quevedo said.

The cardinal's men used their lead well. By the time Don Vincente and Quevedo caught them, they had found, occupied, and hastily forted-up in a small house by the wayside. Don Vincente detailed two men to climb a tree and make sure that the cardinal was not escaping while this defense caught their attention. The man's mule was in evidence, but if he had abandoned it and escaped on foot he might make his escape without raising too much of a telltale dust cloud.

The men reported no sign of a fugitive cardinal anywhere in the vicinity, and the land was flat enough that Don Vincente felt he could take it as good coin. "We have no grenades," he remarked to Quevedo.

"Unfortunate," he agreed. "A direct assault, if you please."

Don Vincente grunted his assent, although he was none too happy about it. He examined the building carefully. Two, perhaps three rooms inside. No upper floor, nor rooftop that a man might stand on. A tiled

roof, pitched. Windows on all four sides and a door
to the roadside and the rear. A fenced-off yard with
a dung heap and chickens, low stone walls on two
sides. An ordinary house, of the more prosperous
sort of peasant. The like could be seen the length
and breadth of Italy.

"Smoke, signor?" Sergeant Ezquerra asked.

"Good idea; see to it." It would have to do. There
wasn't much to make a fire with, although there was
a modest stack of firewood under the eaves of the
house. Firing that would be a challenge if there were
many firearms within the building—as he watched he
could see a loophole appearing in one wall—but it
might serve, with enough brush thrown on it, to raise
enough smoke to force the defenders out. There were
certainly no better options. He left Sergeant Ezquerra
to it, watching from the back of his horse. The animal
seemed to be holding up quite well, despite their
having pressed the pace all morning. It was a little
past noon, now, and if watered and allowed to cool
down the horses ought to be good for the ride back,
barring mishaps.

As he watched, he saw his men encircle the farmhouse, a little beyond effective musket range. That
didn't stop the defenders from trying their luck, and
there was soon a thin haze of gunsmoke around the
place. It was too much to hope that the wadding
would fire the woodpile, Don Vincente supposed,
and then he was surprised by the sight of a lit torch
being thrown over the stone wall. The sergeant had
clearly spotted a covered route up to the house. Don
Vincente made a note to commend Ezquerra and see
he got a bonus. Small bags of powder followed the

torch, loosely tied so they scattered over the woodpile. It was not long before there was a blaze, and loosely tied bundles of green brush were coming over the wall. Don Vincente's eyes began to sting, and he realized he had taken position downwind of the farmhouse without thinking. Chiding himself, he moved around to where Quevedo was watching.

"A good man, that sergeant," Quevedo remarked.

"Indeed," Don Vincente said. "This was well done."

"True. I think the cardinal will come out soon."

It was no more than a few minutes before a white scarf tied on a rake came through the front door. "Parley!" Don Vincente called, urging his horse closer and doing his best to soothe her against the smell of the fire. "Come out if you surrender!" he added.

That was enough. There was a rapid exodus from the farmhouse, and Don Vincente noticed that there was smoke coming out all around the eaves. The roof timbers must have been set afire by the sergeant's blaze. Another five minutes saw the cardinal's men rounded up, and the cardinal himself under guard.

"Release the servants," Quevedo said. "Take their horses and weapons. They will be no threat. We return this one"—he pointed with his chin at Cardinal Francesco Barberini—"back to Rome."

Don Vincente nodded. That was a relief. He had been wondering how they would shepherd twenty prisoners to Rome.

The looting was quick and efficient. The valuables were quickly sorted onto two horses for later division. The remaining horses were burdened with the weapons and armor, all of which could be kept for issue or sold, if no better loot presented itself. The cardinal's servants knelt, eyes downcast, in the road while this was going on, each man with a musketeer to guard him. In the background, the farmhouse blazed merrily now, adding to the discomforts of fatigue and the heat of the day. Don Vincente began to wish he had ordered the captives moved farther away.

Still, they were not there long. The company moved off back to Rome at a much gentler trot than they had left at, Francesco Barberini in the middle of the column with Don Vincente and Quevedo directly behind him. The cardinal had said nothing while his hands were bound and he was boosted onto the back of his mule, and maintained a dignified silence as they rode back to Rome. Doubtless the Inquisition would be causing him to be less taciturn before too long. Which, Don Vincente reflected, was very much not his problem.

Don Vincente noticed that Quevedo kept checking the road behind. After perhaps an hour, he seemed satisfied with something, and drew his sword.

"The cardinal is trying to escape," he said, in a conversational tone, and spurred forward suddenly. The sword swung in a fast and humming arc, the economical and effortless motion of a master swordsman, and bit deep into the back of the cardinal's neck.

"Have your men get that off the road, if you please, Captain," Quevedo said, nodding at the corpse as he cleaned his blade. Barberini lay face down, his ass in the air, all dignity gone as he bled out into the dust. His legs twitched slightly as he died, and Don Vincente noticed that the impact of the sword had caused the cardinal to bite his tongue half off, and it hung at a peculiar angle from between the teeth.

Don Vincente began wondering what the hell this was all about.

Something must have shown in his expression. Quevedo smiled thinly and said: "You are Spanish yourself, Captain, so you should be glad these orders have been given."

Don Vincente wondered through a fatigue-fogged brain what the hell the fact that he was Spanish had to do with anything. Right here, right now, he had thought he was working for Spain's viceroy in Naples, who had ordered him and a large number of other troops to follow the orders of Cardinal Borja.

Don Vincente frowned. Whatever Quevedo was driving at, he couldn't see it. He nodded, out of politeness, and gave the orders to have the body dumped in the ditch. The cardinal had already been thoroughly robbed when he had been captured, so this took no time at all.

"Speak to no one of what you have seen!" Quevedo called out, addressing the men. "The extra pay for this day's work is in part for your silence."

Don Vincente saw a few eyes roll heavenward at that. Had Quevedo said nothing, most of them wouldn't have bothered mentioning it to anyone. One dead priest more or less was nothing to them, when there was an entire city to loot.

"And now, Captain," the agent said, "I have another special mission for you. In Rome."

Seeing Don Vincente's sour expression—"special mission" was sure to translate into "no or very little loot"—the cardinal's man chuckled. "There will be extra pay, of course."

Chapter 33

Rome

The evacuation was rapidly turning into a small slice of hell for Sharon. It was beginning to look like just loading the carriages yesterday and getting while the getting was good would have been the best plan.

Right now, there was a small crowd of would-be evacuees catching a few hours sleep, wrapped in blankets in the embassy ballroom. The carriages and the three carts that the Marines had managed to acquire—Sharon decided she really didn't need to know where or how, although they had spent money to get them—were standing idle. The plans to retain remounts for their cavalrymen had pretty much gone up in smoke. There was a pack made up for every horse that was not carrying an armed man. It would take more than a couple of hours to get everything moving again after Sharon had decided, shortly after midnight, that everyone that could should get some rest before they moved out.

This, on top of learning that Frank had decided to stay, and more than likely make some kind of Heroic

Last Stand. Ruy had ventured the opinion that if Frank felt his honor and duty called him to it, it would be wrong to argue with him about it. Late last night, when word came back, Sharon had been in no mood or condition to debate the point. Frank might have decided on the life of a subversive, and good luck to him, but Sharon was keenly aware that Stoner, his dad, and Magda, his stepmom, were two of her best friends in the world. The last thing Sharon wanted to have to do was send a "deeply regret" letter to either of them. Worse, have to explain to them that he'd stayed in a city about to be invaded because she'd not personally gone down there and dragged him and his wife out.

It had been the first fight she and Ruy had had as a married couple. The mayhem that was the embassy had gotten on her nerves, she'd been tired, she was royally pissed off that this had had to happen on her *fucking wedding day* and she'd given Ruy both barrels. He'd been visibly hurt, and she'd regretted it instantly. The thing was, she wasn't sure how to go about making it up. She'd apologized, explained that she was stressed over the evacuation and upset by Frank's decision and what it might cost her, and Ruy had been all care and consideration after that.

With a reservation. "Sharon, my heart," he'd said, "I, too, am saddened that Frank may not survive these next few days. But I will not regret—*not for one instant*—that he has chosen to fulfill the demands of his honor. Without such as he, this new world whose birth you seek to bring about will never come to be."

Hate it though she did, she knew he was right. "Go in the morning," she'd said, "and if he still thinks he can hold on there, at least see if he'll evacuate the women and kids with us. Pregnant women in particular."

And so Ruy was away in the first few moments of quiet that Sharon had had since walking out of the church yesterday. Right when Sharon needed a strong arm to lean on—

"I'd ask if you were okay, honey," came her father's voice from behind her, "but right now I think that would be the dumbest possible question I could ask."

She felt her mouth twitch a little. She almost, but didn't quite, have the energy to smile at the little joke. "I can't escape the feeling that we're all screwed anyway," she said.

"Evacuations are always bad. I was already back home and in college when Saigon fell, but I saw plenty of refugees trying to get out. You saw what they looked like when they got to Grantville, back in the early days—"

"Hell."

"Like hell, yes. Think about what it takes to get people in that kind of condition. Unless we're good and lucky, that's what we're about to go through." Her dad's voice didn't have any of its accustomed warm humor. If anything, it sounded like the tone he had in the operating room, doing trauma work. Describing the injuries in detail to his support team, so they would know what to expect from the coming work. A tone of voice for describing flesh torn, bones broken, and blood leaking away. Or, for the optimistic, a voice enumerating the things that had to be done to save another life. Businesslike or dispassionate, take your pick.

It was a callousness Sharon hadn't yet acquired. She knew her own operating manner was a lot more involved. Which was showing in the way she was handling this godawful mess.

Her dad put his arms around her. "You'll be okay, princess. You're doing fine. Better at this kind of thing than pretty much anyone I know. So long as we start before they get here, we'll be okay. You heard the report, no cavalry worth talking about. So long as we move quicker than guys who keep stopping to loot, we'll be fine. Other than that, it's bandits, and between the Marines and everyone else here who's got a gun, those are going to be some mighty sorry bandits if they try anything."

Sharon chuckled. "Daddy's going to keep me safe," she said, in a little girl's singsong voice.

"Heh. Daddy's going to kick back and let that fiery young Catalan feller do all the hard work."

"Young?" Sharon turned and smiled at him.

"Young. Man's at least two years younger'n I am—maybe even as much as five—and has the attitudes of a teenager to boot. Not like my own august and reserved demeanor, at all." He puffed up his chest and thumbed a lapel.

"Hooey," came Melissa's voice. Sharon was starting to think of the former schoolteacher as her stepmother, in a way she'd never really expected to. She and Melissa had become friends before Melissa had moved in with her dad, and she'd thought the relationship would stay on that basis. She'd thoroughly approved of her getting together with her father, of course. Mom had been Mom, and couldn't ever be replaced, but it was just plain *right* that Dad should be happy again.

That it was her friend Melissa, her best friend's old history teacher, was just a happy bonus.

"Really? My dad's claim to be respectable is all just a front?" Sharon caught the ball and ran with it, "Who'd a' thunk it?"

"Really. I woke this morning to the sight of him cleaning his pistol. And him a doctor as well."

"Nothing wrong with drumming up a little trade in a righteous cause," he protested.

"Leave it to the young men, you ageing juvenile," Melissa said. "They've got the energy for it."

"Oh, I've not got the energy, have I? That wasn't what you said—"

"Dad!" Adult or not, there were some things Sharon really didn't need to know about. Not, at least, in any detail.

Melissa's heavenward roll of the eyes was all the agreement anyone could want from that quarter. "Are things getting moving yet?" she asked.

"Soon." Sharon hadn't been the only one to remain awake all night. Adolf had kept watch too, and she'd found him just beginning to rouse his people to get the evacuees marshaled. "We'll be a couple of hours after dawn, I think. We have to get the horses loaded up again, breakfast for everyone, and then hit the road. Normally, that's an hour, tops, but here . . ."

"But everything becomes simple, and the simple becomes difficult," Melissa said. "As an old warmonger once observed. I think it'll be midmorning before we finally get moving, myself."

"Still plenty of time, though," Sharon said. "The Spanish were in Ostia yesterday afternoon. They simply can't be here before noon."

Melissa frowned. "I don't want to suggest that they're superhuman or anything, but is there any way they could be here earlier? I think Ruy was assuming that the Spanish commander would rest his troops before marching into town. What if he doesn't?"

"I asked him that," Doctor Nichols said. "He thinks that he's better assuming that we're up against someone with some smarts, and that he'll want his troops reasonably fresh today. Plus, if he tries to push them too hard, they'll just refuse to move. It's not *quite* that following orders is an optional extra for these guys, but it can look that way sometimes. I think I'll take Ruy's judgment on that one."

"Still, perhaps we could get at least some of our people on the road quickly?" Melissa asked. "I find myself thinking that there are a lot of children coming with us, and giving them as much of a head start as we can might be . . ." She let the suggestion hang in the air.

Sharon decided it was a good one. "If we can, Melissa, would you take charge of that convoy? I'll get with Captain Taggart and figure out how best to split the Marines. Having some of us staying until the last minute would be a good idea in any event. There might be people we need to get out who won't be ready to leave until we've got the Spanish breathing down our necks."

Melissa nodded. "Adolf was in the ballroom a few minutes ago, I'll go and find him and we'll get started. Come on, James, the sooner we start—"

Doctor Nichols was holding up his hand. "Actually, Melissa, I'll go with the second party. I'd guess that Captain Taggart is going to want to send most of his Marines with the first group, since they'll have the kids with them and move slowest. If we can, we should confine the stay-behind party to people who can handle a gun and move quickly. And if we're just ahead of the real trouble, I think we're going to need more trained medics with us. If Rita goes with you, she'll be enough medic for the advance group, and Tom can boss the Marines if the good captain stays with us."

Melissa chuckled. "So long as Tom doesn't get all macho and insist on staying with the rearguard."

"No, he won't. Unlike my daughter, who by rights should be going with the lead party, but will insist on standing her post until the last minute. I've got more sense than to try to persuade her otherwise."

Sharon snorted. "Enough. Let's get things moving. It'll be dawn in a few minutes."

They had a convoy of women and children and most of the baggage ready to go within an hour of dawn. The kids were chattering and running about the horses, in some cases still munching on the bread-and-cheese breakfast they had been given. Tom, who in truth had grumbled a little about being sent on, was on foot, having ceded his horse to two pregnant women. "I wish we could get the kids to line up and hold hands," he said, looking about.

Melissa smiled, gently. "It's not something they learn in grade school here. Besides, it'll do the Marines good to have kids to herd while we get outside the city. Keep 'em alert." Sharon had seen her eyes constantly flicking back and forth. The motion looked practiced, and Sharon guessed that Melissa had taken enough field trips in her time that keeping track of dozens of rambunctious youngsters at once had become second nature. Rita was in the middle of a small swarm of children—*where did they all come from? We didn't have this many last night!*—and was comforting a little girl who had already skinned her knee.

Tom had stationed most of the cavalrymen at the back of the column he had formed up in the street outside the embassy, on the theory that they could watch over the kids and herd them back in line if they strayed and their mothers didn't notice. Two of them already had kids riding up with them, which Sharon worried about a little if there was any trouble. Having to put a child down gently could slow them down. Still, the defense of the column had been bolstered by including the menfolk of the embassy staff with cudgels, knives and down-time muskets. They were mostly on foot and would be keeping the kids in line as well. For the time being, though, their attitude seemed to be that if the kids wanted to play, let 'em.

Tom waved it all aside. "Well, we've got what we've got. Anything else is going to have to come out with the rest of you."

"Or be burnt," Sharon said, thinking of the large pile of brushwood, broken-up furniture, classified documents and sprinkled gunpowder that was out back of the embassy awaiting a match to send it up. They were still finding things to go on that pile even now. "Whatever happens, we're not staying past noon."

"See you don't," Tom said, giving Sharon a few watts of his best commanding-officer glare.

With that, he bellowed the order to move out. The kids, to Sharon's surprise, fell into reasonable order quite quickly, and she guessed they would keep up the quick walking pace for quite a while. They didn't have the automobile to make them prone to get bored with a walk of any great length.

Sharon watched them down the street and out of sight as they turned on to the Via Calabria to leave the city by the Porta Salaria. They had a rendezvous point at a village about ten miles away, which they should reach by sundown. The ten people left behind would make better time, of course, and in theory would overtake them on the road. If they didn't, Tom and Rita would have to take their best guess as to what to do. They had the radio crew with them, at least, so they would be able to consult with Magdeburg if they truly had to.

At least most of the people she was responsible for were out of harm's way. Adolf would be pleased that the final clear-up would be done with fifty or sixty fewer bodies underfoot. She was about to turn and go back inside and help when Ruy appeared, trotting his horse around the corner and coming back to the front door.

"Is he coming with us?" Sharon asked, as he dismounted to lead his horse through the arch to the stable.

Ruy sighed. "No, Sharon, he is not. He was not offended that I asked."

"Do you think he'll make it?"

"In truth? With only moderate good fortune, Sharon. He has disguised his tavern to appear derelict, and proposes to hide as many as he may on the upper floors. He has created rear entrances, the women are on upper floors and have pulled the ladders up after them, and I could see nothing left undone in the matter of defenses. Should there be a general sack, he may well escape entirely. In that sense, he is at less risk than we who are evacuating."

"Really?" Sharon felt at least a little relief. If Frank was hiding, that was only a little worse than if he was running. And, surely, looters would not bother with a poor neighborhood. *The Spanish ones won't, at least. And Frank should be able to handle local hooligans. Has before, at any rate.*

She sighed, deeply. "Ruy, I should apologize for my remarks last night. I'm afraid for Frank and Giovanna, truly I am, but I shouldn't have let that make me mad at you."

Ruy didn't trouble to answer that, but simply took hold of her and hugged her, hard, not troubling with who might be watching. Verbose he might be, but when words wouldn't do it, he could say just as much without opening his mouth.

Two hours later, she gathered everyone around her. "Well," she said, "We're ready. Can anyone think of a good reason to wait for—" She was interrupted by the sound of pealing bells, one that rapidly multiplied.

"Early," her dad remarked.

"It may be that a fast horse was posted along the likely approach," Ruy added. "But your assumption is the prudent one. Sharon, we should leave now. We will have something between a half hour and two hours to be clear of the city."

"Let's do it, then," Sharon said. "Are all the horses ready?"

Captain Taggart nodded. "Aye, that they are, mistress."

"Then there's no reason to wait. No, wait. Someone

light the fire. We'll wait to be sure it's going good and hot."

Half an hour later, they were at the Porta Salaria themselves. The structure hardly merited the name it had; the walls on either side were long since derelict and, being nothing more than medieval curtain walls, were not likely to stop a determined attacker for more than perhaps half an hour. Even if Rome had had the troops to man them.

As it was, the gate was simply an arch, in poor repair, with no actual gate in the arch. Off to one side, scaffolding where the modernization work was in its early stages had been left up, so that even if a defense had been mounted, there was a clear route over the wall for soldiers prepared to exert themselves only slightly more than if they had marched through the gate. Sharon had played tourist in her first few weeks, and knew that pretty much every other way into the city was in a similar condition. The gates were customs posts, not serious defensive works.

She looked back. The column of smoke from the fire at the embassy was barely visible. The fire had been burning hot, with little smoke, when they had left, having flared up well. What smoke existed was simply part of the general smudge that covered any city in this day and age. Barely noticeable, in other words. Lighter than usual today, in fact, since so many people had gotten out of town, even if only to sleep rough in the countryside for a few days. And then she saw, to the south, a column of thicker, darker smoke starting to rise, and heard the distant crackle of muskets, volley firing. And the deeper boom of cannon-fire.

"It begins," Ruy said, shading his eyes and peering southward for more clues as to what action was taking place. "It may be that some horse were able to ride ahead of the main body of foot."

"I'm still worried about Frank," she said.

"I will make one final visit, so at least we can be sure that the invaders are truly bypassing Frank's *taverna*."

"That's not safe, surely," Sharon said, realizing as the words came out that that was *precisely* the wrong way to persuade Ruy against anything.

He chuckled. "It is actually perfectly safe," he answered. "A Spaniard, in a city invaded by Spaniards? I can *order* soldiers not to attack me. Indeed, I can ask what their orders are."

Crazy, but it would work. "Make sure you don't get recognized," she said.

"It would be to my advantage if I was recognized," he countered. "I may well have old friends among that army, who will greet me as such and tell me all they can in return for an honest enquiry."

"I guess operational security hasn't been invented yet," Sharon's dad observed. He, too, was peering to the south. Sharon guessed his own days as a soldier were coming back.

Ruy paused a moment, turning the new phrase over in his mind. "No, Doctor Nichols," he said. "We have operational bragging, instead. I intend to take advantage. By your leave, Doctor Ambassador wife of mine?"

"Be careful, Ruy," she said, "and try to make it to the rendezvous by dusk, please."

Chapter 34

Rome

As he watched the citizenry of Rome panic and run
in circles and other geometric forms beyond even
the wit of Pythagoras, Ruy decided that there was
no profit to be made in hurrying about this matter.
A man hurrying, in these streets on this day, was apt
to be considered about military business. One side
would demand of him that he attend to the defense,
and the other that he make himself busy in the attack.
He could, indeed, legitimately claim to be too old to
trouble with either, further that he was not gainfully
employed by either side and in conclusion that he
had duties to a power not party to the conflict, to
wit, his new and most delightful wife. However, the
question was better avoided by simply pretending a
calm disinterest and attracting no attention.

It would, naturally, not do to proceed straight to
the Borgo to visit again with the young Señor Stone.
He had left there scarcely two hours before, by the
watch on his wrist. Consulting the thing, he realized
that removing it and placing it in a pocket would

413

be wise. He would variously have to pass for an out-of-town Italian or a Spaniard unattached to the invading forces. A timepiece not notably available to either group would be a telltale. And, while he was about it, the up-time firearms would have to go into his saddlebags.

The first order of business, then, would be to scout the approach of his countrymen—and the assorted Castilians, Aragonese, Andalusians, Italians, Germans and whatever other mercenaries had rounded out the attacking forces. The obvious approach would have been along the unimaginatively-named Via Ostiensis. Around the city wall would be quicker, but through the city itself would glean more information. He would not have to leave Rome for another few hours, and so through the city seemed the best approach. He urged his horse to a trot. It was a gelding he had selected for characteristics suggesting stamina, but otherwise undistinguished.

Were it not for the cacophony of the bells and the occasional party of persons in a state of panic, it would be a fine morning for a gentle promenade through the city. Indeed, had events not intervened, he would have suggested as much to Sharon. The sun was bright enough for everything to seem clear and fresh, it was too early in the year to be copiously dusty, the thin overcast took much of the fire from the sun without interfering with the blue of the sky overhead, and the streets were quiet as Monday mornings were apt to be.

Twice, as he proceeded through the ancient Palatine, he saw bands of local volunteers erecting barricades. He wished them luck, although doubtless they would need little. A small detachment to ensure that they did not remain loose in the Spanish rear and the main force would simply pass around them to the targets farther on in the city. It was, perhaps, the attackers' intention to cross the river a little downstream of the city proper and approach their more likely targets along the right bank of the Tiber. Much, of course, depended on how well-found for crossing-points the attackers were downstream of the city. Sanchez had not, himself, troubled to reconnoiter the matter, seeing no particular need before today.

It became clear, some few minutes later, that the intent was to use the city's own bridges to procure access to the Vatican across the Tiber. Wishing to use the Via Ostiensis, the advancing army had remained on the left bank and ignored the ferries—time consuming—and ford—likewise—that they had doubtless passed as they marched. Rome itself was much supplied with bridges and the Spanish commander would surely have a realistic appreciation of the pitiful opposition he would face.

Arriving at the Piazza di Porta San Paolo, Sanchez paid himself the small wager he had made. Sitting his horse at the inner side of the piazza, he could see that a group of volunteers, under the direction of what seemed to be a militia officer, was preparing a barricade across the gateway. As with many of the other gates in Rome's walls, it lacked an actual portal in the archway, and the small fortification that guarded it had been built in Caesar's time, from the look of the thing. Sanchez allowed perhaps half an hour for the defense to be reduced using only field pieces, if the opposing commander took a fool notion to do such a thing. Looking through the gate, Sanchez could see a tercio forming up some few hundred paces away. He could also see that the formation was being stuck together in a manner almost random, quite unlike the methodical efficiency practiced by most Italian *condottieri.* He mulled that for a moment. Either improvising in haste, or creating a distraction while the real assault proceeded to one of the many other gaps in Rome's walls. If that were so, then an assault on the defenders' rear would be arriving at any moment. Sanchez removed himself from the main street to a discreet position in a small alleyway.

Not five minutes passed before, indeed, the sound of arquebuses and a brief surge of cheers told of a breach in the walls. Mined for building materials, over the decades, the walls of Rome were as much breach as defense in any event, for all that the current pope had begun many repairs and improvements. They were obviously being carried against minimal opposition.

The defenders at this gate worked on, oblivious. Sanchez wondered if he should warn them, and then reminded himself that he was not involved. He had orders to return safely with intelligence, and would like as not be shot by some nervous boy handling an arquebus for the first time if he ventured closer. So, he waited.

The assault on the defenders' rear, when it came, was short, sharp, and efficient. Sanchez marked their alertness to the militia officer's credit. When the company of pike and arquebusiers formed on the piazza almost exactly where Sanchez had been sitting only moments before, the defenders turned around, snatched up their weapons, and formed a ragged line on the near side of the defenses they had so painstakingly constructed, anchored at one end on a pyramidal tomb that had been incorporated into the wall at some remote date. The Spanish troops—from the look of them, more than likely Italian mercenaries—lowered their pikes and advanced at a fast walk, and halted for the arquebusiers mixed among them to present and fire.

Perhaps twenty pieces discharged, scarcely enough to obscure Sanchez's view of the defenders. Four of them were down, and the rest began to look shaky. Whether any of the defenders had returned fire, and with what effect, was not apparent. The militia officer was waving his back-sword vigorously, and the men nearest him lowered their weapons to countercharge. To either side, however, the men bearing their various aged or improvised pole-arms at the ends of the line began dropping their weapons and running. When the Spanish line advanced at the slow, grim pace of men determined to engage in press of pike, the amateurs simply melted away and the professionals let them. A small knot of defenders remained and, their chances of running lost as the wicked points closed almost to touching, they dropped their weapons and raised their hands.

The leader of the mercenaries called out the command to halt, and the little battle was over. Even from fifty paces away, Sanchez could see that the militia officer was openly weeping, while to either side of him, mercenaries went to dismantle his barricade. Down the Via Ostiensis, the makeshift tercio began breaking up into column of march to advance once more on the city.

As he rode away to secure a vantage to see more of the action develop, Sanchez began to feel hopeful. An army that had not had to bleed to enter a city would not be maddened enough to make serious work of a sack. The city would be comprehensively looted, of course, but in all likelihood the whores and tavern-keepers would earn most of it back over the coming weeks.

"I wish the bells would stop," Benito said, squatting on his heels under one of the windows.

"Me too," Frank said, sitting on a low stool and keeping one eye on the deserted street through a slit in the boards over the window. "I mean, we already know the city's about to be invaded. The only people who don't are deaf. Don't the bellringers have something better to do? Nothing else, all the folks sheltering in churches are getting deafened."

"I'm going deaf and the nearest church is three streets away." Benito was idly whittling at a piece of scrap wood, betraying his bad nerves. Everyone was a little on edge, hardly any of which was due to getting no sleep the night before. In the end, there were twenty guys and twenty-eight women in the place. The women and the disabled folks were all upstairs, and had pulled the ladder up after them through the gap where they'd taken the stairs out. While a lot of folks had gone and sheltered in churches, even Rome didn't have enough church buildings to hold the whole population at once. A lot of people were hiding in cellars or attics, or out of town. The ones in the Committee who'd come and hid were the ones who would likely get grief off respectable folks if they tried sheltering in a church, or who couldn't move very far. Three of the people upstairs were bed-bound, and had had to be carried up.

Downstairs, they had all the doors and windows nailed shut and boarded outside and in, and barricaded. Three rows of barricades, in fact, and with a little luck at least one of the back ways out would be left unguarded. There was a route out through the cellar that came up two doors down the street; with the city under siege Frank had lost his compunctions about knocking cellars through and taking advantage of the centuries-old excavations under the city. He'd wondered if there was any possibility of getting down into the catacombs, which he'd vaguely heard about but never seen. No one had any idea where they might be, or how one got into them, so he'd abandoned the idea. And it was too late now.

There were eight *lefferti* in the place, who'd decided their self-image required that they defend the one tiny oasis of American values that Rome held, or at least the one that they could hang out in regularly. Frank found that kind of funny. The main values his place stood for, looking at it from a practical point of view, were fast food and reasonably priced drinks. All run by a hippie kid from a West Virginia commune. Not *quite* the American Values that the high-school jocks had been so freaking keen on. Still, in his own biased opinion, good ones to stand up for. No one ever invaded a neighboring country to bring them pizza and beer. Maybe if they did, wars would be more civilized affairs.

Although the Geneva Convention would have to be rewritten to forbid anchovies. And Lite beer.

The *lefferti* were, at least, a calming influence at the moment. None of them wanted anyone to think he was anything other than the coolest of cool hands, for which Frank was grateful. They were all playing cards, Harry having introduced the young blades of Rome to the game of poker. The place might be turned upside down with every single exit boarded up, an invading army somewhere in the city outside and a sack about to happen some time in the next few hours, but it was hard to get really worked up when there was a bunch of guys having a quiet card game and sharing a jug or two of wine. Frank wished he hadn't decided that smoke from the chimney couldn't be risked. Firing up the oven and getting a round of pizzas on would be a good idea right now. No one seemed to be objecting to the fact that the provisions were nothing but bread and cheese and onions and cold sausage, but Frank knew that a hot meal would lift everyone's spirits. If they got to nightfall without the Spanish army descending on them, Frank decided, he'd fire up the oven when the darkness would cover the smoke.

For now, Frank was wondering whether it would be the boredom or the tension that would make him wig out first. Or sheer freaking tiredness. His eyelids were stinging, and felt sticky with sweat. There was a coppery taste in his mouth. For some reason, all the muscles up the left side of his back ached. The way his feet felt didn't bear thinking about. He wondered, a little dizzily, if he'd be able to sleep, and then decided that being seen to make the effort would help everyone else's nerves.

"Benito, spell me on watch, will you. I've been up all night."

."Sure." Benito's grin was cheeky and infectious.
"You old guys gotta get your shut-eye."

Frank flipped him the bird as he hauled himself to
his feet. He went over to the bar, grabbed a blanket
from the stack they'd fetched down to use as blackout
if things continued past nightfall, and clambered slowly
up onto the bar. He pillowed his head on the folded
blanket, tugged his cap down over his eyes, and set
himself to the best imitation of a man unconcerned
by events that he could manage.

Shortly, he was pretty certain that Spanish soldiers hadn't installed trapdoors all over the barroom,
and knew that they couldn't spring up like jacks-in-
the-box—or was it jack-in-the-boxes? It was vitally
important that he remember. But he still had to stop
them, but all he had was a big frying pan, from the
kitchens, but he couldn't seem to swing it with any
force and all it made the soldiers do was turn around
for a moment and all the other guys would do was
ask him to keep it down and—

"Frank! Frank! Wake up!" He felt Benito's hand on
his arm, shaking him. He came wide awake with an
electric jolt that left him feeling weak and rubbery
as he half-slid, half-fell off the bar and stood rubber-
legged looking around.

"What's up? What's going on?" he managed, realizing that the thing that had fallen to the floor was
his hat. He bent to pick it up, grunting slightly as his
back unstiffened. "How long was I asleep?"

"Since this morning. It's just after noon."

Frank blinked to clear his eyes and looked around
to get a better idea of what was going on. Everyone
in the room was up close to the windows, peering

through. He looked at Benito, letting his expression ask the question.

"The Spaniards are here," Benito said, in what Frank realized was the loudest whisper he'd heard in a while.

His senses began catching up with what was going on. Somewhere, guns were being fired. A lot of guns. The rattling coughs of arquebuses and other small arms, and occasionally the boom of cannon. There was a general background that sounded like a crowd roar and some yelling. There was fighting in the city, pretty close by. It didn't sound like it was happening right out in the street, though.

"Here?" Frank asked, "Or *right* here?"

"Right here," Benito said, tugging at Frank's sleeve, "out in the street."

Frank cricked his neck a little. Sleeping on the bar, whatever it might have done for morale, had left him more than a bit stiff. He'd likely start aching in a moment, when he managed to wake all the way up. He started to shuffle over to the front, then stopped himself. Best not to look like he was half-dead. He hitched up his pants a little and managed a slightly more purposeful walk.

He found a vacant spot next to Dino, and peered out. After the cool dimness of the barroom, the street was eye-wateringly bright to his just-awakened eyes. He blinked a couple of times to clear them, and looked again. The other side of the street had five, no, six soldiers within his field of view. Four with muskets, leaning against the wall opposite with their weapons grounded, one guy with one of those broad-bladed spear things with the spikes on either side of the blades and one with a sword, who looked like an officer type. They were all looking right across the street at Frank's Place, from maybe seven or eight yards away.

Frank looked away a moment, to murmur, "How long?" to Dino.

"A few minutes. Benito went straight to wake you up."

"Right." Frank looked back. The guy with the spear had moved away. Swiveling his eye around and looking at as much of the street as he could, Frank counted fifteen soldiers. That was along maybe twenty yards of street. This close to the front, the sounds of nearby fighting were a lot louder. If there were other guys moving around out there, Frank realized, no way was he going to track them by the sound of their boots.

And then a couple more guys with guns appeared and joined the ones across the street. They were more of the same, with the almost-in-uniform look to them that the few regular soldiers of the seventeenth century had when they weren't quite elite enough to be wearing some kind of special livery. Frank realized, and it wasn't a comfortable thought, that this meant someone had picked them out for special attention. They weren't just a random group of soldiers looking for easy pickings, a head start on the looting. Mercenaries after stuff to steal wouldn't come in this neighborhood at all, unless they were on the way somewhere else, and this bunch looked like they were here for a purpose. Frank didn't have to think too hard to figure out what that purpose was.

"Benito!" he hissed.

"Frank?" Benito was behind him.

"Get a couple of other guys and check what's going on where our back entrances come out, yeah? And be careful. If they're as smart as they look they might have the whole block covered. Don't get spotted."

"Right." Benito scuttled off.

It took Benito ten minutes and when he came back it wasn't good news, either way. The number of soldiers out front had doubled, at least, and guesses about how many there were ranged up to two hundred. Benito was panting slightly and his eyes were shining. "You were right, Frank, they have the whole block covered. We won't be able to get out by daylight."

Damn right they wouldn't. Even if they figured out a way to sneak out before the shooting started.

Frank figured it was only a matter of time, certainly before dusk, before they had enough soldiers to rush the place. And he had four pregnant women—*including Giovanna!* his little mental voice shrieked at him—and six disabled to think about. Only three of those were bedridden, but the others had at least some trouble getting around. In one case, only one leg. Frank had little doubt that anyone captured would get the Inquisition's idea of due process. The Spanish Inquisition, to boot, which had a far worse reputation than the papal variety.

And no one coming to help, either. They were going to have to hold the place until nightfall at least and then scope out a way to get out.

A thud from in back nearly made Frank jump out of his skin and everyone at the front wall look around. "Steady," he called out softly. A rattle and the sound of someone climbing down the ladder settled everyone. Sure enough, Giovanna appeared in the doorway behind the bar.

She came over. "I counted eighteen of the bastards out front." She looked furious. "As soon as the shooting starts, we have bottles of oil ready to throw. Unless you have a better plan?"

"Can't think of anything," he said, shrugging and fighting the urge to turn back to the slit he'd been looking through. "I figure we hold on until it's dark enough to get out. Leave the ladder down unless you have to pull it up. Benito? Which exit looks easiest to get out of?"

"The cellar one. I figure they might expect us to get out by going through the back wall." There was a hole there now that led into a tenement house, the ground floor of which had been abandoned when news of the invasion came. "They have a whole bunch of guys out there. Same for the houses either side. The cellars, we can go up the street a little and there's that alley opposite, the one that cuts through to—"

"That'll do," Frank said. "Giovanna, we can't fight this. We're outnumbered and surrounded and ain't no one coming to help. We have to get out if we can, if only to tell people."

"Fuck," someone said from the other end of the front wall.

Frank looked, and saw that the musketeers were blowing on the matchcords of their locks, getting them to glow nice and bright. "Giovanna," he said, putting as much urgency into his voice as he could, "back upstairs now and get everyone ready."

When he didn't hear her move at once, heard her take a breath to ask or say something, he barked: "Now!"

Louder than he'd intended.

In a room full of nervous guys with guns.

And so the Committee of Correspondence fired the first shots at their attackers.

Chapter 35

Rome

Ruy Sanchez de Casador y Ortiz was not, with his many years of experience, often wrong. Much mistaken in his youth, occasionally wide of the mark in his middle years. Now, ripe in experience, being wrong was something of an unusual feeling.

In this instance, a somewhat nauseating one. The proper action, the correct action, when advancing against scattered and disorganized defenses, was to secure each strong point against the possibility of action against the flanks or rear and press on. A barricade held by twenty men could be pinned in place by fifty, while the remaining thousands took alternate routes. Barricades across main streets only prevented the passage of cavalry; infantrymen could readily pass through alleyways and side streets at only moderate hazard. There was a price in disorganization of the main body, of course, although that could readily be remedied at some point short of the ultimate objective. And Sanchez felt he must perforce allow that the troops leading this assault were at least above the

426

ordinary quality and would be unlikely to make too much of a muddle of complicated maneuvers.

Such, at least, was the received wisdom of the profession of arms. Other orders seemed to have been given. Alternate routes were being found, but only after time was taken to organize serious assaults on each barricade. It was as if a special effort was being made to either make the main force bleed, enrage them, as a *picador* would, or they were being deliberately advanced slowly to some other purpose. The three barricades whose fall Sanchez had watched had not taken long to succumb. A small volley of arquebus fire did nothing to check the advance of pikes and sword-and-buckler men, supported by muskets. There were few of the older, clumsier weapons in evidence on the attacking side, further bolstering Sanchez's view that these were, if not elites, troops of quality. A few losses were taken each time in making the defenders leap down from their makeshift ramparts and run for hiding places. The defenders, in their turn, were dying, and effort was being expended on chasing as many down as possible.

It was, from any conventional point of view, folly. The tactic was dispersing large bands of men, roused to the attack, throughout the city. While sack and rapine was an accepted if regrettable part of warfare, most commanders sought to do all they could to prevent it save as a punishment for futile resistance. On *those* occasions it was ordered. Here, it appeared that who-ever was giving the orders was attempting to provoke atrocity without being seen to give the order.

But why? Borja's pretext had long since vanished. It would have been trivial to leave word at Ostia to prevent the march. Doubtless the defenders of Ostia, such as they were, expected the fleet that was arriving to sail straight back once they learned of the calmed situation in Rome. Had, in all likelihood, looked forward to the profit in revictualling those ships.

It was a conundrum indeed. A further insight came as he rode past the Colosseum. The advancing army had passed to the west of the Palatine, staying close to the river. Rather than attempt to guess their route through that district so as to maintain scouting contact with them, Sanchez passed around the east and north sides along the wider streets, urging his mount into a trot. Only the officers of that army were mounted, and that advantage of mobility was there to be used. Having thus moved away from the line of advance of the invaders, Sanchez noticed no less than four parties of armed men, moving with determination and clear purpose. The smallest, at a rough count, of thirty men, all musketeers.

Sanchez could not *swear* that he had seen no such parties splitting from the main column, although in order to be ranging so far ahead as they were some of them must surely have sprinted through the streets, a practice no soldier with even the slightest experience of fighting in a town would wish to indulge in. Or, for that matter, any soldier out of sight of senior officers would indulge in on a warm day in full battle gear. As a great likelihood, therefore, parties of soldiers had been force-marched ahead of even the rapid advance of the main body and had entered the city from other directions. To what purpose? Raiding and harrying in the rear of the pitiful defenses of Rome was at best a waste of effort. That left—

He was passing Trajan's column when he saw the disturbance outside the Palazzo Colonna. A cloud of gunsmoke, the sight of figures within it. The sound was barely distinguishable amid the bells and the general sound of fighting elsewhere, although the smoke was thickening rapidly. Several of those small parties seemed to be busy about something there.

So, particular targets, then? Sanchez turned left and bade his horse pick up the pace slightly. A more rapid trot. He considered taking a sharp right and establishing whether the embassy had been a target, but discarded the notion. There was nothing there worth anyone's concern and, indeed, it would be better to wait until whatever was happening there was complete, that a more detailed picture could be gleaned from the evidence left behind. He would pick over the wreckage at his leisure before leaving the city.

He skirted the trouble at the Palazzo Colonna—doubtless a family that boasted so many generals would need no aid in its defense—and maintained the rapid pace. It would be hard to select a bridge that was not likely defended, uncomfortably close to a likely focus of trouble, or denied him by the need to cross the path of the invading army. That was scarcely more than trivial—boldness and a simple polite request to make way would see him through, letting all assume he was simply some officer about official business, but would be an unwanted delay.

However, the Ponte Ripetta proved easy of access. The Palazzo Borghese, the nearest place by the river at that point, was thus far unmolested. There were no guards, no barricades and thus far no invading forces using it. It was, of course, out of the direct path of the invaders, although it provided a useful route into either side's rear. The Ripetta itself was also the scene of no activity, although Sanchez had half expected to see troops being landed there.

Suspicion was awarded the tribute of proof when he neared the north side of the Borgo. The place gave the appearance of recently having experienced a brief, but heavy, rain of soldiers, perhaps sixty all told, circling the small block of buildings that was home to Frank's Place, but remaining out of view of the front, which told its own story. The street looked scorched, and there was a heavy smell of lamp smoke in the breezeless air. Most of the soldiers were musketeers, well-found ones at that. A few pikes and partisans were in evidence, and a leavening of back-swords largely in the hands of obvious officers. Sanchez elected to go no closer than he had to. He reined in his horse behind a sergeant, who was leaning on his partisan, watching the front of Frank's Place from a safe position down the street, and waiting for something to happen.

"Which of the targets is this?" he inquired, refining his tones to his best hidalgo sneer.

The sergeant straightened and turned with commendable swiftness. "The revolutionaries, señor. The witches from the future. They have defenses, señor, and we are waiting for more men before we assault. They opened fire without warning, and have burning oil to throw down. If the señor will wait a moment, I will inform the captain—"

"No, no, my good man." Sanchez waved the offer aside. It was helpful that the man was a Spaniard, though. While habits of deference to the hidalgo varied widely, in a military context a hidalgo manner usually said *officer* to most troops. Someone from another country might be more critically minded. Sanchez prefaced his remark with a chilly glare along the street at the knots of soldiers watching and waiting as the sergeant had been. "I am in the correct place, it seems. We may have the use of some small field pieces, perhaps powder for blasting breaches, if the ground is suitable. I shall make a survey of the buildings and their yards."

He smiled, as if sharing a small confidence with an inferior. "Thus obtaining the benefit of cool shade while my subalterns sweat over gun-carriages."

"Very good, señor," said the sergeant, smiling and nodding in deference.

Sanchez was even able to tip the man a piece of eight to find him a horse-holder while he went inside to find Frank's emergency escape route.

The sight of columns of smoke rising over the eternal city was to be regretted, certainly. Much that was valuable would be damaged, destroyed, looted. Such was the price of turning loose soldiers. It was a price that it was necessary to pay. Cardinal Borja looked down from the high window of the Palazzo Borghese he had chosen for his vantage and post of command. A lone horseman trotted across the riverside terrace toward the bridge, doubtless about some necessary military undertaking.

Borja wondered idly who it was, and then, dismissing the man from his mind, looked downriver. White smoke was already rising from around the Castel Sant'Angelo. The Barberini pope had clearly ensconced himself there and was doubtless resisting.

Good. Borja had been worried that the Barberini pope would somehow manage to escape the city altogether.

Behind Borja there was a brief disturbance.

"What news, Ferrigno?" he asked, without turning his gaze away from the bluish-white haze rising around the fortress of his enemy.

Father Ferrigno cleared his throat. "Your Eminence, the embassy of the Swede was deserted. All belongings of the Americans had been removed, and the remains of a bonfire were found in the courtyard. The building has been set on fire, pursuant to Your Eminence's order."

So they had fled. He was not surprised. Satan imbued his followers with no true virtue, least of all courage. "And the subversives? The alchemist's whelp?"

"His den, Your Eminence, is occupied and appears to have been fortified. Quevedo's unit has surrounded it and await reinforcements in order to commence the assault. The subversives opened fire without warning, Your Eminence, before any attempt could be made to arrest them."

Borja nodded. At least some of the snakes had been caught. And if they desired to play the game by the rule of the knife, Borja saw every reason to oblige them. "Send word to the officer in charge that if further resistance is offered, no quarter is to be given."

"Very good, Your Eminence," said Ferrigno.

It was a miracle no one had been killed yet. Or seriously injured. Frank had a whole lot of little splinters in one cheek that were itching like a bitch, but that was it. They'd cleared all the soldiers away from the front—one or two of them had been hurt, but their buddies had got them away leaving only sprays of blood on the far wall. In getting the hell away from the firing, they'd fired their muskets right back. The boards on the window weren't worth a damn for stopping musket balls, and made things worse when they splintered, as Frank could attest.

Frank had grabbed for his revolver, but by the time he got it out of his belt the street was filling with flames and smoke from puddles of oil dropped from above. That, of course, was cover for the soldiers to get the hell out of the way. Not that it had stopped any of the guys with guns from banging away like woodpeckers on crack. When they'd calmed down and the flames subsided—and hadn't *that* been a great few minutes, while they wondered if they hadn't burnt their own little fortress down by mistake—the street outside was clear.

The celebration had been brief. A sneaked peek from an upper-floor window showed that the soldiers were just holding the street further down, and more kept arriving, in small groups. No one had been driven off, and all the exchange of fire seemed to have done was piss everyone off, on both sides. Not to the point of making a serious assault, but still things were tense.

"Frank?" It was Fabrizio.

"What?"

"I think I hear something downstairs." Salvatore was in back, getting everyone something to drink. The place was full of smoke, and tension, and both were making everyone thirsty.

Frank frowned. They'd piled junk in the gaps in the walls downstairs, in the hope of their escape route not being noticed. By the owners of those buildings, if no one else. Only one of the buildings the makeshift tunnel went through was empty. He got up from behind the table he was using as extra cover—between it and the front wall, he figured he was mostly safe from musket balls except where he had to peer over it—and went back. The stairs down were in the back hall, through a kind of low archway under where the stairs up had been. Frank realized he could hear stuff shifting about down there, like—like someone pulling aside that barricade. He had to do something, quick, but not on his own. He looked back into the main bar and tried to pick out one or two guys who—

There was a clatter down below and a stream of curses in what sounded like Spanish. Frank pulled his pistol out and thumbed the hammer, pulling it back until he heard a nice reassuring click. He leaned over to Salvatore and whispered, "Get Piero and a couple of his guys over here, *quick.*" He leveled the pistol at the archway, preparing himself to shoot at the first Spaniard to show himself.

How the hell did they find it that fast? He realized that what this probably meant was that they were in surrender-or-die country right about now, and maybe there wasn't going to be much of a chance to surrender.

"Frank? Señor Stone?" The voice came up from the cellar below.

Frank let out a breath, sagging with relief, and very carefully made the revolver safe. "Señor Sanchez? Anyone with you?"

The sound of boots on the steps. "No, I am alone."

Frank waved Piero back. "Don't worry, guys. False alarm."

Ruy appeared in the archway, stooped over on the barrel ramp, his hat in his hand and grinning. "How goes it, Frank?"

"'Bout as well as can be expected," Frank replied, grinning ruefully. "Surrounded and outnumbered and we can't get all our people out."

"One of those houses I came through looked to be deserted," Ruy said. "Could you get your women and invalids that far?"

"I wondered, but what good would that do? We'd still be inside the ring the soldiers put around this whole block. They'd see us escaping."

"They will not see those who hide on an upper floor, Frank."

"Yeah, but they'll search if they find this place abandoned."

Ruy shrugged. "Then do not abandon it."

Frank could feel the penny dropping. "Ah, I get it. We get the women and kids—" *and Giovanna! and Giovanna!*—"out while a few of us stay here and make trouble. We make a real obvious try to escape and hope like hell we can outrun 'em at night in all these alleys, and the soldiers don't think to check for who we left behind?"

Ruy beamed like a high-school teacher about to award a straight A. Then grew serious. "It is not certain of success, I must remind you. It may be that the other buildings will be searched. But those whom you place in the other hiding places can say they were always hiding there."

"It's better than what we got," Frank said, mentally

kicking himself for not thinking of that. Of course, Giovanna had chewed him out so badly for suggesting she hide outside the city that he hadn't stopped to think that she might hide close by. Then he realized she probably wouldn't go for that either. Perhaps if he asked her to lead the second site?

Ruy was looking around. "You have no wounded, as yet?"

"No," Frank said. "Yet." And that word was a world of depression all on its own. There were going to *be* wounded, no question.

"May I be permitted to offer some small suggestions?" Ruy asked, fanning himself with his hat.

"Sure. I'm not what you'd call a military genius. I need all the help I can get, here."

"First, the soldiers had orders to capture you, not kill you."

"That's kind of what I was afraid of." The Inquisition had had their hands on Frank once. Only briefly, true, and it had all worked out okay in the end. But the experience had still been enough to scare him out of a year's growth. And he'd been a prisoner under the eye of a whole lot of powerful and influential people, who'd pretty much wanted to see him walk out of that cell alive and unharmed. He didn't think that this time he was going to be so lucky. There was a lot of shooting going on down by the Vatican and the Castel Sant'Angelo, and Frank figured they were probably in for a change of pope real soon.

"Indeed," Ruy said. "A sojourn in the hands of the Inquisition is no laughing matter. But"—he held up a finger—"these soldiers are Spaniards, and regular troops, not mercenaries. They have no love for the Inquisition."

"Eh?" Frank would have thought the opposite would be true.

"The Inquisition is at the very least a nuisance for most of the common people of Spain. They torture few and execute less, but they meddle everywhere, and there is hardly a family that does not have at least one member's name hung up in the parish church as a heretic. It is an embarrassment, a source of shame, and the shame is very nearly permanent. So, Frank, make your women and children safe, and resist valiantly, but not too valiantly. Shoot with your enemy at long range, throw your bottles of oil early so that no man has to listen to his comrade burn to death, but can withdraw in good time. And then *surrender*. Honorably. Demand a parley. Demand to give your parole and keep your sword. Once that is done, you are a military prisoner, and may not in honor be harmed unless you break your parole not to fight against His Most Catholic Majesty. Many officers will regard surrendering you to the Inquisition while under parole as dishonorable. Play upon the fact that you are not a Christian—much less a Catholic—were never baptized, and so cannot be accused of heresy. Explain this to the officer who holds your parole, and that any action by the Inquisition would be plain and simple abuse of a paroled prisoner."

"Ruy, everyone else in here is Catholic," Frank said. "That won't wash for them."

"Good treatment for your men is a standard term of parole. Insist that as far as you know, they are all good Catholics, and no accusation of heresy has been made. I will wager that the only name they have on their list from the Inquisition is yours, Frank. And possibly your wife's, although she should escape. They will assume that all others here were servants, and ignore them."

"You think this will work?"

"It is the best I could think of while I was clearing aside the trash in the cellar to get in here," Ruy said, with a smile of disarming candor. "In truth, I think it your best chance, if you cannot find a way to sneak out by night. You might achieve that, with the help of God, but the moon will not be dark for another two weeks and there have been few cloudy nights lately."

Frank shrugged. "We can hope. We can at least get the women and kids and the invalids out of here. How many soldiers out there?"

"Forty at least, perhaps fifty. I could not count accurately. More have been sent for, although they will not be here in numbers for some time. The troops in the city so far were advance parties, sent to seize particular places. The main body was at the Palatine when I left them, and will be across the river by now. You have a little time, perhaps half an hour."

Frank nodded. "Everyone at the embassy get out okay?"

Ruy smiled. "I would imagine that Borja will be disappointed by what his men find there. I remained behind to gather intelligence; the last of our people departed the city half an hour before the advance parties began to arrive."

"Good to hear," Frank said. "I guess we'd better get on with it. Give my regards to Sharon and everyone."

Ruy flourished his hat in salute. "I wish you every joy of the day, Señor Stone, and when next we meet,

I crave the honor of buying you all the drink you could want."

Frank waved a salute back. "Look forward to it," he said, trying hard to feel as confident as he managed to sound.

A little while later, while he was helping get an old lady down the ladder and into the cellar that he was damned well going to watch a whole lot better from here on in, he realized that Ruy had meant that offer as a real salute to what he was doing.

And if Ruy Sanchez de Casador y Ortiz thinks I've got cojones to be doing this, it's got to be good and crazy. Seems like marrying a Marcoli turned me into one.

Chapter 36

Rome

"Your Eminence!" Mazarini senior, excitable as usual, was pointing out of the window. "Gun smoke, from the Castel Sant'Angelo!"

Barberini walked over, making himself retain his dignity and decorum when all he wanted was to dash madly and press his face against the glass, or hurl the window wide and lean out to see. No doubt remained. The assault on Rome was devoted to removing his uncle from the chair of Saint Peter.

"We will hasten our departure," he said, staring at the columns of dirty-looking white smoke that were appearing over the roofline in the direction Mazarini was pointing. Barberini wished idly, for a moment, that it was the calm, icy-nerved son, now a cardinal in France, that was his majordomo, not the father. That apple had fallen a goodly ways from the tree.

"As Your Eminence wishes," Mazarini said, and bustled away to see to whatever fine details remained. There would be little. The majority of the people of Casa Barberini had gone either the night before or with first light, the morning's party going ahead under the command of Cardinal Francesco Barberini. Where others had implied that he was starting at shadows, Cardinal Antonio Barberini—essentially, left to mind the store while older and wiser heads were about the business of the house—had quietly but firmly made all of the necessary preparations for flight. And had been ruthless. It was sad to think of it, but a large proportion of the art he had so painstakingly assembled, on top of the centuries-old collection that his fore-bears had amassed, would soon be gone. Looted, if the world was fortunate. Destroyed, if the historical tales of how a sack proceeded were correct. Paintings tossed aside while the frames were taken for their gilt. Fine pieces pried apart to make change for whores. Sculpture knocked aside; its value unrecognized or too heavy to carry. Or worse, hurled from upper floors, as Barberini had once seen small boys do with bottles, for the amusing sound as they shattered below.

The more portable pieces, items that would be a worthy kernel of a future collection, had been sent away. A pitiful salvage from what would surely be a terrible wreck. It was all he could do not to weep. He had remained behind to at least see, with his own eyes, what this latest wave of barbarians proposed to do with the Eternal city. And his family. And his church. And, in some sense, because it felt right to be the last of his house to leave. Honorable. And, finally, to take one last look at what it was that was about to be lost.

"Your Eminence?" Mazarini's voice interrupted his morose thoughts. "We are ready, if Your Eminence pleases."

Barberini could not contain the deep sigh. It was that or begin sobbing. His eyes were hot, and stung. Only the firmest of self-control permitted him to turn away from the window without being unmanned. "Lead on, Mazarini," he said. "This must surely be the last moment."

Mazarini did not answer, but the expression on his face betrayed his opinion that the last moment had passed some time since. Outside in the palazzo mews he reflected that the weather had no sense of dramatic unity. Such deeds should not be done on a balmy early-summer day, in bright sunshine with a light scatter of fleecy cloud in the sky. Stormy winds, lightning and thunder would have suited the mood better.

The streets were deserted, the populace hiding or fled. Barberini looked about himself. A small party, and Barberini had taken the precaution of shedding his clerical garb in favor of more modest attire. Of course, there was a limit to how modest the attire he possessed was. He was still at risk of a robbery, but at the least there was much less chance of him being recognized and captured. And the last few of the Casa Barberini guardsmen were gathered about him. A dozen troopers surrounding the cardinal and his majordomo.

"Very good," he said after a moment. "Let us go."

The street outside looked empty, or at least the first trooper out waved back to say as much. As he rode out into the street, Barberini realized that there was another disadvantage to the good weather. He felt as though the entire world could see him, a sensation that hitherto he had found quite pleasant, rewarding even. Now, it made him want to leap from his horse and curl up in whatever hole he could find quickly. He felt sure that the sweat that was starting all over him, and trickling down the small of his back, had little to do with the heat of the morning. He tried looking around to distract himself. The piazza for which he had decided upon a new fountain was away to his left; he saw figures moving there, some of whom seemed to be pointing and starting to move in his direction, but his horse was following that of the lead trooper and he quickly lost them. Trying to look behind oneself from a moving horse, unless one was a much more expert horseman than the cardinal had ever had the inclination to become, was a sure route to a painful fall, or at least a very confused horse. He turned to face ahead.

The troopers ahead—Barberini realized, as suddenly they exploded into action, that he knew none of their names and the thought choked off the question he wanted to ask. He could hardly believe that ill manners were preventing him—and he still could not see why all of the dozen troopers ahead of him had suddenly spurred their mounts and drawn pistols. He looked about himself frantically, tried to rise in his stirrups for a better view—

"*DOWN*, Your Eminence!" It was Mazarini shouting that, although several other voices said the same without the honorific, in one case with an insult. The horse, startled by the sudden motion and then Barberini's antics, began to rear, and then began to dance sideways, shaking its head.

The sound of shots rang out, and Barberini's horse began to turn around. He was still turning his head frantically, looking for the source of the trouble, and tried to control the beast by pulling at its reins. One of the rearguard troopers leaned from the saddle and grabbed the rein, his twisted expression supplying the snarling condemnation of idiot priests who could not ride that he did not speak. Barberini let the man pull his horse back around, still seeking—*there!* Puffs of gunsmoke from either side of the street they had been riding along. One of the troopers slumping in the saddle, a bright red mist puffing from the back of his coat. Barberini's horse becoming frantic again, wrenching its head away to try to escape the grip on its reins.

More shots. Another trooper, this one falling from his horse with his face scattering small pieces into the morning sunshine and his head smacking wetly into the cobblestones, spattering blood and brains in a bright and glistening red star. The trooper who was trying to control Barberini's horse losing his fight with the animal and his seat at the same time.

Barberini realized he was screaming, and that his leg was burning and cold at the same time. His right leg. His thigh. A mist of blood, his own blood, was settling out of the air around a red gash that had somehow appeared there. *I have been shot*, he thought, his mind suddenly clear. There were men on foot near him in the street, men with muskets, with swords, and with pikes. His horse screamed.

He was vaguely aware of falling, and then the world was suddenly bright with a dark border, and he could not breathe, or hear. Someone was grabbing him and hauling him up, and his vision began to clear, although he still could not breathe and his back was a single mass of pain. *I fell from my horse.* He had done that before, although not since he had been a boy disappointing his riding-master.

It was Mazarini helping him up, and now he could hear the ring of weapons clashing. More shooting. Something punched him, this time in the left arm, and he spun round. He staggered once, twice, and then regained his balance. He groaned. It *hurt*.

And then he was being lifted bodily, thrown over a saddle. He fainted.

Not for long. When next he had his wits, he could still hear fighting. Every jolt as the horse galloped hurt. His leg, his back, his chest, his arm. He fainted again.

"Your Eminence? Your Eminence?" Mazarini's voice seemed to come from a very long way away.

"What time is it?" That somehow seemed important. Did he have a morning appointment? He was cold, and thirsty. "Have water brought, Mazarini," he murmured.

Something wet, suddenly, on his face. And cold. Wakefulness came like fire, and he groaned. Memory returned. "I've been shot," he said, not entirely believing it himself.

Mazarini pulled the wet cloth off. "Yes, Your Eminence. My most humble apologies."

"Why? Was it you that shot me?" It was all Barberini could think of that Mazarini might be apologizing for. With the cold compress off his eyes, he could see that they were in a small and noisome back alley. Trash was heaped everywhere, and several mangy cats were watching to see if the strangers were going to do something interesting. The smell was . . . remarkable.

Mazarini looked puzzled. "It was for the manner of

waking Your Eminence I apologized, Your Eminence," he said. "I was able to escape; the party of soldiers we encountered were nearly overmatched by our own troopers, and so I caught up Your Eminence onto my own horse and made good our escape from the fighting. Our enemies mounted their principal assault at the front of the palazzo while we were leaving at the rear, Your Eminence, and—"

"Mazarini, you are babbling," Barberini said. He looked again at the ageing majordomo. "And bleeding."

Mazarini fingered the cut on his neck, which was weeping small drops of fresh blood from where it had not already scabbed. "A mere scratch," he said.

"Where are we?" Barberini asked, looking around again for more clues. A poor neighborhood, certainly. And one that did not seem to object much to the streets being largely paved with cat-shit.

"Near the mausoleum of Augustus, Your Eminence. Close to the docks."

A *very* rough neighborhood, then. Another throb from his shoulder, arm, whatever it was that hurt so much—he dared not look—made him groan.

"Your Eminence, it was the only place I could find where there was no fighting, or sound of it. I have lost the horse, Your Eminence."

"Stolen?"

"By now, certainly, Your Eminence. I perforce had to bring Your Eminence where the horse would not come."

"Sensible animal. What are they doing?" Barberini could hear more and more shooting, now. It was reassuringly distant, though.

"I do not know," Mazarini said, in tones that were even more lugubrious than all he had said so far. "If

Your Eminence will permit, I will attempt to bind
your wounds. The arm needs a sling, I think. I have
already—"

"Please, just get on with it," Barberini said, gritting
his teeth. He looked. There was a neat hole in his
jacket, just above his left collarbone. He could not turn
his head further to look without unbearable pain; his
back felt as though his every rib was broken.

Ten minutes of fiddling and more pain later, Barberini had to admit he felt more comfortable with
his arm in a sling. With a lot of groaning and effort,
he was able to get to his feet. When the flashing in
his eyes and the dizziness had faded, he answered
Mazarini's look of concern. "What now? Have you
made a plan?"

"Your Eminence, I must counsel escape from the
city."

Barberini forced a smile. "Indeed. Shall we discuss
a plan for doing so? I will advance, for learned dis-
putation, the proposition that any member of Casa
Barberini is wanted dead at this time. Or captured,
which will likely be worse." Oh, yes, much worse.
Borja was scarcely the most moderate man to wear a
cardinal's hat, and he was a Spanish inquisitor. There
were things one *expected* of such a man. Barberini
could only hope that his uncle would be protected in
at least some measure by the office he held. However,
it was not a day to inspire optimism.

Mazarini looked nervously to where the alley they
were in—a small passage, barely open to the sky,
wide enough for two men to walk abreast if they
were close friends—turned left toward somewhere
rather better lit.

"I saw many parties of soldiers about the city as we fled the battle in which Your Eminence was wounded. We were gifted by providence with the great good fortune of being pursued solely by foot soldiers, and for much of our flight we retained the horse. Alas, Your Eminence, every attempt I made to strike north, east or south proved to be fruitless at first. I decided later to seek cover in some such alley as this one, but I could not move in such with a horse. The invaders had not reached this quarter yet, so I turned the horse loose, hoping to rouse you and bind your wounds that we might make a better escape on foot."

"Reasonable," Barberini said, and indeed it was. Military ignoramus that he was, even he knew that Rome's defenses were, more or less, nonexistent. That, with only modest preparation or a little effort, there were dozens of places where the walls were no defense at all without extensive preparation. The gates were all still present, but functioned only as customs posts, and those during daylight hours only. Only cargoes too big and heavy to be brought to one of the unrepaired breaches got taxed. At night, a modest bribe to the gate guards brought any cargo through. So, it would have been trivial to send ahead parties of men tasked with taking important points—and people—and charging them to find their way into the city however they could. Doubtless many of them would include local guides; it was too much to expect that the mercenaries who were originally from Rome would scruple overmuch about it. In truth, knowing firsthand the wealth in Rome, they would be more eager than most for a sack.

Why? Barberini found he need not think too long or

hard about that. It would avail Borja nothing to take Rome if he could not hold it, in any and every sense save the purely military. In the military sense, he had rather better prospects of holding the city than the present defenders had had. It was the *political* holding of the city that would matter now. And that certainly meant one Antonio Barberini the Younger would do well not to be caught escaping. Or, indeed, that he would *not* be caught escaping, but would simply turn up dead, a regrettable victim of "the chaos attendant on the civil disorder in Rome."

The best hope Rome had was that Osuna, or Gentili, or one of the other figures fomenting revolt in Naples took advantage of this draw-down of troops from their city. Naples, right now, was likely simply overdefended rather than home to overwhelming force. But any such hope would be weeks away, nothing that could be depended on right now.

And if Borja had flooded the city with raiders as thoroughly as Mazarini was suggesting, it was not stopping at Casa Barberini. There was time enough to be sure of that, though. "Let us move," Barberini said. "We gain nothing by remaining here. I can walk, if slowly, and if we remain on the back routes, we may well evade capture."

"But, Your Eminence, how will we leave the city? The gates are surely guarded."

"We will deal with that when we must," Barberini said, "although I invite you to consider that defenses that fail to keep attackers from coming in will also serve to permit fugitives to go out."

"Your Eminence is most perceptive," Mazarini said, offering his arm for Barberini to lean on.

It was only a short walk through winding alleys to the Via di Ripetta. This was by no means a salubrious district of Rome, being as it was close by the docks. The area around the Palazzo Borghese to the south was somewhat better, but north and south of that particular piece of riverfront it was dilapidated at best. The Via di Ripetta had been carved through the neighborhood some years before, to improve access to the docks, and as such remained a wide and straight street uncluttered by encroaching buildings. It was, therefore, dangerous to cross in broad daylight with hostile soldiers in the area. Mazarini was leaning around the corner and checking both ways. Barberini wished that the musketry was not echoing around the city so promiscuously, so that he could hear what was going on. Over Mazarini's shoulder, despite being somewhat dazzled by the sunlight in the street against eyes that had been in shady alleys for the last half-hour, Barberini could see that the previous cowering of the citizens of Rome had ended, and there were many already trying to flee through the streets. *That will help*, he thought, feeling a slight remorse over being so callous. Many of those people would be hurt, even killed, as the soldiery sought to move about the city and simply swept them aside.

"There are soldiers, Your Eminence, but the streets grow busy. We are unlikely to have a better prospect of—"

"Yes, yes," Barberini said. "Move. I think we should make for the east. Salaria or Pia, I think, and if those are guarded we may try the broken section of wall south of the Castra Pretoria. If nothing else, there may be Jesuits there who might help us."

"Yes, Your Eminence," Mazarini said, and began sidling out into the street. It was comical to watch; the man was all but tiptoeing.

"Come, Mazarini," Barberini said, affecting as normal a walk as he could with his leg burning with pain and his back and shoulder contorted into the only position he could find that even approached comfort. "Let us not skulk. Courage and honor demand it, and in any event a man attempting stealth on a sunlit street may attract attention."

As they made their way across, Barberini realized that they had inadvertently disguised themselves. Between the dirt and the pieces he had torn from his clothing to make bandages, Mazarini looked like a vagabond. Barberini realized that he could look little better, and likely worse. As a prince of the church, he made a good pauper. *Did critics of my lavish living see me now, they would expire of shock.*

They were perhaps halfway across when a carriage, guarded by four outriders, came rumbling by. Barberini cringed away from the thing, not knowing which cardinal was present in it. He took note of the arms painted on the door and saw that it was the carriage of Cardinal Bischi. An ally, by God! And not just an ally—Lelio Bischi was a personal friend and fellow enthusiast of literature and the arts. Barberini offered up a silent prayer of thanks and turned to try to—but no, there was no hope. Lelio was making good his escape, and doubtless none of his men would be looking back along the road to see if there were stray scions of the pope's house scattered in their path.

The point was moot within seconds. The carriage had proceeded barely fifty yards farther when a group of soldiers Barberini had not noticed dashed into the street and lined up to block the carriage's progress. The driver halted, as a man will when he has a dozen muskets pointed at him and his team. Men came forward to take custody of the outriders, the driver, the footman and the postillions. Another man, some manner of officer, judging by the sword and the better clothes, came forward and spoke to whoever was in the carriage.

Barberini heard nothing of what was said. The officer stepped away from the carriage door and waved his sword in an idle gesture of some kind. Four musketeers leveled their pieces at a range of perhaps three paces, and fired. Screams issued from the carriage, and it began rocking. The officer stepped forward, opened the door, and reached inside. With some apparent effort he dragged the occupant—who was wearing a cardinal's purple, although Barberini could not have sworn to the identity of the mewling, bleeding thing that was within those clothes.

The struggle was brief. The cardinal, if it was he, clung to the sides of the carriage door for a moment. A flash of the sword, hitting the wood of the carriage with a thump and sending at least one finger spinning through the air, ended that. The cardinal fell on to the cobbles. The officer planted his sword in the cardinal's throat and leaned on it, as if on a walking stick on a pleasant country stroll.

Barberini could not watch, flinching away. When he looked back, the officer was wiping his blade on the hem of his victim's garment, apparently oblivious to the spattering of blood that now coated him from shoulder to knee down his right side.

Barberini shuddered. Cardinal Lelio Bischi, a lively wit and gifted lawyer, a man of letters with few equals in Rome or anywhere, a man responsible for nurturing several literary talents and an avid collector of books, snuffed out with four bullets and two strokes of the sword. Simply, it would seem, because he was publicly and clearly a Barberini man. Borja truly meant to have Rome for his own. Or for his master's own.

"Mazarini?" he said, after a few seconds of silence, noting as he spoke that the people were starting to move all the faster to get away from something to the south, giving this small party of troops a wide berth but still flowing northward.

"Yes, Your Eminence?"

"We are leaving. Now."

It was another two hours before they reached the Porta Salaria by roundabout ways, back alleys and much circumspection. As Barberini had guessed, the ancient gate was now manned, and Barberini suspected that the guard was both more numerous and less bribable than the customs men who ordinarily stood there. They had reached a small shop doorway before the little piazza that opened out before the gate, and tried not to attract suspicion as they looked carefully over the situation.

There were troops on the piazza, apparently lounging about any old how, but Barberini decided that that was probably deception. Surely they would spring to more efficient action if any person tried to flee the city? Still, it was a quiet gate. As they had crossed the city, each main street that they had had to scurry across like mice had been less and less crowded with refugees. Whatever was rousting the common folk from their homes was happening in the south of the city, and to the west. The last blocks had been incredibly nerve-wracking, as they grew distant from the sound of gunfire that might have covered their own sounds. The crowds in which they had vanished as simply two more frightened citizens had thinned until, in this final quarter, people were again hiding behind bolted doors and shutters.

Behind them, the sound of hooves on cobbles. Barberini turned to look, and it was all he could do not to fall to his knees and praise God in his most extravagant voice. It was Ruy Sanchez de Casador y Ortiz, in the flesh, turning a corner into the street that Barberini and his man were lurking on. Even if the man could not help directly, there was no reason why he should not pass on information.

"Mazarini, wait here," Barberini said. "If I have made a misjudgment, your task is to survive to bring word of my death to such of my house as survive."

He left before Mazarini could say anything, and stepped out of the shady doorway into the street and shuffled over to meet Sanchez. Between the gash in his thigh, the ache in his back and the nagging pain of the wound to his shoulder, he moved like a mendicant. A perverse whim made him want to stretch out his hand in supplication for alms, but he suppressed it.

"Señor Sanchez," he said, as the intended of the USE's ambassador— or had he actually married her? He had been told the date of the wedding but could not now remember when it was, or had been supposed to be. "I must most humbly apologize for my most unbecoming attire." His voice was cracked and choked.

Even for a day as warm as this was promising to be, and for the amount of unwonted exercise he had had to take, Barberini's throat was dry with thirst.

Sanchez reined in his horse before he came too close to Barberini and stared at him for a long moment. "Your Eminence?" he asked, frowning.

"Señor Sanchez," he said, smiling as much as he could while working his jaw to try to get his mouth to moisten, "I have had a long and trying day, but I surely am not entirely so disheveled—"

Sanchez dismounted, a smooth and flowing motion that surprised Barberini, who knew how old the man was. "My apologies, Your Eminence. I had completed my business in Rome and was distracted by thoughts of my return to my wife. How may I be of assistance?"

So, married after all, Barberini thought, trying to calculate the angles while framing his response. "I am desirous of escaping the city while I still can. I delayed my departure—"

Sanchez held up a hand. "My own people also. It seems our timing was slightly better than yours, Your Eminence. By perhaps half an hour. You were set upon? In your palazzo or while evacuating?"

"In the street," Barberini said, interrupted by a cough that rasped his throat and sent ice-hot needles of pain dancing up his back and left side. He screwed up his eyes, despite the way that brought back the sight of Cardinal Bischi, dumped like refuse in the street. "I think we interrupted their preparations to storm the palazzo. We were ambushed. There was confusion. My man Mazarini brought me away after I was shot and fell from my horse." Since that moment he had felt nothing but fear and a constant sense of being hunted, at least during those times when he had not been groaning in pain or unconscious.

Sanchez seemed to notice his hoarse voice for the first time, and handed him a metal bottle that turned out to contain water. "I thank you," he said, after taking a swig. "Mazarini found a hiding place near the Ripetta while I recovered enough to walk. We made our way here, but the gate is guarded. Señor Sanchez, how were you proposing to leave?"

Sanchez laughed. "I had every intention of riding to the gate, calling a surprise inspection, damning every one of them for slovenly curs not fit to bear the name of soldiers of His Most Catholic Majesty before riding out of the gate threatening condign punishments for every last one. A stratagem I have used before. It is of less effect with mercenaries, who tend to listen only to their own officers, but few of those are among these raiding parties."

Barberini chuckled—there was something about Sanchez that simply demanded good humor—but winced as all the ribs up his back twinged at once. "A stratagem that will not work for me, alas. Have you seen whether any of the ruined wall by the Castra Praetoria is guarded?"

"I have not," Sanchez said, his face suddenly becoming blank. A moment of thought. "I shall assist you in your escape. I cannot speak for the USE embassy as to any further aid, but I shall see you safe to a doctor and shelter."

It was all Barberini could do not to faint with relief.

Chapter 37

The countryside, near Rome

"Tough little guy," said Doctor Nichols, rolling his sleeves down as they came out of the back room the taverna's proprietor had let them have as an impromptu consulting room. "Give him an hour or so for it all to catch up with him, though, and he's going to be out like a light. I prescribed a good meal and a night's sleep, but he says he's going to be up and about for a little while."

"What's he doing now?" Melissa asked.

"His servant's helping him get dressed. Rita scared up some fresh clothes for them both. That'll be half the recovery right there. I don't think they were either of 'em used to being dirty and ragged." He ambled over to the serving counter and waved for attention.

Sharon decided to butt in. "Did he ask for any help?" That was going to be an interesting question. The radio guys were upstairs in what would, later, be Sharon's bedroom, getting ready for the broadcast window that wouldn't be open for a short while yet. On the one hand, the fact that they had to relay through the embassy station at Basel was a pain in the ass if Sharon wanted to have a conversation with someone at the State Department. On the other, it was a real help if she had the distinct feeling that a *fait accompli* was exactly the right way to Do The Right Thing as it appeared to the woman on the spot.

"Beyond stitching him up? No." Her dad hoisted a large glass of wine and offered a silent toast before taking a gulp. The watered wine they served like it was a cold soda was actually quite refreshing, and if you were careful about it you kept a clear head. The kitchen had boiled some drinking water for them, money being a perfectly good explanation for any oddity, but it wouldn't be cool enough to drink for a while yet. Except for Melissa, who'd made tea. "Although I think we might well have a foot in that particular door, what with my new son-in-law making up policy on the hoof."

There was no particular note of disapproval in her dad's voice, Sharon noted. He was a doctor, and before that a Marine, and picking up the wounded and getting them to a doctor pulled some fairly well-worn levers in her dad's mind. In her own, come right to it. Rita was nodding her approval as well.

Sharon still had no particular inspiration about how to proceed from here, though. "How bad was he?" she asked, covering her lack of clear ideas with small talk.

"Two, maybe three busted ribs, a cracked collarbone, two nasty cuts and assorted scrapes and bruises. I've strapped the ribs and immobilized the arm, and the cuts just needed cleaning and a few stitches. Nothing a few weeks' rest won't cure," her dad said. "He kept moving all day after being shot up, though, which won't have helped. Adrenaline's powerful stuff, and like I say he's a tough little guy under the flab, but he's going to be one sorry little cardinal tomorrow."

Sharon chuckled. Cardinal Barberini had looked like death warmed up when Ruy had brought him in earlier. His servant, Mazarini, who was apparently the father of the diplomat Sharon had briefly met in Venice, had looked less battered but a lot more tired. Ruy had made him stirrup all the way from Rome, nearly seven miles, while the wounded cardinal had been given a ride behind Ruy on the horse. Ruy had, since handing the two refugees over for care and attention, been out of sight in the stables with a Marine helping him get started on fixing the poor animal up after the strain they had put him under. "Did he tell you how they got out of Rome?" she asked. Ruy would be making his own report once he'd finished caring for his horse, a sense of priorities Sharon wasn't prepared to overrule right now.

"Apparently Ruy found them trying to figure out how to get past a bunch of gate guards, used a rope to get them over the wall well away from any Spanish soldiers and then went back to bullshit his way past the guards so he could get his horse out. Apparently he conned 'em into thinking he was an officer of the Spanish army, pulled a surprise inspection and just rode out while they were still braced up and sweating. Way Barberini tells it, Ruy was still chuckling when they got in sight of this place."

"Sounds like Ruy," Rita said, grinning. She'd only known him a couple of weeks, but there were some things that you learned about Ruy quite quickly. The main one was his low sense of humor.

"Actually," Sharon said, "Ruy wasn't fooling. He *is* an officer in the Spanish army. I don't think he ever resigned his commission. Or sold it, if that's what they do."

"Sold it," her dad agreed. "Came as a bit of a shock to the guys who joined the new army, that. They were expecting to have to buy their commissions and have something in the bank for their old age. Getting given a commission and a pension plan messed with their heads a little, till they got used to the notion."

Melissa had been looking pensive throughout the conversation. "Any thoughts, Sharon?" she asked.

Sharon sighed. She knew exactly what Melissa was driving at, and she pretty much had to have made a decision before the transmission window opened up, or she'd be stuck with whatever State came up with in about a week's time. One thing she *did* know was that the time to act was right now, while there was still fighting in Rome. The sound of cannon had started coming out of the city, silhouetted as it was against the setting sun, and the columns of smoke had been rising since mid-morning and were now probably visible from hundreds of miles away. The USE presence right here right now was small enough to fit into this tavern and rented space in half a dozen nearby farmhouses and barns. So if they were going to do anything to intervene against the USE's avowed enemies, then they'd have to do something very well focused and accurate. Which meant doing it now, before whatever Borja was up to came off completely and he was settled in to—what, exactly? Knowing that would be half the decision made for her.

And that would be the half she was missing. Truth

to tell, she *liked* Cardinal Barberini. He was an easy man to like, being a cheerful little butterball most of the time. She'd been to a few of his salons, seen the kind of company he liked to keep, gotten more than a little giddy on the kind of art he collected, and marked him down as Good People. Politically, he was humane, forward-thinking, liberal and—leaving aside some unthinking assumptions that went with being a nobleman—quite decent. Not the brightest light in the harbor, maybe, but you couldn't have everything.

"Not right now, Melissa," she admitted. "I think maybe we should get something to eat. I'll take suggestions over dinner, have a talk with Cardinal Antonio, hear Ruy's report and then see how it looks." Ruy had come in from the stable yard while she was speaking, still looking travel-stained and a little weary around the edges. "Hi, Ruy. Is the horse okay?"

Ruy rocked a hand in a gesture he'd picked up from the up-timers. "Two or three days of rest, I think. A noble beast, to be sure, to bear the strain I asked of him without complaint. The Marines are coddling him yet, assuring him all will be well. I fear I may have gone down in their estimation for straining the poor animal so." His mouth quirked a little in a tired smile. Sharon found Ruy looking tired and vulnerable rather appealing and realized that they hadn't had a proper wedding night quite yet.

Down, girl.

"I think you need a little coddling yourself, Ruy," she said. "Get yourself cleaned up and I'll order dinner. You can tell me what's going on in Rome while we eat."

Dinner was, as with all rural Italian food, what a

good Italian restaurant was a pale imitation of. What was more, it was fresh and there was plenty of it. Ruy, who plainly hadn't troubled to stop and eat while riding around Rome, got through enough for about four and washed it down with plenty of wine. He still managed to keep up a constant stream of narrative. The news from the Committee saddened Sharon, although if Ruy was right and Frank followed the advice he'd been given there was a good chance he'd come out of it alive. Adolf, for whom Sharon made a mental note to see that there was something left for him to eat, managed to get all of it down on paper.

The news wasn't good. Barberini, who was taking his meal in the room they'd found for him, had seen one other cardinal summarily executed. Ruy had chatted with several soldiers and learned that they had been force-marching all through the night across country and, after a short rest to give the main body time to catch up, had gone into the city with a whole list of targets, chief among which had been the homes or lodgings of several dozen senior churchmen. Quevedo had been busy throughout the time he had vanished from home, as well. The fortifications at Ostia had more or less been sold to the incoming fleet at Naples, and the lighter pieces of artillery kept there would likely have arrived in Rome by now.

There was heavy fighting around the Vatican and Castel Sant'Angelo, but Ruy had not gone close. If there was anyone who might recognize him among the invading army, that was where they would be, and pretty much all the information he needed had been in the sounds of gunfire and the screams of the wounded from that quarter.

What it added up to was another question. The obvious answer was that there would shortly be a new pope, one who was probably sympathetic to Spain and certainly hostile to the USE. The official papal neutrality on the current wars would come to an end. For the USE, a nation with a significant Catholic presence, that was likely going to be a problem. Not all, or even many, of the Catholic clergy in the USE would be beating Spain's drum as a result. Spain having invaded Rome in order to install a new pope would result in a lot of consciences feeling a lot freer than they might otherwise.

But some would. And that would be a problem, in a nation with freedom of religion. A big problem. Not least because there was a sizeable chunk of the Protestant confession that *already* regarded the Catholic population as a fifth column. Of course, the fact that the USE's cardinal, thankfully not in Rome right now, was Larry Mazzare, would mitigate that to some extent. Only the loopier pamphleteers claimed that an up-timer from Chicago was a Habsburg agent. But putting Larry, one of Sharon's closer friends after all they'd been through in Venice, in that position by not acting right now was definitely not something Sharon was prepared to do.

When Ruy finished, and people were sitting back and looking contented with a good meal, Sharon opened the floor for debate. "Suggestions?" she said.

Melissa was first. "We're already committed," she said. "We've helped one of the Barberini."

"Not much, though," Tom said. "Just some medical treatment and a bed for the night. Devil's advocate says we can send him on his way in the morning, keep all our options open. Can't say I like the idea myself, but it's an option."

"Right," Melissa said. "I have to say I can't see what that would gain us, even if it wasn't flat wrong. There's no point doing favors for someone who's going to hate us come what may."

"Is it your belief, Doña Melissa, that Borja intends to make himself pope?" Ruy sat up straighter. "I find myself wondering whether even Madrid is capable of so foolish an order."

"Perhaps," Melissa said. "I think from what you've seen that it's certain that he intends to control the papacy. Another Captivity, a puppet pope—you saw yourself that the Borghese weren't being touched, and they hold the balance right now, if I understand the factions correctly. Making himself the next pope is just one of the options."

"Can we stop him?" Tom asked. "There're three tercios in Rome right now, give or take. We've got maybe twenty effectives."

"Señor Simpson has the right of it," Ruy said, "there is no practical military solution. If there is some other action we might take, we lack the intelligence to determine what it is. I confess that I am bereft of inspiration in this business."

"Have we asked Cardinal Barberini whether he wants help?"

"Not as such, no," Doctor Nichols said. "He was pretty grateful for the help we've given him, and gracious about it. He didn't ask for more than he was getting, either."

Ruy tapped a finger on the table once, twice. "Now that I think on the matter, I recall that His Eminence did not specifically request my aid either. He greeted me, told me what his aims were, and made some small talk. He requested advice on how to escape, but did so obliquely, as I recall."

Sharon thought back to lessons in formal diplomacy she'd had from Don Francisco. "Ceding us the advantage," she said.

"Right," Melissa said. "If he comes right out and asks, he makes himself our client. Until he figures the angles, he's not going to do that. Remember, he's pretty junior inside Casa Barberini; he's not even the senior cardinal. So while he'll accept what we offer and be grateful for it, he's not going to come right out and ask. Not for a moment."

"Rita?" Sharon asked, seeing that her friend had a brow furrowed in careful concentration.

"I think," Rita said slowly, "we should just stick to doing the right thing. I'm not sure of all the angles yet, I got a lot of sympathy for the little cardinal that way, but if we go wrong by doing good, at least we'll do it with a clear conscience. And like Melissa says, we're going to get nowhere by helping folks who're definitely against us."

"Can we do that, Rita?" Tom asked.

"I reckon we have to," Rita said. "The Barberini are pretty much finished in the Vatican, unless there's something we missed, but they're the only faction in Rome who might be friendly and right thing or not we should grab what we can while we can."

Melissa was frowning too. "It might be that the Barberini go the same way now that they did in the other history. They ended up seeking sanctuary in France after Urban died."

"We'd still lose nothing," Rita said. "If we want friends in Rome, they're pretty much all we can get in the big leagues. I say we take the chance we've got."

"Plus," Doctor Nichols added, "if we help the Barberini, any survivors of their faction are going to be friendly as. well."

Ruy harrumphed. "How many of them will still be friends of the Barberini by next week remains to be seen. A wind from Spain will cause many of them to trim their sails accordingly. The loyalties of churchmen and Italians are notoriously fickle. Italian churchmen may well prove to be poor things in which to repose a confidence."

"Maybe is still better than nothing," Rita said.

Ruy nodded. "It is as you say, Doña Rita. I offer the warning that it might inform your thinking, and that of my wife the ambassadora, over the coming days."

"That's certainly worth bearing in mind," Melissa said.

"Getting back to the point I raised," Tom said, "I wasn't so much thinking about whether it was practical to help the Barberini, but more whether we, I mean Sharon, can do it on her own authority."

"Did State give you plenipotentiary powers, Sharon?" Rita asked.

"Yep," Sharon said. Knowing that the buck stopped with her had been a nagging worry since Barberini walked through the tavern door.

"Gustavus won't be pleased," Melissa put in.

"Man'll shit a nut," Tom said.

"Thank you, Tom," Melissa said, giving him an

old-fashioned look. "I wouldn't put it that way myself, but he was somewhat unhappy with the way last year's dealings with the Holy See turned out. Then again, if he's presented with a *fait accompli* he will likely confine himself to grumbling. He'll see that cutting the religious justifications out from under his Catholic enemies is well worth the minor embarrassment in front of his Protestant allies."

"I think that settles it, then," Sharon said, glad at last for a justification for what she wanted to do. "Adolf, see if the cardinal is done eating, and tell him I'd like a word when he's ready. I'll make the offer and we'll let Magdeburg know what's what when the radio's working."

Chapter 38

The countryside, near Rome

Barberini was sipping his wine and wondering how much longer he could keep his eyes open when one of the Americans' servants invited him to join Ambassadora Nichols as soon as was convenient. He looked over the remains of the dinner he and Mazarini had shared and decided that if he did not go now, he would be unable to before morning. "Please ask the ambassadora if now would be convenient," he said.

While he waited for the fellow to return, he stood and walked to the window, throwing the shutters wide to try to allow the cool evening air to refresh him. He might, perhaps, have wished for a room that did not have so commanding a view of the western skyline, for in the distance, some few miles away, he could see the smoke rising from the city and hear the thunder and crash of cannon. He could only hope that meant the Castel Sant'Angelo still held. There were still some hours of daylight left, and the fighting continued. Would the soldiers continue into the night, he wondered? He knew too little of military matters to guess. As far as he could recall, Mazarini had not been a soldier either, so he would not know. Barberini, not for the first time today, missed the younger Mazarini, who as well as having the supple mind and smooth tongue he would likely need for the meeting he was about to have, had had some few years of experience as a soldier and would know the answer to questions such as that.

Enough of wishing. Hopes were enough to torment him now. Another roaring crash of artillery. How much had the Spanish brought? The defensive works that Bernini was supervising were only partially complete. Doubtless the Spaniards would have found some way to get past those, leaving only the older fortifications. Bernini had waxed eloquent on how poor those would be at resisting modern cannon. Some of what he had had to say would surely have been the architect seeking to pad his commission. Fortunately, the additional cannon Bernini had recommended had been cast and installed, for the most part, and for the sake of the additional bombards to protect his uncle, Barberini no longer cared what had been written on Rome's talking statues.

"Your Eminence?" The servant had returned and spoke to Mazarini, who was now setting himself to pull Barberini out of his funk.

"Coming, Mazarini," Barberini said. Fortunately, moving was considerably easier after a few glasses of wine to numb the pain, or he would have been unable to make his way down the steep wooden stairs.

Ambassadora Nichols was in the taverna's main room with all of her party. Barberini's first impression was that this was likely to be an easy negotiation, at least as to the most vital items. While the ambassadora was most commendably impassive in the course of such discussions, as much so as she was animated and charming when Barberini had had chance to observe her in discussion with the few natural philosophers he had had at his salons, it was those around her who gave the game away. They seemed friendly, welcoming even. Whatever discussion these people had had while Barberini had been eating, the conclusion had been that they would at least be friendly, and might even extend some further boon to him.

"Your Excellency, Ambassadora," he said, "permit me once again to express my gratitude for the assistance you have given me. I am personally most humbly in your debt, not least for my life." The personal debt, at least, he could acknowledge. And, assuming that the day finished with him anything but a pauper, one he would do all he could to repay. Would Borja even permit him to remain a cardinal? There was precedent for the summary dismissal of cardinals by a reigning pope—but the ambassadora was replying.

"Your Eminence is welcome," she said, "and I would like to know what else the United States of Europe can do for Casa Barberini."

Barberini nearly fainted. That was as good as a blank promissory note; there would be practical limits, but those would be the only ones. "I—I know not, Your Excellency," he managed to stammer out. "I have little information on the situation in Rome. My people escaped the city early this morning for Castel Gandolfo and perhaps there is somewhat—"

He realized he was babbling and shut his mouth. Then, after a deep breath to calm himself: "Forgive my surprise, Your Excellency. I have had a day of hardship and am much tempted to the sin of despair."

Is God truly with our party? he wondered. "For the moment, I can advance no practical proposition in which your most gracious offer of assistance might be reckoned of account. Perhaps I might inquire, in my turn, what Casa Barberini might do for the USE? I would not have my house thought ungrateful in such a matter."

Better, Barberini decided, to get the price settled quickly. By all accounts, Dottoressa Nichols was something of a merchant princess in her own right and as such would not be embarrassed by what might be construed as haggling.

"For now, Your Eminence," she said, "the status of your house as our only friends within Rome commands whatever service we might render."

Barberini nodded. *That* made sense. If Borja did contrive control of whoever became pope—and he was, he realized, abandoning all hope of his uncle's survival—then it was for certain that there would be no love lost between the USE and the See of Rome. "I shall, Dottoressa, think most deeply about what we each may do for the other. I shall speak for my house in this matter; we are glad to find friends among your embassy, and, we hope, your government. For the moment, Dottoressa, I am tired and hurt and in need of rest. I hope that with the morning my poor wits will be of better service?" There was no shame, he realized, in asking permission to be excused from this company, however obliquely. He was very much the supplicant and, he discovered, a grateful one.

The ambassadora was about to speak when a servant

scurried over to where she sat and whispered in her ear. "See him in," she said. "Your Eminence, I think you should remain for this."

The servant went out again, and moments later ushered in a small group of men in priestly soutanes. Leading them was Father-General Muzio Vitelleschi.

"Father-General," Ambassadora Sanchez y Nichols said, apparently unfazed by the man's appearance. "I was just inquiring of His Eminence what the USE might do for Casa Barberini. Including, naturally, his uncle. Is His Holiness Urban still pope?"

Very well briefed, Barberini realized through the shock. The Society of Jesus would be loyal to the pope, not one particular man. A change would require Vitelleschi and his brothers to shift their loyalties to follow.

"Your Excellency," Vitelleschi said, "to the best of my personal knowledge he is. If the Ambassadora would care for the most recent information in the Society's possession?"

Dottoressa Nichols nodded her assent. Barberini listened carefully as Vitelleschi reported the news he had from Rome, which seemed to be from some hours after Barberini himself had left. The Castel Sant'Angelo was likely to fall in the morning, defended as it was only by the Swiss Guard and the few members of the Palatine Guard—part-time soldiers who seldom drilled—who had gotten to their posts in time. The Spanish had a sufficiency of cannon to force the gates and more than enough soldiers for an escalade. As soon as dawn was close enough for the men with ladders to see what they were doing, the ancient fortress would be overrun. Although, to hear Vitelleschi tell

it, most of the cannonade was from inside the fort;
the damage they were doing to their attackers would
be scant consolation come morning.

Elsewhere in Rome, fully half of the cardinals whom
the Barberini might have counted on for support in
the consistory were confirmed dead. Of those who
remained, exactly two were accounted for as being
alive and escaped from the city. For the rest, there
was no news and less hope.

"And so, Your Excellency," Vitelleschi concluded, "we
of the Society of Jesus anticipate suppression of our
order in the event of the fall of Castel Sant'Angelo.
Our archives have been moved to places of safety, our
brethren are evacuated. Our concern is that there may
be persons who will require asylum. We are confident
of sanctuary from His Eminence Cardinal Mazzare
during such time as he remains a cardinal. We fear
that should he be dismissed that office, secular asylum
will be required. The present state of the Church
makes Catholic nations unsafe, and Protestant ones are
unlikely to become safer. A right to remain for certain
persons is, therefore, the matter in which I am most
humbly come to petition Your Excellency."

Barberini tried not to giggle. Many though Vitelleschi's excellent qualities were, horse trading was not
a talent he possessed. Listening to the man try was
almost embarrassing. Fortunately, Barberini realized,
this particular horse had already been bought and
paid for.

"Your Excellency," he interrupted, "if it lies within
your power, securing the person of my uncle from that
siege would be the greatest service your nation might do
for me, my house, and the Most Holy Roman Catholic

Church. His Holiness will not leave of his own accord, I must add. Any rescue must be prepared to drag him out by main force."

"How?" The man who spoke was, if Barberini remembered correctly, the son of the USE's Admiral Simpson. Certainly there could not be two men answering such a description—that of a giant from out of legend.

"I know not," Barberini said, shrugging with the one shoulder that was not immobilized in bandages. He still winced; the ribs might be bound tightly to help them heal but any more than the slightest movement was agonizing. "If no means can be found in time, so be it. But if His Holiness yet lives and can be brought out from that place, there remains hope for the Church."

"His Eminence speaks truly," Vitelleschi said. "If this thing can be done . . ." He left the question hanging.

"Surely," Simpson said, "the worst that happens is that you get a new pope?"

"Perhaps the Church will survive this, as it once did," Vitelleschi said, "but she will not be the stronger for it. An antipope is no longer a thing unremarkable."

And, his own interests apart, Barberini realized that there was something true in that. The last effort to use military pressure on the pope had been a century ago. The future histories showed that it would happen only once again, and then expressly only in his capacity as temporal ruler of the Papal States. Would the church, as an institution of men, survive once more having its spiritual leader in the thrall of a temporal king? Would His Most Catholic Majesty, who had surely not ordered this, whatever the tendency of his actual orders and the folly of the choice of agent to carry them out, take full advantage of the control he thus acquired over the church?

Certainly, there had long been Catholics who regarded their consciences as less than fully bound as a result of the See of Rome's partiality in this and other wars. The Church in France took pains, every few decades, to ensure that its willingness, under sufficient pressure, to go the way of the Church in England was sufficiently pointed out to Rome.

Other schisms would happen, once France was lost. The Church would shatter, and the legacy entrusted to Peter would be lost. Did Borja realize this? Probably not. The man was, at bottom, an ass.

"Forgive me, Father-General," Sanchez was saying, after a whispered conference with Simpson, "but how recent is your information regarding the state of the siege at Castel Sant'Angelo?"

"One hour. No more."

"And the Swiss Guard still holds the inner ward?" Sanchez's questioning was intent, the earnest concentration of a man seeking information pertinent to his profession. Vitelleschi had mentioned something about the various military technicalities of the siege, but Barberini had not been able to follow them.

"They do. The outer ward fell shortly after noon. It is the belief of those informing me that only a token resistance was made, in order to buy time for the inner ward to be secured."

Sanchez nodded. "And all of the artillery in use at the siege is field pieces?"

"So I understand. The Spanish could bring only light field pieces on the fast march they made. A siege train may be en route, but I have no information as to that."

"How long can they hold?" Simpson asked.

The captain of the horse who guarded the USE embassy spoke up. "I've seen yon fortress. Two hundred men could hold it for days, wi' no siege artillery tae fret on, unless there's an escalade."

"Escalade?" asked Simpson's wife. She, like the ambassadora, was a doctor, and doubtless even more ignorant of matters military than Barberini. At least he could say he knew what an escalade was.

"An assault on the walls by men wi' ladders, mistress," the captain said. "I dinnae ken how long it'll take 'em tae get ladders enough to carry the walls, but it's the quickest way. The Spanish general will have to be ready to spend men like water, mind ye."

"True," Sanchez said. "We may count on a certain delay while ladders are found or made. The besiegers have men enough to assault the whole wall of the inner ward at once, and that will ensure success."

"The butcher's bill's going to be . . . bad," Simpson said. "Even with only two hundred men that wall's a tough one to get over."

"True," Sanchez said. "The assault will likely be at dawn tomorrow."

"So soon?" Barberini asked. Hearing about the need for enough ladders to go all the way around the walls of Castel Sant'Angelo had given him hope that the fort might hold a while yet.

"So soon," Sanchez said. "Were I commanding that siege, I would have the docks raided for every timber in the boatyards and press every carpenter I could find. The ladders need not be perfect, just good enough.

A mast with planks nailed to it is all that is needed, with some ropes to steady it. One ladder at every five to ten paces, and the besiegers have men enough to man them. The first few hundred men over will be a forlorn hope, but eventually grenadiers will reach high enough, an establishment will be made, and then the defense will collapse quickly. They will lose perhaps a thousand men, but they have ten thousand and no fear of counterattack."

"I thought sieges took longer," the Ambassadora remarked.

"Ordinarily, yes," Simpson said. "Sounds like these guys have a massive advantage of numbers and nearly all the resources they could want. And they're already inside the outer defenses, trying to take the citadel."

"Oh," the ambassadora said. "Can we get the pope out of there?" She addressed the question to Sanchez. Knowing what he knew of the man, Barberini would have done the same.

Sanchez shrugged. "Maybe. I would perhaps be able to bring a small party within the inner ward and attempt something. This is not to say that the same idea will not occur to Quevedo, of course."

"He'd assassinate the pope?" Simpson's expression was one of honest curiosity. For all their cheerfulness and generosity, these Americans could take a bloodthirsty turn at times, Barberini reflected. The first thing *he* had thought of when Sanchez mentioned an infiltrator into the fortress was a gate being surreptitiously opened to let the besiegers in.

"Likely enough," Sanchez said, shrugging. "My heart," he went on, addressing the ambassadora, "this may be something we can do, or it may not. I will need to take a party of men back to Rome tonight and look more closely. With your permission?"

The ambassadora frowned a moment, then looked around the room at the other members of her party. "Comments?" she asked.

"Do it," Dottoressa Simpson said.

"Only if you can manage it without getting yourselves killed," Dottore Nichols added. "Forlorn hopes do no one any good. And I'll come along. Not in the raid itself, but you'll need someone holding horses outside, and a trained medic."

"You sure, Dad?" the ambassadora asked.

"I'm a shoo-in for this one," he said, leaving Barberini slightly confused. The sense of it was clear enough, though. "I've been a Marine, and I know my trauma medicine well enough to play corpsman. Although I could wish we had Harry along here."

"He's got a good resumé for it," Signora Mailey added, smiling at some private joke, doubtless connected with the fact that she had escaped a similar fortress only the year before. Perhaps the infamous Harry Lefferts had been involved in that? "But like James said, don't do it if it looks too risky."

There were no further objections. "Do it, then," the ambassadora said. "I'll go and compose a dispatch for Magdeburg. They won't be able to tell us not to, fortunately."

Naturally not, Barberini thought. He wondered what diplomacy would be like when the day came that the great radio towers were built all across the world, and princes could speak to each other directly. Would peace result, once everything could be discussed at length, directly between rulers? More likely, Barberini thought, that such ease of communication would make it more likely that they would take offense more easily. A plenipotentiary could be disowned, deratified, apologized for. Insults direct from the prince's mouth were less easily remedied. The radio diplomacy his uncle had engaged in the year before had certainly caused plenty of trouble.

Magdeburg

"I thought you should see that before anyone else," Francisco Nasi said.

Mike was rereading the lengthy dispatch. "You weren't wrong. Did we have any warning of this?"

"None at all. Shortly after we last spoke on this subject, I received intelligence that confirmed our initial assessment. Borja's orders were to create political confusion in Rome, to prevent Urban from taking any further effective action. To create, as you remarked, a lame-duck pope. The troops came from Naples, but our news from there has been concentrating on the domestic turmoil. The troops were there to suppress trouble in that part of Spain's possessions, and moving them is a strategic error unless they can be returned swiftly enough that the rebellion is not encouraged by their absence. And plans to move them were held closely enough that we got no wind. I will admit that our assets in that part of the world are not as comprehensive as I would like. We are still not sure what Osuna is up to; he has become remarkably quiet these few months past."

"So basically the situation is that Borja got a wild

hair up his ass and Olivares is going to be as surprised as we are?"

Nasi chuckled. Some rulers would not have been so understanding. A failure on this scale—and Nasi planned to light a few metaphorical fires under several figurative backsides come the morning, on general principles—would have seen him personally lucky to be allowed to resign alive. "Most succinctly put. More surprising still is the response of our embassy in Rome. Without for one moment wishing to ensure the embarrassment is spread as widely as possible, I think State will be responsible for the brick that will be found, come the morning, in the royal privy of Gustavus Adolphus. But we do have some radio time left. Do you wish me to instruct Sharon to call it off?"

Mike closed his eyes, and appeared to be thinking very hard and very fast. "No, she's done the right thing. She's given me a *fait accompli* that I've pretty much got to play along with. Remember, my sister signed off on that deal as well. Be kind of hard to go back on it now, and I'd prefer us to have a good name for keeping our bargains. We're helping the only friends we're likely to have in Italy for a long time to come, if Borja pulls this off, and we're trying to toss a wrench into the works for the biggest enemy we've got. I can't see that anyone's going to blame us, or even be surprised, much."

"So we go with it?"

"We go with it," Mike said. "Get a message back to Sharon, tell her that all her actions to date are ratified, ask for a list of persons desiring asylum as soon as she can plausibly claim to have had a message back to us and, uh, wish her and the team she sent in to Rome luck."

"Luck?"

"Yep." Mike grinned, broadly. "How many divisions has the pope? Right now, quite a few, even if they're in the wrong place to do him any good. Next week, if he gets out of Castel Sant'Angelo, none. I think the results might be, ah, interesting. And *very* embarrassing for Spain."

Chapter 39

Rome

Frank clutched his left hand tight in against himself, squatting down and pressing it between his thigh and belly. It wouldn't be so bad if it would just settle down and hurt. But just when he thought he'd gotten used to it, it'd start throbbing again. And he'd get to thinking about the fact that he had only three fingers on his left hand now.

That was better than poor Benito, who had a splinter of one of the tables he'd waited take one of his ears off and rip his cheek down to the bone. Dino had taken a nasty crack to the head diving for cover when they sent the last volley of musket fire into the building. Both of them were sitting in back, watching the cellar stairs and feeling sorry for themselves. Everyone else had various cuts and bruises and there was a lot of coughing going on.

But at least no one had been killed yet, on either side, as far as Frank could tell. And the two near-things they'd had with fires starting about the place had been put out before they did more than make the air in the place foul and vile to breathe. It had all just been one little accident after another. They had plenty of furniture to hide behind, and that, behind solid brick walls, made pretty effective protection against musket balls. Some of the ricochets were a little scary, but by the time they'd made a couple of bounces they were pretty much spent. One of Piero's friends had gotten hit in the ass, which had made him yelp, but the bullet hadn't even gone through his coattails. There was a bit of a scorch mark and he'd have a bruise, but everyone had gotten a laugh out of it.

They'd run out of lamp oil on the upper floors nearly an hour ago. The soldiers out front, who'd got themselves into positions in the house across the street so they weren't standing in the open to shoot, had settled down to occasionally letting fly with a few shots, as far as Frank could tell, just to let everyone inside know they were there.

"Time, yet?" Piero asked, "Only it's getting late, and there's this girl—"

"There's always a girl," Frank retorted, grinning back with only a slight flinch as another couple of musket balls splintered through the increasingly threadbare shutters to ping and whine around the room. "But, yes, it's getting about that time. Nearly dusk." They'd decided on that, earlier, so that when the women and kids and invalids were making their escape they'd have the best chance they could. And the guys who surrendered could say they'd only been doing it to buy them some time to get away. That was assuming they hadn't got out already. There probably wasn't anything stopping anyone in one of the other houses on this street from just going out and walking away. None of the soldiers seemed to be paying any attention to them, either as places to sack or possible routes into Frank's Place.

"Do we even have a white flag?" Piero asked.

"Bound to be a shirt we can use," Frank said. "And I think there's a broom handle behind the bar. That ought to do it."

"You realize we're probably going to get a beating even before the Inquisition starts asking us questions, right?" Piero was looking serious for a moment.

"Yeah, I'd figured," Frank said, although he hadn't. Made sense, though. These guys could've been off robbing the Vatican while they'd been trying to get in here, and a couple of them had been winged or scorched right at the start of the day. They'd be pissed. And Frank knew all about what jocks did when they got pissed. They found someone smaller and weaker than them to take it out on. Somehow Frank didn't think he'd be running any pranks on these guys, either.

It was, as his dad would say, a bummer. Still, it beat being dead. "I'll get the white flag and tell the wounded guys to get out," he said. "You remind everyone that when we get taken to the Inquisition, we tell 'em everything. No sense getting tortured, and we haven't committed any heresy, so the worst they can do is lock us up for a while."

"I wish I shared your confidence that that would stop them," Piero said. "I have heard *stories* about the Spanish Inquisition."

"It's that or total despair, right at the moment," Frank said.

"Despair has this to say for it, Frank: why did they come straight here?"

Frank heaved a sigh. He'd been hoping that the silence on that subject was because no one but him had noticed. "They want me, Piero. When I go out, I'll ask if me surrendering will mean the rest of you get out, okay? I wasn't going to say anything, and don't tell anyone because I don't want anyone trying to be a hero on my account."

Piero frowned. "What? And let you be a hero on our account?" Frank's expression must have been all the answer he needed. "Fine, fine. Whatever, we've saved nearly everyone, yes? Do what you feel you have to, but I'll not be running if it comes to it."

Frank shook his head. "Nuts, all of you," he said, and scuttled off to find a white flag.

Waiting for a lull in the shooting was a nervous few moments for Frank, because to get where he could poke the flag out through a ruined shutter he needed to get in front of the barricade of furniture. Someone over the street must've spotted the movement, because suddenly every single bullet that came over came through the window he was crouched under. Bits of glass and splinters of wood fell all over him and he couldn't help screwing up his eyes and trying to burrow into cracks in the plaster. Muskets might not be real accurate weapons, but across the width of a street they did just fine. A few seconds pause, and he thrust the broom handle with its dirty dishrag attached out into the evening sunlight.

A couple more shots and then there was shouting from outside. No more shooting. He got up and looked out of the window, holding the flag out and waving it as vigorously as he dared. Every last bit of him wanted to dive back behind the barricade and cower there like a mouse.

Someone across the street leaned out of *his* window and shouted something at Frank. *Problem number one,* he thought. "No hablo español!" he shouted back, hoping that that was the right language, and at the same time using pretty much the whole of his vocabulary in it.

"*Momento!*" came the shout back, followed by something that included what sounded like "*capitan.*" Were they telling him to wait for an officer? He hoped so.

A nervous wait. Five minutes? An hour? The soldiers across the street were leaning out of their windows and hollering to where, Frank could now see, they had a barricade of their own up. Somewhere to watch the action from shelter. Their barricade was a lot more professional looking than the ones Frank had been squatting behind all day, and there seemed to be a fair number of horses down there, too.

Frank squinted against the glare of the setting sun, which had now moved around to shine the other way along the street. Definitely horses, maybe two dozen. What use were cavalry going to be? Or maybe they just had a lot of officers here. And then Frank remembered what else horses did on battlefields. He couldn't see them from where he was, but he was willing to bet there were at least a couple of cannon waiting behind that barricade. *Looks like we did this just in the nick of time,* he thought.

Then a couple of guys emerged from behind the barricade and began walking briskly up to where Frank was. One of them was holding a pole-arm of some sort, Frank couldn't remember which name went with which weapon, but it was the one with a big spike and an axe-blade. Some sort of white cloth had been tied to it.

Frank sighed in relief. They were willing to talk, then. Best news he'd had all day. When the two soldiers got closer, Frank saw that they were an officer-type, all fancy clothes and waxed moustaches and wearing a sword, and another, older guy who, if you cut him in half, probably had "sergeant" written right through him. When they reached Frank, the sergeant immediately planted the staff of his weapon and began to lean on it with the air of a man who could, in that position, loaf all day. The officer took a considerably more martial stance, feet apart, hands clasped behind him.

"I am Don Vincente Jose-Maria Castro y Papas, Captain in the army of His Most Catholic Majesty of Spain," he said, in good, if accented, formal Italian. "To whom do I have the honor of speaking?"

"Uh, Frank Stone, of Lothlorien." Frank was impressed in spite of himself. This guy was being polite and civil even though he and his men had spent all day being shot at and firebombed by Frank and his guys. Maybe the fact that no one had gotten badly hurt yet helped. "I was hoping we could discuss surrender," he went on, realizing as he did so that, hippie upbringing or not, sensible tactical decision or not, he felt deeply ashamed.

Don Vincente's iron mask slipped a moment. He seemed, for just an instant, genuinely saddened. When he spoke again, he had softened his tone still further.

"Señor Stone," he said, "I am a man under authority. I have orders to accept no surrender and to reduce your resistance by force of arms. Apparently the Inquisition does not want you to surrender voluntarily. The most I can say is that I have no orders to ensure the death of you and all your comrades, and, more, that I would refuse orders to fire on a flag of parley. But I cannot take your surrender."

Frank looked back at Don Vincente. The man seemed genuinely upset by what he was being ordered to do. "Is there some way around your orders?" he asked. "We've only held out long enough to let the women and children get away."

"Some of them," Don Vincente said.

Frank just looked at him, hoping like hell that that didn't mean—

"We discovered a woman, a cripple and some children attempting to escape from where you had hidden them along the street, there." Don Vincente shrugged. "One of them was identified as your wife. If there were more, and note that I carefully do not ask that question of you for I would not have you stain your honor with even a ruse of war, the search the inquisitor ordered me to make did not reveal them."

Frank suspected there was a whole other story behind that little summary, not least because the sergeant there was grinning his head off. But he was too overtaken by shock to process it properly. *Giovanna captured!*

Don Vincente must have figured out how Frank was feeling, because he went on to say, "Alas for my good name with the inquisitor, the cripple and the children made good their escape. The sergeant here, you will note, is being punished for it. I am making him carry that heavy burden"—the sergeant flicked the white cloth tied to his weapon to show which burden was meant—"in the hopes that it will cure his most unmilitary sloth. I fear the man is irredeemably lazy. Had I known of his shirking tendencies earlier, I might have ordered some other man to search the building. Who knows what he missed?"

The wide, eagle-wing mustachios flickered once, briefly. Even Frank, standing close enough to smell the man, could not swear that he had smiled.

Giovanna captured! He could see how it had gone. They had tried to sneak out in small groups. Giovanna would have insisted on making the first, riskiest, run. And someone, probably someone who'd been a regular at Frank's Place, had taken money to point her out to the inquisitor. And if the inquisitor hadn't pissed this Captain Don Vincente-whatever off, everyone else would've been caught too. Or maybe the inquisitor hadn't done it by himself. Everything about Don Vincente said he was a man who might be a first-class bastard any way you looked at him, but he had his honor and orders could go right to hell. Ordering him to knowingly slaughter civilians—especially cripples and children—probably grated like a bitch with the guy. *Yay for hidalgo honor,* Frank thought.

Frank reckoned he'd probably have got on okay with the guy, another time and place. Hell, Ruy was a nice guy once you got past the weirdness and the constant stream of wisecracks. He took a deep breath. "Don Vincente, is there any chance your inquisitor would be satisfied with just my surrender?"

"My orders are for everyone," Don Vincente said,

his eyes narrowing, like he was weighing Frank up afresh. "I will inquire as to the specifics. I will offer no great hope in the matter, please understand." He turned and barked a stream of Spanish at the sergeant, who snapped up straight, brought his weapon up in some kind of salute, and marched off at a surprising turn of speed for a man supposed to be such a layabout.

"I see you brought cannon," Frank said, trying to combine small talk and intelligence-gathering in one fell swoop.

"Indeed," Don Vincente said, apparently not too troubled about what Frank knew. "Only the horses can be seen from here, but I have been given three medium field pieces with which to blast a way into your dwelling. A shot or two through your front door, now that your burning oil is exhausted, will open it handily. Except, of course, that this street is not wide enough for the gun to recoil without smashing against the house behind me. But, the inquisitor ordered cannon, so cannon I must use. I will fire on the oblique, from along the street. No more than a few hours cannonade will create a small breach, certain to be a death-trap to any man attempting to force it. But force it we shall. I have nearly three hundred men in this neighborhood now, as various parties of men have been sent to reinforce my company."

"Right," Frank said. "And, maybe, if those guys got through the breach and didn't get slaughtered doing it, they might be inclined to take prisoners?"

"Indeed," Don Vincente said, not cracking his face one bit. "And the inquisitor would be most disappointed if we did not take one or two prisoners. I will order a most careful search of the remainder of the premises for anyone who might be hiding, for example on an upper floor or in a cellar. It might be that my sergeant will redeem himself of his besetting sin of sloth? I certainly pray God that the fellow takes the path of righteousness."

Frank smiled, then. "He has an excellent example to follow, Don Vincente," he said. "I see that you follow every order you are given to the letter."

Don Vincente inclined his head briefly to acknowledge the compliment. "I see that my worthless layabout of a sergeant is returned."

Another exchange of Spanish, and Don Vincente turned back to Frank. "I must regretfully inform you that this parley is concluded. The inquisitor demands to know why I have not shot or arrested you. May I request a further half-hour's truce while I explain to the tiresome fellow what a white flag actually signifies?"

"By all means," Frank said, grinning in spite of himself.

"I shall have a bugle blown at the end of the half-hour, Señor Stone. Until we meet again, I wish you much joy of the day."

With that, and no further ceremony, Don Vincente and his sergeant walked away.

"Shit," Frank said, and went inside to tell the other guys.

Chapter 40

Rome

"Ruy Sanchez de Casador y Ortiz, you are just plain freakin' *nuts*."

Even in the gathering gloom, Tom could see the man's grin and the way the mustachios flared like the wings of a bird. Tom knew what kind of bird, too. A loon. "No, my way is perfect sanity. I, Ruy Sanchez de Casador y Ortiz, am perfectly sound of wits. It is those who would turn down the chance for such a magnificent adventure who are, as you say, freakin' nuts. And if we succeed, it will be spoken of in a thousand years."

Tom snickered. "Yeah, they'll be saying *jeez, were those guys nuts, or what?* Or possibly, *man, that was a horrible way to die!*"

Darkness had all but fallen, the sky a pale and purplish hue and the sun well down behind the skyline of Rome, if not fully over the horizon quite yet. And here they were, loafing about in plain view on the left bank of the Tiber, looking across the river at the Castel Sant'Angelo. The Ponte Sant'Angelo was out of the question, but Ruy was talking about boats as a way out of the city, and, now, a way across to the Castel itself. Two birds with one stone.

They'd left Doctor Nichols and a couple of Marines downriver a ways. They'd ridden around to the south, right through the gate as bold as brass, and left the horses, the doctor, and a small guard with orders to pick their way out of the city. The doctor had gotten away with his rather distinctive appearance so far by being dressed up as a Spanish soldier. They didn't have many black soldiers, but there were nevertheless a few who, through one misadventure or another, ended up bouncing around Europe. Tom had seen a couple as far north as Thuringia, although hadn't had much chance to talk to them. Ruy said that in a soldier's outfit, Doctor Nichols would attract mild curiosity, but would pose no particular problem.

Now, though, having seen what Ruy thought amounted to a perfectly reasonable proposition, Tom was beginning to doubt the man's sanity. To start with, there was the Castel Sant'Angelo itself. The walls were, from the looks, thirty to forty feet high. And guarded by enough men to keep up a constant cannonade from behind them. There was no telling if, or when, they'd take it into their heads to lob a few shells over to this side of the river. For now, they were pasting the general area around their fortress with a bombard shell every thirty seconds or so.

There didn't seem to be any pattern to it. Just, every now and then, a loud crash and, against the softly glowing evening sky, a trail of sparks would shoot up from somewhere inside the fort, arch over, and drop with a crash somewhere in the buildings around the fort. About every fourth shot was a dud, but otherwise there would then, a moment or two later, be a crack and a puff of smoke shot through with a flare of yellow flame. Sometimes, if the bombardiers got lucky, a few screams.

Which was bad enough. But to get a chance to get blown up on the way to the sheer walls and alert guards, they first had to get past what looked like, allowing for the dim light, the entire Spanish army. All of whom had their attention very, very firmly fixed on the aforementioned sheer-walled fortress and its alert guards, *et cetera*.

The plan to get across the river seemed sound enough. Most of the wall was pretty well lit up with bonfires that the besiegers had lit, just outside accurate shooting distance. The exception was on this near side, where the fortress stood right at the riverside. The main defense here was the river itself, and getting across the river to the esplanade under the fort walls basically meant coming right under the fort's guns. So there were no fires there, and the fires to either side cast long, deep shadows right along the wall. Once they got that far, they would be all but invisible. The Spanish commander had apparently decided that sending men over there was a waste, a certain slaughter as there was no cover anywhere on the Ponte Sant'Angelo. He had simply left a guard force on the near end of the bridge to contain any sally the defenders might make.

Those guys, apart from a couple of sentries watching along the bridge, had taken the sensible view that two hundred Swiss Guards weren't going to be attempting a daring breakout any time soon and had gotten comfortable, with small fires here and there and a fair few of them stretched out either side of the road exercising a soldier's privilege of racking out when nothing interesting was happening.

Meanwhile, down on the river, there was actually still some river traffic. There were boatmen who ran a taxi service, and a few were still plying for hire. Tom had no doubt that some of those boats were carrying refugees, sneaking out of the city by one of the many routes the invaders couldn't watch. There weren't many, though. Just enough for cover. The rest of the boats were clustered at piers up and down the river, tied up against the day when the shooting stopped and people wanted rides again. If they could just get the pope on one of those boats and downstream out of the city, they could retrieve the horses and get the hell out of Dodge a lot faster than any pursuit could be organized and get after them. That would give them a chance to break contact, and once they did that and lit out across country, the chances of getting caught before they had the pope well on his way to whatever sanctuary his people thought best were actually pretty small.

The trick was going to be bringing that happy outcome about without indulging in what looked like a messy and elaborate suicide.

"Did we even bring a rope?" Tom asked, trying to figure out how the hell they were going to get over that wall.

"Have faith, Señor Simpson," Ruy said. "We are about the Lord's work."

"On a mission from God, eh? Put like that, I've no reason to worry at all. I'm certainly not thinking that, in fact, you don't have a plan of any kind at all for this. Not in the least."

"Plans? Faugh. The playthings of lesser intellects. I, Ruy Sanchez de Casador y Ortiz, need no plan. Insult me no further with such talk, Señor Simpson. We must steal, I think, four boats."

"Four boats?" Tom looked around, wondering what kind of counting system the old guy was using. They'd started out with Ruy, Tom himself, Doctor Nichols, Captain Taggart and six Marines. Three of the Marines had stayed with Doctor Nichols, leaving six to get across the river. Either Sanchez was planning on stealing really, really small boats, or he was improvising madly and a spare or three were going to come in to it somewhere.

"Indeed. Four boats. To ensure that none of them sink. Listen, Señor Simpson, to the voice of experience."

"This is going to be good, isn't it?" ,

"The best advice always is. As you are aware, all pursuit of the profession of arms is attended by a most malign imp, a hell-spawn shat from the very asshole of Satan himself, whose sole delight is in ensuring that if, in the affairs of mortal men, it can go wrong, it will."

Tom nodded. "We Americans call him 'Murphy.'"

"Truly? Then you are not a people as wholly divorced from reality as I had thought. But no matter. Were we to steal exactly sufficient boats to accomplish our task, nothing is surer that one of them would spring a leak, or we should be struck by a random shot in the dark. Nothing, but nothing, would be surer. But if we provide ourselves with more boats than we need—"

"Then if all of them float, then we've gone to a lot of wasted time and effort, yes, I see what you're saying."

"Logic. Reason. I, Ruy Sanchez de Casador y Ortiz, am truly a master of these disciplines. Ah, here are the very craft we require."

While they had been talking Ruy had been leading them down a set of steps to where a wooden jetty was home to a large number of rowboats. Most of them looked like they could take a couple of passengers at least in addition to whoever was going to be rowing them. There were even a couple of bigger models. They were all unattended. And all lacked oars. Well, that made sense. Like not leaving the keys in your car. Tom looked around for somewhere that might be an oar-storage shed, but wasn't seeing one anywhere. And then he heard the sound of splintering wood over the sounds of the battle on the far side of the river.

Ruy's direct approach in action again. He had gotten the Marines organized ripping the simple bench seats out of several of the boats, to use as paddles, it looked like. They were using their forage axes to pry the things out, and had so far manage to free one of them. *Well, if it's that simple*, Tom thought, and stepped into one of the smaller boats that they almost certainly wouldn't be using. Now, the Marines were all well-built guys, tough, wiry customers that no one would want to mess with casually. Tom, on the other hand, still had the build of a nearly-pro footballer and hadn't stinted any on his exercise regime since the Ring of Fire. One swift tug, and a thwart came up in his hand. A twist and the pegs at the other end gave way. He ripped out three in quick succession, during which time the Marines had gotten one more out. "How many more do we need?" he asked brightly, noting the look on Ruy's face.

"Three more should suffice," Ruy said, momentarily at a loss for words, which Tom judged entirely worth the grazed knuckles he'd picked up.

Tom looked across. It was maybe two hundred yards, and the river didn't seem to be in full flood; there was a little mud showing under the jetty on this side, and the same on one a little upstream of the fortress on the other. It wouldn't be so bad. From here, with a little effort, they could get across to the shadows under the bridge on the other side. Hopefully, the boats wouldn't be noticed, because with only Captain Taggart and three Marines to keep an eye on them, they were relying entirely on stealth for that part of the mission. Tom couldn't help feeling that maybe, just maybe, they needed a bit more planning than they were doing. On the other hand, Ruy had been pulling crazy stunts like this for longer than Tom had been alive, so maybe he was approaching this as just another routine rescue of a major spiritual leader against thousand-to-one odds. *Done it a dozen times before. Could do it again in my sleep.* Suitably embellished with appropriately Catalan curlicues and declarations of honor and willingness to dare all in pursuit of his goal, of course.

Tom couldn't help thinking, as he helped drag the boats off the mud and into the water, of Sean Connery in all those action-movie roles he had played well into his fifties or sixties. Not that that was any guide to reality, but it was getting remarkably easy to imagine Ruy with a Scots accent.

The paddle across the river, the sweating, sore back and blistered hands apart, proved to be fairly easy. Pulling the boats up on to the mud below the river wall, only a little trickier. Tom's boots, filled as they were with a hair over two hundred and seventy pounds of footballer, sunk a bit deeper than everyone else's, and it was all he could do not to lose one of them.

There were steps up to the esplanade. Tom was just craning his neck to see if there was any cover at the top when Ruy started strolling up them, for all the world as if he was on a pleasant evening promenade without a care in the world.

"Are you *nuts*?" Tom hissed, wondering as he did so why he was trying to whisper. Between all the shouting and shooting and the regular firing of bombards from inside the fort, even if he could have been heard, anyone who might have been listening was probably halfway to deaf anyway.

Ruy turned back and the low light of the evening, the moon not yet risen, revealed a wide grin. "Señor Simpson, nothing is surer to make a sentry want to shoot than the sight of a man creeping up on the fortress he guards. So, we do not creep up."

"But *those guys*," Tom said, jerking a thumb over his shoulder to indicate the several hundred soldiers waiting on the opposite bank of the Tiber. "They're going to see you for sure."

"Are they? A man, two hundred yards away, in the dark, with fires there"—he pointed toward one side of the fort—"and there"—he pointed to the other—"to dazzle their eyes? I think not, Señor Simpson. In this place, señor, we are in the safest place in Rome this evening."

Put like that, it did make a twisted kind of sense. There was the old joke about walking confidently with a piece of paper in your hand. Tom hadn't ever tried it, and suspected that like a great many such things that "everyone" knew, it was a lot of hooey. Still—

"I hope you know what you're doing," he muttered as he followed Ruy up the steps.

"A' ken richt weel whit he's deein,'" Tom heard from behind him. "Bein' a mad bampot Spaniard, like always." It did nothing for Tom's confidence that the Marine who'd said it had known Ruy a lot longer than he had.

Ruy had got out of sight briefly at the top of the steps, and when Tom got to the top and saw what Ruy was doing, it was all he could do not to turn tail and flee, gibbering in terror. Ruy was striding across the esplanade, looking up at the battlements of one of the corner bastions where the wall was a little lower, maybe twenty feet, and waving his hat.

From above, a helmet was just visible, peering down at the apparent lunatic making a one-man, unarmed assault without a ladder on a battlemented fortress wall. There was a musket up there, and even in the dim light Tom could see that it wasn't leveled. Yet.

"Hello the fort!" Ruy called out, in what sounded like the Roman dialect of Italian that Tom had been hearing about the place this last couple of weeks.

Tom couldn't quite catch what got shouted back, being a few yards behind the lunatic Catalan and more occupied with looking around for the small horde of Spanish soldiers who were, he was sure, going to come thundering into view at any moment to do for the pair of them.

He heard Ruy's response, though. "My name is Ruy Sanchez de Casador y Ortiz. I'm here to rescue the pope. Please lower a rope!"

Tom groaned. The *least* they could expect now was to learn some Swiss swearwords. He strained his ears for the sound of muskets being cocked, peered into the shadows between the battlements for the glow of matches being blown on for a shot. He had maybe three, four paces to go and if he dived down the steps he probably wouldn't suffer more than minor scrapes and bruises.

Whatever the answer actually was, and again Tom didn't quite catch it, Ruy turned and smiled. "Did I, Ruy Sanchez de Casador y Ortiz, not counsel faith? A humble trust in divine providence? He has gone to fetch an officer."

"He needs orders to shoot us?"

Ruy shrugged. "This they will not do. We are no threat. If there is an assault sent from across the bridge, *then* they will shoot us. For now, we are simply two men outside the walls. We are no threat, nor likely to be one."

"Can't you get them to open a gate for us?" Tom said, not liking the idea of climbing a rope to get up over that wall. Right here they were in fairly deep shadow, cast along the wall by the corner bastion from the bonfire further along the riverbank. They'd have to go into the light some to reach the door at the midpoint of the wall, but it looked like an easier bet all round than trying to get over the wall just here.

"It will be barricaded. They will suspect a trick if we insist on that being opened," Ruy said. "Besides, what cause have you to complain? You are young, and strong. I am the aged and infirm member of this party."

"Aged and infirm maybe," Tom muttered, "but with the mind of a teenager."

There was movement above, and a shout of "*Who did you say you were?*"

"Ruy Sanchez de Casador y Ortiz, and with me is Signor Thomas Simpson of the Embassy of the United States of Europe. We are here to rescue His Holiness." Ruy was now standing right in the shadows under the wall, practically invisible even from five feet away where Tom was standing. *Method in his madness,* Tom thought.

The madness part had been spotted by whoever was on top of the wall. Tom didn't quite catch all of the idiom, but he figured "madder than a hatful of assholes" was probably a fair translation.

"Precisely!" Ruy shouted back, "No one will be expecting it! May we come in and discuss the matter like gentlemen, or will you keep us out here all night like unwelcome peddlers?"

A shout came back that they should wait. A few nervous minutes later and a pair of thick ropes dropped over the wall.

"See?" Ruy said, grabbing a rope and bracing one boot against the wall to begin the climb. "Now for the *difficult* part."

"Getting out alive?" Tom said, giving the rope an experimental tug. It seemed to be securely attached. It better be, given what he weighed.

"No," Ruy said, between grunts of effort. "Persuading His Holiness to come with us."

It would pretty much figure that the pope would be as nuts as everyone else was acting tonight and want to stay in here. *He's nuts? Tom Simpson, you're going in there with him.* "Right," Tom said, and began to climb.

Chapter 41

Rome

"I cannot believe that just worked," Tom said, as he hauled himself over the parapet onto the lower battlement of the Bastion of St. John of the Castel Sant'Angelo. "Did someone forget to pay the reality bill?"

That got him a whole series of frowns. From Ruy, because he'd used an idiom that wouldn't mean squat for about three hun—well, maybe a hundred years, if electricity caught on here the way it had up-time. From about a dozen suspicious-looking Swiss Guards, a really suspicious-looking Swiss Guard officer and several incredibly suspicious-looking priests, because he'd said it in English, and they didn't appear to understand the language. All of the guards were armed; halberds, slung matchlock muskets and each with his own individual assortment of close-quarter mayhem. Plus grenades. He noticed that Ruy was very ostentatiously keeping his hands well clear of his weapons, and he did the same. "Hi!" he said, brightly and with a big smile. "Tom Simpson, pleased to meet you," he added, almost certain he'd mangled the Italian he'd switched to.

The Swiss Guard officer nodded. "Adolf Weisser, and it is an honor to meet you also, Signor Simpson. I understand you are one of the Americans who are said to be from the future? For the moment I take it on trust that you gentlemen are who you claim to be."

"I am, although these days I'm from the United States of Europe," he said. "Has Señor Sanchez already asked for an audience with the Holy Father?"

"I had not," Ruy said, "but this is indeed why we are here."

"I do not see that this is a good idea," Weisser said. "This man is a Spaniard, and while you claim to be one of the Americans, I have no way of knowing if what you say is true. An assassin, at this time, would spare those outside our walls a great deal of trouble."

"I understand your problem," Tom said. "Have you heard about the technical marvels we Americans are capable of?"

"I have," one of the priests said, not bothering to introduce himself.

Tom decided the man was probably an inquisitor, or whatever branch of the church it was that did the pope's spying for him. He'd boned up a little on the distinctive dress of the various religious orders within the Catholic Church and from the looks, this guy was a Jesuit. "If I could just show you one or two things, I think I can prove I'm not with the Spanish army. For what it's worth, Señor Sanchez here is married to Dottoressa Nichols, our ambassadora to the Holy See, and the prime minister of the United States,

Michael Stearns, is my brother-in-law. Now," he dug in his pocket, "see here—"

They'd anticipated this problem during the brief— very brief—planning session they'd had before riding back to Rome. As well as getting a short message from Cardinal Barberini that would identify them to the pope—committed to memory, as it would work pretty well for anyone who captured the message—Tom had picked up a few items that they had had among the embassy party that were unquestionably up-time in origin. A solar-powered four-function calculator, a little flashlight whose batteries were currently charged courtesy of a great deal of sweat from one of the radio guys and the pedal generator that usually went to working the radio, and his own personal shotgun. Originally belonging to Dan Frost, it was a real hit with the Swiss Guards, who politely asked to see it fire. Tom had brought a whole satchelful of rounds for it, some of the first coming out of the new munitions works at Suhl producing percussion-cap rounds for the private market, and let off three cartridges of buckshot in the general direction of the Spanish army by way of demonstration.

Naturally, they wanted to know how it worked, and they took turns away from trying to see what the Spaniards were doing past the ring of bonfires to listen attentively while he explained the cartridges and the pump-action mechanism. The questions were intelligent, and they were all professionally impressed with such a convenient and useful weapon.

Tom decided he could get to like the Swiss Guards. He still kept in touch with the German ex-mercenaries in the regiment he'd helped organize just after the

Ring of Fire, and the Swiss Guards were from a similar mold. A little less rough-and-ready, what with having to be on their best behavior at various church functions all the time, but basically the same. And after having dealt with a dozen different dialects of German, Tom found the Swiss dialect pretty easy to understand within a few minutes. While he was chatting with the Guards, Ruy had been convincing the Jesuit who had spoken that they were safe to be allowed into the papal presence, even agreeing that they would check their weapons at the door of the audience chamber. The Guards seemed fairly sorry to see the shotgun go, if nothing else.

Getting to see the pope turned out to be something of a trek. Once out of the bastion, the interior of the Castel Sant'Angelo's citadel was a lot more convoluted than it had been when Tom had played tourist there as a teenager, when it had been a museum. The building had had a nearly two thousand year history by then and Tom had found it confusing. Now, at sixteen hundred years and a working fortress and prison rather than a museum, it was even worse. There was the detritus of extensive renovation and building works shoved aside everywhere, and the place was full of scurrying priests, nuns, and assorted guys with guns and other weapons who were being soldiers for the day.

The route up through the central keep of the Castel Sant'Angelo, which had begun life as the Mausoleum of the Emperor Hadrian, was like traveling through a layered history of Roman architecture, starting with the remains of the original tomb at the bottom, a spiral corridor up through the monument, proceeding to the medieval prison level and thence up to the renaissance apartments built on the top of the fortress, an oblong block of papal luxury standing across the drum of classical fortification.

His Holiness was, of all places, on the roof. He was dressed in what Tom had to suppose had to be called "civilian" clothes, although they were a couple of decades out of fashion and rather expensive-looking. There was a small breastplate in evidence and a helmet on the table next to him. Clearly what the well-dressed pope wore to a battle. In fact, there seemed to be no cardinals nor bishops nor any other senior clergy in evidence. The only priests Tom could see were in the regular dress of ordinary priests or Jesuits and one or two other orders of priests that Tom didn't know well enough to tell apart.

That figured. If what Barberini had seen was typical, any senior priest in this place was on a hit-list of some kind. Either they'd heard the same story or were smart enough to figure it out, and were ready to take it on the lam incognito. And the fact that they were all ready to run pretty much summed up the way they were thinking inside the Castel Sant'Angelo.

One of the priests who had guided them up to the papal presence went over to converse with the aides surrounding the pope. Looking around, Tom could see that the rooftop had a commanding view of the defenses, although if the army outside got any artillery worth the name organized it was going to be a place they'd have to get the hell out of pretty quickly.

While they waited, he turned to Ruy, who was leaning over the parapet watching the gunners below heave and grunt to service their bombards. "You reckon they can hold here?" he asked, quietly.

"No," Ruy said, not taking his eyes from the sight of the men laboring over the bombards by torchlight below. "The first escalade will carry the wall, possibly in many places at once. With more men, more time to prepare, or the outer defenses intact, or any of a hundred other things not as they are, there might be hope for some days. As it is?" Ruy shrugged. "And they know it. But these are the Swiss Guard. It is a little more than a hundred years since they died, almost to the last man, guarding a pope. They will not surrender so long as His Holiness still stands here, his flag flying."

"I wonder if they've tried asking for terms."

"I know not. It would certainly seem like the prudent course, and there is no good reason why they should not leave with full military honors." Ruy sucked at his mustachios a moment. "No reason for a reasonable besieger to refuse such, of course. They would wish His Holiness given into their captivity first, which of course they cannot do, but if His Holiness surrendered himself—"

"I wonder if he offered?"

Ruy shrugged. "We will discover this momentarily," he said.

There was time for four more bombard shots to go off. From here, Tom could see that they were mounted on the battlements of the inner keep, three stories below. They were being worked by crews that consisted mostly of uniformed Swiss Guards, another sign that the fortress had been caught woefully unprepared. If there were professional gunners to work those cannon, they had been caught outside the castle. Tom wondered what they were achieving with all that effort, other than to piss the attackers off. There were regular cannon on the walls as well, guns fixed to fire out over the outer defenses, and maybe cover the outer part of the outer ward. Maybe they could be depressed to cover the inner ward, but it didn't look like it. They might be some help if the walls of the inner ward were about to fall, but again it didn't appear as though they'd depress to fire that close. Maybe there were guns lower down that would serve. Ruy didn't seem to think so, though. And, when it came down to it, with thousands of attackers in the assault there would be little the cannon would achieve anyway. They took minutes to load, and were hard to aim accurately. The medieval inner defenses of the Castel Sant'Angelo depended on having a great deal of manpower to make them effective. Tom had to admire the poor doomed bastards who were going to try anyway. *And if the army outside is really alert for escapers, we'll end up joining 'em.*

"His Holiness will see you now," said the priest who had guided them up.

Tom had been expecting an old guy—somehow he had been imagining someone who looked like John Paul II, the only pope he had ever known back up-time.

"Your Holiness does us much honor," Ruy said, and knelt. Tom wasn't sure of protocol for a non-Catholic visiting a pope, so he followed what Ruy was doing.

"A rescue party of two?" the pope asked, when they had regained their feet. "I have heard much of the marvelous machines possessed by the Americans. Can it be that some such contrivance is to be employed? An airplane, perhaps?" There seemed to be genuine yearning in his voice at that last.

"Your Holiness," Ruy said, "no great wonders, simply myself and some few brave companions. We bring an offer of the assistance of the United States of Europe, and asylum in that nation if Your Holiness so desires."

"Alas, I cannot abandon—"

"Your Holiness," Tom said, "that's so much crap. It's you they want to kill."

The pope's old-fashioned look in reply had a good three hundred years' head start on any such look Tom had ever had before. "Did they desire only that, Signor Simpson, they would have accepted my offer to give myself into their hands. As it is, all offers of parley have been rejected."

"That figures," Tom said. "They can't just shoot you after taking you prisoner; that makes you a martyr. Have you heard what's happening to cardinals who support you?"

The pope inclined his head and cocked an eyebrow in silent inquiry.

"They are being assassinated," Ruy said. "We have word of nearly a dozen dead so far, from the father-general, and your own nephew saw Cardinal Bischi done to death in the street only this morning. It is the father-general's estimation that any cardinal who might not cooperate with Borja in the next conclave is being killed, if there is any chance he might be in Rome in time for the conclave. He has no conclusive information in relation to the cardinals elsewhere in Italy, but—" Ruy's silence, and small, discarding gesture with his left hand, was as suggestive as a whole litany of dead priests.

"We suspected . . ." the pope said. His face had

gone from drawn and tired and harassed-looking to masklike. Almost as if the undertakers had been at work. Serene, even.

"Now the Holy Father knows." Ruy's tone was flat. "I have a message from Cardinal Antonio Barberini the Younger by way of authentication, if Your Holiness' advisors are in any doubt."

Tom caught the parsing. One look at the face of His Holiness Urban VIII would reassure anyone that he doubted not a single word, and would have believed if it had come from Satan himself.

Some of the papal aides began to get it. "He means to make himself pope," one of them murmured, and there were several gasps and not a few angry mutters.

Urban was shaking his head slowly. "Then I must ask myself whether, in these most difficult of times, Holy Mother Church can survive an antipope." He turned on its aides. "*Can it?* Advise me."

A lot of blank looks was the reply. A lot of blank, worried looks.

"Your Holiness," Tom said, "if I understood Father-General Vitelleschi correctly, there is going to be an antipope come what may. I don't know the law of the church, but assassinating your predecessor, even if it's covered up as confusion of the battle, has to make an election invalid, doesn't it?"

"Debatable, my son," the pope said. "There is precedent." His mouth twisted into a wry grin. "Not all of what the Protestants say about previous holders of my office is entirely slanderous."

"Your Holiness, would you have the likes of *Borja* as the true pope?" Ruy asked, and there was venom in his voice as he said the name. That figured. Ruy had seen more of what Borja had ordered done in Rome today than anyone else here, if Tom's guess was right. "If he holds the throne of Saint Peter, he can do so only as antipope while you yet live."

For long moments, no one spoke over the sound of the cannon roaring and the hubbub of the defenders about their work. "I must think about this," the pope said, at length. "And I must pray for guidance. There remain yet some hours—"

There came a distant roar, as of hundreds, thousands of throats yelling defiance. All along the parapet, heads turned, men leaned over and peered into the darkness. Tom looked himself, as did everyone in the party around the pope.

Beyond the fires that the besiegers had lit in the outer ward, the outer defenses were visible as vague firelit blurs. Only now they seemed to heave and writhe and move, and gleam here and there as the firelight caught on helmets, breastplates, and weapons.

"They begin the escalade early," Ruy said. "Foolish. Many more will die than might have in a dawn attack. Your Holiness, if you will go, you must go *now*."

Outside, in the firelight, the advancing columns were plainly visible, lit by the fires they themselves had set. From within the advancing columns—merging into a crowd as they neared the walls—little jets of flame marked where musketeers were optimistically shooting at the walls. From the walls themselves, jets of flame in answer as Guards emptied their pieces at the oncoming horde. It wasn't enough. It would never have been enough. Tom could already see ladders beginning to rise.

That sparked a thought, and he dashed over to the

far side to check the riverside wall. Nothing so far, and he could see the Guards on that wall running to either end to hold the bastions. "Ruy," he called out, "we can get out through the gate in the river wall if we go now. I don't see an assault coming over the bridge."

Ruy had been urgently addressing the pope, then appealing to the bodyguard who were with him even here. Now he headed for the stairs down, surrounded by Swiss Guards and holding the pope's arm. He managed to make it look like a gesture of support for an elderly gentleman—only a few years older than he himself was, but in attitude the gap was decades wide—but in truth it was the nearest he could get to frogmarching the pope.

Tom carefully kept his face straight as he joined them. "His Holiness tried to order the Guard to surrender while we escape," Ruy said. "Their commander has refused the order. They will fight to the last to cover our flight."

The pope began to say something.

"No, Holy Father," Ruy said, cutting him off, "do not waste this. These men serve the Church in their way, serve her in yours that they do not do so in vain."

The laughing adventurer, making light of every difficulty, was gone of a sudden, Tom noticed. Ruy's face had set hard into the mask of a conquistador, intent on deadly purpose and grim slaughter to all who stood in his way. A far cry from the joker who'd waltzed into a fortress under siege simply by asking nicely.

Oh shit, Tom thought, *if Ruy's getting serious, we are in deep, deep shit.*

Chapter 42

Rome

Frank looked at the gun on the shelf under the bar in front of him. He'd been halfway to giving the thing to the guys upstairs for the last hour. He'd kept it in case he needed it, but made sure it wasn't actually in his hand in case the assault started. He wanted to be down and in a posture of abject surrender immediately and with no possibility of being mistaken for a threat by even the most nervous musketeer. Which meant that it was pretty silly to have it here where it was *guaranteed* to be no use whatsoever. And it wasn't like he was in any shape to fight either. What with splinters in various bits of him, cuts and bruises and the pain from his hand, he really didn't feel like fighting at all.

The street outside was getting dim, and inside the bar it was almost pitch black. Frank had allowed one small candle, and made sure to stand well away from it. Maybe that Captain Don Vincente was a reasonably decent sort of guy and wouldn't order a massacre. That didn't mean that the musketeers across the street wouldn't do their level best to make sure there wasn't any resistance inside. The end of the bar where the candle was flickering and dancing was taking all the musket fire, with balls crashing into that part of the room a couple of times a minute. Piero, who was doing his level best to look nonchalant on a kicked-back chair with his heels on the bar, had tried running bets on how long it would take for the musketeers to succeed in shooting the flame out, but the joke had got old an hour ago.

Frank cringed again as the cannon along the street banged—where, Frank wondered, did all those guys writing about old battles get the notion that cannon roared? This one made a huge bang and then shook the building and Frank's teeth. A roar was more drawn out, kind of. He tensed up for the crash, not that he ever did so in time, and then relaxed as he realized they'd missed again. That had made him giggle at first. Missing the broad side of a building was *the* standard of bad marksmanship. And then Frank had remembered what the captain had said; if he didn't want to simply smash up the cannon, he had to fire from along the street and make a hole in Frank's wall by bouncing cannonballs off it at an angle. A lot of that façade was wooden paneling between brick arches, and a fair proportion of that was already pretty busted up. Only the door was closed completely, although there was a chunk of the brickwork missing from one side of it already.

It wouldn't be long, anyway. They were getting a shot off every three or four minutes. Frank had no idea whether that was quick or slow for three guns, but they'd kept it up for two hours now. They'd only missed a few shots, and the ones that had hit had got in between the columns of the brick arches that made up the front of the ground floor of his place and smashed the woodwork out of its supports. Frank wasn't too happy about what was happening to the brickwork, either. He wasn't an engineer, but there was one column that looked like it had had most of its outer face smashed away. And this building had been standing hundreds of years on those columns; Frank wasn't sure about how well they'd hold up with one of them shot away and all the others battered by a couple of dozen cannonballs.

Piero coughed on the falling dust. It was pretty constant now, although when the cannons hit they produced a massive shower. Which was damn strange, actually. Given how much housework Giovanna had them all doing upstairs, it wasn't like there was any dust left in the place. "Seems like cannon are harder to aim than they look, eh?" he said.

"Looks like," Frank said. "That makes, what, three or four misses?"

"I count five, with that. I don't like the look of that wall, either."

"I was wondering about that, too." Piero's presence was helping a lot. If he'd been on his own, he'd have gone completely nuts by now. One or two prisoners, the captain had said, and they'd decided on two. Piero was the only other realistic candidate. The Inquisition *had* to have Frank, no question. Of everyone who was left, Piero was the one with the most family connections and money and so had the best chance of getting off with the aid of a good lawyer and a little luck, probably with no more than a dose of intimidation by being shown a fully stocked torture room. Which was, apparently, standard procedure before questioning anyone. Piero planned to confess to a couple of years' worth of drunkenness, adultery and general misbehavior to keep them from torturing him because they suspected he was hiding something. He'd joked that if he was lurid enough in the details he could get the Inquisition to boot him out just to keep him from killing the priests with jealousy.

Piero took a swig of wine. "I could wish it was safe to step out in the street and surrender."

"We'd get shot. Whoever that inquisitor is, he got those guys with the muskets plenty stirred up." Most of the day had passed with no more than a desultory few volleys of fire from across the street, which had scattered a few splinters of glass and wood about the place and served to keep everyone's heads down. But being mostly out of sight of officers and not being in any position to do much other than waste ammo, the soldiers had settled into a rhythm of a shot every few minutes, apparently more for looks' sake rather than anything else. When the cannon opened up, the musketeers had stopped for a little while, and for a few minutes after the rest of the guys had gotten safely hidden upstairs Frank and Piero had considered going out and surrendering in the street so they didn't have to endure any more cannonballs crashing into the front of the bar.

Then someone—or something—had made them go into high gear. There seemed to be more of them over there, too. From a shot every few minutes it went to two or three a minute, with occasional flurries that had Frank and Piero forgetting the nonchalance they were trying to display and crouching behind the invitingly solid bulk of the bar. Even the regular rate of shooting put paid to the notion of going out there. If nothing else, the sight of any movement in here would attract every would-be Hawkeye across the street.

Same with the stable yard, which had a lot less cover and was overlooked by all of the buildings across the street. There was maybe three or four feet out front where a shooter on the roof opposite couldn't get them.

Piero sighed between musket shots. "I know. What is keeping them? Surely even a Spanish soldier could make his way through what is left of your front wall? My great uncle Pierpaolo could get through some of those gaps, and he is famous for eating six meals a day."

"Maybe they want to see a hole in—"

Frank winced and hunkered down some more as another cannon-shot sounded, and this time hit the front of the building. A brief cacophony of bangs and crashes and a gentle shower of wood splinters and chips of brick told Frank that the thing had ricocheted inside the taverna. It sounded like someone had taken the entire contents of the building up to the roof and tipped the lot four stories down on to the cobbles in one go, and finished with the sound of breaking glass.

"Shit," he said, with feeling, once he was sure the little lump of hot iron had stopped bouncing around. "Second time that's happened."

He risked a peek, surveying the piles of furniture in the main bar room area. There was just enough light to tell that what had already been a messy heap had now been stirred up and trashed even more. As he watched, a pile that had been tottering gave way, either knocked askew or with some crucial support smashed out. Another crash, this time a little less flinch-inducing. It looked like the cannonball had left through one of the windows to the yard; there was a little more light from the evening sky filtering in that way now. The next musket ball came by uncomfortably close, no more than eighteen inches above his head, and Frank ducked back down, his pulse suddenly hammering in his ears and his mouth full of the cold coppery taste of fear. Clearly he'd been visible, the movement maybe. Missing by eighteen inches was about par for what they were able to do with those weapons at fifteen, twenty yards, Frank recalled. So clearly they'd been aiming at him, not at the light at the other end of the bar.

Sure enough, whatever it was that periodically put a wild hair up the asses of the musketeers started biting again. A ragged volley of shots passed over Frank's head, and he heard the dull tock—tock—tock of rounds hitting the wood of the bar. *Thank God for cheap carpentry,* he thought. They'd saved on building the bar by doing it themselves. The counter itself had been installed by a pro, but the structure of the thing was something he and Salvatore had knocked together themselves using the parts from a couple of old, heavy tables they'd found when they moved in. The things had been something like the picnic tables Frank had known back in Grantville, except without the gaps between the planks, which were three or four inches thick. *If I'd known, I'd have bought some sheet iron for 'em,* he thought to himself.

"I don't think those fellows like you all that much," Piero said, and the mournful tone in his voice gave Frank a fit of the giggles.

"You think? I thought it was just the guys with the cannon who were pissed at me."

"No, those fellows are just crude in their wooing, Frank," Piero said, deadpan, and then, in the faggiest falsetto he could manage, *"Look what a big gun I've got, Frank, let me fire it for you!"*

Frank knew he shouldn't, but he laughed anyway. What the hell, he was three hundred years away from Gay Rights, or whatever it was. *And probably going to die anyway*, a little voice at the back of his mind added. He laughed long and loud, and hoped the musketeers across the road could hear him. Even if they did, they slacked off the fire a little.

Which meant that he heard the creaking start. "You hear that, Piero?" he asked.

Frank could hear Piero swallow nervously before he answered. "A kind of groaning noise?"

"I was thinking creaking," Frank said, wondering how in hell he was managing to fix on something so freaking trivial at a time like this. "I'm also thinking that this place isn't going to take much more punishment before it falls down. You want to take a look, see what you think? I think they're watching for me to poke my head up here."

Which was true enough. But more to the point, Frank wasn't sure he *could* get up again, he was fast coming to realize. He'd tried to will his legs to stand up under him so he could poke his head over the bar, and found they wouldn't budge. He felt down each trouser-leg while Piero was risking a glance, and came up dry. He hadn't been shot. *So this is what it feels like*, Frank thought, *being too terrified to move.* He didn't feel like he was a gibbering wreck at all. In fact, he felt quite clear-headed. And he knew what he had to do, or ought to do, at least. He just couldn't make himself do it. He decided he'd shift a bit away from the position he'd been in, and found he could move quite handily if he didn't think about getting up. There was nothing wrong with his legs.

He tried to stand up again, and couldn't. Even the thought of doing it made him feel nauseated, now, and his legs shook in their rebellion at what Frank was trying to make them do. And there was a constant whine of musket balls overhead and the occasional hammer-blow of a ball into the front of the bar to remind him of why this was so.

Piero grunted a swearword and sat down heavily on the floor. The musketfire shifted over to his spot, and that wild hair seemed to have gotten back up the musketeers. It was like being in a giant popcorn-maker for a few seconds. When it settled down, Piero called softly, "You okay, Frank?"

So he'd noticed Frank shuffling about. "Yeah, just getting comfortable," he said, and blushed at the lie. In the dark, Piero saw nothing. Frank hoped like hell his voice wouldn't give him away. "What'd you see?" he asked.

"One of the pillars, to the left of the door, looks like it's about to give way. That last shot must've knocked out a big lump, there's about four, five bricks left right now, and the top part is leaning over. I think I see the ceiling sagging down some."

Frank found his mouth going dry and his stomach

churning. He needed the bathroom, and needed it real bad. He'd read an Edgar Allan Poe story when he was a kid, about some guy who got bricked up in a wall, and ever since then the thought of getting buried or shut in had creeped him out completely. Having it happen on top of an entire day of getting shot at was moving Frank's mental needle clear over to "wig out." He couldn't stop himself whimpering a little. *Get a grip, Frank.* "What about the guys upstairs?" he wondered aloud.

There was a long pause from Piero. Frank took comfort from the fact that the thought of the ceiling coming down was getting to Piero too. Finally, Piero said, "Frank, at this time and in this place, sorry specimen of Christian charity that I am, I could not give a fuck about the guys upstairs. Their corpses will be on *top* of the wreckage."

Frank thought he heard Piero's voice catch on the word *corpses*. Then he realized something else. "Hey, when did we last get shot at?"

"You're right. Maybe it's about to be over." The sheer hope and yearning in Piero's voice almost made Frank laugh out loud.

A loud and violent crunch, followed by a really loud creak interrupted the moment of good humor. And then there were loud, popping cracks, as of big pieces of timber splitting and breaking.

"Piero, cellar! Now! It's going!"

Piero was moving before Frank was done yelling, and made it into the mouth of the cellar stairwell before Frank had properly got his legs under him. They'd planned to retreat here if the musket fire got too intense, if it started coming through the wood of the bar. They hadn't figured to shelter in it if the place collapsed around their ears. Frank made it into the mouth of the stairwell just as the noises stopped. He checked to make sure that the stairwell was still a solid brick construction, thanked any gods that might be around for medieval standards of design—*if in doubt, overbuild*—and peered around to see what the rest of the building was doing. The ceiling at the front of the bar was now sagging four feet lower in the middle than it was at the sides. Some of the brickwork out front was still standing, but it looked like the collapse of the ceiling had knocked some of the pillars out. In fact, there was a huge pile of rubble out there, illuminated by something burning. Silhouetted by it, in fact. Frank hoped like hell that it was just a whole bunch of torches. If this neighborhood caught fire, they were all dead if the Spanish weren't real, real understanding about letting people escape.

There's an inquisitor out there, dummy. Probably call it God's Will and a great saving in firewood if we burn to death of natural causes. Frank realized that the little voice in the back of his mind was back. Good timing. *Great* timing.

"Are they beginning the assault?" Piero asked, real hope in his voice.

That better not be because you're looking forward to a fight, Frank thought. "Can't tell," he said out loud, listening carefully. "Even if I could understand Spanish, I can't make out what they're yelling at each other."

"Sounds like proper military shouting," Piero observed, and Frank quietly agreed that it did have that kind of sergeant-like flavor that jocks loved to imitate so much.

On the other hand . . .

"I can't tell if it's 'line up you guys and storm that building' or 'line up you guys and wait while we toss a couple grenades in there.' I reckon the difference could be important."

"Grenades?" Piero spat. "Filthy weapons."

Frank couldn't help but be amused. When all was said and done he reckoned violence and weapons were pretty much all as bad as each other, and the people who made them necessary didn't have much cause to complain if the other guy turned out to be more fiendishly inventive when it came to dishing out the pain and misery. Right up until the roof started collapsing he'd been thinking that he'd been in with a fair chance of ending this with nobody else getting hurt, and as such was ahead of the game. "You reckon?" he said, looking back at where Piero was displaying an authentic *lefferto* scowl. "Me, I think dead is dead. And from their point of view, tossing a couple of grenades in here would be a good way for them not to get hurt so bad, what with marching into a notorious nest of bloody-handed revolutionists and all."

"True," Piero said. "But right now I don't feel like seeing the other fellow's point of view."

Frank listened again. The shouting was still going on, and the firelight was moving about in a way that suggested torches. Frank had seen people lighting their way along the streets with the things and recognized the way they made the shadows shift and dance. It was one of the regular sights in a poor neighborhood such as this one, after dark.

That was a relief. They weren't going to burn to death. There was still no shooting, which was another.

"Reckon we can surrender now? Trying to defend a building that's falling down strikes me as hopeless enough that they'll respect us for giving in before they have to come in and get us."

"Has to be worth a try," Piero said. "How are we going to do this?"

"Let's keep it simple," Frank said, and cupped his hands around his mouth. "We surrender!" he yelled, hoping like hell someone out there could understand his Italian. He got up and walked toward the front of the barroom. "We surrender!" he yelled again, looking nervously at the sagging ceiling, which picked that moment to creak forebodingly. *None of you guys hiding upstairs better move suddenly,* he thought. And then, in one of those thoroughly helpful contributions from his Inner Pessimist, *and loud noises can start avalanches, can't they?*

He got near the front, picking his way though the mangled and shattered furniture, and yelled again. There was a sudden stop to the shouting outside. "Say that again," a distant shouted voice from outside called.

"We surrender!" Frank yelled back. "The building is about to collapse!"

There was a long silence, long enough for Piero to make it up next to Frank. "What'd he say?" he whispered.

"Just asked me to repeat it," he whispered back. "He hasn't answered yet, though."

"If they accept, let me go first," Piero said.

"Why?"

"You, they may shoot out of hand. Stay behind me until we are among them. They may not shoot if they do not realize who you are until too late."

"Uh, right," Frank said. There were any number of holes in that argument, not least of which was that if they were going to be shooting captives out of hand they wouldn't be getting picky. That Don Vincente guy had said there was an inquisitor trying to run the show for him out there, and wasn't it the Inquisition who'd come up with *Kill them all, God will know his own*? Besides, if they wanted to make sure Frank was dead, all they had to do was wait. Maybe toss in a couple of grenades to help matters along a bit. Something cracked in the timbers above, and the ceiling shifted a little, causing a shower of dust and grit. Frank could hear it pattering around him on the floor and on the broken furniture.

"How many of you are there?" came a shout from outside, followed by a white scarf on a stick poked in through a hole in the shattered wall.

"Two," Frank called back. "We're coming out, unarmed."

The white rag was followed by a face under a helmet, who looked into the darkened interior, said something over his shoulder and reached back for a torch. It turned out to be the sergeant Frank had met earlier, once it was lit up. Frank could see that the torch was a chairleg with some rags wrapped around it. Clearly these guys had had to improvise on the spot as well. Half of the sergeant's face was covered in black soot, the way soldiers got to be when they'd been shooting a lot with black-powder weapons. He was grinning, which Frank hoped was a good sign. He shouted something over his shoulder, out of which Frank picked out the word "dos," which he recognized as being Spanish for "two."

The sergeant vanished, and after a moment— punctuated by another groan from the ceiling timbers— the shout came back: "Come out, one at a time! With your hands up!"

Frank heaved a sigh of relief. "You first, Piero," he said, looking nervously at the ceiling. *Yeah, that's right, bartender's last to leave a sinking bar. Tradition.*

Piero nodded. "There is nothing left to say, Frank, except that when we meet again after this, the drinks are very much on me, yes?"

"Get gone," Frank said, suddenly remembering what he was walking out into. *At least most of the people who came here for shelter got away,* he thought. *Just me, Giovanna and Piero got caught.* Then the little voice added, *So long as the falling building doesn't kill the rest of the guys.*

"First one coming out!" he yelled, as Piero stepped up to the gap the sergeant had used, his hands in the air.

Frank listened to Piero's scramble over the rubble. There were voices, and then a crash from somewhere up above. The ceiling groaned, and Frank hunkered down into the doubtful shelter of a broken table. He peered upward, nervously, squinting against the falling dust and grit, and then curled up tight with his eyes closed when he saw the ceiling begin to drop again. A few seconds, and then he opened them again. In the middle, at the front, the ceiling was maybe five feet from the ground, where it had been nearly ten feet moments before. *Please let that be where it gets stable,* Frank prayed. *Please.*

"Next one! Come out now! Hands up!" It was a miracle Frank heard the shout over the sound of his pulse hammering in his ears. He stood up and made himself walk, not run, over to the gap. As he stood in the gap, blinking in the too-bright torchlight, something began to give way in the collapsing floor behind and above him. Nails began to rip free and timbers cracked. *Sounds like gunshots*, he thought.

The musketeers across the street thought so too.

The last thing Frank remembered was fire, blooming like time-lapsed roses across the street, and swirls of dirty white smoke that seemed to glow like pearls in the torchlight. And Piero's face, horrified where he stood between two soldiers, under guard.

It all went dark.

Chapter 43

Rome

There was shouting by the time Ruy, Tom and the pope reached the stairs down to the lower levels of the fortress. By the time they'd gotten to the main part of the old fortress, there was screaming.

"We must leave while the inner ward holds," Ruy said. "Over the wall or through the door?"

"Which door?" the pope asked.

"The one in the riverside wall," Tom said.

"It is barricaded."

"I saw as we entered." Ruy was negotiating the final turn of the staircase and emerging into the circular corridor that ringed the wall of the inner tower. "Without help, it will take much time to clear a way through."

"Can't we just climb over the blockage?" Tom asked. "His Holiness seems pretty spry."

Ruy chuckled. "The gate opens inward, Señor Simpson. The barricade keeps it closed. I did not examine closely—ah, excuse me." He flattened against the wall as a bunch of middle-aged men with arquebuses that looked like they'd had the rust hastily scraped off quite recently came up through the stairs they were about to use. "But I suspect that the barricade is nailed in place," he concluded.

"It is," the pope said. "I saw it done."

"Over the wall it is, I guess," Tom said. "We'll need rope."

"Rope we shall find," Ruy said. "Or anything that might serve. Please to be observant as we pass along."

Down two more flights of stairs, through a courtyard and a mad dash down the spiral corridor around the old tomb, and out in to the courtyard. They were on the east side, facing the river, which ran more or less due north-south by the fortress.

All along the wall ahead of them, Tom could see guardsmen on the parapet, hastening in either direction toward the walls that had been threatened, while others remained to guard against the possibility of a further attack taking advantage of the diversion. Although if an attack came in, with half the men on this wall gone, they were screwed. Still, it should be pretty much impossible to get ladders around to this side without bringing them over the bridge, and there hadn't been any when Tom had been over that side before.

To Tom's left, just visible above the storage houses built close-under the wall in the northeast corner, he could see Guardsmen leaning out with guns to fire at targets right at the foot of the wall. As he watched, one of them jerked, his head fountaining up as someone below shot him. The body pitched back and then slumped forward. Beside him, he heard the pope mutter, *"Requiem aeternam dona eis domine . . ."*

Tom felt his stomach heave. *I've seen worse, lots worse,* he told himself sternly. Somehow it still seemed to get to him.

Ruy was taking in the scene as well. "We have perhaps five minutes before they gain the walls," he said, in tones that spoke of a judgment formed from long experience. "The whole wall is engaged. There are no reserves. If the towers were not heavily engaged, those men would not need to lean over so. We may hope that the towers are protecting each other for the moment."

There was a loud cheer from beyond the wall, and Tom saw the head of a long, crudely lashed ladder slam into the wall close to the corner tower to their left. Seconds later, two more appeared farther along the wall. "Ruy," he said, "I think we should be leaving. That's right next to our way out, if we're going over the lowest part of the wall."

"A moment." Ruy was rummaging among a pile of planks and spars roughly stacked against the fortress wall. Tom recalled that the whole place had been sheathed in scaffolding a few days before, and realized that half of the work of readying the place for defense must have been taking all that down. And in these days before steel scaffolding poles and other modern conveniences of the building trade, scaffolding was *lashed* together. He joined Ruy.

Ruy beat him to it. "Here." He lifted up a sizeable coil of hempen rope. "Not ideal climbing rope, but it will serve."

"Right. I'll go first, we may need to clear a way. And, respect to you, Señor Sanchez, I do brute force and ignorance a whole lot better than you."

"The province of the young," Ruy said, smiling. Tom could swear there was a hint of sadness in that smile. Whether it was for youthful folly or in remembrance of his own days of brute force and ignorance, Tom didn't know.

The lack of reserves Sanchez had commented on had been more profound than Tom had thought. Men were streaming across the courtyard to get up to the walls, but they were few, pitifully few. There were a couple of hundred yards of wall to hold, and probably no more than three hundred men to do it. Tom didn't even bother to try to estimate the numbers as he strode—*don't run, you might need the wind*—around the inner castle toward the tower they had climbed in by.

Tom recalled that it had a lower parapet on the river side. If the Spaniards hadn't troubled to get around to that side, there might be an easier way over there. They were just reaching the door of that tower when he heard the sounds of hand-to-hand fighting, the clangs and screams of men close enough to smell each other locked in a struggle with edged weapons. Somewhere, someone was using grenades. The fizzing crack of the little iron pots of black powder seemed to be coming from the other side of the wall, so maybe that meant the defense was holding well somewhere. *Other hand, they've got grenades too.*

Twice in the time it took to get to the tower door, men fell from the parapet, and Tom couldn't help feeling glad he'd never been in this kind of fight. The sight of the oncoming Swabians at Suhl dying in dozen lots still woke him at night with the cold sweats. The last screams of wounded men falling thirty

feet onto paving stones wasn't going to leave him any
time soon either. Ruy was behind him, bringing the
pope along.

Once inside the tower, the noise was if anything
worse. "They're on the tower, Ruy," Tom said, guessing
from the sounds he was hearing from above. "Do we
fight our way through or look for another route?"

"I may have been optimistic," Ruy said, "but this
is the quickest way to the top of the wall now. Señor
Simpson, ensure your gun is fully charged."

"Right," Tom said. He worked the slide, checked
that the magazine was full, and checked the safety.
"Ready," he said. This was, if anything, going to be
the easy part. Without even trying too hard he could
get a shot off every second or so, and at these ranges
even his notoriously poor marksmanship would be no
handicap. And the guys coming over the wall were
coming over with swords and knives and pikes. So long
as he didn't let any of them in range, he was fine.
Rate of fire, he murmured to himself, trying not to
think about what actually happened to men who took
a blast of heavy shot at close range. Especially when
he'd have to be at close range to see it happen.

Another body fell from the wall, this time right
opposite where Tom was standing waiting to go into
the tower. He had his back to the grain-store that
was built under the wall here, side-on to the door
ready to dash through it, gun at the ready. He had
no idea whether that was the right way to do it, but
he'd seen cops doing something like it on TV. In the
absence of any actual training, it was all he had to
go on. His own troops had been hot as you could
wish for on standing up and taking it like men in a

firing-line. This SWAT stuff was pretty much beyond them. Or they grew up in cities and were used to casual violence at close quarters.

"In your own time, Señor Simpson," Ruy said. "I have His Holiness behind me."

"Okay," Tom said, and took a deep breath. "Let's go."

He made the turn into the door look a lot more casual than he felt and moved quickly but without running across to the stairs. There wasn't much to see down here. On the way in, there had been guys sitting around waiting their turn on watch or catching some shut-eye. Now, it was empty with the remains of a meal and drinks spilled off the table in the middle of the floor. Up the stairs, one step at a time. The sounds of combat got louder, and Tom flinched as he heard another grenade go off. "Where are they getting all those grenades?" he asked. "I thought those things were rare?"

"There are armories here and at Ostia," the pope said. "They have had ample time to fill them." Tom realized the old man—it was possible to think of him as an old man in a way it wasn't of the not-much-younger Sanchez—had spoken English. Quite good English, as well. So it was true about him being a whiz with languages. He realized he'd stopped to woolgather, and took a look up the stairs before continuing.

"What is it, Señor Simpson?" Ruy asked. "Is there a problem?"

"No, just a pause for thought."

"This may be the voice of instinct," Ruy said. "Do you counsel finding another route?"

There was a flurry of screams and curses among the clashes of metal above, and a sudden crack and a puff of smoke in through one of the arrow slits. "Not yet," he said. "I think that means they're still holding up there." He began to walk forward and up the stairs.

"I find one must trust instinct in these matters, you know," Ruy said, almost casually, as he followed Tom. "To place faith in reason when battle is joined is to submit to rank superstition. No man can think fast enough."

"True," Tom said. "Although all the battles I've been in have been a mite more formal." He held up a hand to signal a halt. The door onto the lower level of the tower's fighting platform was right ahead. "Let me check if they're still friendly."

He leaned his head out of the door and saw that the platform was elbow-to-elbow with Swiss guards, or at least the part he could see was. He had no idea what was going on up at the top. Two of them had grenades and were lighting fuses, while another dozen or so were gathered around the tops of two ladders with their halberds at the ready, the closer ones jabbing at whoever was trying his luck. Tom decided to establish their bona fides the best way he could, and stepped smartly over to the nearest ladder, shotgun at the ready. The guy on the ladder looked at Tom, away from the halberd he was trying to get past one-handed for a critical moment and squawked as the back-spike of the thing laid open one side of his face. He clutched at the wound with the hand that still held his sword and lost his footing. Trying to hold his face and his grip on the ladder with nothing but his hands proved too much and he fell. Fifteen feet, at least. Tom winced.

He worked the slide, and without letting himself pause to see what was happening, walked the shots down the ladder. Screams and cries and a round of cheers were the result he got. That, and a bunch of shots from below. He stepped back hurriedly as near-misses flung up chips of stone from the wall he'd been leaning over.

Ruy joined him. "His Holiness is waiting in the tower," he said. "I think we should try elsewhere, yes?"

"Maybe," Tom said. There were Spanish soldiers all around the bottom of the tower, some trying to aim arquebuses in the press and others waiting their turn at the ladders. In the firelight from the bonfires atop the outer defenses they seemed like a lot of demons, jostling for a chance at the condemned sinners. The shadows under their helmets made them seem faceless and sinister, and the forest of bright-whetted weapons they were carrying reflected the firelight so that they swam in a sea of flames. The view along the riverside wall was little better. Some of the soldiers had spilled around and were in the shadows along that wall, but there seemed to be a nice long section of wall with no attackers. Tom couldn't see anyone coming over the bridge, but the other side was a hundred yards away, easily, and there was no real light over there to see what was going on.

More shots spanged from the breastwork, and a guardsman staggered back clutching his face, blood starting between his fingers. Tom was about to go to the man's aid, dithering briefly between that and reloading his shotgun, when something landed on the parapet next to him. Something small and round and black and shiny, with a fizzing fuse.

He was halfway back to the doorway before he yelled "Grenade!" and Ruy was ahead of him. Naturally faster reflexes and less mass to get moving. *It's going to go off any second,* Tom thought—and then his back and legs were on fire and he was pressed up against the opposite wall of the stairwell he'd come up and there was a flashing somewhere in front of his eyes and darkness to either side and he could hear a strange noise. He felt, suddenly, very tired.

"—Señor Simpson? Now is not the time to—" Ruy was shaking his shoulder, gently but firmly. "Ah, you are awake, I see."

"What . . . ?" Tom muttered. It sounded like an alarm clock going off, if he could just hit snooze—and then he remembered where he was. Or where he had been. "How long was I—ow!" The pain in his back and legs returned.

"A few seconds, no more," Ruy said. "And thank you for shielding me from the blast. You don't seem badly hurt. Some fragments, no more."

"Feels worse," Tom grunted. He tried to look around to see how bad it was, but his back hurt like hell.

"Some small cuts to your legs, and one in your ass, Señor Simpson," Ruy said. "Your buff-coat prevented the worst elsewhere, and you were already out of the worst of the blast."

"Got to get out," Tom said, grabbing hold of what he decided was the salient point. "Got to get the pope out."

"Yes, but are you well enough to—"

Tom had been here before. It wasn't the first time he'd taken a mild stomping and played on, after all. He stood up, took a deep breath, winced at the literal pain in the ass, and said, "If we've got to, we've got to. How's the wall doing?"

"*Hijo de—*" was Ruy's only response. There was a sound of metal moving very, very fast. A scream, and a gurgle, and Tom turned round to see that the doorway out to the tower's lower fighting platform was blocked by Spanish soldiers, the first of whom was already collapsing with his face a mess of blood and his crotch bleeding out. Sanchez was holding the door with a sword in one hand and a dagger in the other.

Tom spotted the shotgun he'd dropped, but it was too far away. So he reached for his pistol instead. One of the soldiers in the doorway was struggling to get his halberd through, while another was armed with either a very long knife or a short sword. The kind they called a hanger, Tom recalled. The short blade was no use where Sanchez was concerned. The tip of the saber he had brought licked out like the tongue of a snake and opened the man's gut in a neat thrust-and-twist action after batting the man's blade just fractionally aside. As he hunched forward over the wound Sanchez punched the blade in again, making a neat gouge in the man's throat. The halberd the next man had was now in play, but Sanchez caught the thing with his dagger and, hardly moving his arm, flicked the saber around and across the wielder's face, stepping around the halberd to get in close. The sword came back again to cause the next man to try to get through the doorway to sway back out of reach of the wicked and bloody edge, getting sprayed with drops of his friends' blood for his trouble.

Tom got his pistol up and into the correct stance.

He was a lousy shot, but he couldn't miss at this range, and he began to methodically punch away at centers of mass. Effective though the breastplates these guys wore might have been against down-time firearms at any reasonable range, against a 9mm round at not much more than knife-fighting distance, all they did was make a thunking sound as the bullets went through. Tom shot six times, taking five enemies down.

Just targets, he repeated to himself each time he pulled the trigger, trying not to think about it. Sanchez had stood back.

And then men in Swiss Guard uniforms surged across the doorway, taking advantage of the hole Tom had opened in the melee.

"We need to find another way," Ruy said.

"Reckon you're right," Tom said. "Let's get upstairs, go along the wall."

Chapter 44

Rome

"News, Ferrigno!" Cardinal Borja barked as he stared out over the rooftops of Rome. The terrace atop the Palazzo Borghese afforded a fine view of the Vatican, the Castel Sant'Angelo and the district within the Leonine wall that was the focus of effort of the troops he had wheedled out of the viceroy of Naples.

For hours the Castel Sant'Angelo had spat its defiance at the surrounding troops. The ring of bonfires illuminating its walls and the crash of the bombard shells it was firing lighted, by turns, the assorted vile and filthy little alleys around it. Borja had been assured by some military functionary or other—not one of the generals, he was sure, but some under-officer detailed to keep the prelate happy, in the mistaken belief that Borja would not notice the implied slight in fobbing him off with a second-rank myrmidon. Doubtless it was to do with their embarrassment at the fact that this simple assault on a fortress whose defenses had been out of date a hundred years ago was taking hours, that an operation that had been planned to be complete during a single day had now proceeded beyond sunset. The cardinal-infante had managed the reduction of an entire city in not much more time than this, scarcely two years before.

Borja had grown weary of the excuses some hours before. The just execution of the Barberini was now long overdue and the final prize, the completion of God's holy work in righting the wrongs done Holy Mother Church was close, tantalizingly close. And so he had bid Ferrigno shut his weaselly little mouth and hold the reports this half hour past, while Borja watched the shells fly and prayed furiously for calm.

Now, though, something seemed to be happening. Only a small part of the outer defenses of Castel Sant'Angelo was visible from this vantage, but there seemed to be movement there.

"Well?" he barked again. What was *keeping* the man?

"Your Eminence," Ferrigno said, coming to his side, "word reached us some moments ago that the ladders required for the escalade on the inner ward were prepared and the assault would proceed momentarily. The courier assured Colonel Don Pablo and myself that the first ladders would be reaching the walls only a few moments after he himself arrived here, and indeed—"

"Enough!" Borja held up a hand. Ferrigno was a good enough secretary, if kept well-whipped by his master's tongue. But the man's besetting sin was a tendency to prattle when nervous. Raised to the priesthood from a family barely removed from the common sort of folk, the man had not had the proper composure of a gentleman under fire. Nor, he being from some middle order of persons, did he have the brute indifference to peril that marked the true lower orders. Thus, with the fire of great guns echoing over the tiled roofs of Rome, the man seemed in near danger of soiling himself.

Christian charity bid Borja silently recognize that his own impatience had contributed nothing to helping the man's temerity. Still, it was *unseemly*. He sighed. "Fetch this Don Pablo"—it was a help, at least, to know the man's name; since Borja had not troubled to remember it past the initial introduction—"and bid him explain to me, as will undoubtedly be the case, why the Barberini will not be in our hands before dawn."

"Yes, Your Eminence," Ferrigno said, his relief evident. Where Don Pablo might be was anybody's guess. Borja had made his boredom with the technicalities of the man's explanations—excuses, to give them their right name—entirely plain some hours before.

Borja turned and looked again over the rooftops of Rome. To the east, the seven hills of Rome rose away from the river, their shapes lost amid the nighttime shadows and the shifting light from the explosions of shells and the fires burning round the city. The hills seemed to burn themselves, great rolling waves of fire like ocean swells of dark flame. Here and there, a house, some great palazzo or the town residence of some prelate, burned. There seemed to be no way of preventing it, unfortunately. The confiscation of the worldly goods of those heretics who had thrown in with the Barberini would have done much to defray the costs of this business. God's work it might be, but much of it was done by men who expected to be paid. A company of soldiers sent to ensure that some cardinal was arrested seemed to turn into ravening bandits the instant they were out of sight of responsible oversight. Quevedo was quite clear on the orders he was giving to these men, but deeply regretted, in his every report to his master, that the houses were being looted and the looters giving in to incendiary impulses.

The demise of so many cardinals would doubtless become convenient later. Some would have had to be released from prison in order to see to it that the canon lawyers were satisfied. Sinceri had been quite clear on the forms that would have to be followed to assuage the narrow, pinched consciences of such men. Doubts would otherwise be raised, he had said, and although nothing overt would ever be said and nothing printed that named him specifically, there would be lingering doubt about what had taken place. So there would need to be forms observed to ensure that once Barberini was in custody, he could be kept there without any whispering.

With no suggestion, of course, that whoever replaced him in the ensuing conclave was an antipope. Borja remained mindful of the old saying that he who went into conclave a pope would come out a cardinal, the folk wisdom that reminded all of the Holy Spirit's dispensation to punish presumption and the sin of pride.

"Your Eminence?" Don Pablo's gravelly tones came from behind. It was quite clear why he had been visited with the duty of liaison to the cardinal. An ageing warhorse whose wind and vigor were no longer up to the vicissitudes of combat, he had been shuffled off to the roof of the Palazzo Borghese to be out of the way. Borja could not bring the rest of the man's name to mind, he being of some country-gentry, hare-catching little hidalgo family of scarcely any account whatsoever. The cardinal had never heard of them nor could he place who of consequence they might be related to.

Still, Borja could not shake a vague feeling that the man was laughing at him.

"Enlighten me, Don Pablo," Borja said, turning away from a last glance at the Castel Sant'Angelo. The Barberini's defiance was no longer being hurled by the bombard-shell full from its ramparts, or battlements, or whatever they were called. Bastions, possibly.

"As Your Eminence wishes. I will beg forgiveness if, in describing what may be, beyond the discernment of my eyes, I err in some small detail—"

"Fine, fine," Borja said, waving aside the excuse. "How soon is this assault likely to succeed?"

"Your Eminence strikes for the very nub of the matter." Don Pablo's salt-and-pepper mustachios crinkled upward in an ingratiating smile. "The walls of the inner ward are some hundred paces around, perhaps a hundred and fifty if I am any judge of these matters. Seventy-five to a hundred, leaving out of account the river wall where an escalade is not practical. Along that wall, perhaps two thousand men can be brought to the point of decision. Against two hundred who will be defending the walls."

"Ten to one odds, eh?" Borja said, hearing the first cheerful news in some hours. "Surely the slaughter will be brief?"

"Alas, Your Eminence, would that it were so. There

will be perhaps a dozen ladders, and at the top of each will be a single man. Against him will be ranged two, perhaps three Swiss Guards. Only the very skilled and lucky will achieve the wall, and they in turn must be still luckier to survive long enough atop the wall for their comrades to get over and assist them."

"It will, however, be inevitable? Surely with so many—?" Borja was keen not to let Don Pablo—what was the rest of the man's name again?—make too many excuses and deflate the small moment of hope Borja had felt that the thing would be over soon.

"Your Eminence, the prospects are good. For it is true that we require only one lucky man with the courage of a lion. The Swiss Guard surrounding His Holiness require to be fortunate at the top of every ladder long enough to break the spirit of the attackers."

"How so? With such numbers—"

"Your Eminence, while these men wait at the foot of the walls, they will be showered with bullets and grenades and even rocks thrown from above. Men will be wounded and die. Soldiers will bear much with the scent of victory in their nostrils, Your Eminence, but however willing their spirits, their flesh is weak. If they do not carry the walls quickly, Your Eminence, the defenders might break their spirit."

"And how likely is this?" Borja asked, his earlier ill-humor returning in force.

"Moderately, Your Eminence. Even with the conditions for a successful escalade being as favorable as they are at this time—"

Don Pablo's shrug was very expressive. It expressed hope, great hope, all the hope that a Christian gentleman might bear in an imperfect world where stout hearts stood firm against the sin of despair, yet allowed for those imperfections and admitted that to express true confidence in anything was to admit the cankerous worm of the sin of pride.

Borja sighed. "So it might be that a second attempt would be required?"

"Indeed, Your Eminence. And it would be my recommendation, and a course of action that will naturally suggest itself to your commanders at the Castel Sant'Angelo, that the men be well-rested before a second attempt is made. Waiting for dark tomorrow would also be well advised, at the very least. An escalade by daylight would be far less certain of success, and it would be a counsel of perfection that an assault wait for the following dawn."

"Why not dawn tomorrow?"

"Your Eminence would not flog a horse past its endurance?" Don Pablo's tone was the very model of politeness, but Borja could detect just a hint of testiness. Not sufficient that he might reprimand the man without being unseemly.

"Of course not," Borja said. He was no great horseman, but he could ride and owned several horses in addition to the mule he used on public occasions. A good horse was a valuable animal. In some circles, the suggestion that a man might abuse a horse was a fit subject for a duel—the title of *caballero* being taken very seriously by some.

"It is a similar case with soldiers, Your Eminence." Don Pablo's tone remained equable and patient without ever quite straying over the line into patronization. "These men have marched hard, with little rest, from Ostia after a sea voyage itself a source of discomfort and little sleep for men not habituated to the sea. That they remain able to fight is testimony to how stout their hearts are, Your Eminence, but a prudent commander will not attempt to press them beyond endurance, for in that direction lies certain failure."

"I see," Borja said. That there were limited benefits to flogging a brute beast once it was too tired to work was obvious to even the dullest wit. He sighed. "So we must pray that God grants a swift end to the performance of his will in Rome this night."

"Indeed, Your Eminence." Don Pablo bowed and left the terrace.

"Your Eminence?" It was Ferrigno again.

"What now?" Borja asked. Surely it was too much to hope that this was news of the successful assault *already*?

"The heretics of the Committee of Correspondence, Your Eminence. We have word from Father Gonzalez, who is supervising the arrest."

"There has *been* an arrest?" Borja said, not troubling to hide his disbelief that, for once, there was something going right.

"After a fashion, Your Eminence," Ferrigno said, visibly cringing.

All Borja had to do was raise one eyebrow to complete Ferrigno's collapse.

"Your Eminence," he went on, talking quickly now, "there was a cannonade to force an entrance to the building, which the heretics had fortified against the possibility of their capture. The structure was an old one, Your Eminence, and there was a collapse."

Borja could not see where the trouble was more than a minor annoyance. So the alchemist's whelp would not live to publicly repent of his sins. The loss of a heathen soul to Satan was a matter for the most profound grief, but a commonplace tragedy.

"Send word," he said, "that the search for survivors should be diligent and thorough, but that I am satisfied that the nest of heresy has been destroyed. My compliments to Father Gonzalez and the soldiers assisting him, also."

"Yes, Your Eminence." Ferrigno fled to do the cardinal's bidding.

"Your Eminence?" The next voice Borja heard was one that caused him to delight and groan in dismay in equal measure. And one whose owner took a positive delight in Borja not seeing him enter. As though Borja cared a whit for how well the man did his work of skullduggery, provided results were forthcoming. A matter on which Borja was growing impatient this night.

"Well, Quevedo?" he snapped, turning to see the man. Over his shoulder, the flare and flicker of the battle around the Castel Sant'Angelo was visible against the night sky. A pall of smoke hung over that part of the city and every flash of cannon and the constant flicker of arquebuses and muskets lit it like the visions of hell offered by second-rate country preachers.

"Your Eminence will be pleased to hear that the final reports on the prelates Your Eminence wished to have prevented from working against Your Eminence are received. All are accounted for, albeit that two were overtaken on the road out of Rome. Your Eminence was most wise to disburse monies on the maintenance of horses for the soldiery to use on their arrival."

"I was?" Borja realized that he might well have not

paid complete attention to everything Quevedo had done on his behalf in the last few weeks. The man *had* spent a remarkable amount of money, that was certain. Doubtless he had foreseen the possibility of flight and—Borja pulled himself back to the matter at hand. No matter that Quevedo had planned well, it was the results that mattered. "How many are accounted living?" he asked.

"Three, Your Eminence," Quevedo said, gravely. "Caetani is within the Castel Sant'Angelo, where as Camerlengo of the Holy Roman Church he was required to be, and Vitelleschi seems to have been forewarned and escaped Rome before the arrival of the army."

Borja chuckled. "Vitelleschi, eh? The spider not in his web when you went to catch him?"

"Indeed not, Your Eminence. There are few who may reckon themselves any man's equal in such a business as this one, Your Eminence, but Vitelleschi is one such. And he is master of the Jesuits, to boot. I believe I may have adverted as much to Your Eminence?"

Borja waved it aside. "Religious orders can be suppressed, given sufficient will on the part of the Holy See." And there would be sufficient will. "Who was the third prelate accounted living?"

"The youngest Barberini, Your Eminence, Antonio. He seems to have been better prepared to flee than others. The Palazzo Barberini was, as I mentioned in earlier messages to Your Eminence, largely empty when Your Eminence's men entered it. The cardinal himself was apprehended in the course of his departure, but being by far the youngest man on the list, had the wherewithal to cut himself free of the men who attempted his capture. His guard died to a man covering his escape."

Borja nodded once, slowly, and then shrugged. "It is of little import. The man is a butterfly, of minor consequence save insofar as he bears the Barberini name and wears the purple. He may serve yet as a scapegoat for his family's peculations these ten years past. I am more concerned that there have been no captures alive, Quevedo. I gave orders for capture, not assassination."

"Indeed, Your Eminence, and I tender my most humble apologies. However, the constraints of time and·hands to turn to the task have meant that in many cases those guarding the prelates in question have felt themselves able to make a show of defiance. In all cases, either the subject has died in the fighting or was killed to prevent his escape, a point on which Your Eminence was most forceful. There were to be no fugitives."

Borja sighed, again. "So be it. It seems the Holy Spirit has sentenced each of these men to death, for in the wager of battle is the providence of the Almighty most clearly to be seen. Let us turn to a more happy chance. Is it confirmed that Barberini is within the Castel Sant'Angelo?"

"It is, Your Eminence. The man I set to watch the Leonine wall is most reliable, and positively identified Barberini as he passed from the Vatican to his current redoubt."

"Good, good. I will ask, Quevedo, that you go personally and see to it that there is no escape there, either. I would desire greatly that the man publicly answer for his crimes against the church, but not at the price of his being granted any period of liberty during which he may wreak further mischief."

"I am Your Eminence's to command." Quevedo withdrew with a bow.

Borja turned back to watch over the roofs of Rome, and tried to guess whether the confusion and tumult about the Castel Sant'Angelo meant he would see success before the dawn.

Chapter 45

Rome

Tom rubbed at his eyes. The courtyard between the inner keep and the wall was sheltered from the wind and there were two hundred men in it and on the wall around it doing their level best to burn their own weight in black powder. A few bombards were still firing, lobbing shells out over the walls in an attempt to drive off the crowd of Spaniards at the walls. The assault had been going on for nearly twenty minutes, now, and everyone who could work a gun was doing so. The Swiss Guard knew that an attempt was being made to get the pope to safety, and a few of them had grinned savagely at Tom and Ruy as they cast about for a way to get out.

They'd tried the riverside wall already. By the time they'd got up onto the upper level of the walls and gone along to find a place to rappel down, there was a spillover from the assaults on the north and south walls, and there was only a narrow gap that was not now covered by Spanish soldiers awaiting their turn at the ladders. For all the bravery of the Swiss Guards, there was no driving them off, now.

The grenades had been exhausted in minutes. There were more in the armory, but with everything else that had had to be done to get the fortress into a condition fit for even the little defense they could manage, there had been too few hands available to fill many of them with powder. The men on the walls were reduced to tossing rocks and cannonballs over the walls in an attempt to put the attackers off, but it was unlikely to achieve much.

Possibly, if the defensive works had actually been finished, the fortress might have held longer. Or at all. For now, there were small parties at the top of each ladder who had beaten off three concerted rushes at the wall, but the attackers were not retiring after each attempt. They were ranged at the bottom of the wall and any man who showed himself over the battlements received a hail of bullets for his trouble. There were already forty or fifty casualties, most of them dead. They wouldn't want for last rites, either. The place was full of priests. Tom had stayed with the pope by the river gate while Ruy went to discuss the escape further with the commander of the Swiss Guard. Hopefully, there would be some kind of diversion, but Tom couldn't imagine what.

Another man fell from the wall above them, and hit the ground with the boneless finality that could only mean one thing. The pope started forward. Tom was about to restrain him, when he saw the elderly cleric kneel down by the corpse and make the sign of the cross.

Tom went to one knee beside him. "Your Holiness?

Please be quick," he said as gently as he could over the noise of battle. "The man is surely gone beyond any comfort you can bring him."

"I know," he said, and Tom saw in the firelight that the pope's eyes were bright and shining, his face blank with distress. "But he will not go there without my prayers to speed him on his way. He—will—*not*."

Tom realized that what he had taken for distress was, in fact, overwhelming fury. "It's all wrong, isn't it?" he said, embarrassed at the banality of the sentiment in a place where men were dying every second.

"All wrong, yes," the pope said, closing the dead guardsman's eyes and crossing himself again after a briefly murmured prayer. Tom didn't know enough Latin to understand what he'd said.

"These men"—the pope gestured at the broken thing beside him, the brains leaking onto the ancient flagstones, the smells of shit and blood and piss reeking the man's death even over the stench of powder-smoke—"have pride that they die before I am taken. And Borja knows this. Signor Simpson, I have not learned enough English to say it well, but—"

Tom didn't have enough Italian—or, at least, not enough of that class of Italian—to follow all of it, but the sentiment was clear enough. He hoped that, wherever he was, Borja's ears were burning. And the pope was right. Borja's attempt to capture the pope was as good as a death sentence for all two hundred of these tough, wiry men from the Alps, no matter that they went to their deaths grinning savagely and determined to heap up the corpses of their attackers on the way.

Whatever else he had ordered today in Rome, Borja had ordered the murder of two hundred men who, Tom was sure, he would have gotten along with famously if he had met them elsewhere. His Episcopalianism notwithstanding, Tom couldn't help feeling that there might well be something to a church that had a man like this at its head. Sure, the fellow was a notorious crook when it came to money and nepotism, but still—

He sighed. "Your Holiness, let's get back under cover, please?"

The pope nodded, rose stiffly from his knees and moved back with Tom under the shelter of the wall. "I thank you, Signor Simpson. It seems that once again I am to be saved to continue God's work by the United States of Europe."

Tom grinned. "Any time, Your Holiness. It isn't like we can piss the Spanish off any more than we already did."

The pope smiled back. "This is true. But one Spaniard deserves to be pissed off a great deal, I think."

"You're picking up English idiom quite well, there, Your Holiness," Tom said, trying not to snigger like a schoolboy. The idea of priests swearing was kind of amusing. Hearing the pope do it was *hysterical*.

Tom was saved from bursting out laughing altogether by Ruy reappearing.

"What're we doing?" Tom asked.

"A diversion is arranged, and we should take cover while it comes to pass." Behind him the keep of the Castel Sant'Angelo seemed to explode as people—mostly men, but some women as well—began pouring out of the door and fanning out to head for the bastions and the various buildings under the walls.

Tom wondered about that for a second or two, and

then a horrible thought presented itself. "What have you arranged as a diversion, Ruy?" he asked, with a horrible suspicion that he'd already worked it out.

"The good captain and I discussed it, and it seemed a shame that all that powder would be wasted for want of time to shoot it at the enemy. And it certainly makes for an excellent alternative to surrender, yes?"

"Ruy! That building is a fuckin' world historical monument! Are you out of your—" Tom stopped. "Yes, you are, aren't you?"

"Indeed. And I notice that you have followed me every step of the way, Señor Simpson." It was dark under the wall, and Tom could not see Ruy's face very clearly, but his imagination clearly supplied the grin. A great deal of humor with more than a tint of malicious glee.

"Please, what is the plan?" The pope was also eyeing the stream of people fleeing from the inner keep. Tom noticed also that there seemed to be rather fewer jets of fire from various windows, as the musketeers and arquebusiers fell silent.

"Your Holiness, this fortress will not be surrendered. Shortly, there will be a struggle on the walls as the defenders seek to escape. There will be an explosion, a mighty one although not, we think, sufficient to level the castle."

"You *think*?" Tom was dumbfounded. He'd picked up a little about up-time demolitions, enough to understand that it was a precision business that was done carefully and patiently with calculations to umpteen decimal places. Matters were certainly more rough-and-ready in the seventeenth century, but, still, there were limits.

"We were pressed for time," Ruy said, and Tom could see enough of his silhouette to see that he was shrugging.

"How did you persuade the Guard?" the pope asked. "I had understood that they would fight on here so that the enemy would not suspect—?"

He was switching back and forth between Italian and English in a single sentence. Tom found it surprisingly easy to follow. So long as he didn't switch to Spanish for Ruy's sake, because all Tom could remember how to say in that language was to explain that he *no habla* it.

Ruy shrugged again. "It was not hard. These men are proud that they are known for never surrendering, Your Holiness. But the Swiss are a practical folk, very hardheaded. I explained that the best manner in which to ensure that their mission was successful was create so much confusion that the Spaniards did not realize you were gone until it was too late. I promised on your behalf that word would be given when you reached a place of safety so that the survivors might rally to you. In fact, it was one of the lieutenants of the Guard who suggested evacuating the keep and firing the magazine."

"How are we getting out?" Tom asked, realizing that Ruy was being surprisingly reticent on this subject.

"Ah, now there we have a further trick to play." As he said it, four guardsmen ran up, each carrying a small keg under one arm and a bundle under the other. They headed straight for the barricade piled behind the river gate.

Tom put two and two together and realized that he wasn't going to like this, not one bit. He looked around himself. The wall they were sheltering under was the medieval inner ward, which was a square of four bastions connected by walls, under which an assortment of outbuildings and sheds had been constructed. The spare stonework of the later tourist-attraction castles was something that happened after the castle fell in to disuse. A working fortress needed all kinds of interior structures. Right in the middle of the inner ward was the cylindrical structure that had started as Hadrian's mausoleum and was now the fortified citadel of the papacy. So there was going to be an explosion *there*, and unless Tom missed his guess there was going to be an explosion next to the door right by them. As far as he could see, there was shelter from one, but not both.

The guardsmen came back from the barricade behind the river-wall gate, one of them trailing a stream of powder from the keg under his arm. The other three were pulling on plain clothes from the bundles they'd been carrying. *Makes sense,* Tom thought, *that livery is kind of distinctive*. Which didn't advance the matter at hand one whit.

"Ruy, we are *screwed!*" he yelled, over a sudden and thunderous cheering that seemed to come from every direction at once.

"Not yet, Tom. Not until I finally get to have my wedding night, at any rate."

"Jesus, Ruy," Tom said, suddenly wincing at the thought of blaspheming in front of the pope, who didn't actually seem to mind. "Where do we take cover?"

"There," the pope said, pointing along the wall. There was, maybe twenty yards away, a cluster of blocky stone buildings just under the bastion they'd come in over. "Grain houses. Very strong."

"See?" Ruy was grinning as he stood up in the firelight. "Did I, Ruy Sanchez de Casador y Ortiz, not say that the Almighty would provide? His personal vicar on earth shows us the way."

"Right," Tom said, grinning in spite of himself, "that's what I call *service*."

The grain stores proved to be cool and, relative to the din outside, quiet. Ruy was with the guardsmen at the door doing something with the powder train. Inside, there were already a dozen or more civilians taking shelter, perched on the sacks of grain that lined the walls. Some, with more presence of mind, had found places where the bags were stacked like sandbags. A couple, junior priests from the looks, offered nervous grins when Tom led the pope in with them to crouch down.

Ruy came back, and between him and four guardsmen, the shelter was getting cramped. "The powder-train is lit. Perhaps a minute?"

"What about the men on the walls?" Tom asked, realizing for the first time that unless those guys had noticed what was going on, they had had no warning.

"Most will live," Ruy said, somewhere in the gloom beside Tom. The sounds of battle, the clatter of metal and the hoarse yells of men struggling for life and death, were growing closer. "More than if this assault should continue. Much of the blast will remain inside the fortress, except for our little diversion."

"Yes, but—"

Tom was cut off by a glaring flash and a mighty

slam like the gate of hell. Lights flashed in front of his eyes, and for a panicky moment he could not breathe, felt as though he was submerged under miles of lightless ocean, and then his vision began to come back through the purplish-green afterimage of the doorway.

"Guess you got your earth-shattering kaboom," he said, and then realized he hadn't heard a word. *Shit, deaf on top of everything*, he thought, and staggered to his feet.

He could see nothing. He pulled out his flashlight and tapped it a couple of times to get it to come on. He'd more or less avoided using the thing for months at a time, battery-recharges being as tough to come by as they were, and the little light seemed almost indecently bright in the gloom. The Swiss Guards were blinking and looking about. Two of them hauled the pope gently but firmly to his feet. Tom noticed that everyone in the room had the beginnings of a nosebleed, and he could feel a warm wet trickle on his own top lip.

"The barricade is gone," Tom heard, and looked around. Ruy's voice had sounded like it had come from a very long way away indeed, but the wiry Catalan was stood right next to him, and had been bellowing. He'd already been up and about while Tom was gathering his wits.

How does he do it? he wondered. *If I've got half his energy at that age, I'll be glad. Half his energy now would be good, too.*

"Right!" Tom yelled back. He switched to the rather coarse German he'd used with his mercenaries and hoped the Swiss would understand. "Follow Sanchez! I'll come behind!"

They seemed to get the message. Tom limped after them, checking his gun as he went. Somehow the shock of the explosion had made his ass hurt worse, and it definitely felt like the cut there was bleeding again. Riding back was going to be a stone bitch. *Here's hoping I live long enough to suffer with that*, he thought.

Outside the grain store things seemed eerily quiet and clear, although Tom had to wonder if that was in part due to the deafness. He certainly couldn't hear his own boots on the flagstones of the courtyard. All of the junk that had been out in the courtyard had settled or tumbled over, and there were lumps of shattered masonry everywhere. There were fires here and there. The air had temporarily cleared, but the smoke was already starting again. Here and there shocky-looking survivors were staggering about, looking dazed.

A few short strides, stepping over debris and bodies, brought them to the gate. Before looking more closely there, Tom looked up at Hadrian's mausoleum. The whole top was missing. All of it. The heavy, thick walls at the base had channeled the blast straight up and burst the upper floors like a suppurating boil. The jagged rim of the drum at the top was stark against the flame-lit clouds of smoke above, crowned with a rapidly swelling mushroom cloud, a cloud that looked like a flying saucer lifting off when seen from below as Tom was looking at it. The papal apartments that had stood atop the great drum of the fortress were gone completely. *Probably in orbit*, he thought. *Bits of 'em, anyway.*

He turned to the gate. Ruy was beckoning. The gates were cracked, partially open, but had fallen off their hinges. "Jammed!" Ruy shouted. "Push!"

Again, the words seemed to come from a very long way away. Tom hoped that the dim rumble as of a receding freight train was his hearing coming back.

"Right," he murmured. "Brute force and ignorance, coming right up." He handed off his shotgun to someone, not looking around as he weighed up where best to push. He wasn't quite up to the bulk he'd had as noseguard for his university, but he was still in damned good shape—better, in some ways—and had plenty of mass. He set a shoulder against one leaf of the gate and heaved. A little lift to the push, and he felt it start to shift. *Damn thing must weigh two tons,* he thought, panting with the effort. His right ham began to burn, and the gash in his ass-cheek sprang a leak again. Something in the shoulder he was shoving with began to flare a whining little spike of pain into the joint, but he pushed on.

And then it gave, and he had to clutch at the gate to keep from falling on his face. Ruy, followed by two guardsmen, eeled through the gap, then two more, and finally someone was tugging at his sleeve and offering him his shotgun back.

"Thank you, Your Holiness," he said, and escorted the pope out into the cool night air.

To find the way was blocked. His hearing was definitely coming back. "I have orders, Don Ruy," someone was saying.

"And you are following orders?" Ruy replied. "It seems an age of miracles is upon us."

"Most droll."

"Stand aside, Quevedo," Ruy said.

Tom moved forward to see what the trouble was. There seemed to be only a couple of soldiers there, and one older guy, although still younger than Ruy, who looked like an officer type if Tom was any judge.

"No, Don Ruy," said the other man—*Quevedo? Sharon mentioned him,* Tom realized—"It beggars belief that you do not have His—ah, I see you do."

Tom had the presence of mind to get between Quevedo and the two soldiers with him and the pope. The guardsmen pulled out an assortment of long knives and pistols that Tom hadn't noticed them carrying before. A quick check to either side showed that there didn't seem to be any other soldiers close by. The men under the walls, if they had been as shocked as those inside by the explosion, had recovered by now and the one ladder Tom could see had a steady stream of men going up it. It wouldn't be long before those men started looking for gates to open. He worked the slide of his shotgun. "Ruy," he said, loud and clear, "one side, please."

"No," Ruy said, "I have a debt to pay. Get His Holiness clear."

Tom wasn't about to argue with the crazy old guy. *Fuck it,* he thought, *I'll apologize later,* and raised the shotgun to his shoulder. He got a bead on one of the soldiers and was surprised by a flare of the musket the man was carrying going off. He jerked the trigger compulsively and sent the shot somewhere over the rooftops of Rome. Where the Spaniard's shot had gone, Tom didn't see, but to either side the guardsmen snarled and leapt forward while Ruy went at Quevedo like a springing trap.

In the time it took him to work the slide for a second shot, the two soldiers had gone down under a flurry of knife-thrusts and one pistol-shot, a guardsman was bent over and clutching a wound in his side, and Ruy was booting Quevedo in the face to free his sword from the man's neck, into which it had gone nearly three quarters of the width. Blood was spurting everywhere, and Quevedo's face had gone slack as his head flopped to one side.

"I never did cure him of that fault in his guard with the back-sword," Ruy remarked, casually, as he flourished an already-bloodstained handkerchief to clean his blade. "And I am now glad I did not."

Quevedo thumped to the floor as he spoke the last words, and was clearly dead by the time Ruy sheathed his blade.

Tom turned and saw that the pope was assisting his wounded guardsman. "Not bad," the pontiff remarked when he saw Tom looking. "And you have good doctors, not so?"

"Three of 'em," Tom said, grinning. "Let's git."

They slipped unseen to the boats, while behind them the fires in the ruins of the Castel Sant'Angelo began to take hold and light the night sky once more.

Epilogue

Rome

Giovanna peered into the earthenware jug that the jailer had brought in that morning. She could manage the night despite the thirst. There would be another jug in the morning, as there had been for the last two mornings. She had had to use most of it to get Frank clean, since she had been allowed to share a cell with him. They had let a doctor at him, and the bandages were clean, at least. It was the rest of him, the cuts, the bruises, the scrapes and gouges. And the soot and the dust he'd been covered with, and the dried blood.

He was still breathing, for which Giovanna thanked God. They had left Giovanna her rosary, which had been her mother's. She'd been trying for years to follow her father's revolutionary precepts but she'd not been able to bear to throw the thing away. Here and now, it was a great comfort. She even remembered the right prayers to say.

Would it do any good? They'd told her there was to be a new pope soon, that the old one was dead in the ruins of the Castel Sant'Angelo. The last light of a summer's evening came through the tiny, barred window, and she stared up at the indigo sky in which stars were starting to appear. Outside she could hear the sounds of soldiers marching about. She'd heard only snatches of the sack of the city that was going on outside. Sometimes there was screaming, and earlier in the day she'd heard the grisly sounds of an execution outside. From the window, she'd just been able to see that someone was being garroted. Someone in a priest's clothes. She'd tried to think of it as the inevitable bloodshed when the forces of reaction fell to fighting among themselves, but what she'd *seen* had been an old man being strangled.

It made thinking about anything beyond the next jug of water and loaf of bread . . . hard. The last of the daylight was falling on Frank's face now. His eyes were twitching a little under his eyelids, and his breathing had the rasp of his soft snores. She hoped that was a good sign. The linen of the bandage around his head was crusted with blood, and she had not dared try to change it. There was a finger missing from his left hand, the ring finger. That seemed to have stopped oozing now, and she hoped she'd kept it clean and dry enough. The broken leg seemed to have been set well enough, but she could not tell under the splint and the strapping.

They'd told her that he'd been shot, but only grazed by two bullets, and the rest had happened when the building collapsed. That he had not been beaten, or shot by anyone's order. That the shooting had been an accident in the tension of surrender and the bruises from being buried under rubble.

Why Spanish soldiers should care that she thought

of them any better than she did, she had no idea. But they had put her in here to nurse her husband, which was worth far more than any apologies. She had been weeping, barely able to breathe for grief until they told her Frank was alive. They'd also told her they did not have enough jailers to nurse all the injured prisoners, and needed the cell space anyway.

It helped that the Spaniards were using Roman jailers, who didn't seem all that enthusiastic about keeping prisoners for the Spanish Inquisition. They were doing their best to keep everyone in the cell block healthy and comfortable.

And Frank still slept. She had heard stories of people who never awoke after head injuries, and every hour Frank slept made her think about them some more. He had the beginnings of a fever, too. If any of his wounds became gangrenous, only the mercy of her jailers would bring a doctor to save him from it.

There was a rattle of keys in the corridor. Someone was coming.

"Señora?" The voice wasn't the usual jailer, a native Roman, but a Spanish-accented voice. Giovanna put down the jug and stepped away from the door when the spyhole clacked open. There was murmured conversation outside and then another rattle of keys. The door opened and it was the Spanish captain who had had her captured but let everyone else go. And who had had Frank shot.

She choked down the urge to hurl herself at him and try to choke the life from him. Getting herself killed would not help Frank and, anyway, the man had been under orders from that foul priest who had spent hours making her feel filthy with his eyes.

"Yes?" she said, after taking a deep breath, and then stopped. What else to say to such a man?

"It is no large thing I can do, Señora Stone y Marcoli," the captain said, "but I felt I must make at least some small apology, however humble, for my part in what has happened."

"My husband is still alive—" Giovanna resisted the urge to spit *Spaniard!* at the man in lieu of a name she did not know. "—Spanish soldier. He may awaken any time now."

"I pray for this happy outcome," the man said, and Giovanna wondered to see that he clearly meant it. There was sincerity written all over his face, despite his somewhat cracked Italian.

"Thank you, sir," she said, wondering what the man's name was. She'd caught that he was a captain when she'd been held there on that street, watching them shoot cannons at the place she'd made home for all those months, the place where her husband had been hiding and had come out of to be shot. "He sleeps now. He has slept for days. I worry, but they will not send a doctor again. I have asked and asked, but they will not send a doctor, and I have done all I can."

She ached to ask for his help, and pride would not stop her. What stopped her was fear of what the answer would be. She could keep herself warm with hope in a cold cell. If he said no, even that paltry rag of comfort would be taken away.

The pleading must have shown in her face. "I will ask on your behalf, señora," the captain said. "And while the pleas of Don Vincente Jose-Maria Castro y Papas may count for little, I will not have it said that they were not entered in the right ears. I do not know if you are military prisoners, civil prisoners or in the hands of the Inquisition, señora, but it may be that I can sow some little confusion and see to it that the standards of the military are upheld. Even the standards of the Inquisition would be an improvement, I think."

Giovanna bowed her head in gratitude. Gratitude and not a little fear—would he demand—?

She looked up, and saw no lechery in what she now realized was the face of quite a young man. Thirty-five, no more. And yet a face lined with cares. She had seen him argue with the other Spaniard, the priest, and realized that the argument, and what he had had to do when he lost it, had both cost him in their own way.

."Thank you," she said, her voice barely above a whisper.

"I would say that what happened was entirely against my will, señora," he said, "but this is no comfort. Please, accept my apologies nevertheless. There is little about this business"—he waved a hand in the air, taking in the whole of Rome in one weary little circle—"that I can atone for in any way save what was placed in my hands to do. I did it, but there is no honor in it, no pride."

There was nothing Giovanna could think of to say. Could she even say she forgave him, when she felt no forgiveness, no pity? Even as recompense for the crumb of charity he had offered? The words would not come. After a long and uncomfortable silence, the captain left.

She went to sit by Frank. "Do you hear, my love?"

she whispered to his sleeping ear. "They may send another doctor to help you. I pray they will."

"I pray they will too," he whispered back. "I feel like shit."

"Frank?" she cried aloud. "Are—"

He hissed, and she fell silent. "Not so loud," he said. "I figure so long as they think I'm out they won't do anything. I think I woke up when that guy was in here."

"Captain Papas?" she asked.

"Was that him? I thought that was a dream—" his breath rattled as he spoke—"water?"

She offered the jug, and he drank the last of the water greedily. Giovanna knew she could wait for more, but Frank had had no more than the dribbles she had dripped through his lips for days.

"God, that tastes good," he whispered, his throat still plainly raw. "I feel weak as a kitten. I don't think I could move much even if I wanted to."

"Don't," Giovanna whispered back. "Your leg is broken, and you have other injuries."

"Yeah, I can feel—God, I can't tell. Everything hurts. The leg's bad, though."

"Lie still, Frank, if we can fool them long enough . . ."

"Yeah." His smile seemed to outshine the starlight that lit their cell. "Something's bound to turn up."

Padua, Italy

"Well, that's that," said Tom Simpson, demonstratively slapping his hands together, as if clearing them of dust.

"What's *what*?" demanded Melissa. She was glaring at the Venetian soldiers who were barring the road to Venice—and doing so just as demonstratively.

Tom gave her a sage look. "We've done what we can, come as far as the road takes us. If you give me a minute or two, I can probably drum up a few more clichés."

"Very funny," snapped Melissa.

"He's got a point, hon," said Dr. Nichols. He nodded toward the soldiers. "On the positive side, they've got ten times as many troops guarding the road *into* Padua. I figure the pope's safe enough for the moment, now that we're in Venice's *terraferma*."

"Don't call me 'hon,'" Melissa snapped.

Nichols rolled his eyes. "Sure, babe, whatever you say."

Sharon couldn't suppress a gurgling laugh. Just . . . couldn't. Melissa's face had practically turned purple.

Melissa started to glare at her, but halfway through started a gurgling laugh of her own.

"Okay, I surrender!" she exclaimed. "'Hon' it is. Anything's better than 'babe.' For God's sake, James, I'm sixty years old."

"Don't look a day over fifty-five, hon," Nichols assured her.

"Indeed so!" boomed Ruy, who had just emerged from the door of the very big taverna they were standing not far from. He gave Sharon a smile and a little nod. Then, swept off his hat and gave Melissa a sweeping bow that would have dazzled the court at Madrid. "I, Ruy Sanchez de Casador y Ortiz, swear it is true!"

That was good for a real laugh, and from everybody.

When that was over, Melissa asked: "So now what?"

"At a guess," replied Rita, "Italy starts going up in flames. A good chunk of the rest of Europe as well. With those two over there"—she wiggled a thumb in the direction of the pope and his nephew, who were engaged in some sort of negotiations with three Venetian senators—"pouring on the gasoline."

Tom studied them. The pope and the cardinal were enjoying the shade next to the taverna's wall. Also enjoying a bottle of wine.

"I say we join them," he proposed.

"By all means," said Sharon. "You do so."

"You're not joining us?" asked Rita.

"No. Maybe tomorrow. For the moment . . ." She took Ruy by the hand. "My husband has made arrangements for a room."

"Rooms for everyone," Ruy added. "Separate rooms."

Seeing that everyone was staring at her, Sharon sniffed haughtily. "The stresses of the past period may have scrambled *your* brains and made you forget everything. But not me. Our wedding was interrupted, remember?"

And she was off, Ruy in tow.

"Well, that's that," said Tom.

Madrid, Spain

Philip IV had been staring out the window of the Alcazar throughout the count-duke of Olivares' report on the situation in Rome. Now, his hands still clasped behind his back, he hunched forward a bit. As if he were looking for someone in the gardens below.

"How many assassins do we have in our employ, Gaspar?"

The count-duke had been afraid of that royal reaction. He inhaled, preparatory to launching a little speech on the virtues of caution.

"However many there are," the king of Spain continued—there was a snarl coming into his voice now—"I want each and every one of them dispatched to Rome immediately. With firm and clear instructions to bring me back the head of Cardinal Gaspar Borja y Velasco. Note carefully—make sure to pass this along to the assassins—that I used the title *Cardinal*."

The explosion finally came. The king unclasped his hands and slammed the palm of the right hand against one of the window panes. Fortunately, the glass was thick and well made. "We'll see how much that bastard likes the title 'pope' when he stares down at his severed neck impaled on a pike!"

"Better if we could have him brought back alive," said Don Jerónimo de Villanueva.

Olivares gave him a warning glance, but the Protonotario of the Crown of Aragon was too furious to notice. His own words had been said in a snarl.

"We could then entertain ourselves at leisure, with his torture," he finished.

Fortunately, the other two members of the hastily assembled council present, José González and Antonio de Contreras, were more phlegmatic by temperament— and, unlike Villanueva, had been keeping an eye on their patron's reaction. They knew the count-duke of Olivares quite well, and interpreted the expression on his face correctly.

"I think we need to be cautious here," said González.

He said it cautiously, of course. Granted that Philip IV was not generally a hot-tempered man; granted also, he normally left matters of governance to the count-duke while the king entertained himself with his patronage of art and literature. Still, he *was* the king of Spain, and he *was* in an obvious rage.

The king turned away from the window, bringing his heavy-boned face to bear on that of his advisor. The sweeping royal mustachios were practically quivering, below the prominent nose and above the classic Habsburg chin and lower lip.

"*Why?*" he bellowed. He pointed a rigid finger at the window. "That—that—"

"Traitor," Villanueva unhelpfully supplied. "Madman, also."

"Yes! That *madman*—that *traitor*—has just managed to bring down into ruins Our entire foreign policy! Every bit of it!"

"Ah—not quite, Your Majesty," said Olivares.

The king brought the glare to bear on him. "Indeed? Please explain to me, Count-Duke, which aspect of Our policy the creature Borja has *not* destroyed."

Philip didn't wait for an answer. Although he didn't concern himself with the day-to-day business of ruling the Spanish empire, the king was neither stupid nor ill informed. Most times, Olivares found that a blessing. On some occasions, however—this certainly being one of them—it was something of a curse.

The king brought up his thumb. "Shall We begin with a recitation of the casualties suffered by Our armies in the north? We recall them quite well, Gaspar, even if you seem to have mysteriously forgotten. How, We can't imagine—since those dismal figures were the principal subject of your report to Our council not so very long ago."

The forefinger came up. It was a large finger, and very stiff. Olivares had to restrain a momentary and quite insane urge to giggle. He had no difficulty imagining Borja impaled on that royal digit.

"Let's move on to a consideration of our military situation. We were all agreed that we faced an unavoidable period of retrenchment, did we not? While we scraped up the money—We shall get to *that* subject in a moment!—in order to recruit more troops and arm them with the new weapons that the cursed Swede and his American witches have inflicted on the world.

"Did we not?" he shouted.

A nod of hasty obeisance was called for here, and Olivares—hastily—provided it.

"Splendid," continued the king. The middle finger came up. "Let us now consider Our financial position—which is perilous, as always. The *last* thing we needed was to have a madman—no, a traitor!—produce a situation in Italy which will—unavoidably, Olivares, deny it if you can!—force us to pour bullion into that miserable peninsula."

Olivares tried to say something, but Philip would have none of it. "Deny it if you can! With the troops that madman—no, that traitor!—pulled out of Naples to carry through his adventure, tell me—if you can, Olivares!—that we will not face a rebellion in southern Italy."

"I agree that the financial damage will be extensive, Your Majesty," Olivares said smoothly. He needed to divert the king from too much thought on the subject of Italian rebellions. At least for the moment, when he was in such a fury.

In point of fact, Olivares was quite sure they faced something considerably worse than the usual rebelliousness of Neapolitans. He had not mentioned in his report—and now thanked God that he hadn't—the last item of information. That Borja had not only overthrown the existing pope, but that he had also managed to let Urban *escape*. And to do so, to make the disaster complete, with the assistance of the USE embassy to Rome!

Was it really too much to ask, that a madman not be a complete incompetent as well?

Thankfully, Villanueva was finally coming to his senses. Realizing the precipice that the royal anger might plunge them over, the protonotario hurried to add: "My reports are that the latest bullion fleet from the New World will be bringing more silver than usual, Your Majesty. I think—combined with some tax levies, no way now to avoid them—that we will manage well enough."

That caused the first break in Philip's escalating temper.

"Really?" he asked.

Villanueva gave the king a nod of such assured confidence that Olivares forgave him his recent sins. For all the world, you'd think Don Jerónimo actually knew what he was talking about.

Which, he didn't. Villanueva knew just as well as Olivares did that there was no way, this early, to be sure what amounts of bullion would be coming over from the New World. Even leaving aside the ever-present danger of piracy, which was especially acute now with the remnants of the Dutch fleet still at large in the Caribbean.

But the count-duke was not a man to sneer at blessings, wherever they were found and however gilded they might be.

"Indeed, Your Majesty," he said, lying just as smoothly as Villanueva had. "Furthermore—"

In the end, it worked out as well as Olivares could have hoped for. The king was still furious, but had bowed to necessity.

"We simply have no choice, Your Majesty. Yes, Borja's actions were completely unsanctioned and went far beyond any instructions we gave him. But the fact remains that to disavow him now would simply produce a still worse situation. Your brother's disaffection in the Low Countries"—he was tempted to call it *treason,* but refrained—"is sure to deepen. I fear also that our Austrian cousins will do the same, now that Ferdinand II has been succeeded by his son."

And there was *another* casualty of Borja's insane ambition. In truth, Olivares had looked forward to dealing with Ferdinand III instead of his predecessor. The son was three times as smart and not given to his father's pigheadedness. Unfortunately, that same intelligence would now lead him away from Spain, not toward it. Olivares was just as glumly certain of that as he was that he would soon face rebellions and uprisings all through the Italian peninsula.

"But for all those reasons," he continued, "we have no choice but to hail the restoration of the true faith to the See of Rome. The coming storm is of Borja's making, not ours—but a storm it will surely be. To

throw over Borja would be to throw over our oars as
well as the mast that Borja himself demolished."

That evening, Olivares had two other meetings. No
broad councils, these, but secretive affairs.

The first was with the envoy from Monsieur Gas-
ton. Whom Olivares had carefully ignored in the
past, but could do so no longer. With Spain now
divided still further from both other branches of the
Habsburgs—he cursed Borja yet again—the empire
could no longer afford the luxury of a careful policy
with regard to France.

"Yes," he told him. "We will supply you with money.
Troops also, if need be. But!"

He wagged an admonishing finger under the miserable Capucin's nose. "Only if you can demonstrate
some results."

The second meeting was more secretive still. Olivares even went to the extreme of leaving his palace
in disguise to make the encounter in a taverna.

"You can reach someone in Borja's forces?" he
asked. "It will need to be an officer."

The man he sometimes used as an informal agent
gave him a nod. "I can reach several. More than you
might think. I can assure you, Count-Duke, that you
are not the only one who thinks our beloved former
cardinal is a rogue."

He cocked his head, slightly. "You wish . . ."

Olivares shook his head. "No assassination. The
king was most explicit on the matter."

He hadn't been at all, actually. But there was no
reason to bring that up.

"My concern is not with Borja, at the moment. My concern is with the American prisoner. And his Venetian wife."

The agent nodded. "So I've heard. You want them . . ."

Olivares scowled. "Is it the wine, Pedro?"

He lifted his own glass, which was still mostly full. In truth, the wine was wretched. This taverna was not one that Olivares would have ever frequented on his own behalf.

"That keeps your mind fixed to murder, like a mouse to bait?"

The agent chuckled. "I point out to you—"

"Yes, yes," Olivares said impatiently, "I know what I normally ask of you. But this situation is quite different. We will most likely be at war again with the USE, and much sooner than I had either planned or anticipated. I should think the rest follows."

The agent studied him, for a moment, slowly twirling his glass around. He'd drunk very little of the wine himself.

Then, he smiled, more thinly still. "Yes, I understand. The prisoner is simply a boy. His wife, younger still—and now pregnant, by the accounts. Emotions would run high if they were to meet a sordid end in Borja's dungeon."

"High, indeed."

The agent was almost grinning, now. The expression was quite insufferable, in a way. But Olivares made no reproof. He didn't like the man, not in the least. But he had all the skills of the cursed Quevedo, with none of Quevedo's flamboyance and carelessness.

For this subject, that was all that mattered. The

next few years were going to be stressful enough, for the count-duke of Olivares. He didn't need to add to that burden the constant memory of Wallenstein being struck down at a distance of half a mile—because Borja couldn't resist further exercises in madness.

"Yes, exactly. He's just a boy; and she, just a pregnant girl of a wife. Let's make sure they keep that modest status, shall we? The world has martyrs enough."

Magdeburg

Mike Stearns gave the man slouched in a chair in his office the Official Stern Look. "You understand—given the circumstances—that this is entirely unofficial?"

"Goes without saying," came the reply. Mike hadn't expect the Look to do much good.

"Fine. I hate to do this, but . . ." He shrugged. "I figure you're the best one for the job we've got. Going by the record."

"Hey, Mike, it's no sweat. Really."

Harry Lefferts rose from the chair and donned his wrap-around sunglasses. The ones he loved, that made him look like an extra from a bad thriller. Especially combined with the boots and the Lee Van Cleef cutaway jacket. The less said about the hat the better.

In a chair over in the corner, Francisco Nasi looked to be choking on something.

"One jailbreak, coming up," said Harry. "My specialty."

As he headed for the door, he said: "It'll be the talk of Europe."

On his way out, he added: "Again."

MORE ...
ERIC FLINT

THE SF OF ERIC FLINT

MOTHER OF DEMONS
Humans stranded on an alien world precipitate a revolution.
Also available at the Baen Free Library, www.baen.com.

pb ◆ 0-671-87800-X ◆ $5.99

BOUNDARY with Ryk E. Spoor
A "funny" fossil is found in the American desert, and solving
the mystery of its origins takes paleontologist Helen Sutter all
the way to Mars. . . .

First paperback edition available in 2008

THE COURSE OF EMPIRE
with K.D. Wentworth
Conquered by the Jao twenty years ago, Earth is shackled
under alien tyranny—and threatened by the even more dangerous Ekhat. The humans will fight to the death, but the
battle to free the Earth may destroy it instead!

pb ◆ 0-7434-9893-3 ◆ $7.99

CROWN OF SLAVES with David Weber
A novel set in the *NY Times* best-selling Honor Harrington
universe. Sent on a mission to keep Erewhon from breaking with Manticore, the Star Kingdom's most able agent
and the Queen's niece may not even be able to escape
with their lives. . . .

pb ◆ 0-7434-9899-2 ◆ $7.99

RATS, BATS & VATS with Dave Freer

Never count out the underdog, even if he is a rat. Or a genetically engineered and cybernetically modified bat. Or a vat-bred human. And especially don't count them out if they are working together to kill the aliens who killed their comrades.

pb ◆ 0-671-31828-4 ◆ $7.99

THE RATS, THE BATS & THE UGLY
with Dave Freer

"It's a neat trick to write an old-fashioned SF adventure story that contains elements of romance, humor and the sort of lively ensemble that graced the classic Warner Bros. war movies. Both Flint and Freer know the trick rather well. This is that rarity among SF novels these days: a fun read."—*Starlog*

hc ◆ 0-7434-8846-6 ◆ $24.00
pb ◆ 1-4165-2078-3 ◆ $7.99

THE WIZARD OF KARRES
with Mercedes Lackey & Dave Freer

The rollicking sequel to James H. Schmitz's legendary *The Witches of Karres*.

pb ◆ 1-4165-0967-7 ◆ $7.99

And don't miss Flint's alternate history series
The Ring of Fire and
The Belisarius Saga with David Drake.